Dance Class

Béka and Crip

PAPERCUTZ
New York

Dance Class Graphic Novels Available from PAPERCUTZ

Béka and Crip
Dance Class
So, You Think You Can Hip-Hop?
PAPERCUTZ

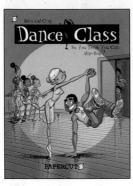

#1 "So, You Think You Can Hip-Hop?"

Béka and Crip
Dance Class
Romeos and Juliet
PAPERCUTZ

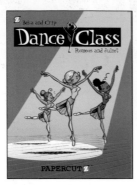

#2 "Romeos and Juliet"

Béka and Crip
Dance Class
African Folk Dance Fever
PAPERCUTZ

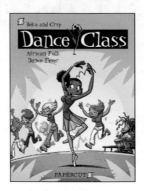

#3 "African Folk Dance Fever"

Dance Class

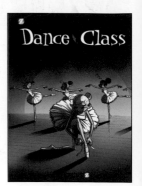

#4 "A Funny Thing Happened on the Way to Paris..."

Béka and Crip
Dance Class
To Russia, With Love
PAPERCUTZ

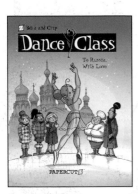

#5 "To Russia, With Love"

Béka and Crip
Dance Class
A Merry Olde Christmas
PAPERCUTZ

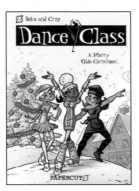

#6 "A Merry Olde Christmas"

Béka and Crip
Dance Class
School Night Fever
PAPERCUTZ

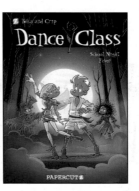

#7 "School Night Fever"

Béka and Crip
Dance Class
Snow White and the Seven Dwarves
PAPERCUTZ

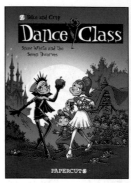

#8 "Snow White and the Seven Dwarves"

COMING SOON

Béka and Crip
Dance Class
Dancing in the Rain
PAPERCUTZ

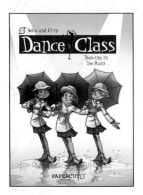

#9 "Dancing in the Rain"

Béka and Crip
Dance Class
Letting It Go
PAPERCUTZ

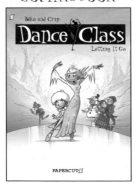

#10 "Letting It Go"

SEE MORE
AT PAPERCUTZ.COM
Also available digitally wherever e-books are sold.

Dance Class 3 in 1

Table of Contents

BACK TO POINTE!
HMMM! THEY'RE PUTTING NEW CAKES IN THE DISPLAY WINDOW!
HEE HEE! EVER SINCE THAT NEW BAKERY OPENED IN FRONT OF THE SCHOOL, LUCIE HAS BEEN DOING EXCEPTIONAL *RELEVÉS*.

GOOD JOB, JULIE! YOU'RE DOING REALLY WELL AT IT!

DON'T FORGET THAT, AT THE END OF THE YEAR, WE'RE STAGING THE BALLET "ROMEO AND JULIET"! YOU MUST ACQUIRE THE GRACE OF A SWAN!
HUFF!
PFFF!
PFFF!

...THE DANCERS' MOVEMENTS, TOO.
TOOM
TOO TOOM
TOOM

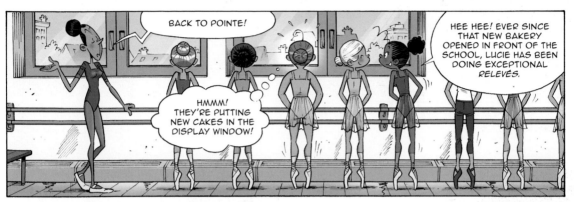

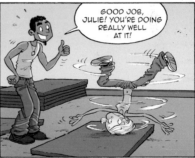

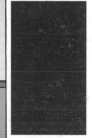

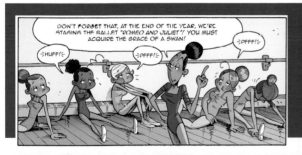

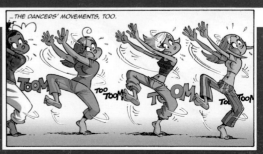

Dance Class

3 IN 1 #1

Originally published in France as Studio Danse [Dance Class] Volumes 1, 2, and 3
©2008-2009, 2019 BAMBOO ÉDITION.
www.bamboo.fr
All other editorial material © 2019 by Papercutz
www.papercutz.com

DANCE CLASS 3 IN 1 #1
"So, You Think You Can Hip-Hop?"
"Romeos and Juliet"
"African Folk Dance Fever"

Béka — Writer
Crip — Artist
Benoît Bekaert — Colorist, "So, You Think You Can Hip-Hop?"
Maëla Cosson — Colorist, "Romeos and Juliet," "African Folk Dance Fever"
Joe Johnson — Translation
Tom Orzechowski — Lettering
Karr Antunes — Editorial Intern
Jeff Whitman — Editor
Jim Salicrup
Editor-in-Chief

ISBN: 978-1-5458-0533-6

Printed in China
February 2019

Papercutz books may be purchased for business or promotional use. For information on bulk purchases
please contact Macmillan Corporate and Premium Sales Department at (800) 221-7945 x5442.

Distributed by Macmillan
First Papercutz printing

So, You Think You Can Hip-Hop?

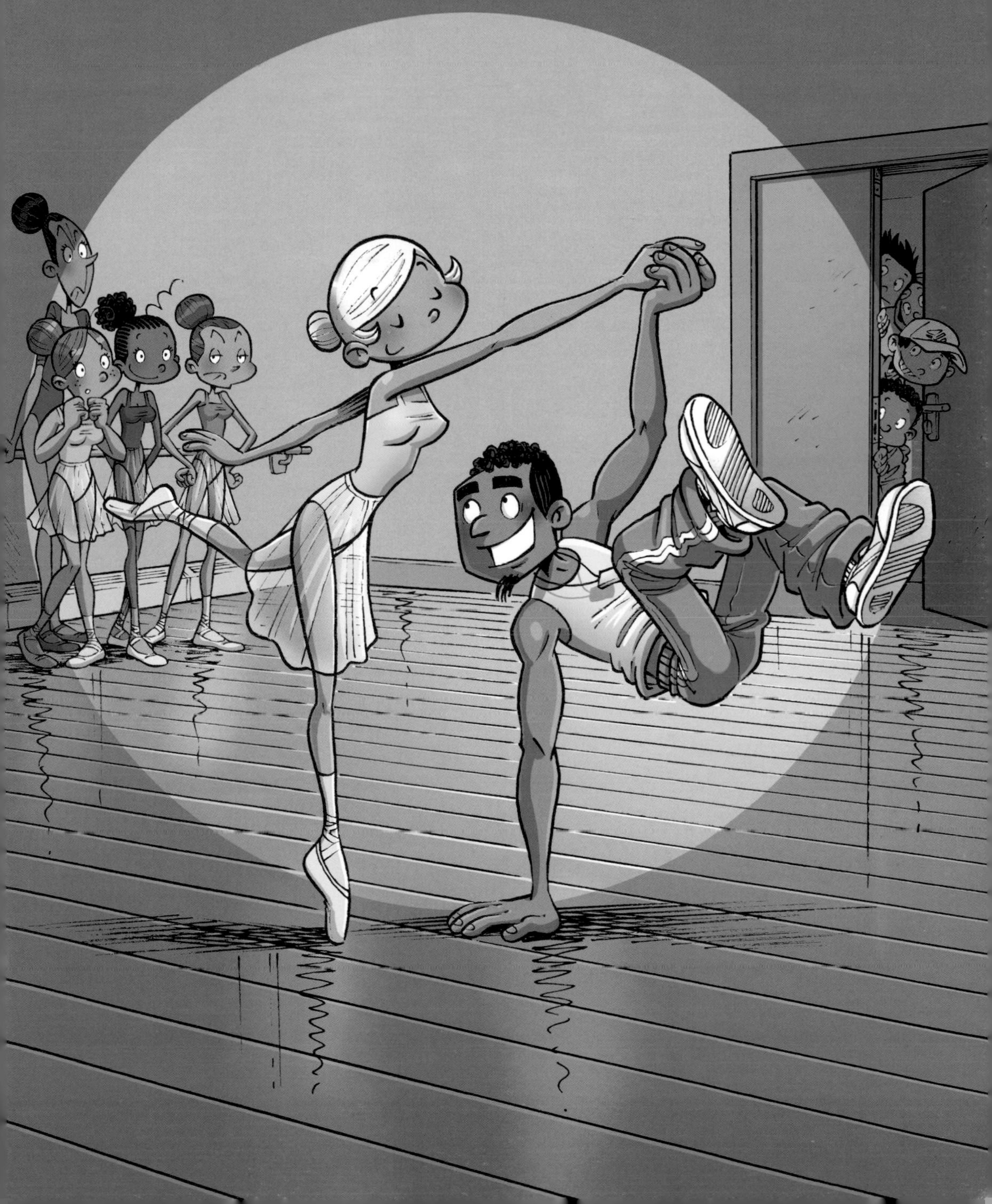

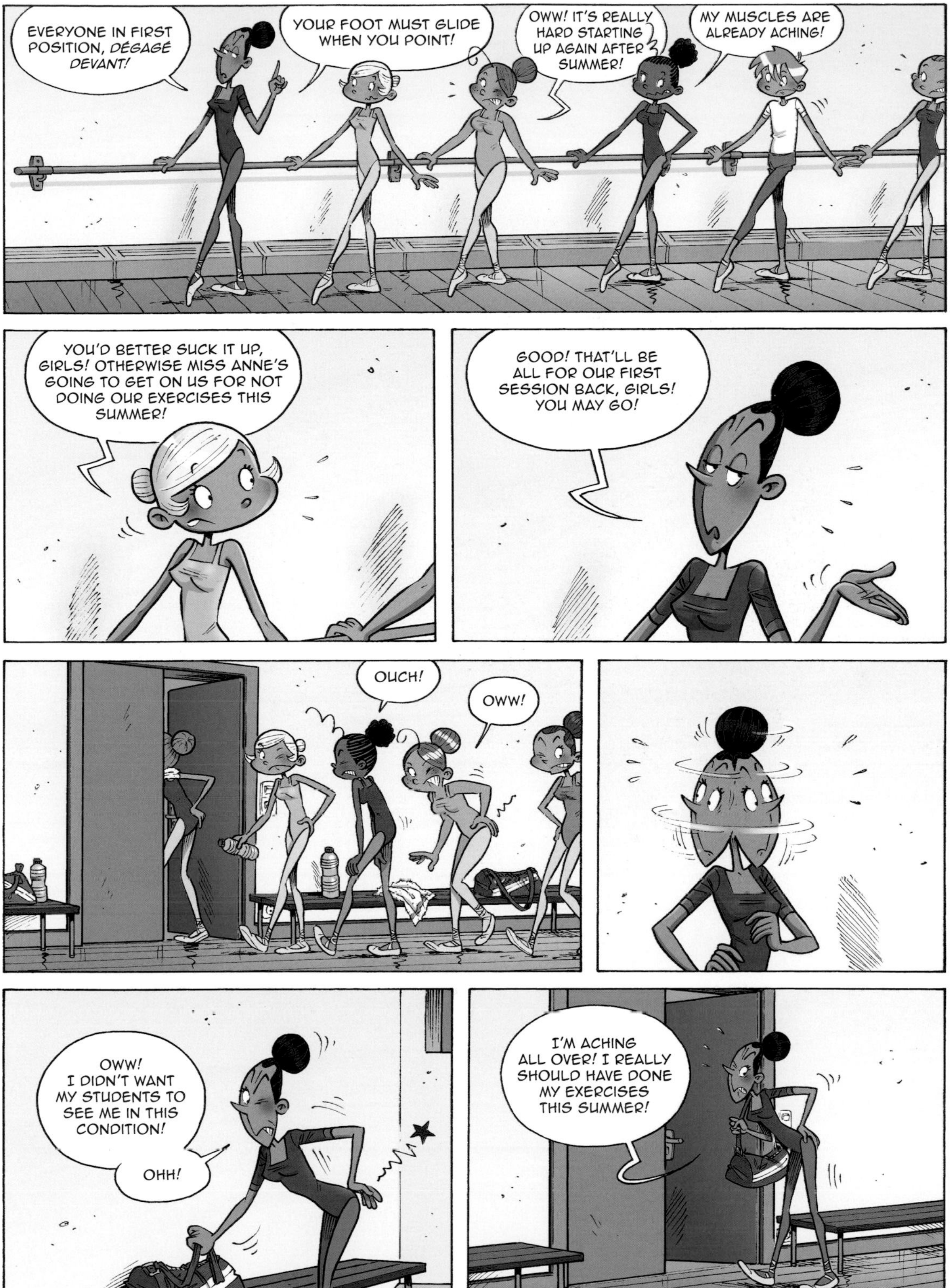
EVERYONE IN FIRST POSITION, *DÉGAGÉ DEVANT!*
YOUR FOOT MUST GLIDE WHEN YOU POINT!
OWW! IT'S REALLY HARD STARTING UP AGAIN AFTER SUMMER!
MY MUSCLES ARE ALREADY ACHING!
YOU'D BETTER SUCK IT UP, GIRLS! OTHERWISE MISS ANNE'S GOING TO GET ON US FOR NOT DOING OUR EXERCISES THIS SUMMER!
GOOD! THAT'LL BE ALL FOR OUR FIRST SESSION BACK, GIRLS! YOU MAY GO!
OUCH!
OWW!
OWW! I DIDN'T WANT MY STUDENTS TO SEE ME IN THIS CONDITION!
OHH!
I'M ACHING ALL OVER! I REALLY SHOULD HAVE DONE MY EXERCISES THIS SUMMER!

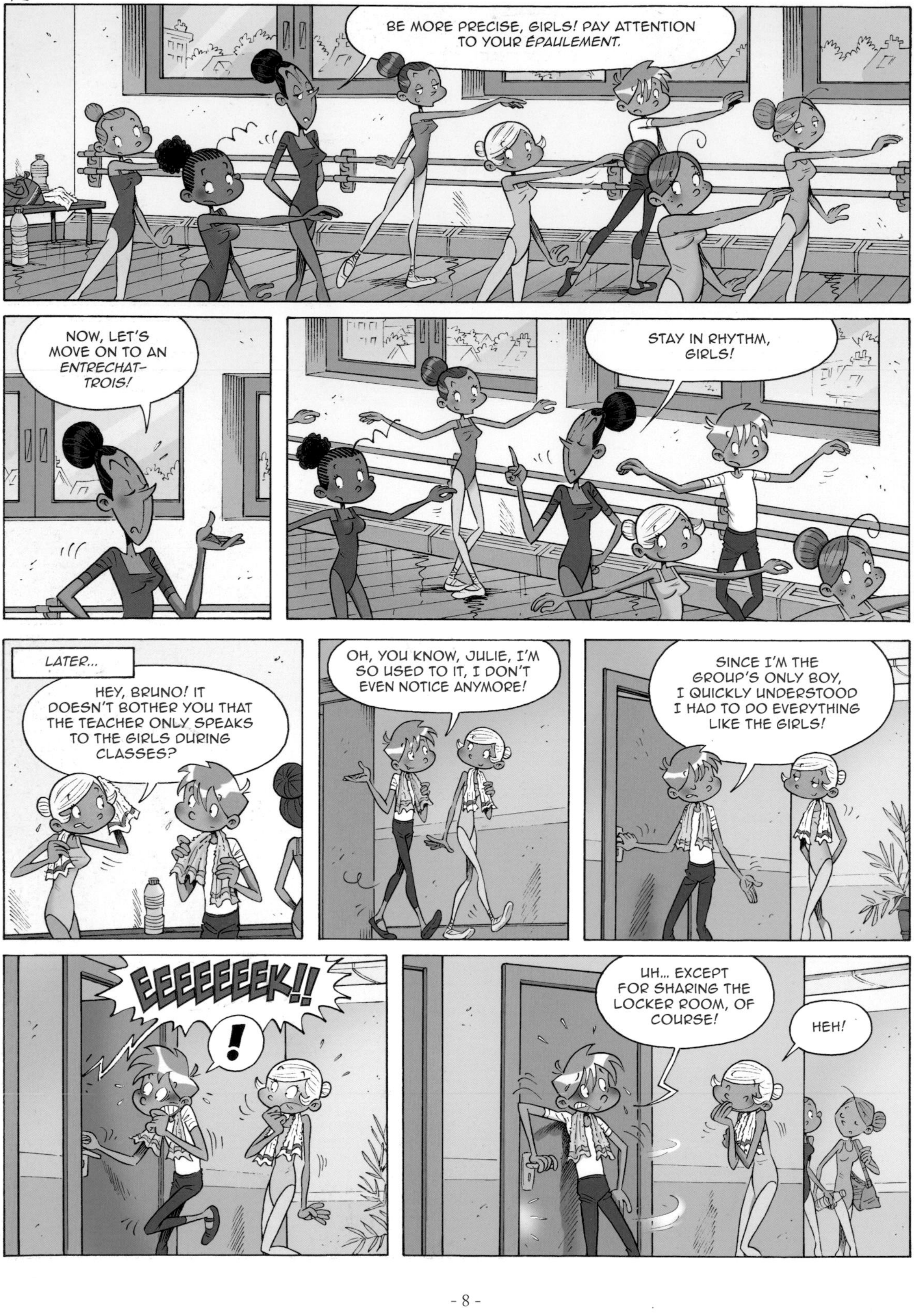
BE MORE PRECISE, GIRLS! PAY ATTENTION TO YOUR ÉPAULEMENT.
NOW, LET'S MOVE ON TO AN ENTRECHAT-TROIS!
STAY IN RHYTHM, GIRLS!
LATER...
HEY, BRUNO! IT DOESN'T BOTHER YOU THAT THE TEACHER ONLY SPEAKS TO THE GIRLS DURING CLASSES?
OH, YOU KNOW, JULIE, I'M SO USED TO IT, I DON'T EVEN NOTICE ANYMORE!
SINCE I'M THE GROUP'S ONLY BOY, I QUICKLY UNDERSTOOD I HAD TO DO EVERYTHING LIKE THE GIRLS!
EEEEEEEK!!
!
UH... EXCEPT FOR SHARING THE LOCKER ROOM, OF COURSE!
HEH!

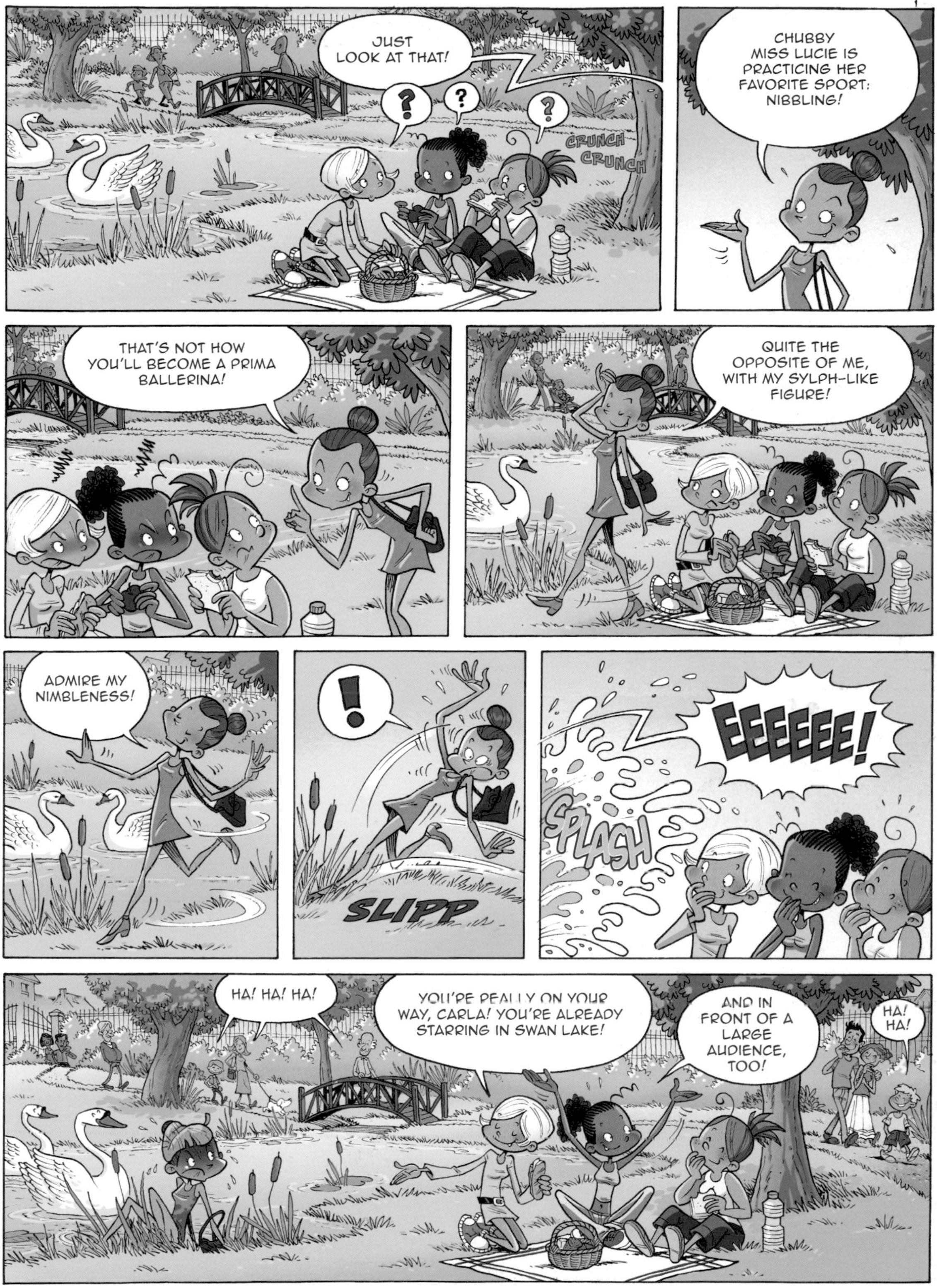

JUST LOOK AT THAT!
?
?
?
CRUNCH CRUNCH
CHUBBY MISS LUCIE IS PRACTICING HER FAVORITE SPORT: NIBBLING!
THAT'S NOT HOW YOU'LL BECOME A PRIMA BALLERINA!
QUITE THE OPPOSITE OF ME, WITH MY SYLPH-LIKE FIGURE!
ADMIRE MY NIMBLENESS!
!
SLIPP
EEEEEE!
SPLASH
HA! HA! HA!
YOU'RE REALLY ON YOUR WAY, CARLA! YOU'RE ALREADY STARRING IN SWAN LAKE!
AND IN FRONT OF A LARGE AUDIENCE, TOO!
HA! HA!

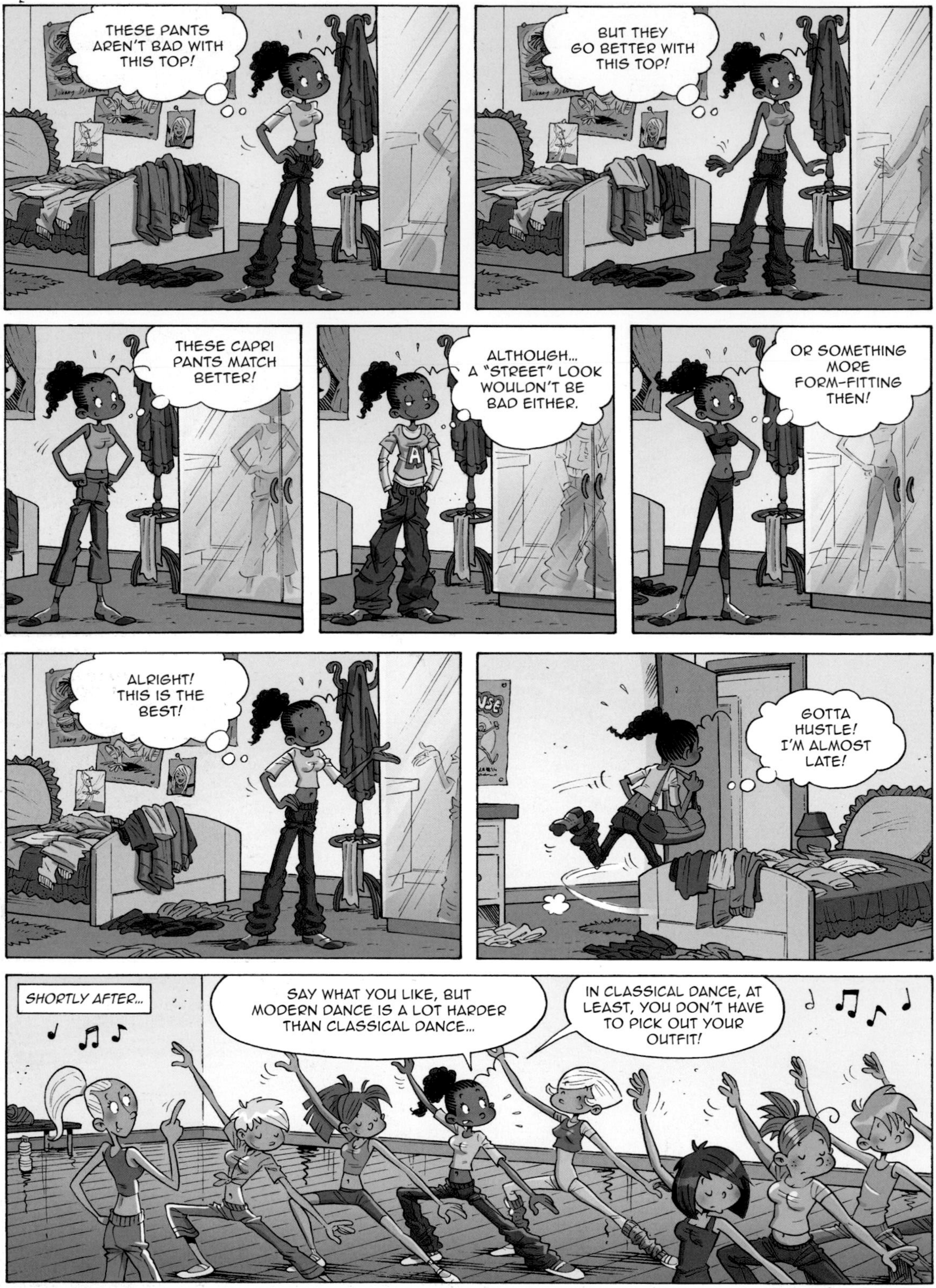
THESE PANTS AREN'T BAD WITH THIS TOP!
BUT THEY GO BETTER WITH THIS TOP!
THESE CAPRI PANTS MATCH BETTER!
ALTHOUGH... A "STREET" LOOK WOULDN'T BE BAD EITHER.
OR SOMETHING MORE FORM-FITTING THEN!
ALRIGHT! THIS IS THE BEST!
GOTTA HUSTLE! I'M ALMOST LATE!
SHORTLY AFTER...
SAY WHAT YOU LIKE, BUT MODERN DANCE IS A LOT HARDER THAN CLASSICAL DANCE...
IN CLASSICAL DANCE, AT LEAST, YOU DON'T HAVE TO PICK OUT YOUR OUTFIT!

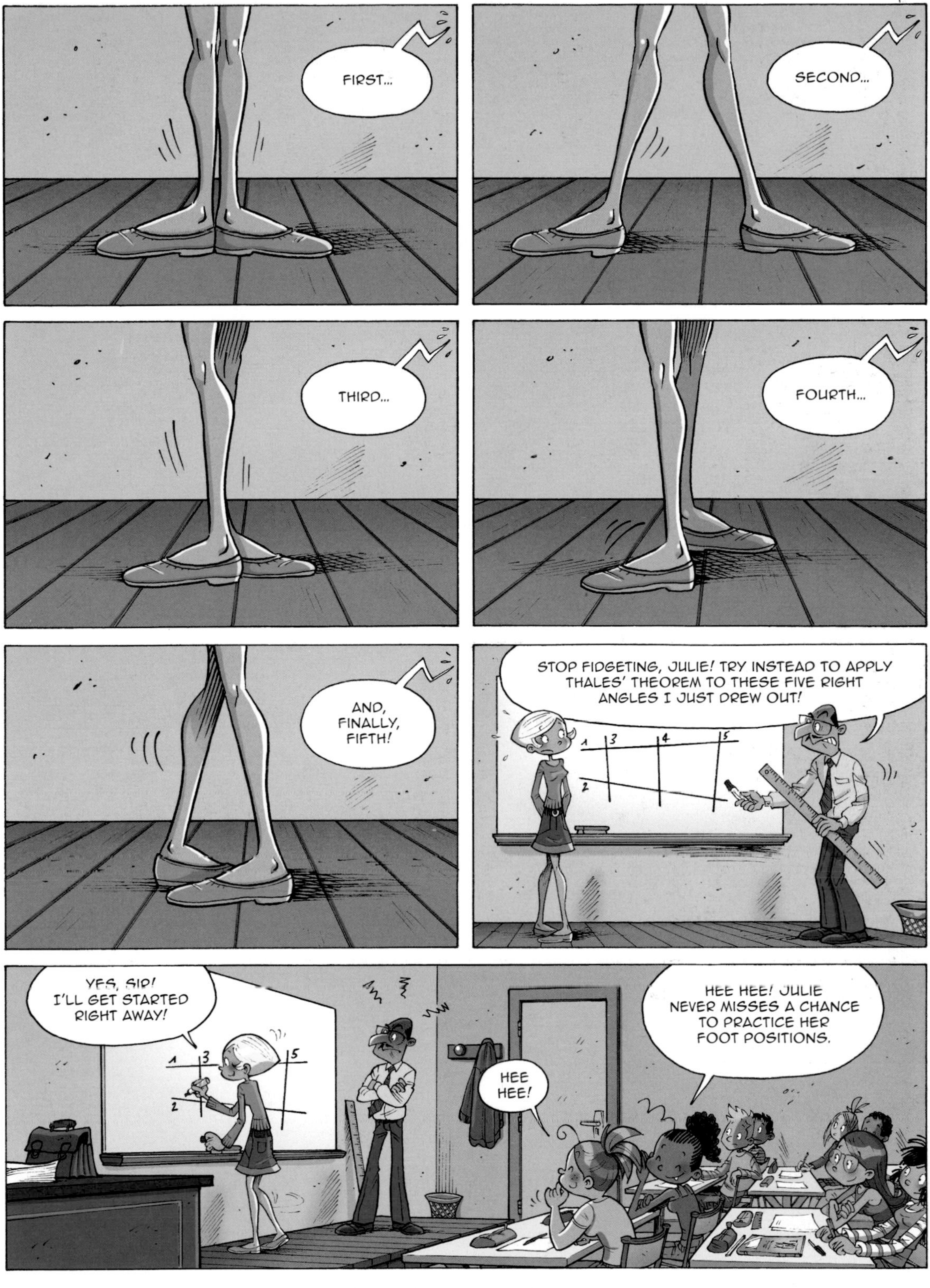

FIRST...
SECOND...
THIRD...
FOURTH...
AND, FINALLY, FIFTH!
STOP FIDGETING, JULIE! TRY INSTEAD TO APPLY THALES' THEOREM TO THESE FIVE RIGHT ANGLES I JUST DREW OUT!
1
2
3
4
5
YES, SIR! I'LL GET STARTED RIGHT AWAY!
HEE HEE!
HEE HEE! JULIE NEVER MISSES A CHANCE TO PRACTICE HER FOOT POSITIONS.

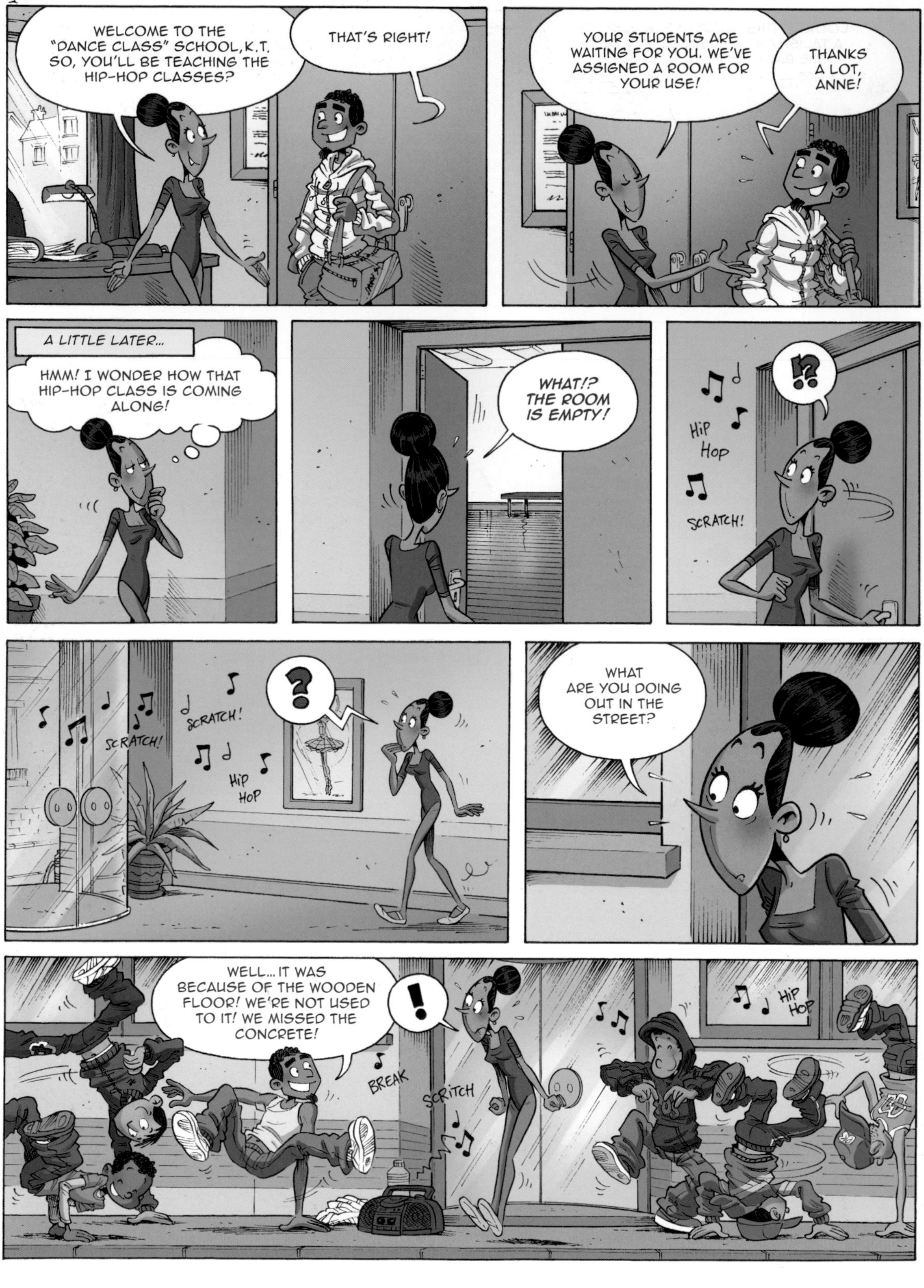
WELCOME TO THE "DANCE CLASS" SCHOOL, K.T. SO, YOU'LL BE TEACHING THE HIP-HOP CLASSES?
THAT'S RIGHT!
YOUR STUDENTS ARE WAITING FOR YOU. WE'VE ASSIGNED A ROOM FOR YOUR USE!
THANKS A LOT, ANNE!
A LITTLE LATER...
HMM! I WONDER HOW THAT HIP-HOP CLASS IS COMING ALONG!
WHAT!? THE ROOM IS EMPTY!
!?
HIP HOP
SCRATCH!
SCRATCH!
SCRATCH!
HIP HOP
?
WHAT ARE YOU DOING OUT IN THE STREET?
WELL... IT WAS BECAUSE OF THE WOODEN FLOOR! WE'RE NOT USED TO IT! WE MISSED THE CONCRETE!
!
BREAK
SCRITCH
HIP HOP

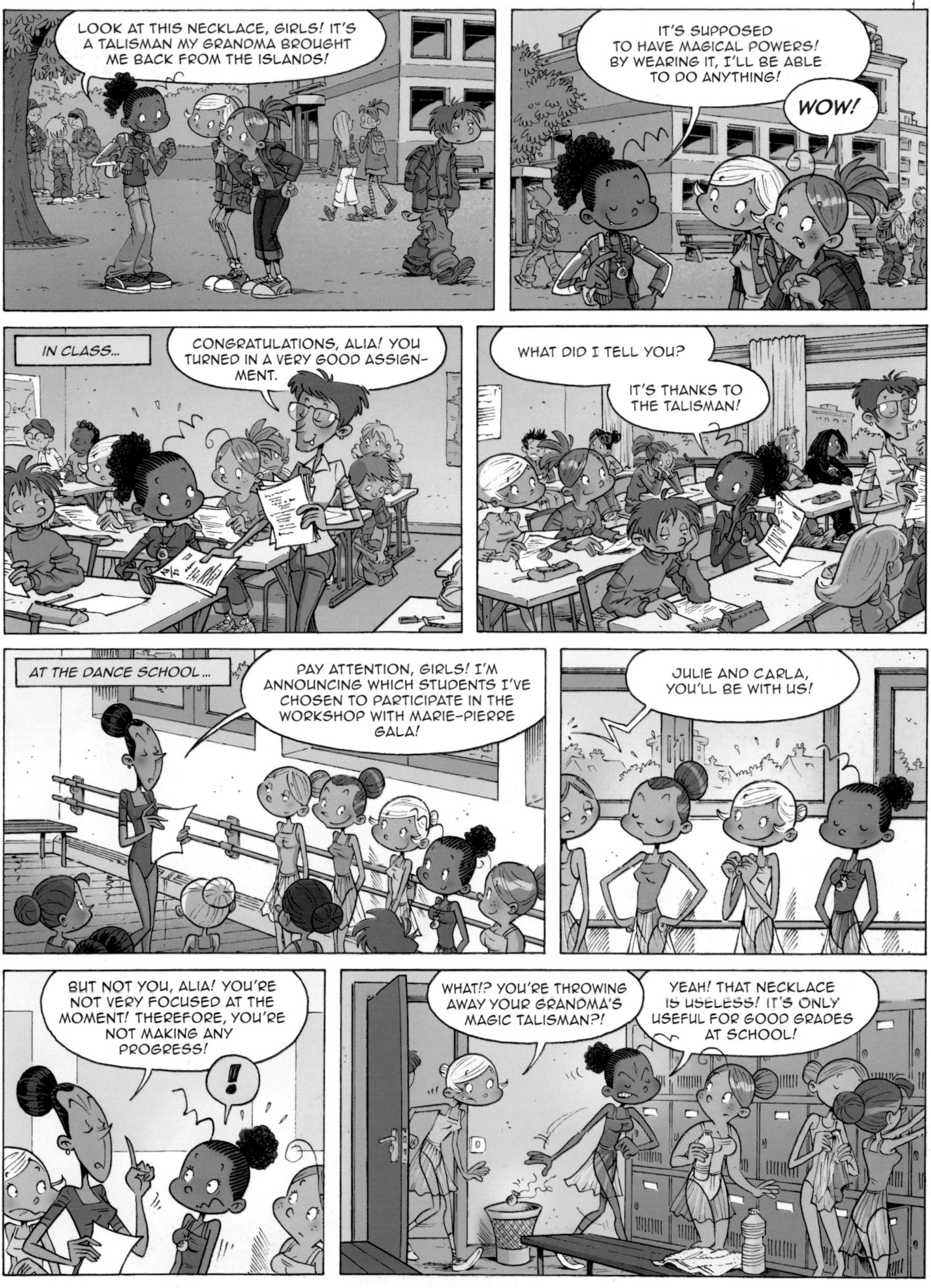
LOOK AT THIS NECKLACE, GIRLS! IT'S A TALISMAN MY GRANDMA BROUGHT ME BACK FROM THE ISLANDS!
IT'S SUPPOSED TO HAVE MAGICAL POWERS! BY WEARING IT, I'LL BE ABLE TO DO ANYTHING!
WOW!
IN CLASS...
CONGRATULATIONS, ALIA! YOU TURNED IN A VERY GOOD ASSIGN-MENT.
WHAT DID I TELL YOU?
IT'S THANKS TO THE TALISMAN!
AT THE DANCE SCHOOL...
PAY ATTENTION, GIRLS! I'M ANNOUNCING WHICH STUDENTS I'VE CHOSEN TO PARTICIPATE IN THE WORKSHOP WITH MARIE-PIERRE GALA!
JULIE AND CARLA, YOU'LL BE WITH US!
BUT NOT YOU, ALIA! YOU'RE NOT VERY FOCUSED AT THE MOMENT! THEREFORE, YOU'RE NOT MAKING ANY PROGRESS!
!
WHAT!? YOU'RE THROWING AWAY YOUR GRANDMA'S MAGIC TALISMAN?!
YEAH! THAT NECKLACE IS USELESS! IT'S ONLY USEFUL FOR GOOD GRADES AT SCHOOL!

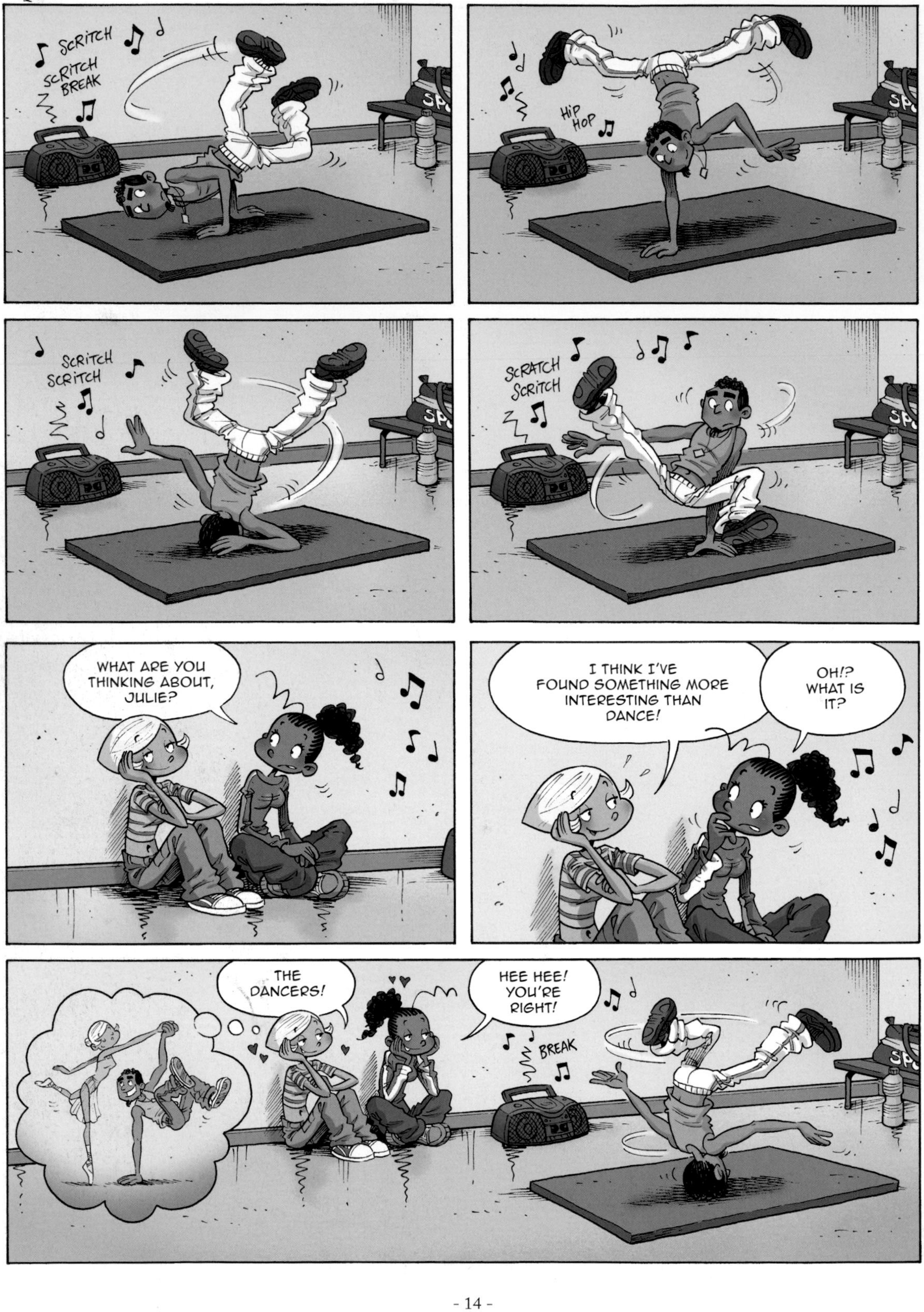

SCRITCH
SCRITCH BREAK
HIP HOP
SCRITCH SCRITCH
SCRATCH SCRITCH
WHAT ARE YOU THINKING ABOUT, JULIE?
I THINK I'VE FOUND SOMETHING MORE INTERESTING THAN DANCE!
OH!? WHAT IS IT?
THE DANCERS!
HEE HEE! YOU'RE RIGHT!
BREAK

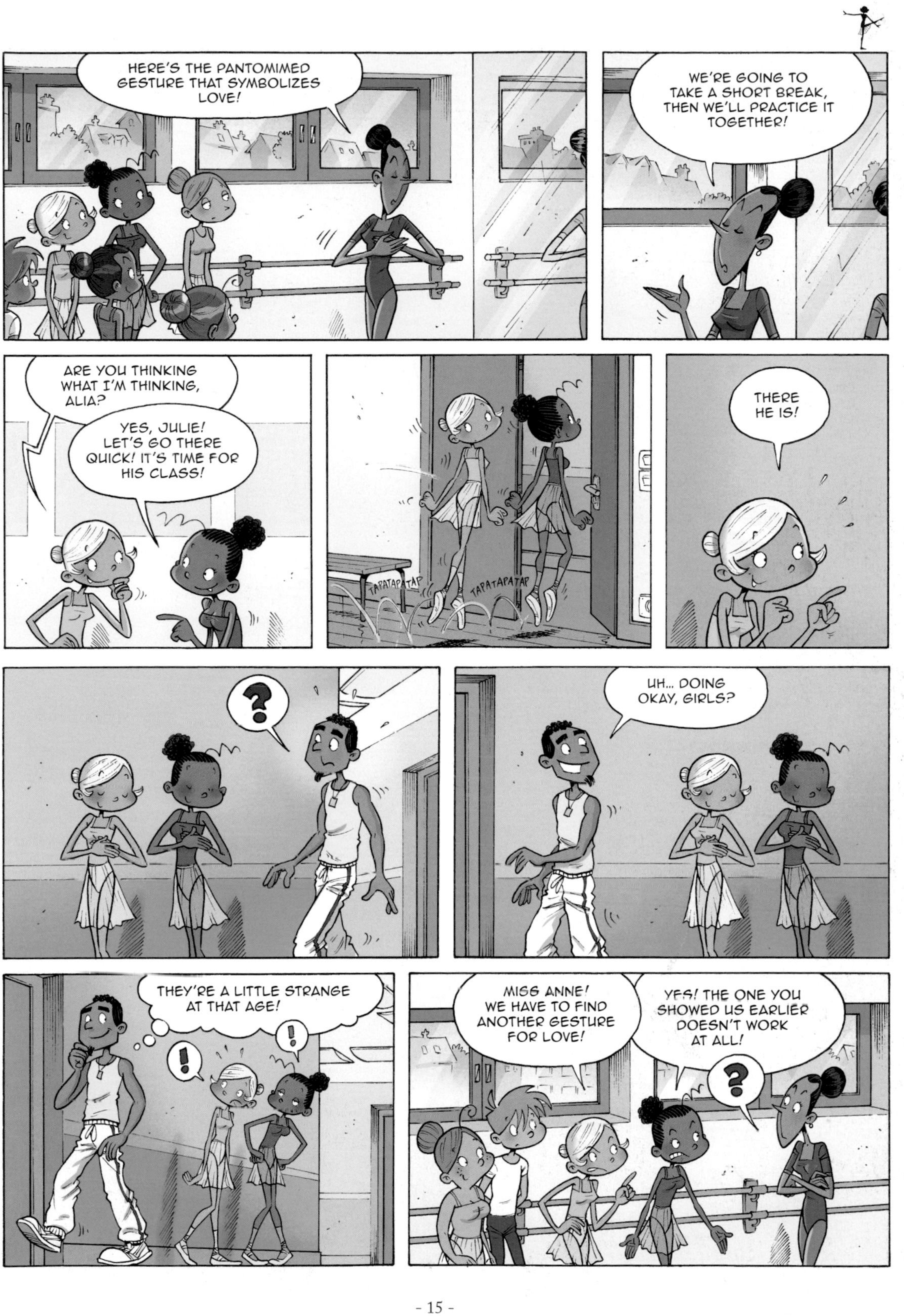
HERE'S THE PANTOMIMED GESTURE THAT SYMBOLIZES LOVE!
WE'RE GOING TO TAKE A SHORT BREAK, THEN WE'LL PRACTICE IT TOGETHER!
ARE YOU THINKING WHAT I'M THINKING, ALIA?
YES, JULIE! LET'S GO THERE QUICK! IT'S TIME FOR HIS CLASS!
TAPATAPATAP
TAPATAPATAP
THERE HE IS!
?
UH... DOING OKAY, GIRLS?
THEY'RE A LITTLE STRANGE AT THAT AGE!
!
!
MISS ANNE! WE HAVE TO FIND ANOTHER GESTURE FOR LOVE!
YES! THE ONE YOU SHOWED US EARLIER DOESN'T WORK AT ALL!
?

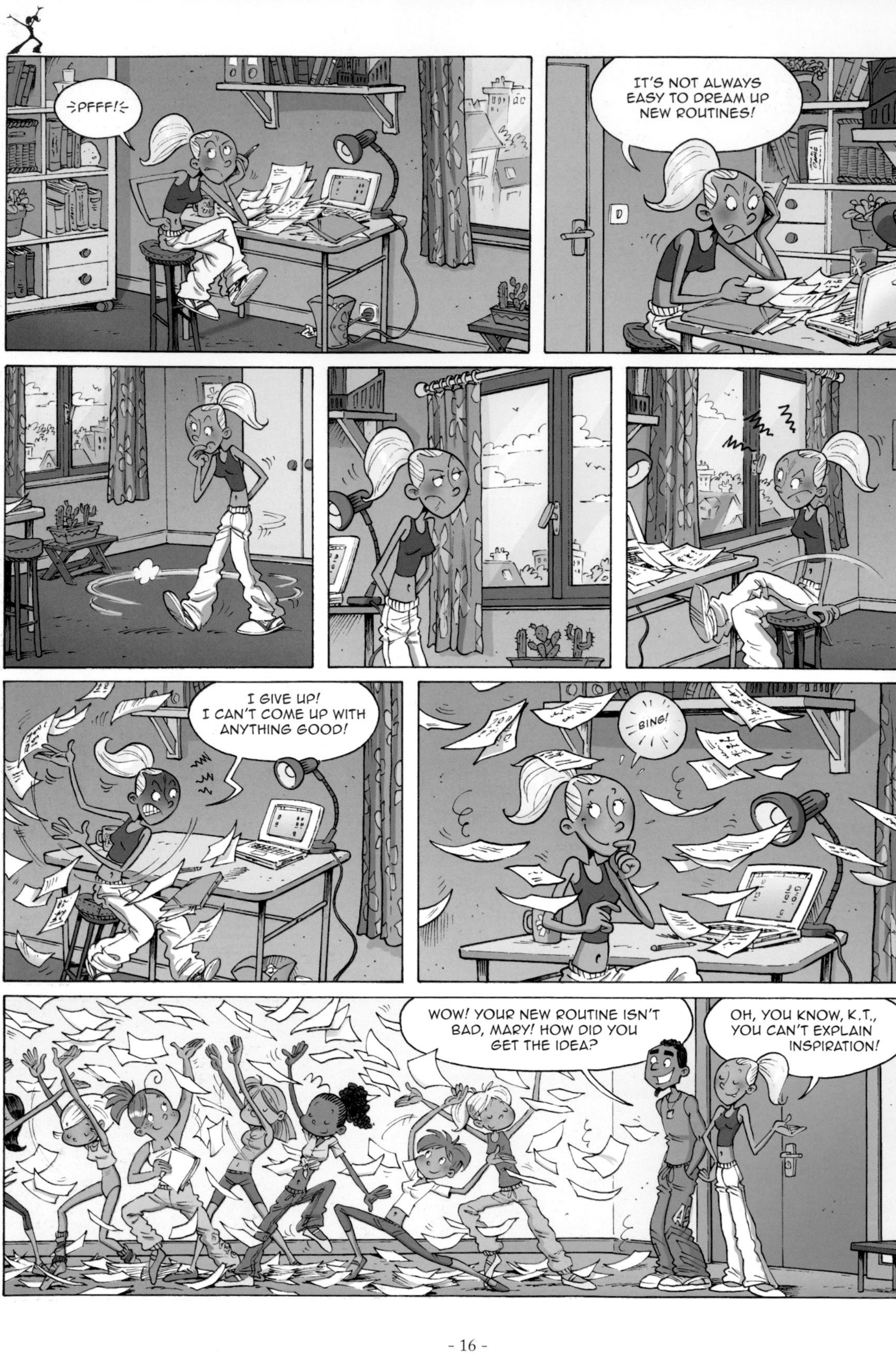
PFFF!
IT'S NOT ALWAYS EASY TO DREAM UP NEW ROUTINES!
I GIVE UP! I CAN'T COME UP WITH ANYTHING GOOD!
BING!
WOW! YOUR NEW ROUTINE ISN'T BAD, MARY! HOW DID YOU GET THE IDEA?
OH, YOU KNOW, K.T., YOU CAN'T EXPLAIN INSPIRATION!

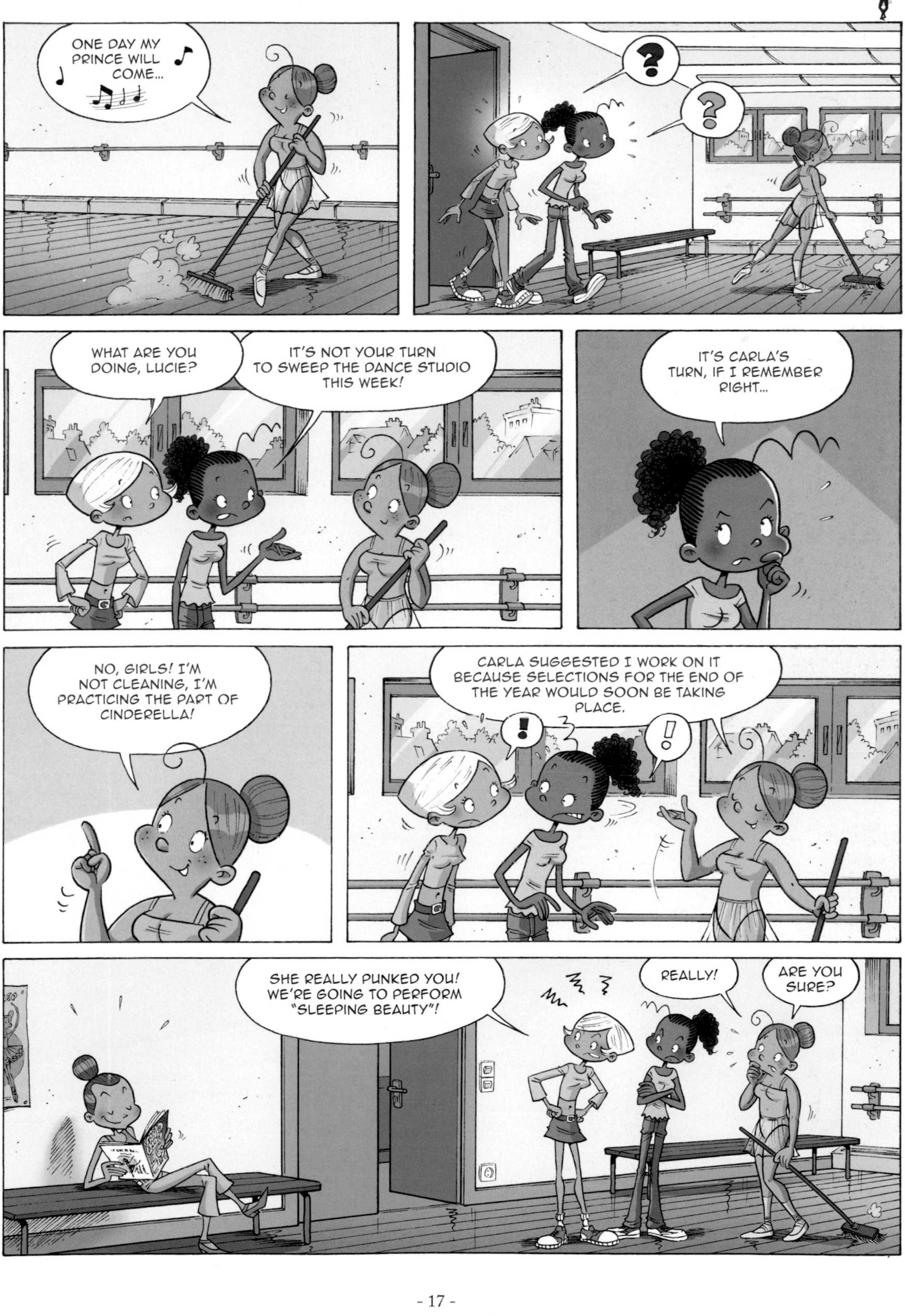
ONE DAY MY PRINCE WILL COME...
?
?
WHAT ARE YOU DOING, LUCIE?
IT'S NOT YOUR TURN TO SWEEP THE DANCE STUDIO THIS WEEK!
IT'S CARLA'S TURN, IF I REMEMBER RIGHT...
NO, GIRLS! I'M NOT CLEANING, I'M PRACTICING THE PART OF CINDERELLA!
CARLA SUGGESTED I WORK ON IT BECAUSE SELECTIONS FOR THE END OF THE YEAR WOULD SOON BE TAKING PLACE.
!
!
SHE REALLY PUNKED YOU! WE'RE GOING TO PERFORM "SLEEPING BEAUTY"!
REALLY!
ARE YOU SURE?

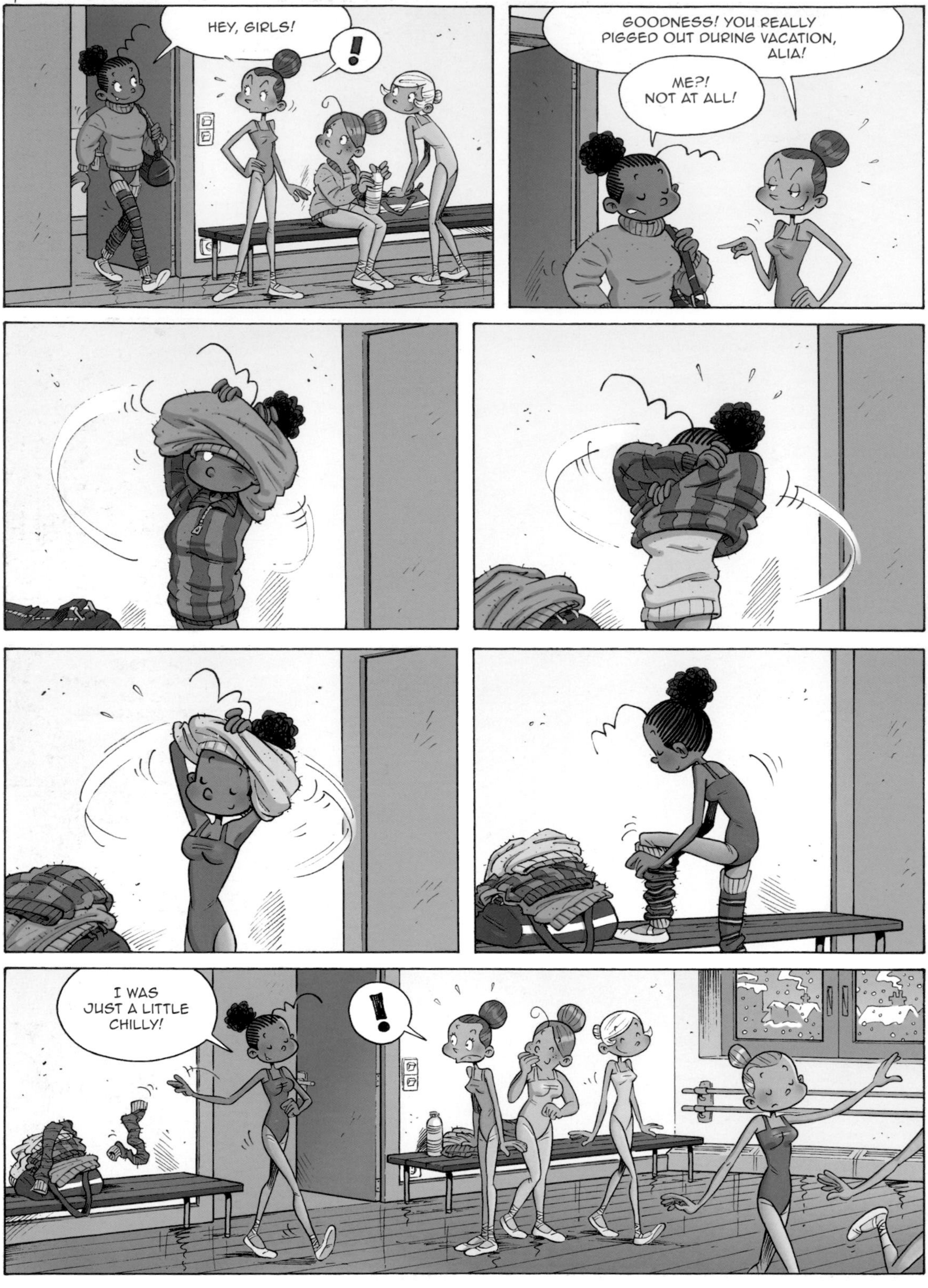
HEY, GIRLS!
!
GOODNESS! YOU REALLY PIGGED OUT DURING VACATION, ALIA!
ME?! NOT AT ALL!
I WAS JUST A LITTLE CHILLY!
!

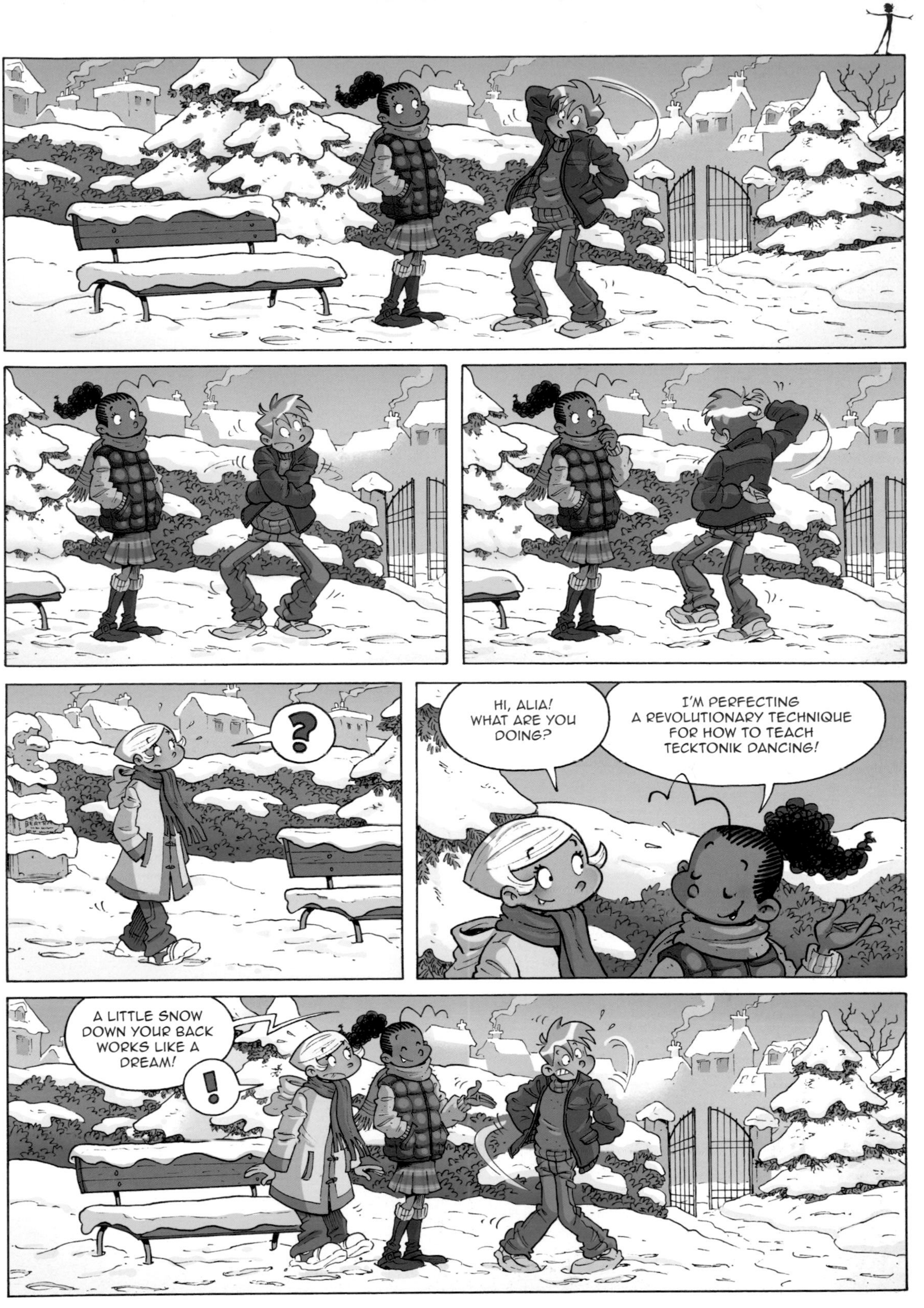
?
HI, ALIA! WHAT ARE YOU DOING?
I'M PERFECTING A REVOLUTIONARY TECHNIQUE FOR HOW TO TEACH TECKTONIK DANCING!
A LITTLE SNOW DOWN YOUR BACK WORKS LIKE A DREAM!
!

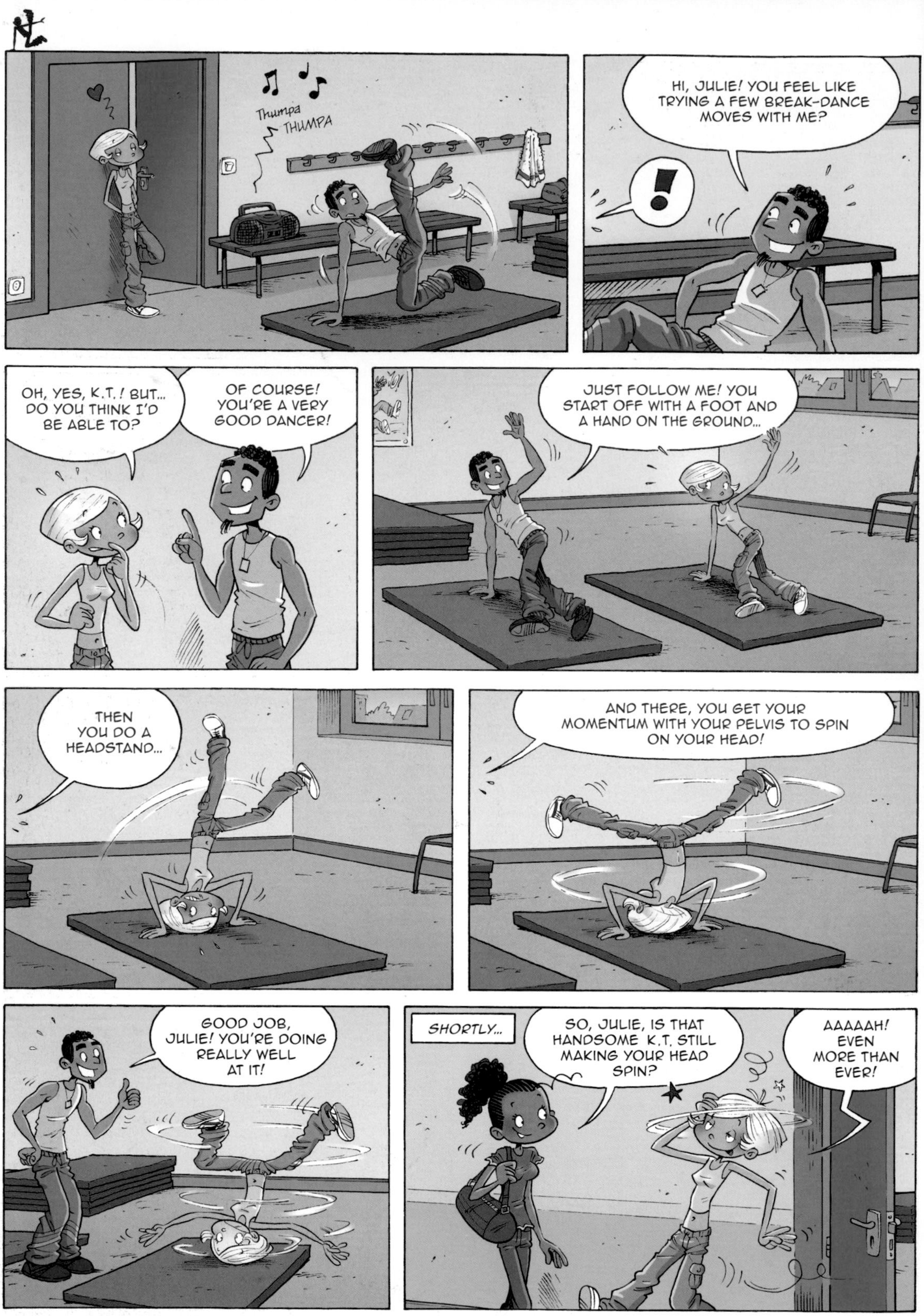
Thumpa
THUMPA
HI, JULIE! YOU FEEL LIKE TRYING A FEW BREAK-DANCE MOVES WITH ME?
!
OH, YES, K.T.! BUT... DO YOU THINK I'D BE ABLE TO?
OF COURSE! YOU'RE A VERY GOOD DANCER!
JUST FOLLOW ME! YOU START OFF WITH A FOOT AND A HAND ON THE GROUND...
THEN YOU DO A HEADSTAND...
AND THERE, YOU GET YOUR MOMENTUM WITH YOUR PELVIS TO SPIN ON YOUR HEAD!
GOOD JOB, JULIE! YOU'RE DOING REALLY WELL AT IT!
SHORTLY...
SO, JULIE, IS THAT HANDSOME K.T. STILL MAKING YOUR HEAD SPIN?
AAAAAH! EVEN MORE THAN EVER!

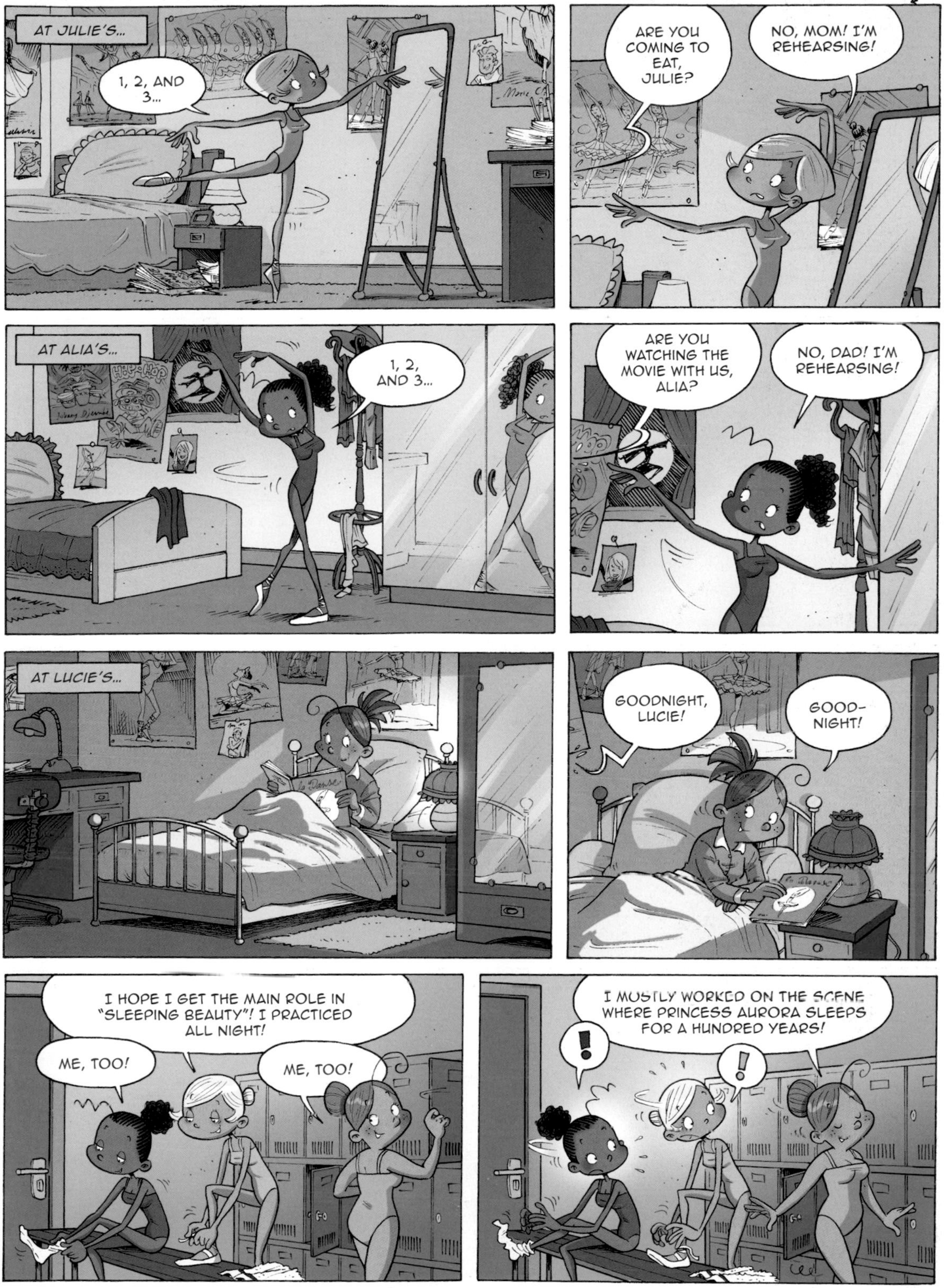

AT JULIE'S...
1, 2, AND 3...
ARE YOU COMING TO EAT, JULIE?
NO, MOM! I'M REHEARSING!
AT ALIA'S...
1, 2, AND 3...
ARE YOU WATCHING THE MOVIE WITH US, ALIA?
NO, DAD! I'M REHEARSING!
AT LUCIE'S...
GOODNIGHT, LUCIE!
GOOD-NIGHT!
I HOPE I GET THE MAIN ROLE IN "SLEEPING BEAUTY"! I PRACTICED ALL NIGHT!
ME, TOO!
ME, TOO!
I MOSTLY WORKED ON THE SCENE WHERE PRINCESS AURORA SLEEPS FOR A HUNDRED YEARS!
!
!

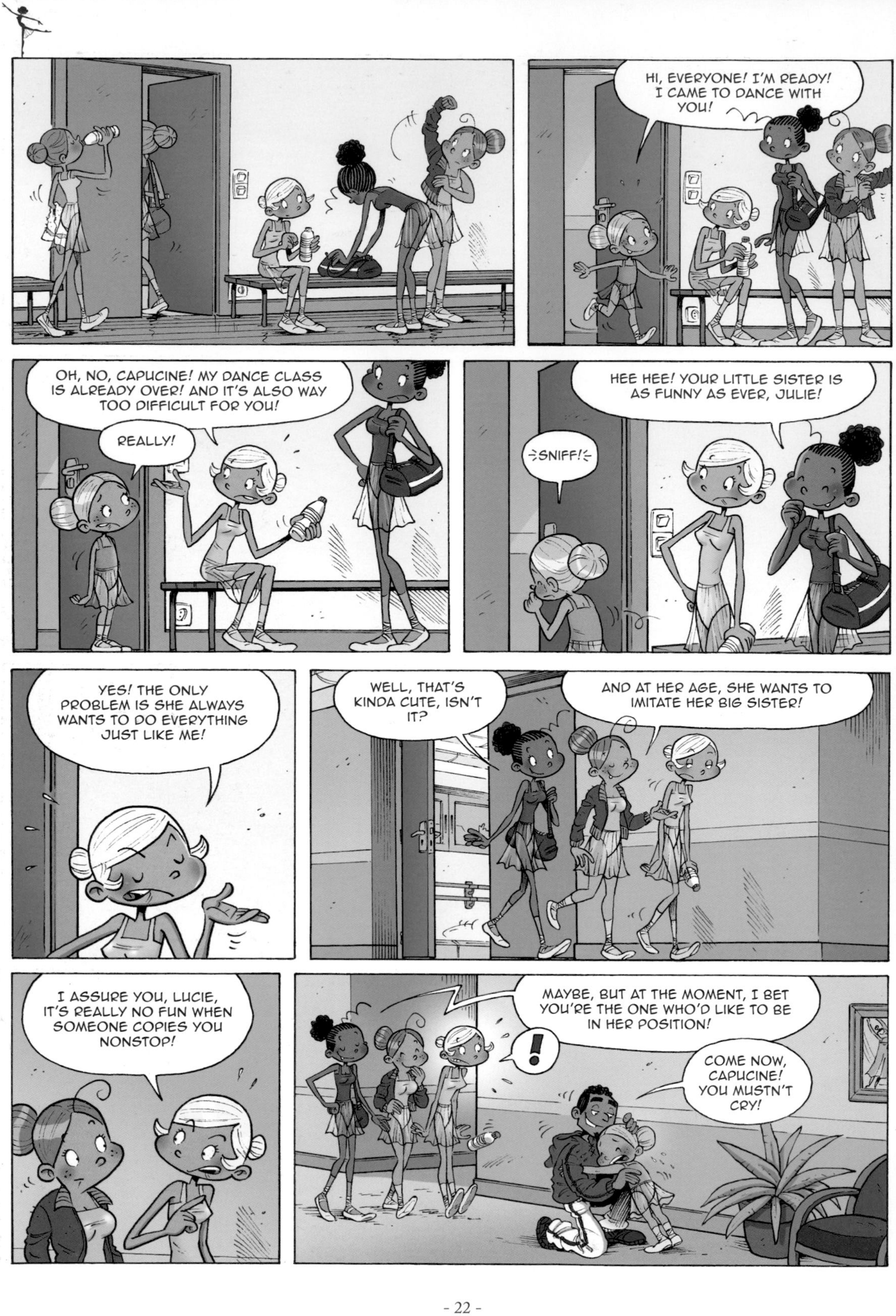
HI, EVERYONE! I'M READY! I CAME TO DANCE WITH YOU!
OH, NO, CAPUCINE! MY DANCE CLASS IS ALREADY OVER! AND IT'S ALSO WAY TOO DIFFICULT FOR YOU!
REALLY!
HEE HEE! YOUR LITTLE SISTER IS AS FUNNY AS EVER, JULIE!
SNIFF!
YES! THE ONLY PROBLEM IS SHE ALWAYS WANTS TO DO EVERYTHING JUST LIKE ME!
WELL, THAT'S KINDA CUTE, ISN'T IT?
AND AT HER AGE, SHE WANTS TO IMITATE HER BIG SISTER!
I ASSURE YOU, LUCIE, IT'S REALLY NO FUN WHEN SOMEONE COPIES YOU NONSTOP!
MAYBE, BUT AT THE MOMENT, I BET YOU'RE THE ONE WHO'D LIKE TO BE IN HER POSITION!
!
COME NOW, CAPUCINE! YOU MUSTN'T CRY!

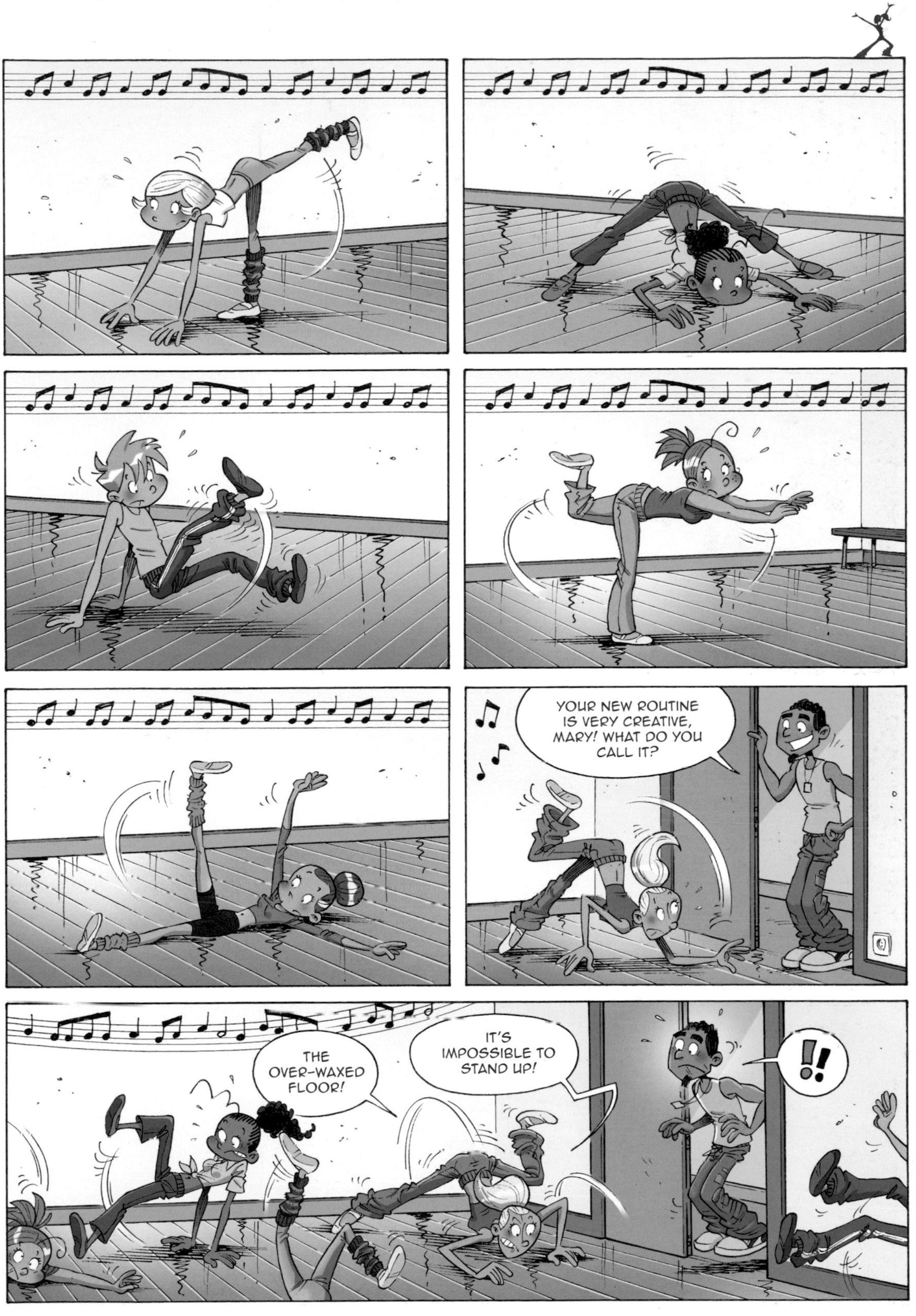
YOUR NEW ROUTINE IS VERY CREATIVE, MARY! WHAT DO YOU CALL IT?
THE OVER-WAXED FLOOR!
IT'S IMPOSSIBLE TO STAND UP!
!!

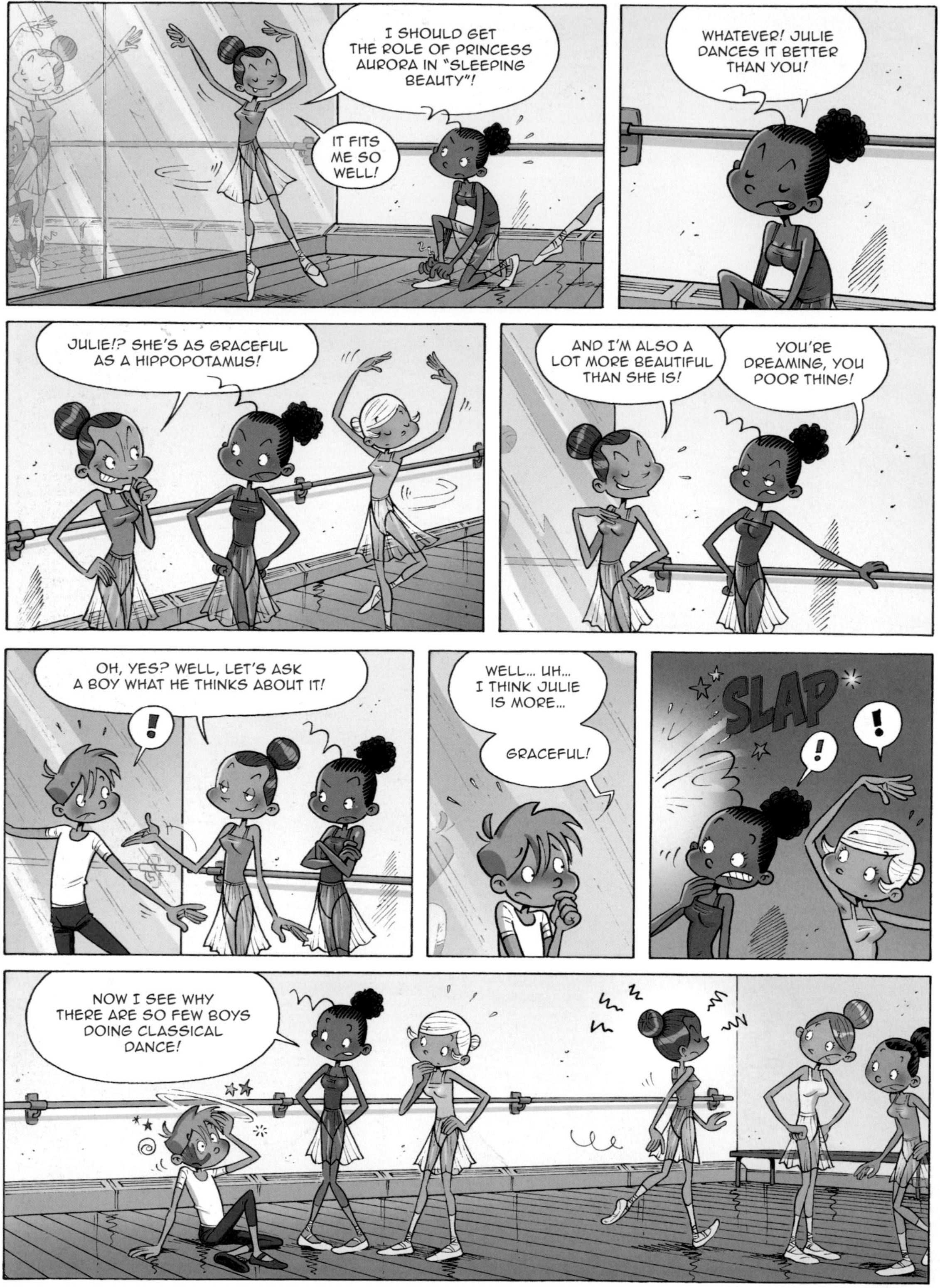

I SHOULD GET THE ROLE OF PRINCESS AURORA IN "SLEEPING BEAUTY"!
IT FITS ME SO WELL!
WHATEVER! JULIE DANCES IT BETTER THAN YOU!
JULIE!? SHE'S AS GRACEFUL AS A HIPPOPOTAMUS!
AND I'M ALSO A LOT MORE BEAUTIFUL THAN SHE IS!
YOU'RE DREAMING, YOU POOR THING!
OH, YES? WELL, LET'S ASK A BOY WHAT HE THINKS ABOUT IT!
!
WELL... UH... I THINK JULIE IS MORE...
GRACEFUL!
SLAP
!
!
NOW I SEE WHY THERE ARE SO FEW BOYS DOING CLASSICAL DANCE!

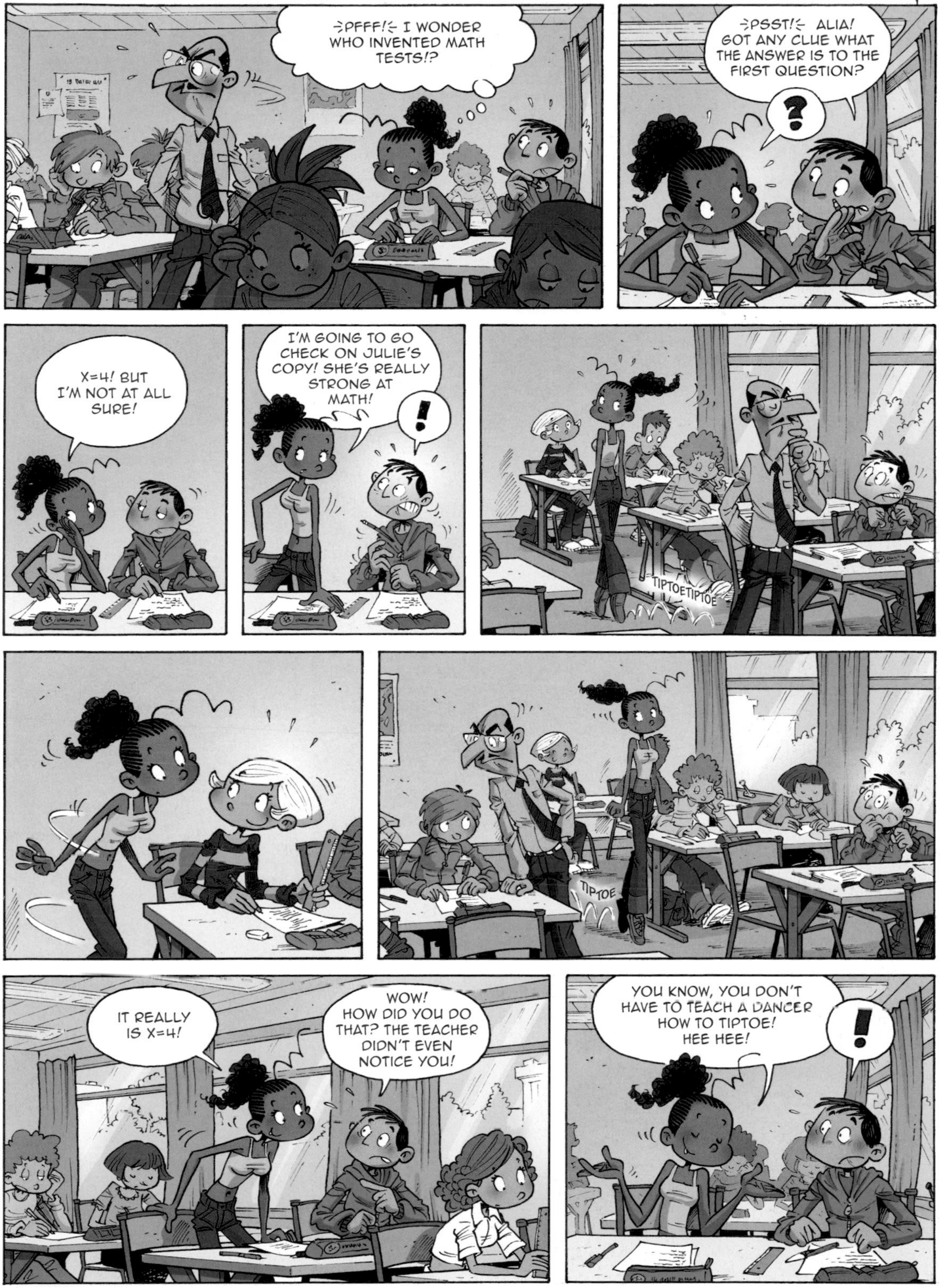

PFFF! I WONDER WHO INVENTED MATH TESTS!?
PSST! ALIA! GOT ANY CLUE WHAT THE ANSWER IS TO THE FIRST QUESTION?
?
X=4! BUT I'M NOT AT ALL SURE!
I'M GOING TO GO CHECK ON JULIE'S COPY! SHE'S REALLY STRONG AT MATH!
!
TIPTOETIPTOE
TIPTOE
IT REALLY IS X=4!
WOW! HOW DID YOU DO THAT? THE TEACHER DIDN'T EVEN NOTICE YOU!
YOU KNOW, YOU DON'T HAVE TO TEACH A DANCER HOW TO TIPTOE! HEE HEE!
!

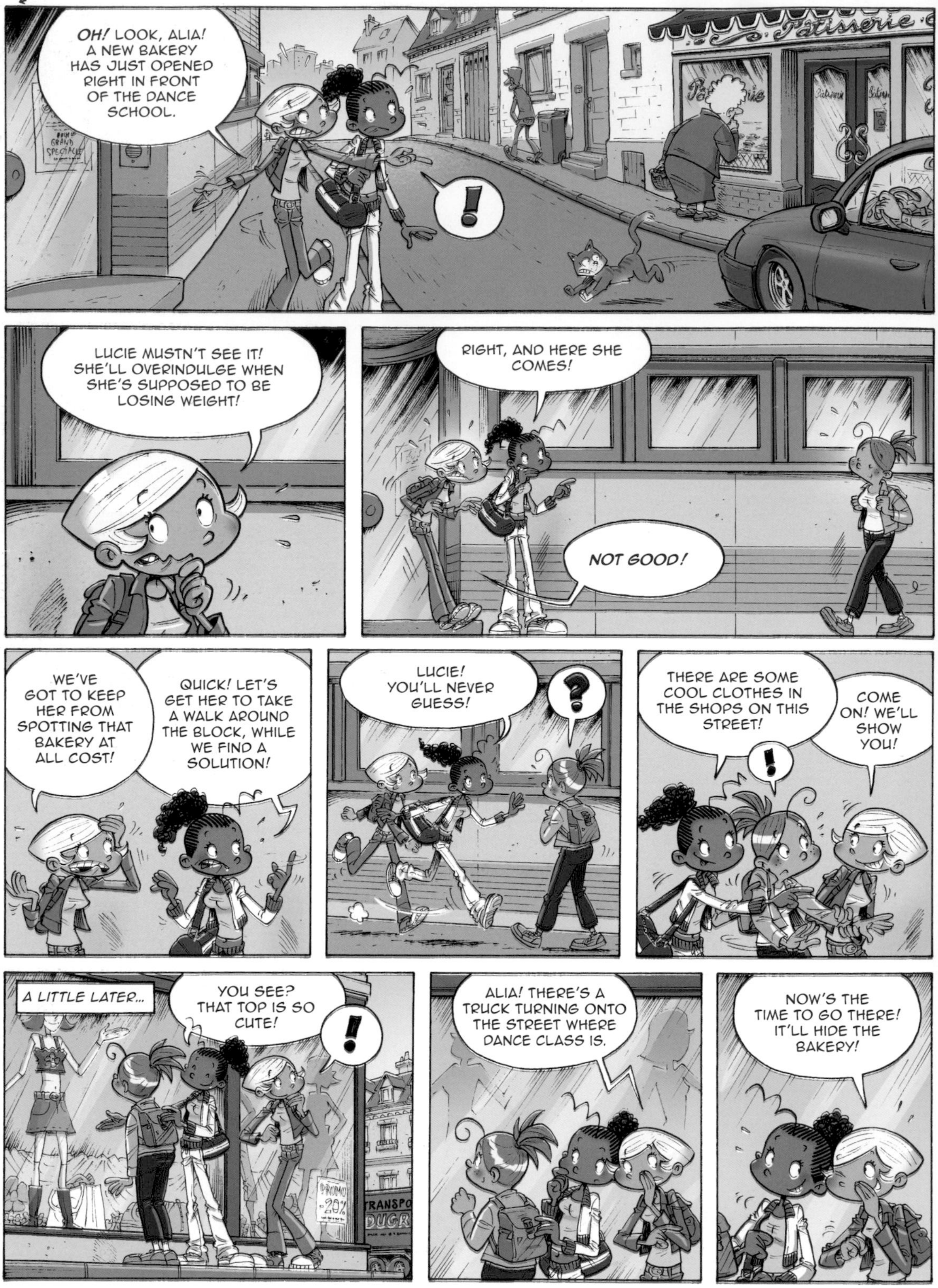

OH! LOOK, ALIA! A NEW BAKERY HAS JUST OPENED RIGHT IN FRONT OF THE DANCE SCHOOL.
!
Pâtisserie
LUCIE MUSTN'T SEE IT! SHE'LL OVERINDULGE WHEN SHE'S SUPPOSED TO BE LOSING WEIGHT!
RIGHT, AND HERE SHE COMES!
NOT GOOD!
WE'VE GOT TO KEEP HER FROM SPOTTING THAT BAKERY AT ALL COST!
QUICK! LET'S GET HER TO TAKE A WALK AROUND THE BLOCK, WHILE WE FIND A SOLUTION!
LUCIE! YOU'LL NEVER GUESS!
?
THERE ARE SOME COOL CLOTHES IN THE SHOPS ON THIS STREET!
!
COME ON! WE'LL SHOW YOU!
A LITTLE LATER...
YOU SEE? THAT TOP IS SO CUTE!
!
PROMO -20%
ALIA! THERE'S A TRUCK TURNING ONTO THE STREET WHERE DANCE CLASS IS.
NOW'S THE TIME TO GO THERE! IT'LL HIDE THE BAKERY!

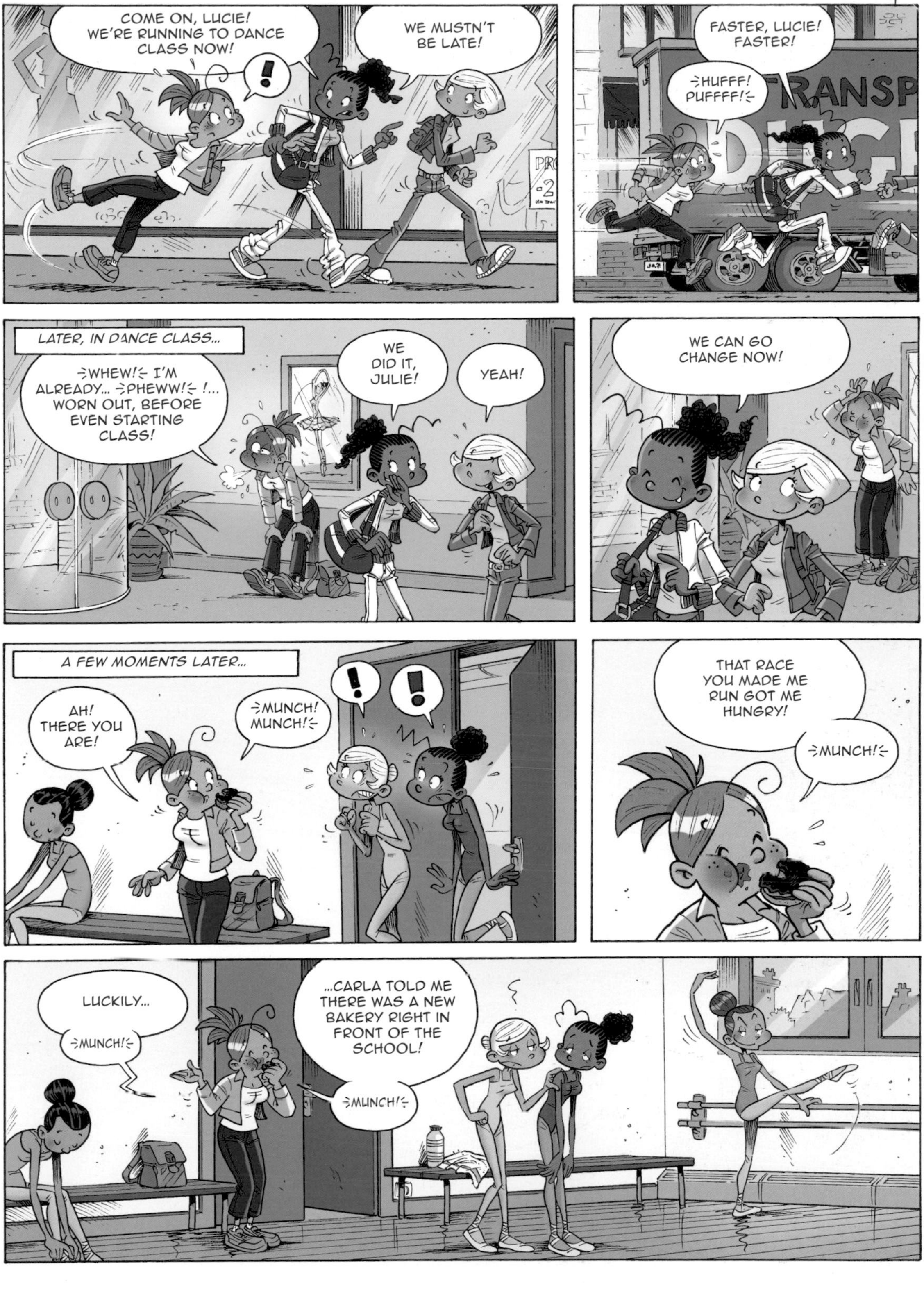
COME ON, LUCIE! WE'RE RUNNING TO DANCE CLASS NOW!
!
WE MUSTN'T BE LATE!
FASTER, LUCIE! FASTER!
HUFFF! PUFFFF!
LATER, IN DANCE CLASS...
WHEW! I'M ALREADY... PHEWW! !... WORN OUT, BEFORE EVEN STARTING CLASS!
WE DID IT, JULIE!
YEAH!
WE CAN GO CHANGE NOW!
A FEW MOMENTS LATER...
AH! THERE YOU ARE!
MUNCH! MUNCH!
!
!
THAT RACE YOU MADE ME RUN GOT ME HUNGRY!
MUNCH!
LUCKILY...
MUNCH!
...CARLA TOLD ME THERE WAS A NEW BAKERY RIGHT IN FRONT OF THE SCHOOL!
MUNCH!

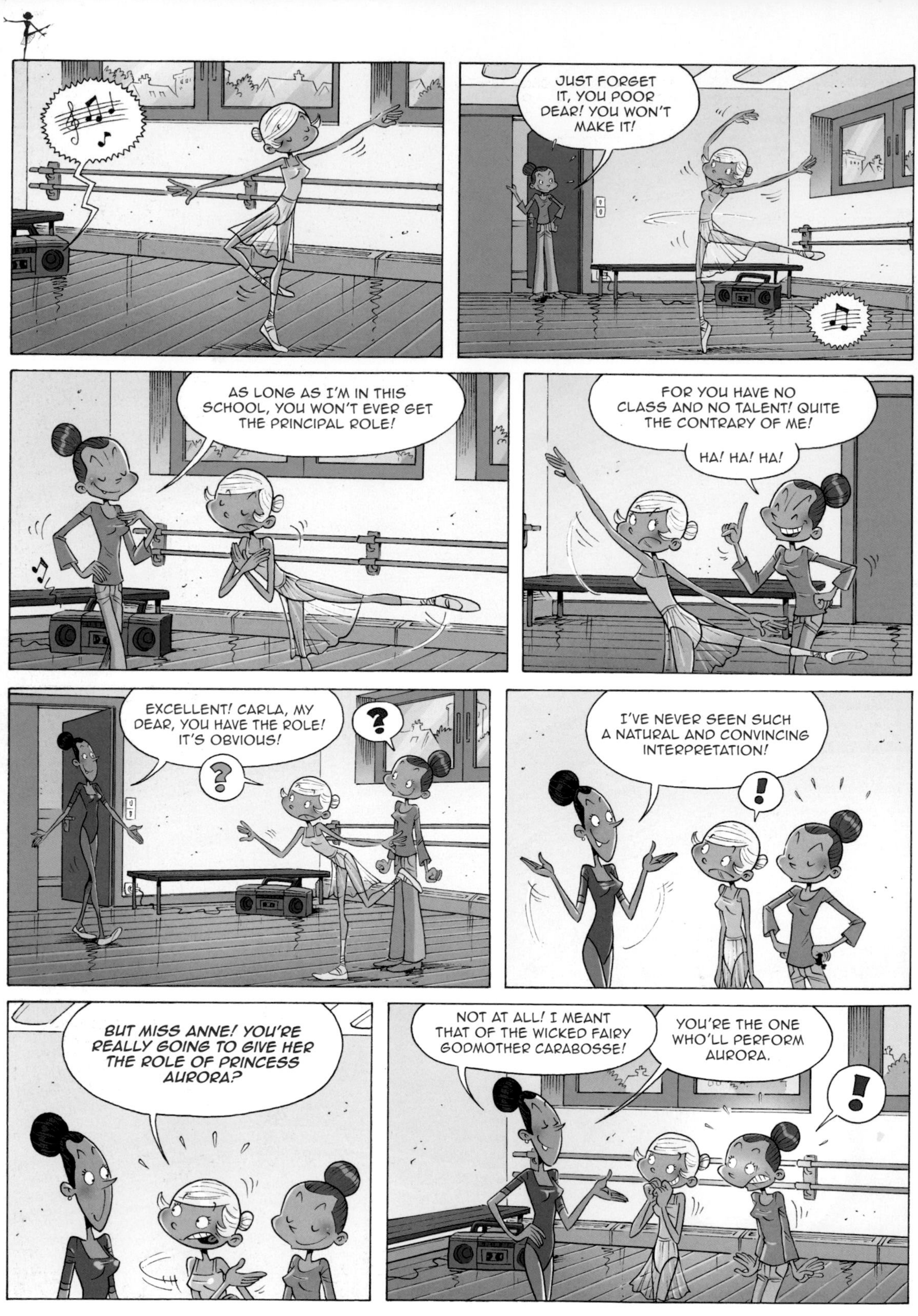
JUST FORGET IT, YOU POOR DEAR! YOU WON'T MAKE IT!
AS LONG AS I'M IN THIS SCHOOL, YOU WON'T EVER GET THE PRINCIPAL ROLE!
FOR YOU HAVE NO CLASS AND NO TALENT! QUITE THE CONTRARY OF ME!
HA! HA! HA!
EXCELLENT! CARLA, MY DEAR, YOU HAVE THE ROLE! IT'S OBVIOUS!
?
?
I'VE NEVER SEEN SUCH A NATURAL AND CONVINCING INTERPRETATION!
!
BUT MISS ANNE! YOU'RE REALLY GOING TO GIVE HER THE ROLE OF PRINCESS AURORA?
NOT AT ALL! I MEANT THAT OF THE WICKED FAIRY GODMOTHER CARABOSSE!
YOU'RE THE ONE WHO'LL PERFORM AURORA.
!

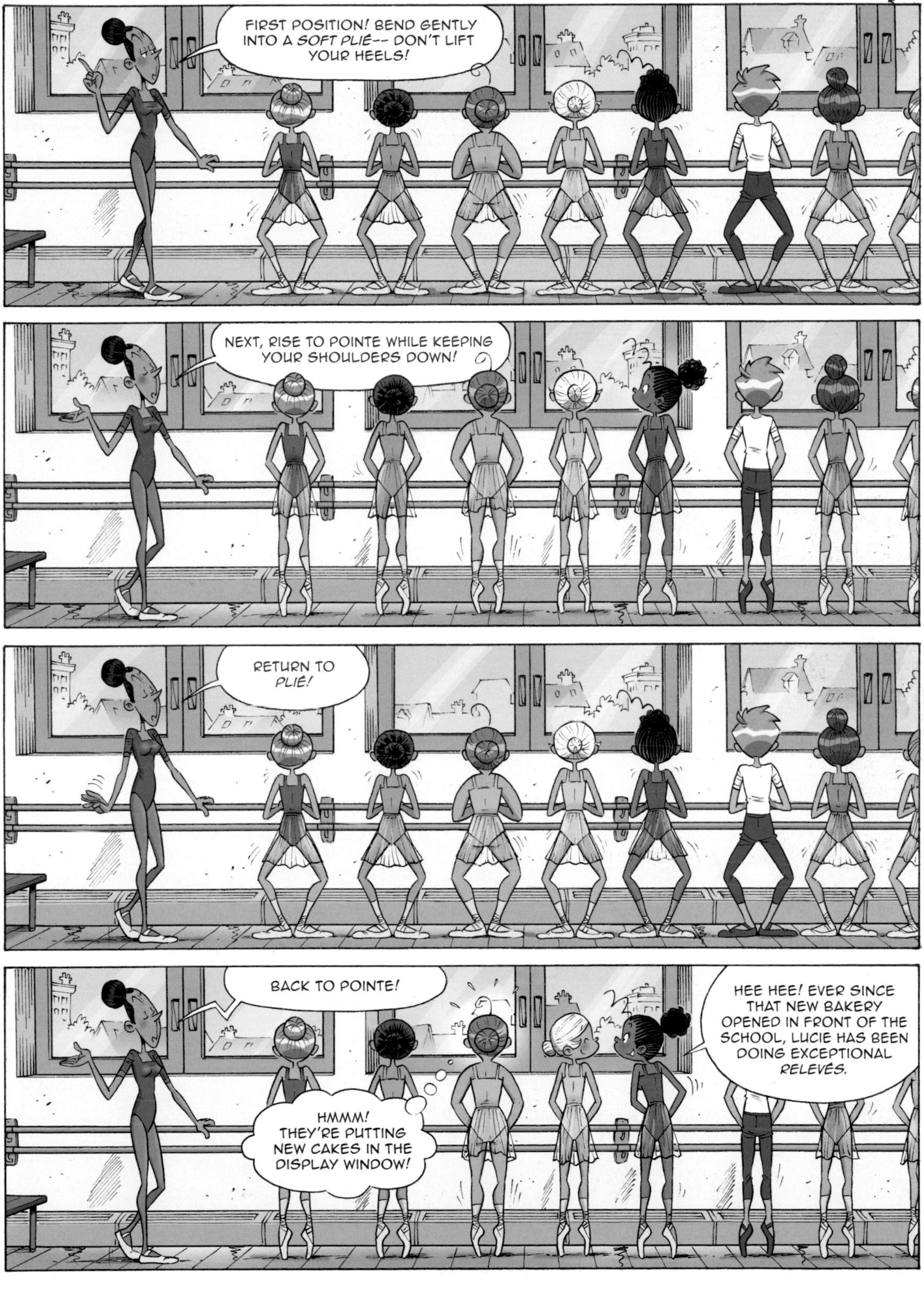

FIRST POSITION! BEND GENTLY INTO A *SOFT PLIÉ*-- DON'T LIFT YOUR HEELS!
NEXT, RISE TO POINTE WHILE KEEPING YOUR SHOULDERS DOWN!
RETURN TO *PLIÉ*!
BACK TO POINTE!
HMMM! THEY'RE PUTTING NEW CAKES IN THE DISPLAY WINDOW!
HEE HEE! EVER SINCE THAT NEW BAKERY OPENED IN FRONT OF THE SCHOOL, LUCIE HAS BEEN DOING EXCEPTIONAL *RELEVÉS*.

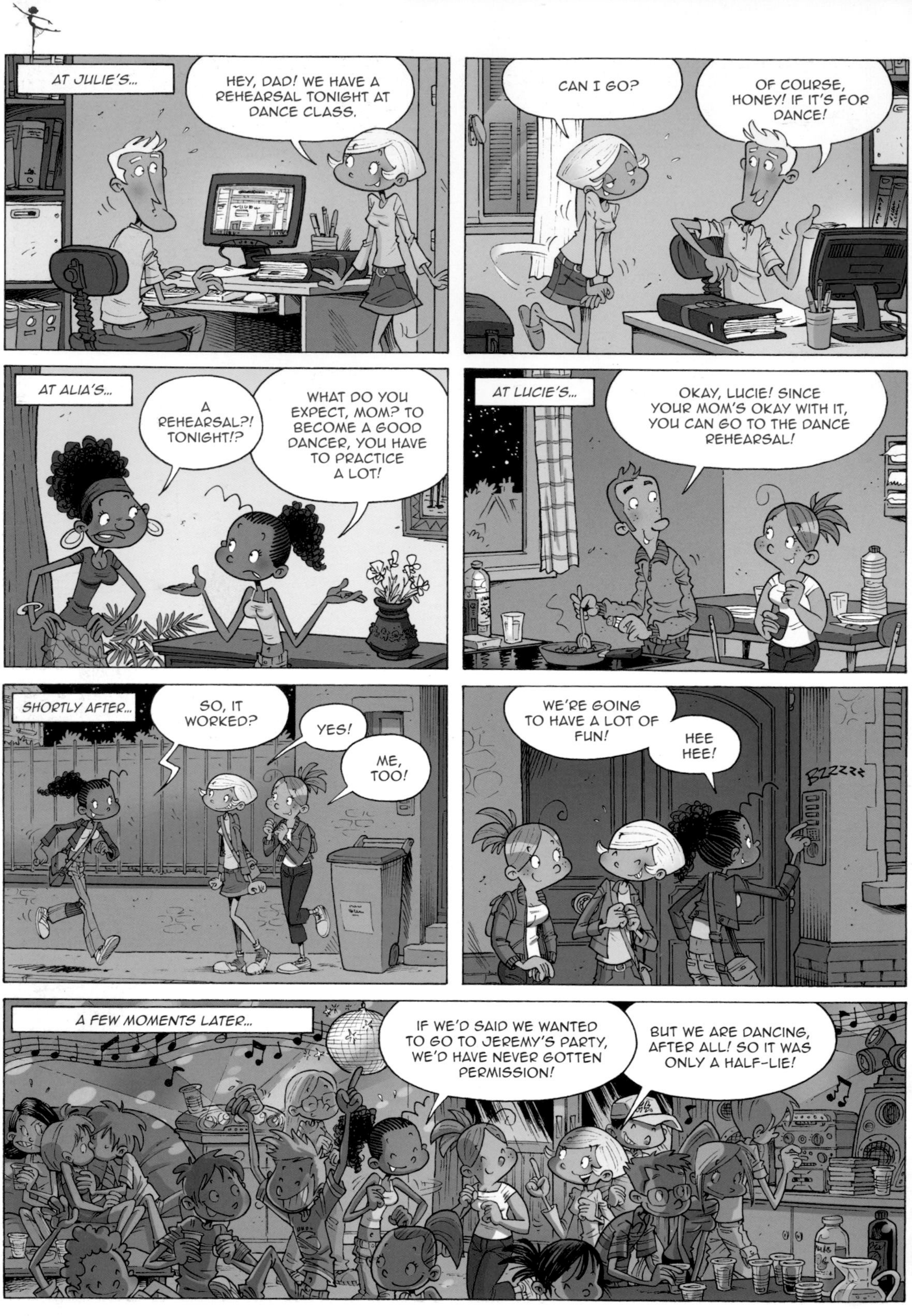
AT JULIE'S...
HEY, DAD! WE HAVE A REHEARSAL TONIGHT AT DANCE CLASS.
CAN I GO?
OF COURSE, HONEY! IF IT'S FOR DANCE!
AT ALIA'S...
A REHEARSAL?! TONIGHT!?
WHAT DO YOU EXPECT, MOM? TO BECOME A GOOD DANCER, YOU HAVE TO PRACTICE A LOT!
AT LUCIE'S...
OKAY, LUCIE! SINCE YOUR MOM'S OKAY WITH IT, YOU CAN GO TO THE DANCE REHEARSAL!
SHORTLY AFTER...
SO, IT WORKED?
YES!
ME, TOO!
WE'RE GOING TO HAVE A LOT OF FUN!
HEE HEE!
BZZZZZ
A FEW MOMENTS LATER...
IF WE'D SAID WE WANTED TO GO TO JEREMY'S PARTY, WE'D HAVE NEVER GOTTEN PERMISSION!
BUT WE ARE DANCING, AFTER ALL! SO IT WAS ONLY A HALF-LIE!

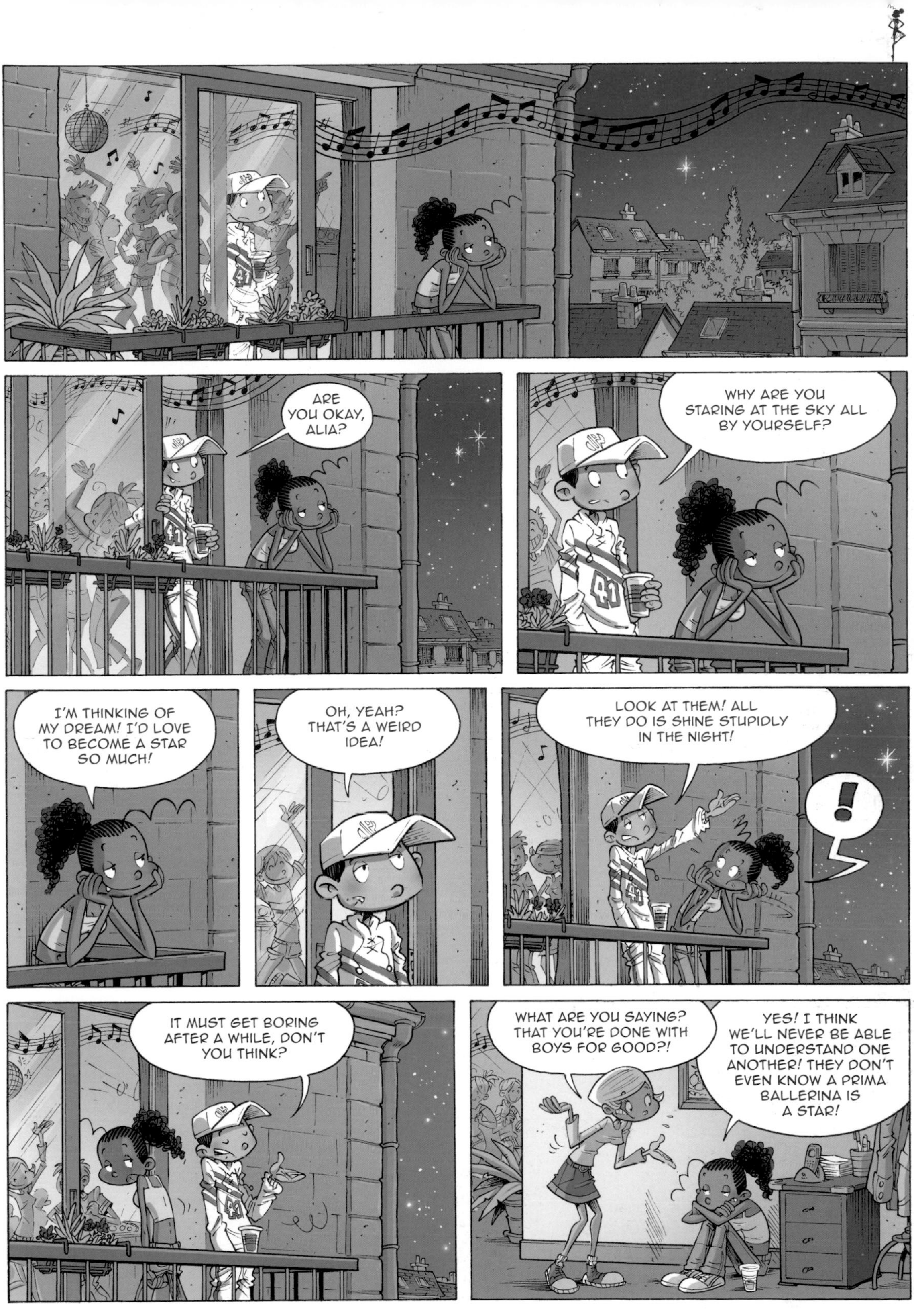
ARE YOU OKAY, ALIA?
WHY ARE YOU STARING AT THE SKY ALL BY YOURSELF?
I'M THINKING OF MY DREAM! I'D LOVE TO BECOME A STAR SO MUCH!
OH, YEAH? THAT'S A WEIRD IDEA!
LOOK AT THEM! ALL THEY DO IS SHINE STUPIDLY IN THE NIGHT!
!
IT MUST GET BORING AFTER A WHILE, DON'T YOU THINK?
WHAT ARE YOU SAYING? THAT YOU'RE DONE WITH BOYS FOR GOOD?!
YES! I THINK WE'LL NEVER BE ABLE TO UNDERSTAND ONE ANOTHER! THEY DON'T EVEN KNOW A PRIMA BALLERINA IS A STAR!

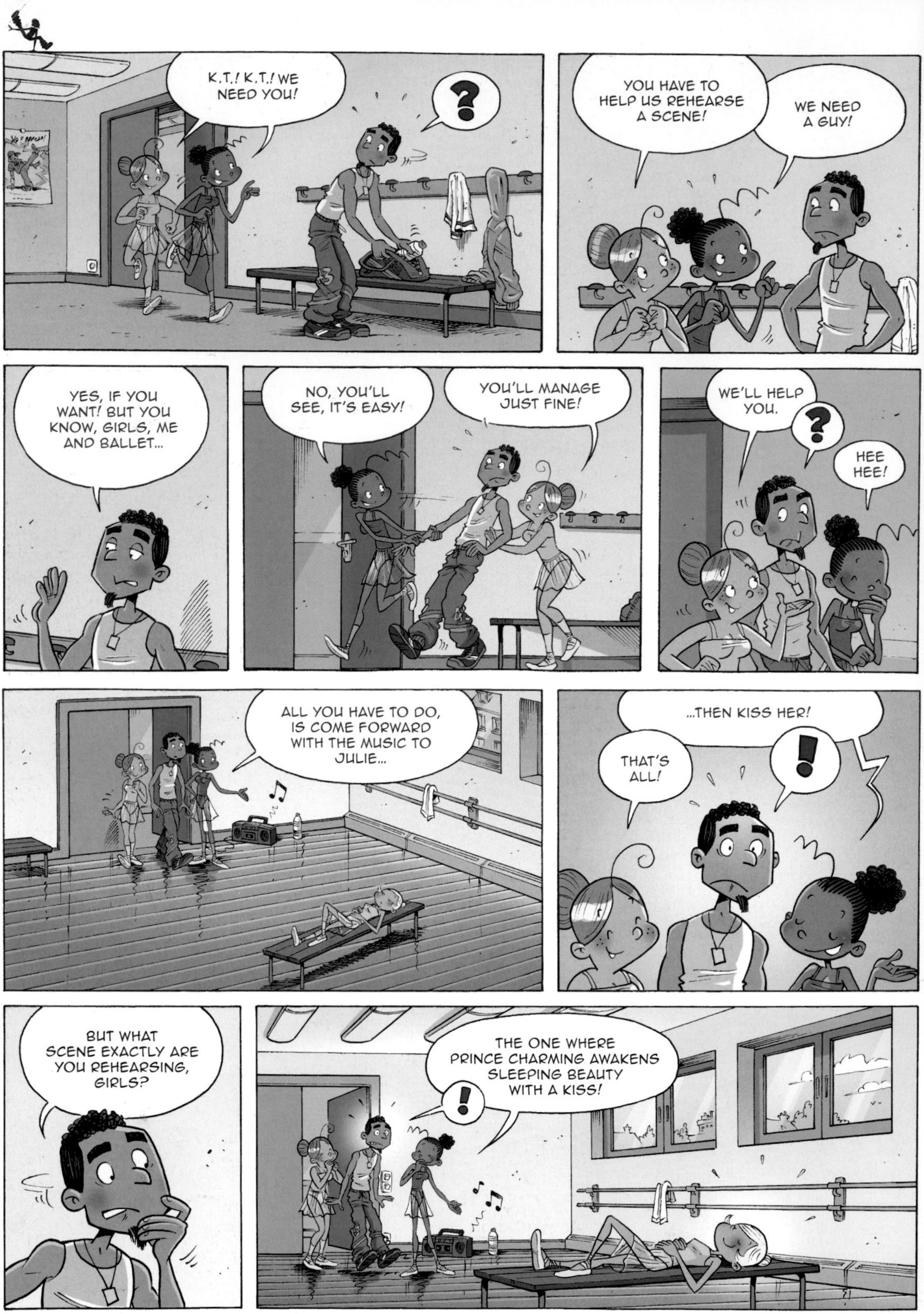

K.T.! K.T.! WE NEED YOU!
?
YOU HAVE TO HELP US REHEARSE A SCENE!
WE NEED A GUY!
YES, IF YOU WANT! BUT YOU KNOW, GIRLS, ME AND BALLET...
NO, YOU'LL SEE, IT'S EASY!
YOU'LL MANAGE JUST FINE!
WE'LL HELP YOU.
?
HEE HEE!
ALL YOU HAVE TO DO, IS COME FORWARD WITH THE MUSIC TO JULIE...
...THEN KISS HER!
THAT'S ALL!
!
BUT WHAT SCENE EXACTLY ARE YOU REHEARSING, GIRLS?
THE ONE WHERE PRINCE CHARMING AWAKENS SLEEPING BEAUTY WITH A KISS!
!

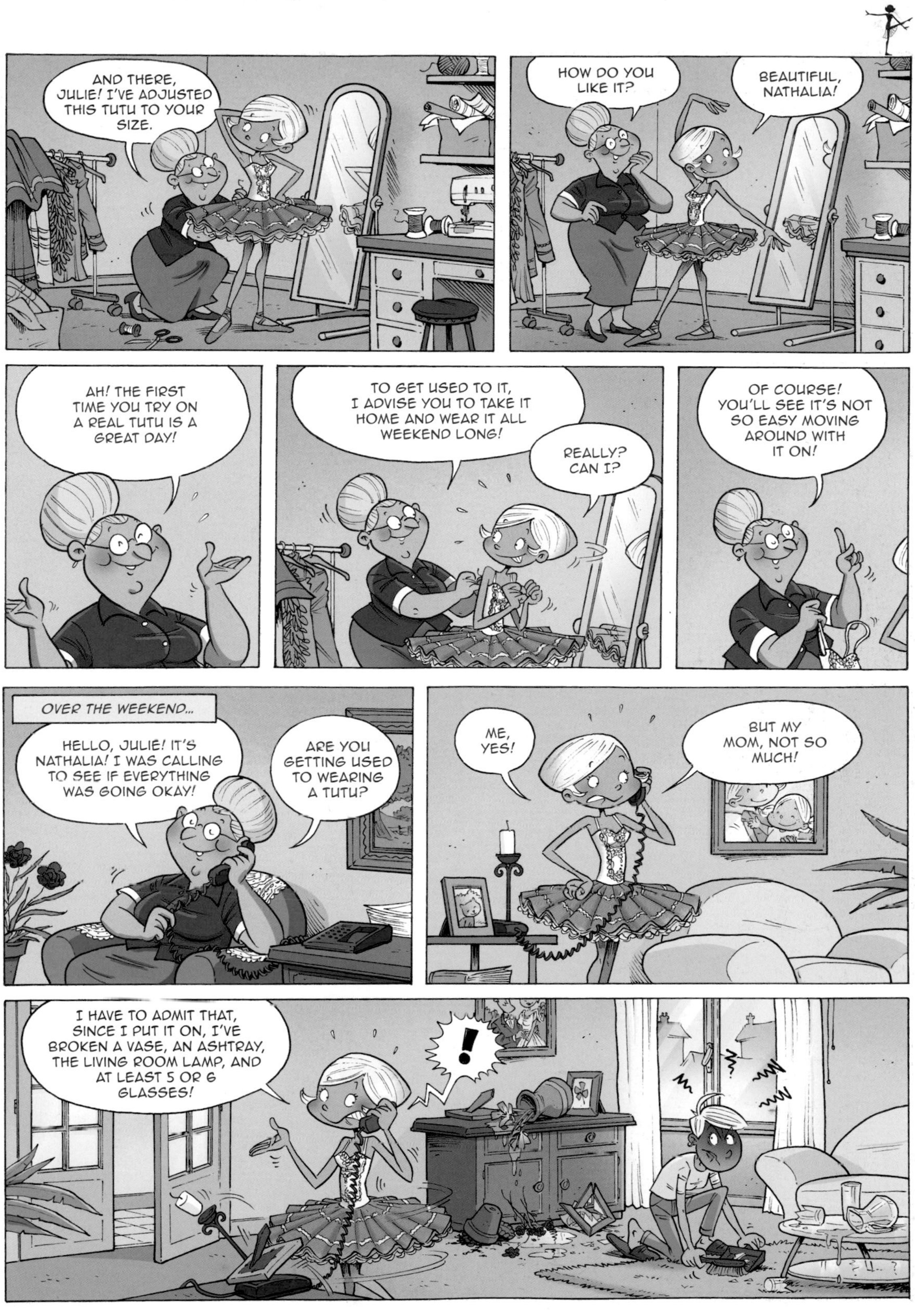
AND THERE, JULIE! I'VE ADJUSTED THIS TUTU TO YOUR SIZE.
HOW DO YOU LIKE IT?
BEAUTIFUL, NATHALIA!
AH! THE FIRST TIME YOU TRY ON A REAL TUTU IS A GREAT DAY!
TO GET USED TO IT, I ADVISE YOU TO TAKE IT HOME AND WEAR IT ALL WEEKEND LONG!
REALLY? CAN I?
OF COURSE! YOU'LL SEE IT'S NOT SO EASY MOVING AROUND WITH IT ON!
OVER THE WEEKEND...
HELLO, JULIE! IT'S NATHALIA! I WAS CALLING TO SEE IF EVERYTHING WAS GOING OKAY!
ARE YOU GETTING USED TO WEARING A TUTU?
ME, YES!
BUT MY MOM, NOT SO MUCH!
I HAVE TO ADMIT THAT, SINCE I PUT IT ON, I'VE BROKEN A VASE, AN ASHTRAY, THE LIVING ROOM LAMP, AND AT LEAST 5 OR 6 GLASSES!
!

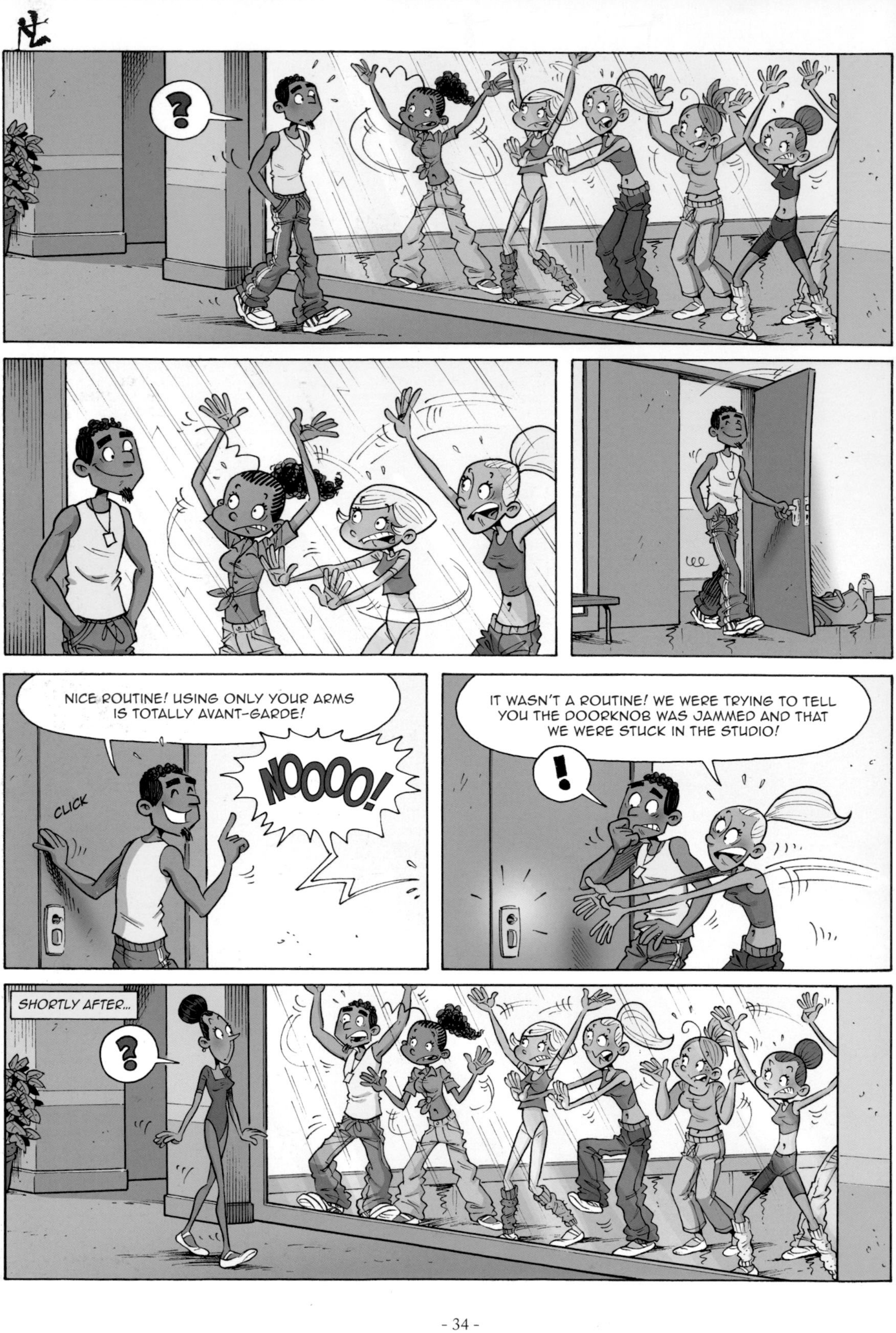
?
NICE ROUTINE! USING ONLY YOUR ARMS IS TOTALLY AVANT-GARDE!
CLICK
NOOOO!
IT WASN'T A ROUTINE! WE WERE TRYING TO TELL YOU THE DOORKNOB WAS JAMMED AND THAT WE WERE STUCK IN THE STUDIO!
!
SHORTLY AFTER...
?

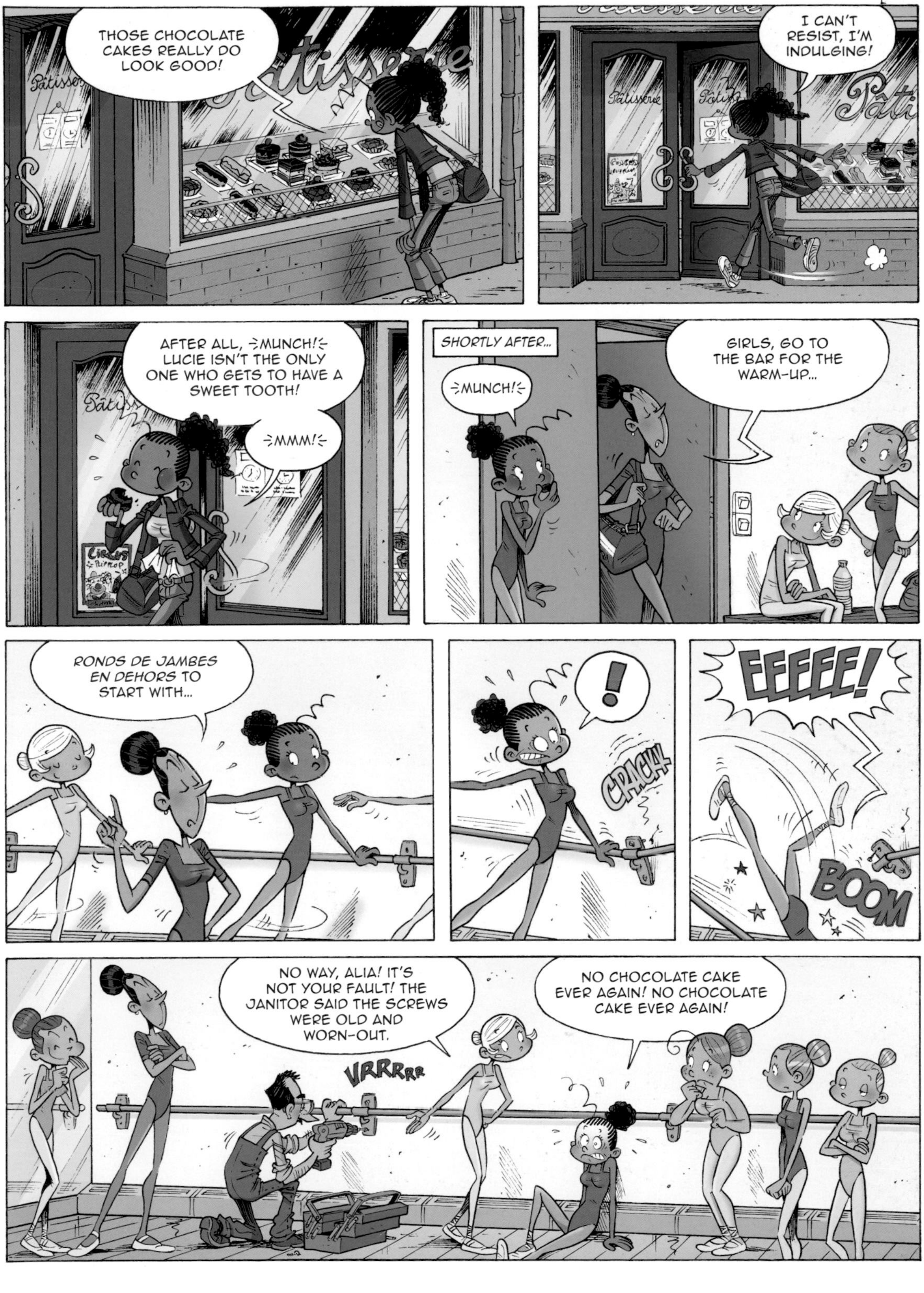

THOSE CHOCOLATE CAKES REALLY DO LOOK GOOD!
I CAN'T RESIST, I'M INDULGING!
AFTER ALL, MUNCH! LUCIE ISN'T THE ONLY ONE WHO GETS TO HAVE A SWEET TOOTH!
MMM!
SHORTLY AFTER...
MUNCH!
GIRLS, GO TO THE BAR FOR THE WARM-UP...
RONDS DE JAMBES EN DEHORS TO START WITH...
!
CRACK!
EEEEE!
BOOM
NO WAY, ALIA! IT'S NOT YOUR FAULT! THE JANITOR SAID THE SCREWS WERE OLD AND WORN-OUT.
VRRRRR
NO CHOCOLATE CAKE EVER AGAIN! NO CHOCOLATE CAKE EVER AGAIN!

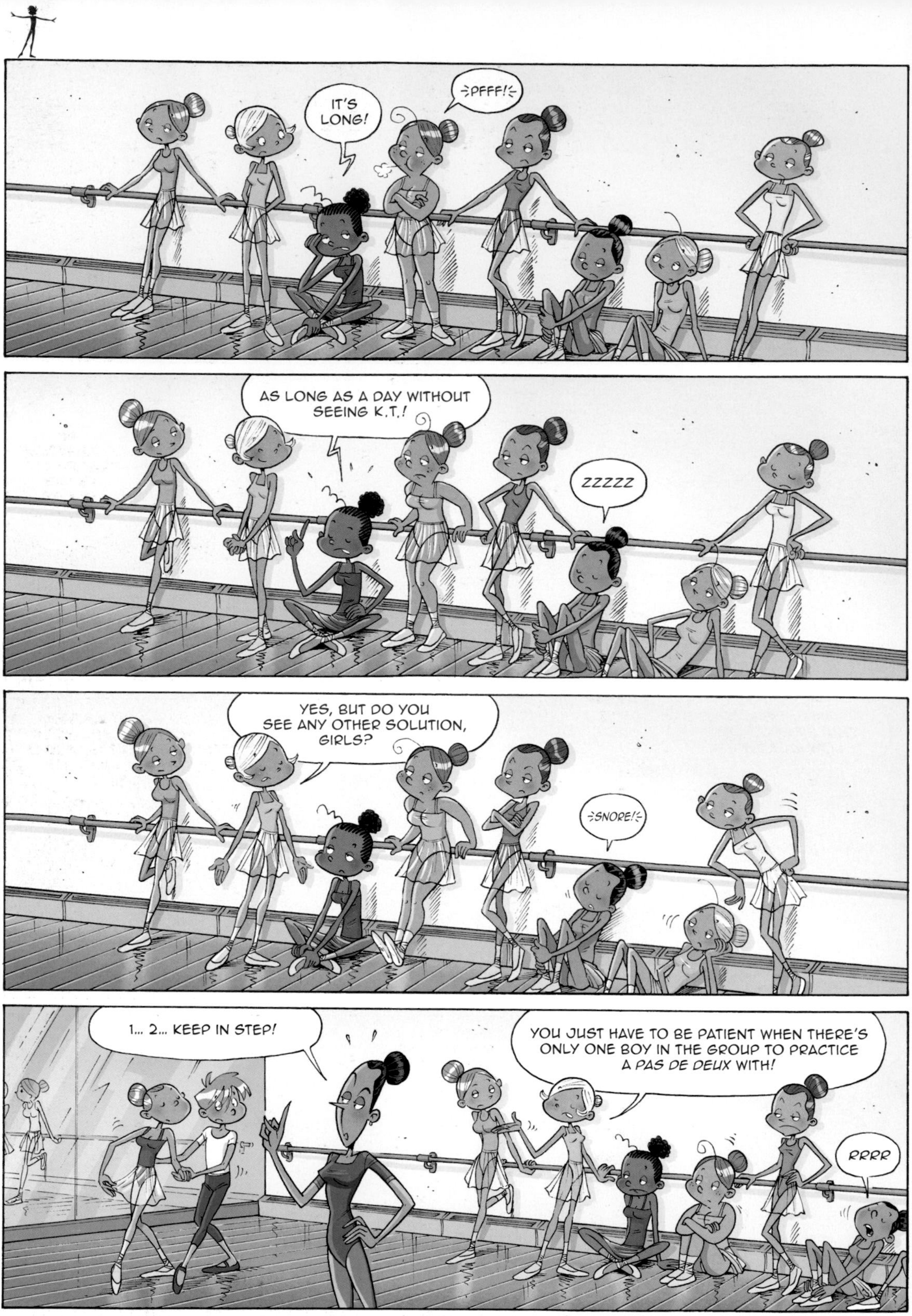
IT'S LONG!
PFFF!
AS LONG AS A DAY WITHOUT SEEING K.T.!
ZZZZZ
YES, BUT DO YOU SEE ANY OTHER SOLUTION, GIRLS?
SNORE!
1... 2... KEEP IN STEP!
YOU JUST HAVE TO BE PATIENT WHEN THERE'S ONLY ONE BOY IN THE GROUP TO PRACTICE A *PAS DE DEUX* WITH!
RRRR

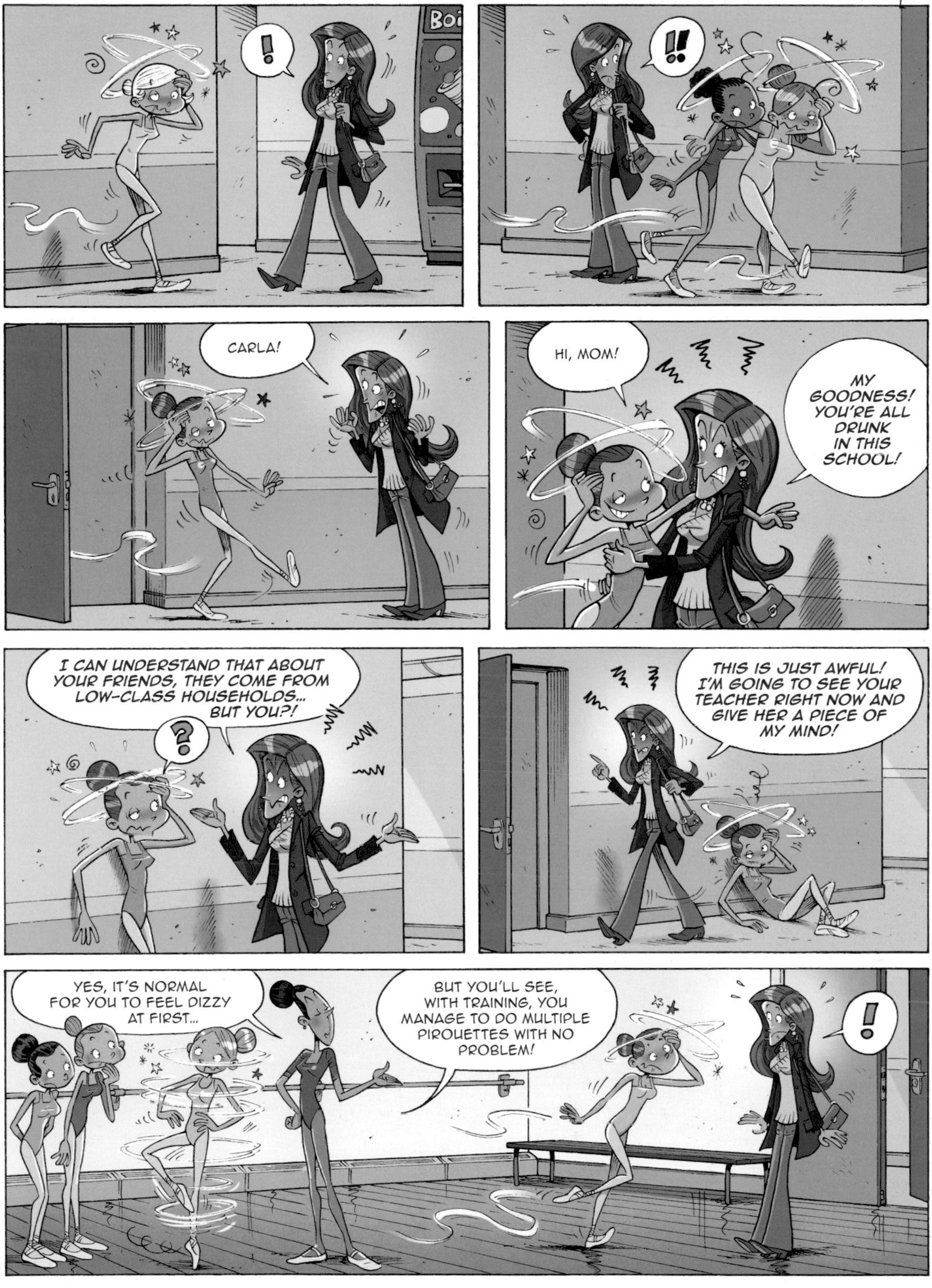
Boi
!
!!
CARLA!
HI, MOM!
MY GOODNESS! YOU'RE ALL DRUNK IN THIS SCHOOL!
I CAN UNDERSTAND THAT ABOUT YOUR FRIENDS, THEY COME FROM LOW-CLASS HOUSEHOLDS... BUT YOU?!
?
THIS IS JUST AWFUL! I'M GOING TO SEE YOUR TEACHER RIGHT NOW AND GIVE HER A PIECE OF MY MIND!
YES, IT'S NORMAL FOR YOU TO FEEL DIZZY AT FIRST...
BUT YOU'LL SEE, WITH TRAINING, YOU MANAGE TO DO MULTIPLE PIROUETTES WITH NO PROBLEM!
!

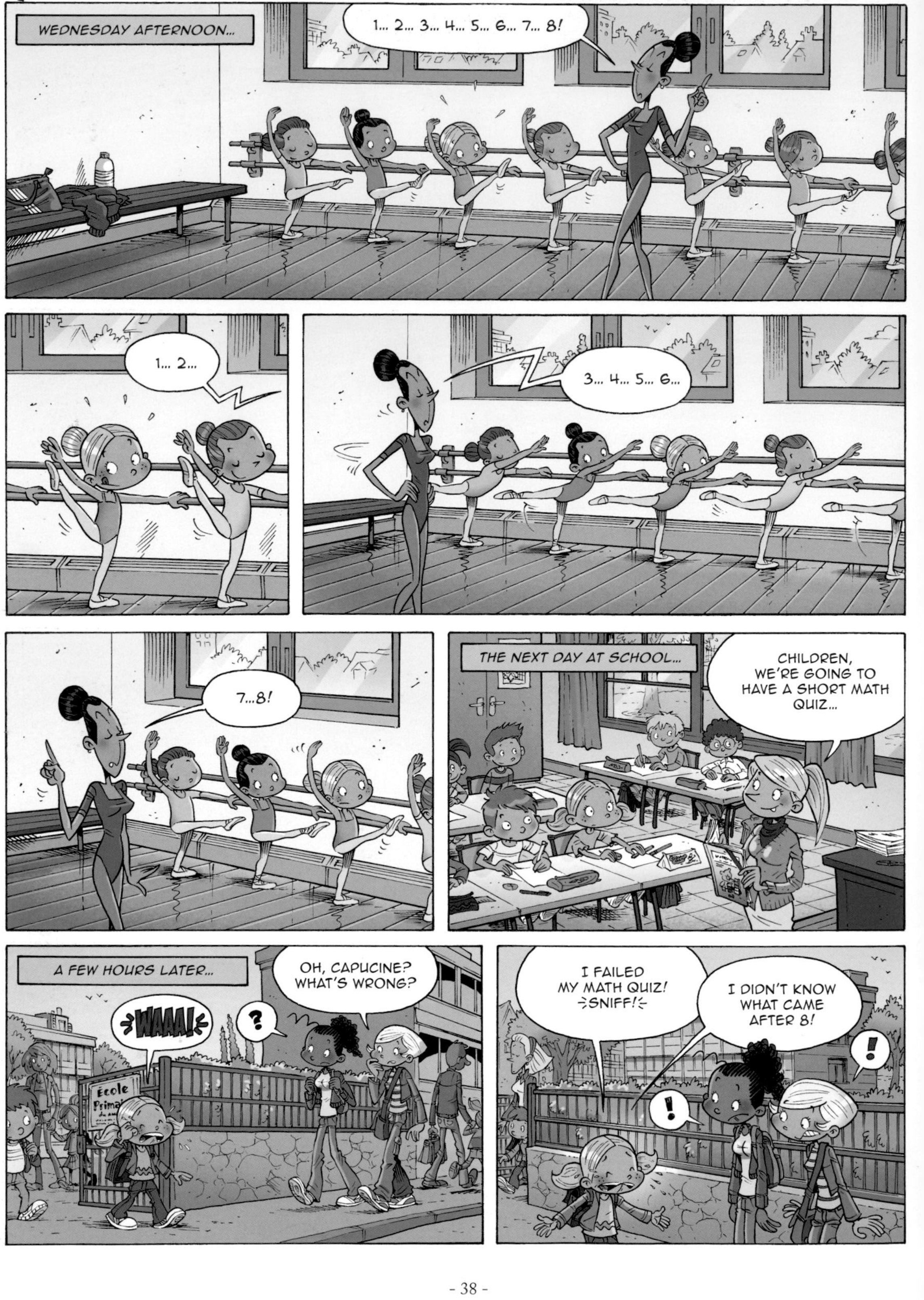
WEDNESDAY AFTERNOON...
1... 2... 3... 4... 5... 6... 7... 8!
1... 2...
3... 4... 5... 6...
7...8!
THE NEXT DAY AT SCHOOL...
CHILDREN, WE'RE GOING TO HAVE A SHORT MATH QUIZ...
A FEW HOURS LATER...
WAAA!
?
OH, CAPUCINE? WHAT'S WRONG?
École
I FAILED MY MATH QUIZ! SNIFF!
I DIDN'T KNOW WHAT CAME AFTER 8!
!
!

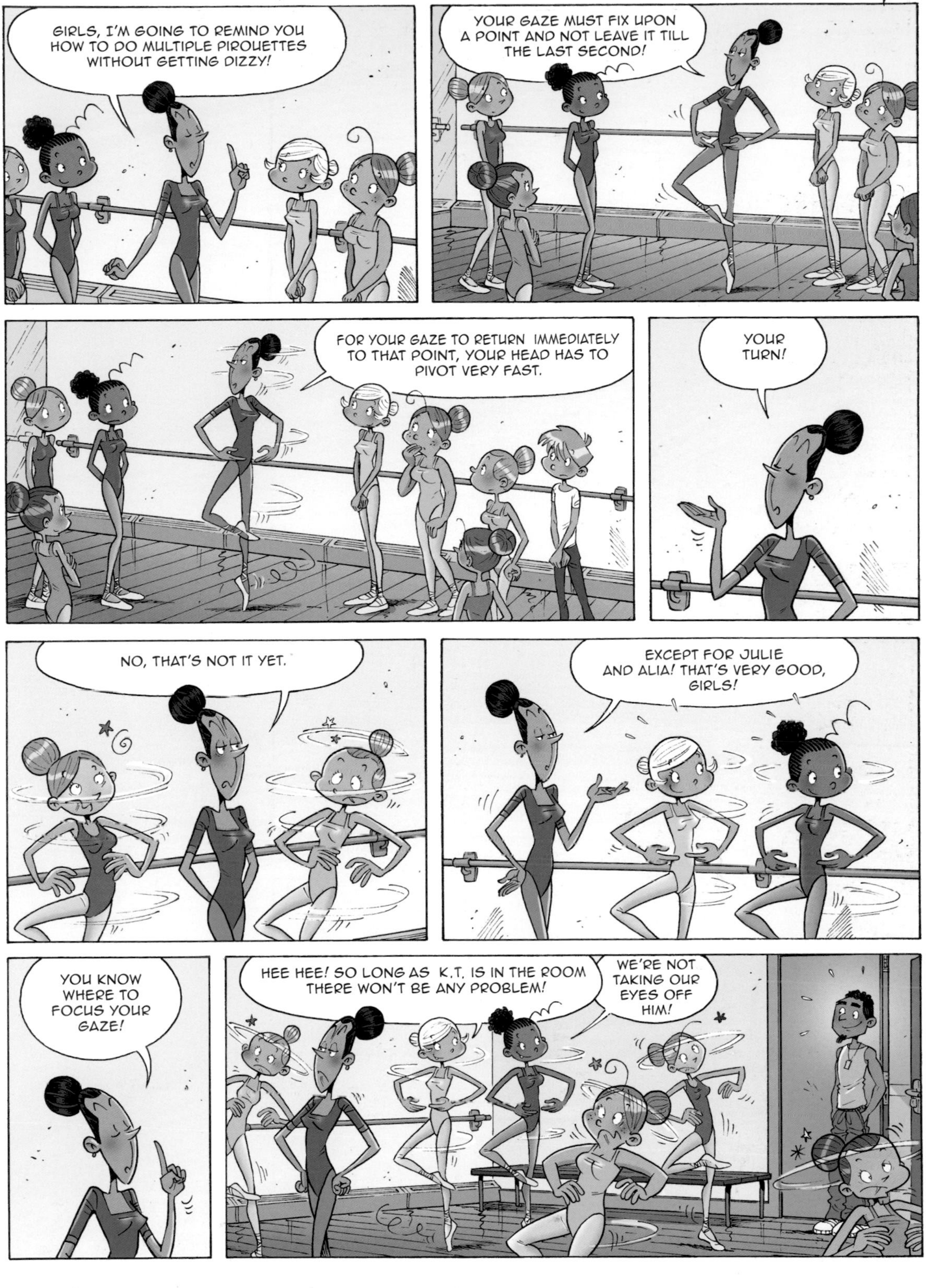
GIRLS, I'M GOING TO REMIND YOU HOW TO DO MULTIPLE PIROUETTES WITHOUT GETTING DIZZY!
YOUR GAZE MUST FIX UPON A POINT AND NOT LEAVE IT TILL THE LAST SECOND!
FOR YOUR GAZE TO RETURN IMMEDIATELY TO THAT POINT, YOUR HEAD HAS TO PIVOT VERY FAST.
YOUR TURN!
NO, THAT'S NOT IT YET.
EXCEPT FOR JULIE AND ALIA! THAT'S VERY GOOD, GIRLS!
YOU KNOW WHERE TO FOCUS YOUR GAZE!
HEE HEE! SO LONG AS K.T. IS IN THE ROOM THERE WON'T BE ANY PROBLEM!
WE'RE NOT TAKING OUR EYES OFF HIM!

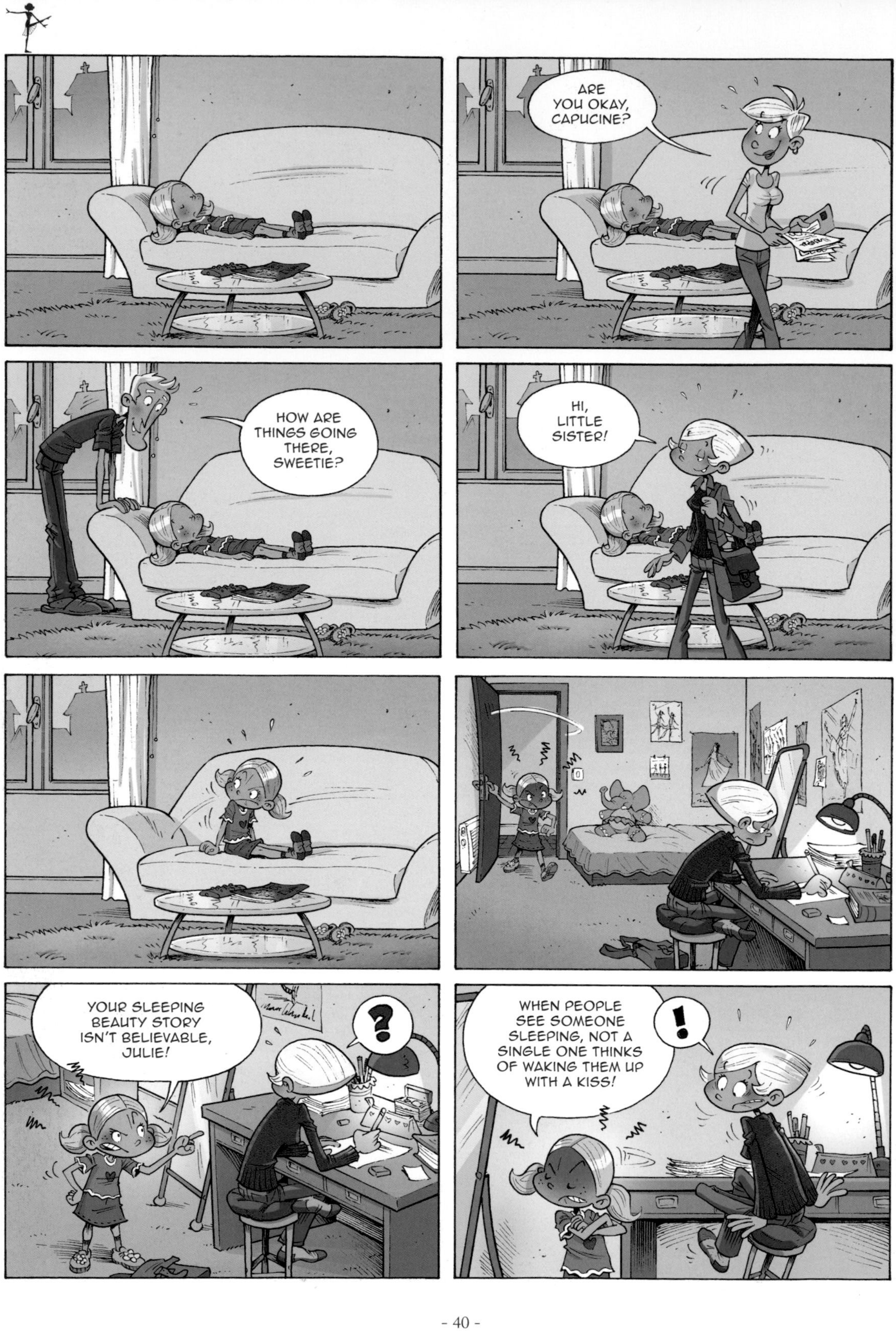
ARE YOU OKAY, CAPUCINE?
HOW ARE THINGS GOING THERE, SWEETIE?
HI, LITTLE SISTER!
YOUR SLEEPING BEAUTY STORY ISN'T BELIEVABLE, JULIE!
?
WHEN PEOPLE SEE SOMEONE SLEEPING, NOT A SINGLE ONE THINKS OF WAKING THEM UP WITH A KISS!
!

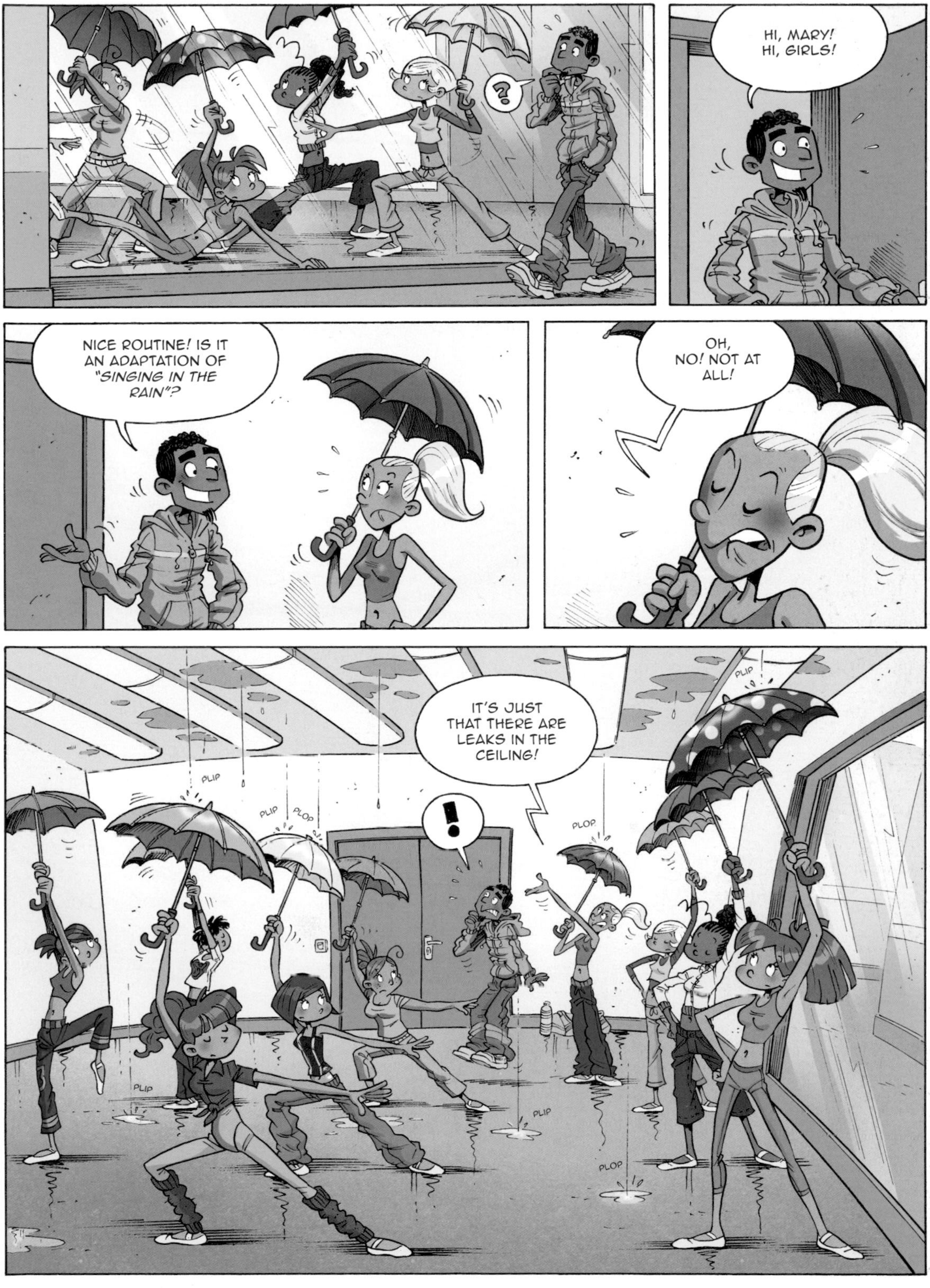
?
HI, MARY! HI, GIRLS!
NICE ROUTINE! IS IT AN ADAPTATION OF "SINGING IN THE RAIN"?
OH, NO! NOT AT ALL!
IT'S JUST THAT THERE ARE LEAKS IN THE CEILING!
!
PLIP
PLIP
PLIP
PLOP
PLOP
PLIP
PLIP
PLOP

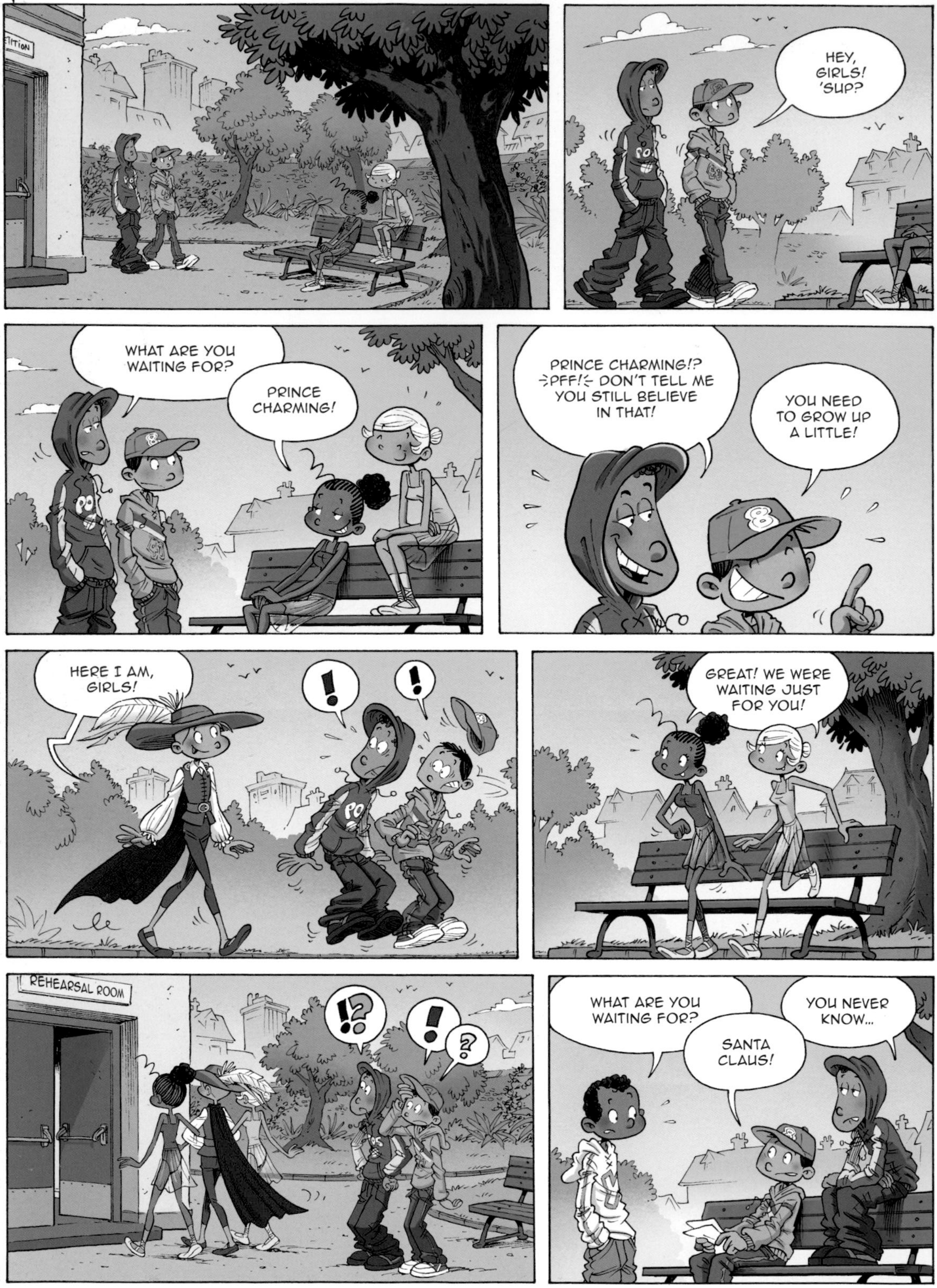
HEY, GIRLS! 'SUP?
WHAT ARE YOU WAITING FOR?
PRINCE CHARMING!
PRINCE CHARMING!? PFF! DON'T TELL ME YOU STILL BELIEVE IN THAT!
YOU NEED TO GROW UP A LITTLE!
HERE I AM, GIRLS!
!
!
GREAT! WE WERE WAITING JUST FOR YOU!
REHEARSAL ROOM
!?
!
?
WHAT ARE YOU WAITING FOR?
SANTA CLAUS!
YOU NEVER KNOW...

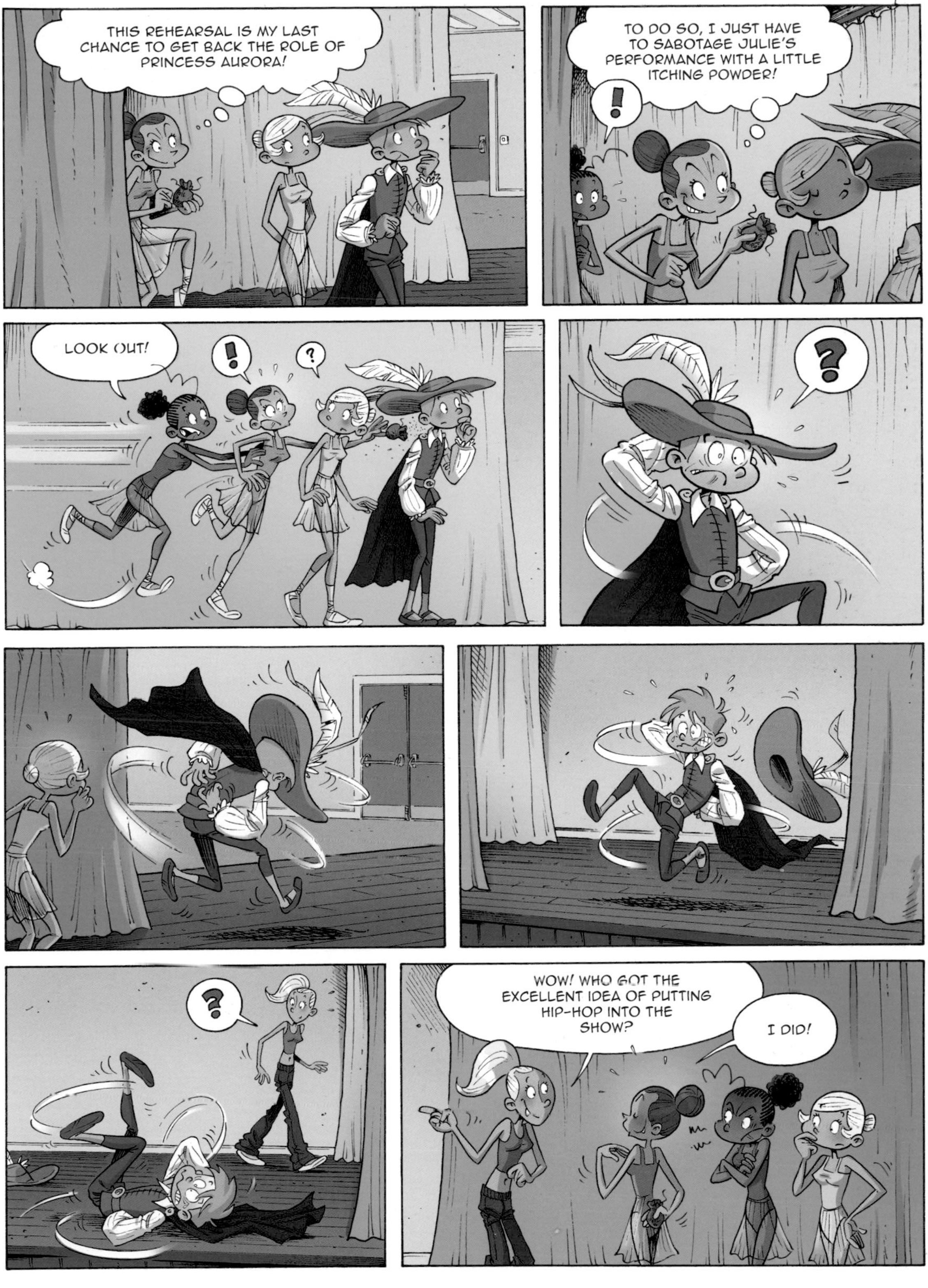
THIS REHEARSAL IS MY LAST CHANCE TO GET BACK THE ROLE OF PRINCESS AURORA!
TO DO SO, I JUST HAVE TO SABOTAGE JULIE'S PERFORMANCE WITH A LITTLE ITCHING POWDER!
!
LOOK OUT!
!
?
?
?
WOW! WHO GOT THE EXCELLENT IDEA OF PUTTING HIP-HOP INTO THE SHOW?
I DID!

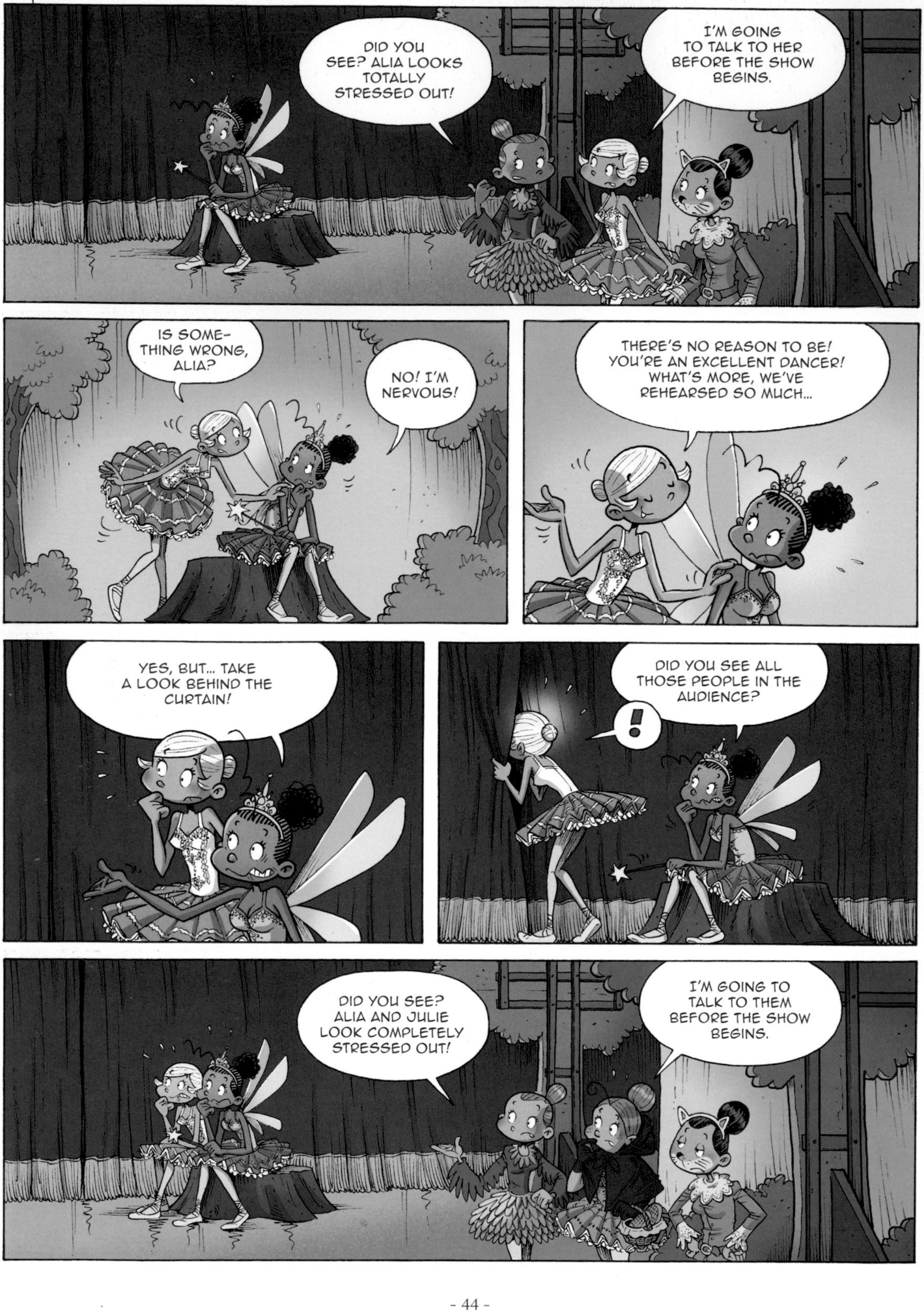
DID YOU SEE? ALIA LOOKS TOTALLY STRESSED OUT!
I'M GOING TO TALK TO HER BEFORE THE SHOW BEGINS.
IS SOMETHING WRONG, ALIA?
NO! I'M NERVOUS!
THERE'S NO REASON TO BE! YOU'RE AN EXCELLENT DANCER! WHAT'S MORE, WE'VE REHEARSED SO MUCH...
YES, BUT... TAKE A LOOK BEHIND THE CURTAIN!
DID YOU SEE ALL THOSE PEOPLE IN THE AUDIENCE?
!
DID YOU SEE? ALIA AND JULIE LOOK COMPLETELY STRESSED OUT!
I'M GOING TO TALK TO THEM BEFORE THE SHOW BEGINS.

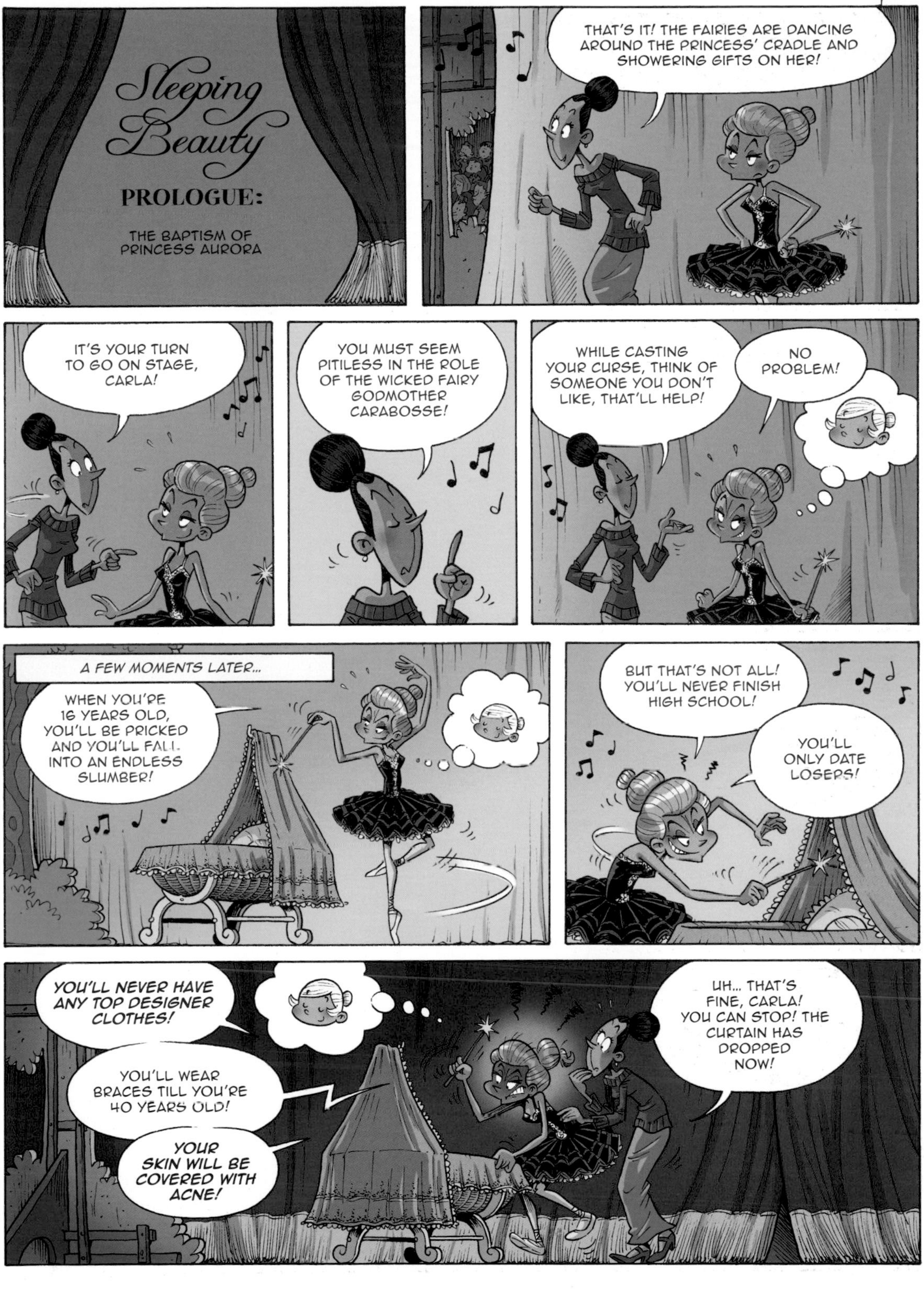
Sleeping Beauty
PROLOGUE:
THE BAPTISM OF PRINCESS AURORA
THAT'S IT! THE FAIRIES ARE DANCING AROUND THE PRINCESS' CRADLE AND SHOWERING GIFTS ON HER!
IT'S YOUR TURN TO GO ON STAGE, CARLA!
YOU MUST SEEM PITILESS IN THE ROLE OF THE WICKED FAIRY GODMOTHER CARABOSSE!
WHILE CASTING YOUR CURSE, THINK OF SOMEONE YOU DON'T LIKE, THAT'LL HELP!
NO PROBLEM!
A FEW MOMENTS LATER...
WHEN YOU'RE 16 YEARS OLD, YOU'LL BE PRICKED AND YOU'LL FALL INTO AN ENDLESS SLUMBER!
BUT THAT'S NOT ALL! YOU'LL NEVER FINISH HIGH SCHOOL!
YOU'LL ONLY DATE LOSERS!
YOU'LL NEVER HAVE ANY TOP DESIGNER CLOTHES!
YOU'LL WEAR BRACES TILL YOU'RE 40 YEARS OLD!
YOUR SKIN WILL BE COVERED WITH ACNE!
UH... THAT'S FINE, CARLA! YOU CAN STOP! THE CURTAIN HAS DROPPED NOW!

Sleeping Beauty

ACT 1:

FOR HER SIXTEENTH BIRTHDAY, PRINCESS AURORA RECEIVES A BOUQUET FROM AN OLD WOMAN. A SPINDLE WAS HIDDEN WITHIN IT, WHICH PRICKS HER HAND.

BRAVO!

CLAP CLAP CLAP

MAGNIFICENT!

BRAVO!

BRAVO!

CLAP CLAP CLAP CLAP CLAP CLAP

WOW! THAT WAS GOOD, JULIE! IT WAS REALLY BELIEVABLE YOU WERE HURT BY PRICKING YOURSELF!

BUT I **WAS** HURTING!

NATHALIA, THE COSTUME DESIGNER, LEFT A NEEDLE IN MY TUTU!

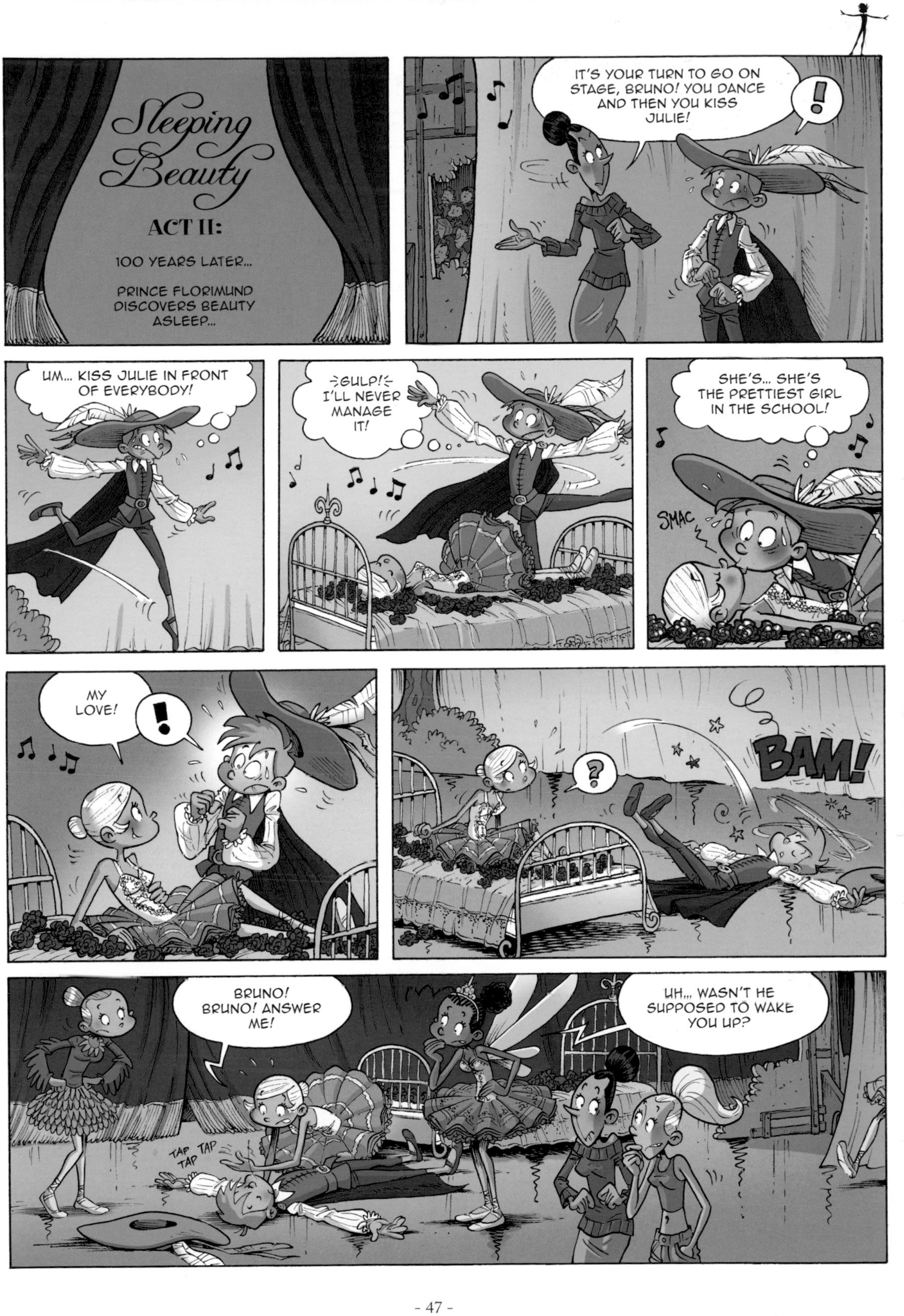
Sleeping Beauty
ACT II:
100 YEARS LATER...
PRINCE FLORIMUND DISCOVERS BEAUTY ASLEEP...
IT'S YOUR TURN TO GO ON STAGE, BRUNO! YOU DANCE AND THEN YOU KISS JULIE!
!
UM... KISS JULIE IN FRONT OF EVERYBODY!
GULP! I'LL NEVER MANAGE IT!
SHE'S... SHE'S THE PRETTIEST GIRL IN THE SCHOOL!
SMAC
MY LOVE!
!
?
BAM!
BRUNO! BRUNO! ANSWER ME!
TAP TAP TAP
UH... WASN'T HE SUPPOSED TO WAKE YOU UP?

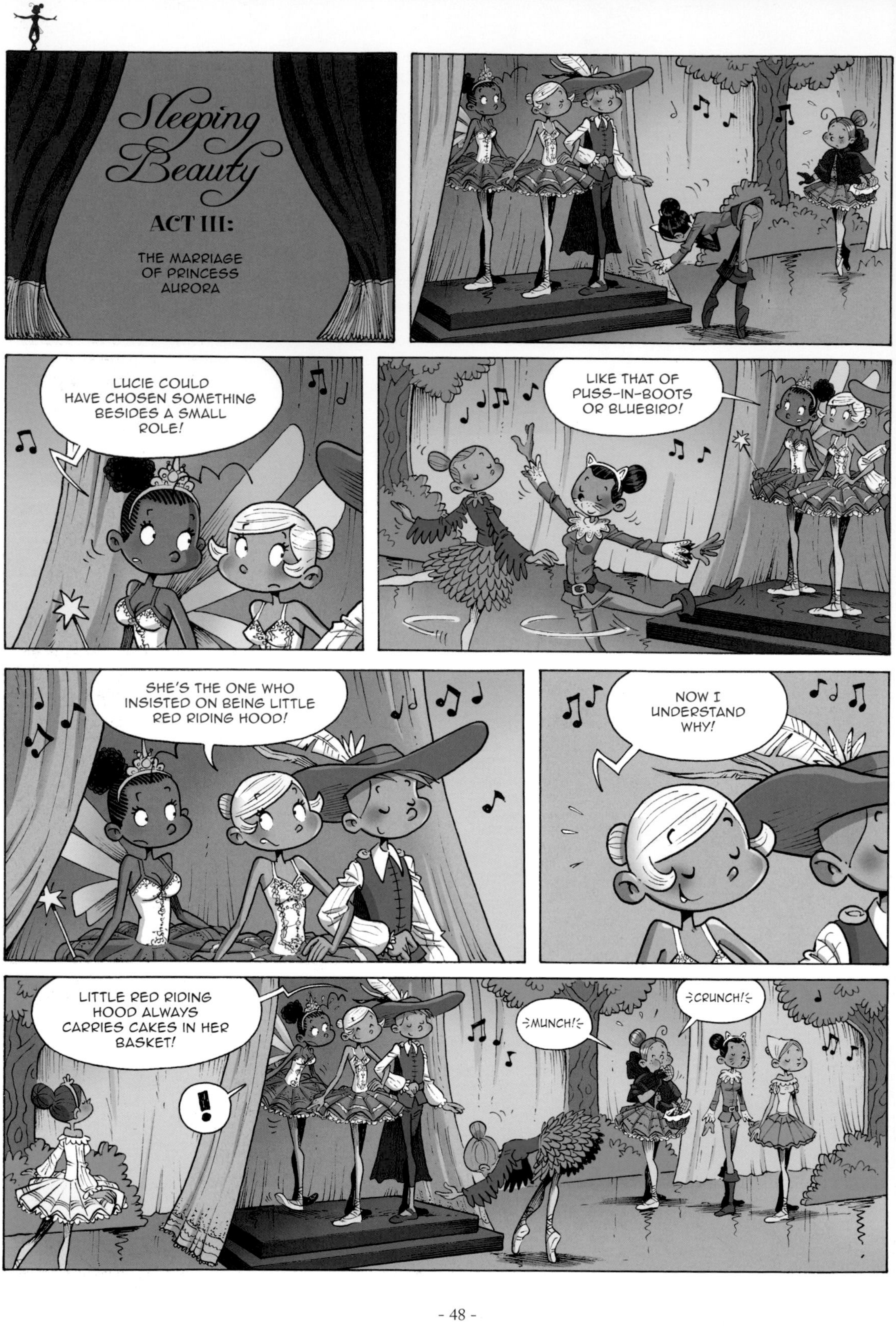

Sleeping Beauty
ACT III:
THE MARRIAGE OF PRINCESS AURORA
LUCIE COULD HAVE CHOSEN SOMETHING BESIDES A SMALL ROLE!
LIKE THAT OF PUSS-IN-BOOTS OR BLUEBIRD!
SHE'S THE ONE WHO INSISTED ON BEING LITTLE RED RIDING HOOD!
NOW I UNDERSTAND WHY!
LITTLE RED RIDING HOOD ALWAYS CARRIES CAKES IN HER BASKET!
MUNCH!
CRUNCH!
!

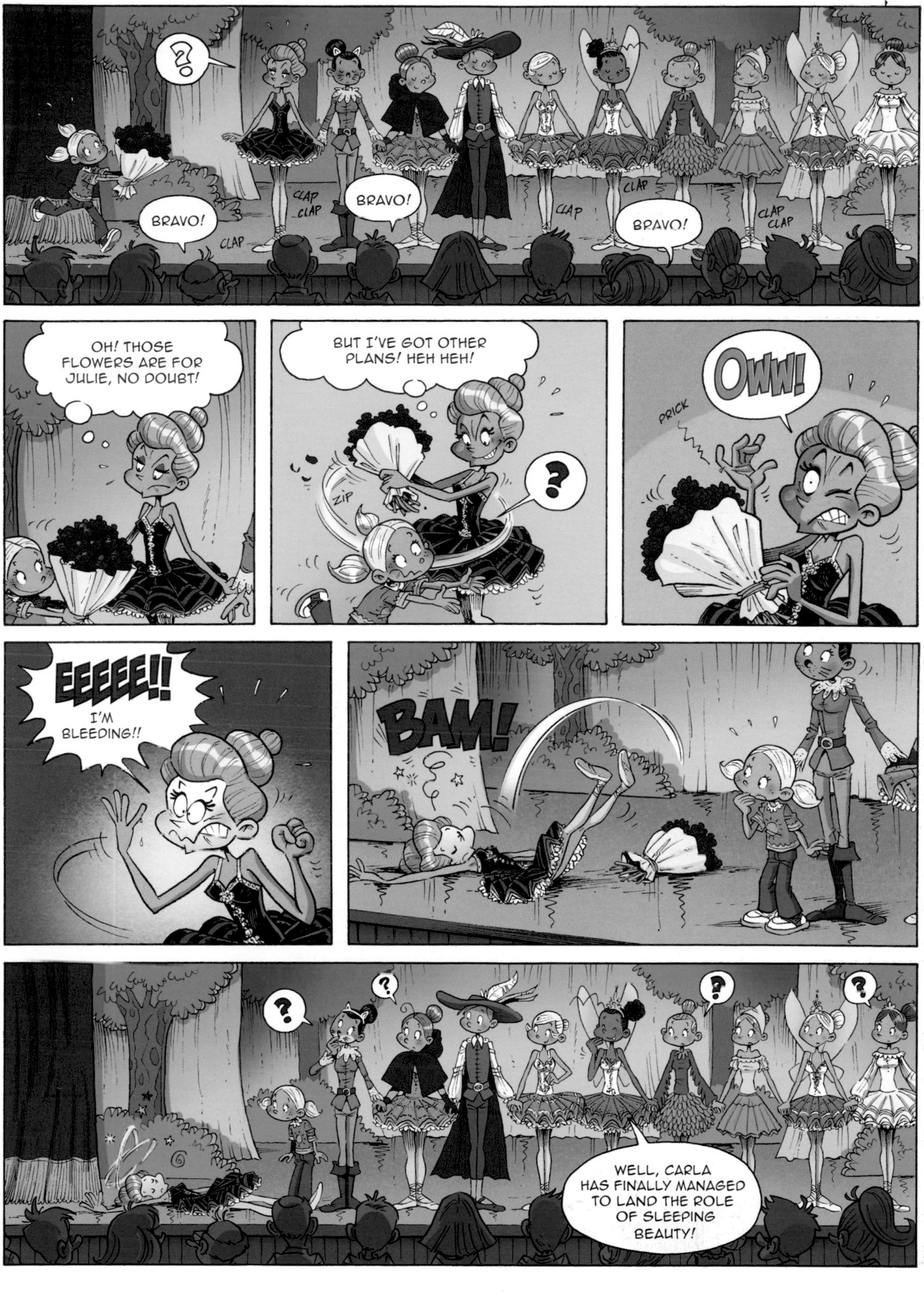
?
BRAVO!
CLAP
CLAP CLAP
BRAVO!
CLAP
CLAP
BRAVO!
CLAP CLAP
OH! THOSE FLOWERS ARE FOR JULIE, NO DOUBT!
BUT I'VE GOT OTHER PLANS! HEH HEH!
ZIP
?
PRICK
OWW!
EEEEE!! I'M BLEEDING!!
BAM!
?
?
?
?
WELL, CARLA HAS FINALLY MANAGED TO LAND THE ROLE OF SLEEPING BEAUTY!

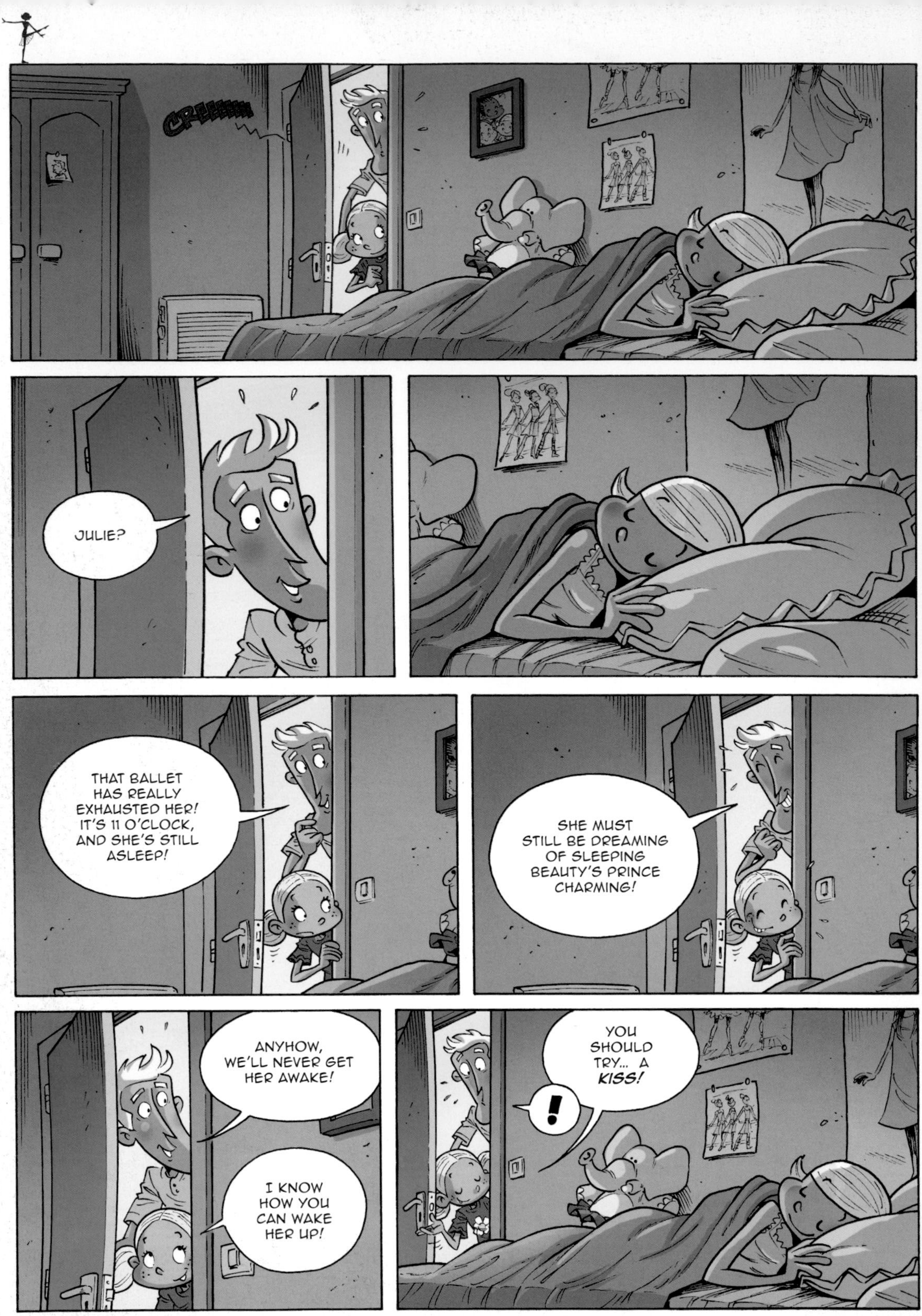
CREEEEEE
JULIE?
THAT BALLET HAS REALLY EXHAUSTED HER! IT'S 11 O'CLOCK, AND SHE'S STILL ASLEEP!
SHE MUST STILL BE DREAMING OF SLEEPING BEAUTY'S PRINCE CHARMING!
ANYHOW, WE'LL NEVER GET HER AWAKE!
I KNOW HOW YOU CAN WAKE HER UP!
YOU SHOULD TRY... A *KISS!*
!

Romeos and Juliet

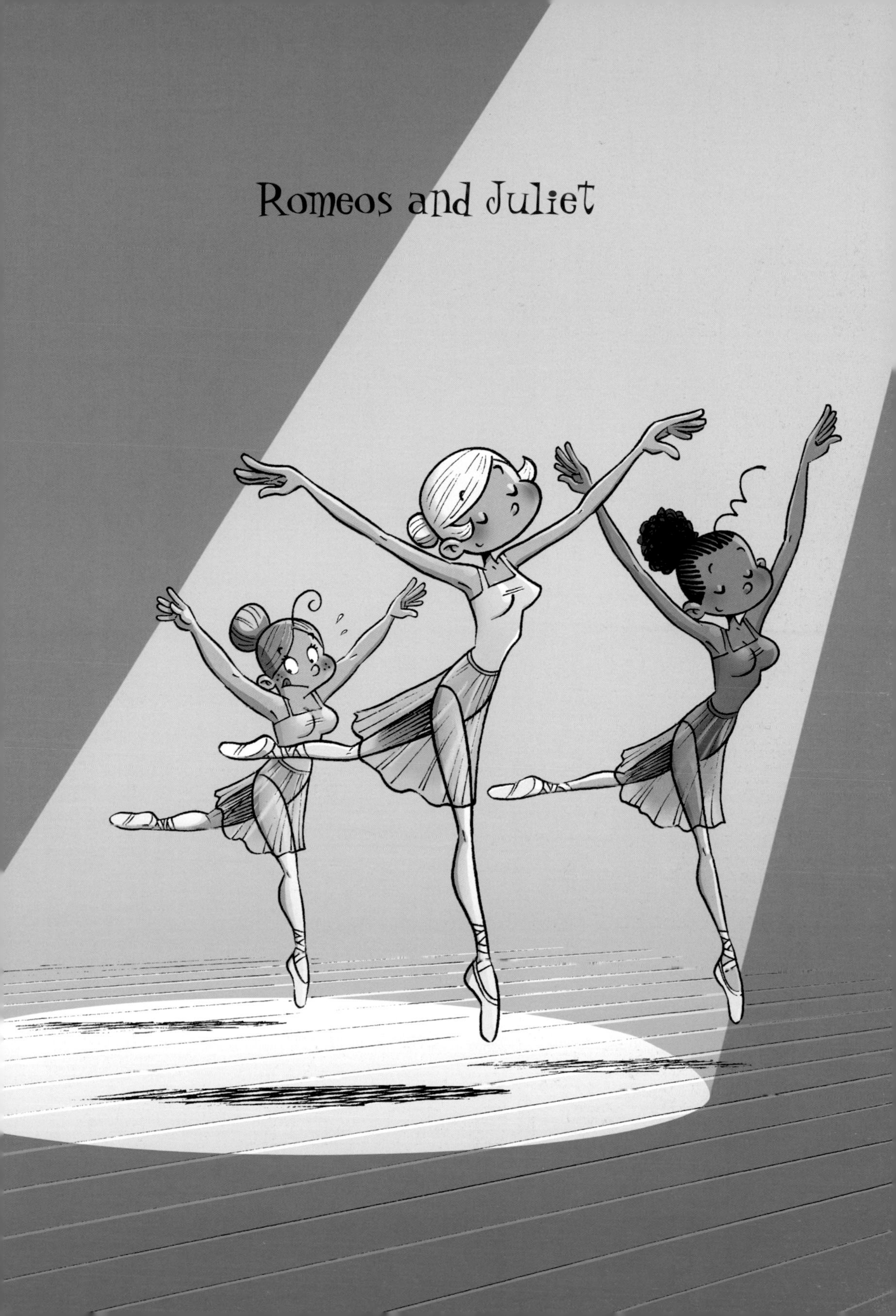

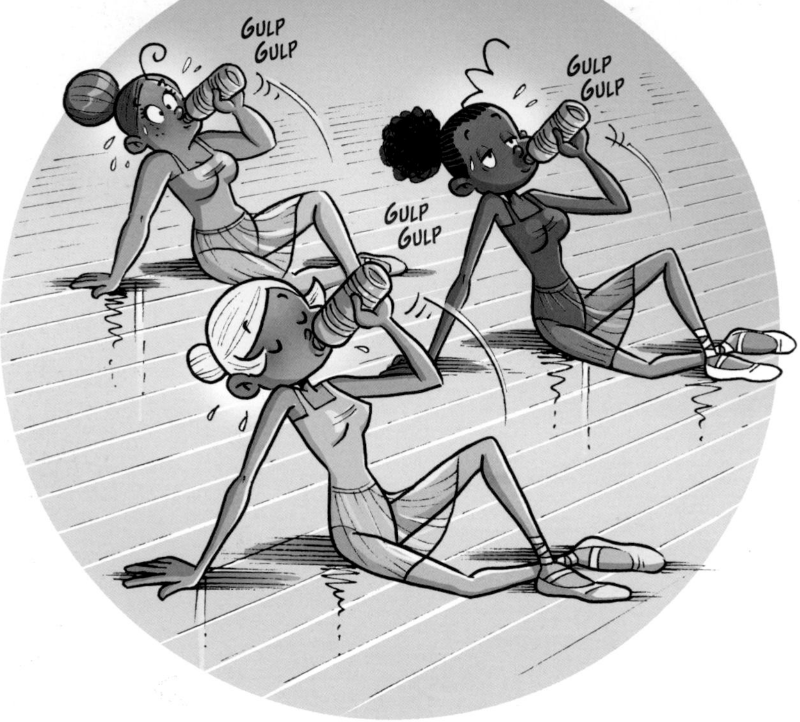
GULP GULP
GULP GULP
GULP GULP

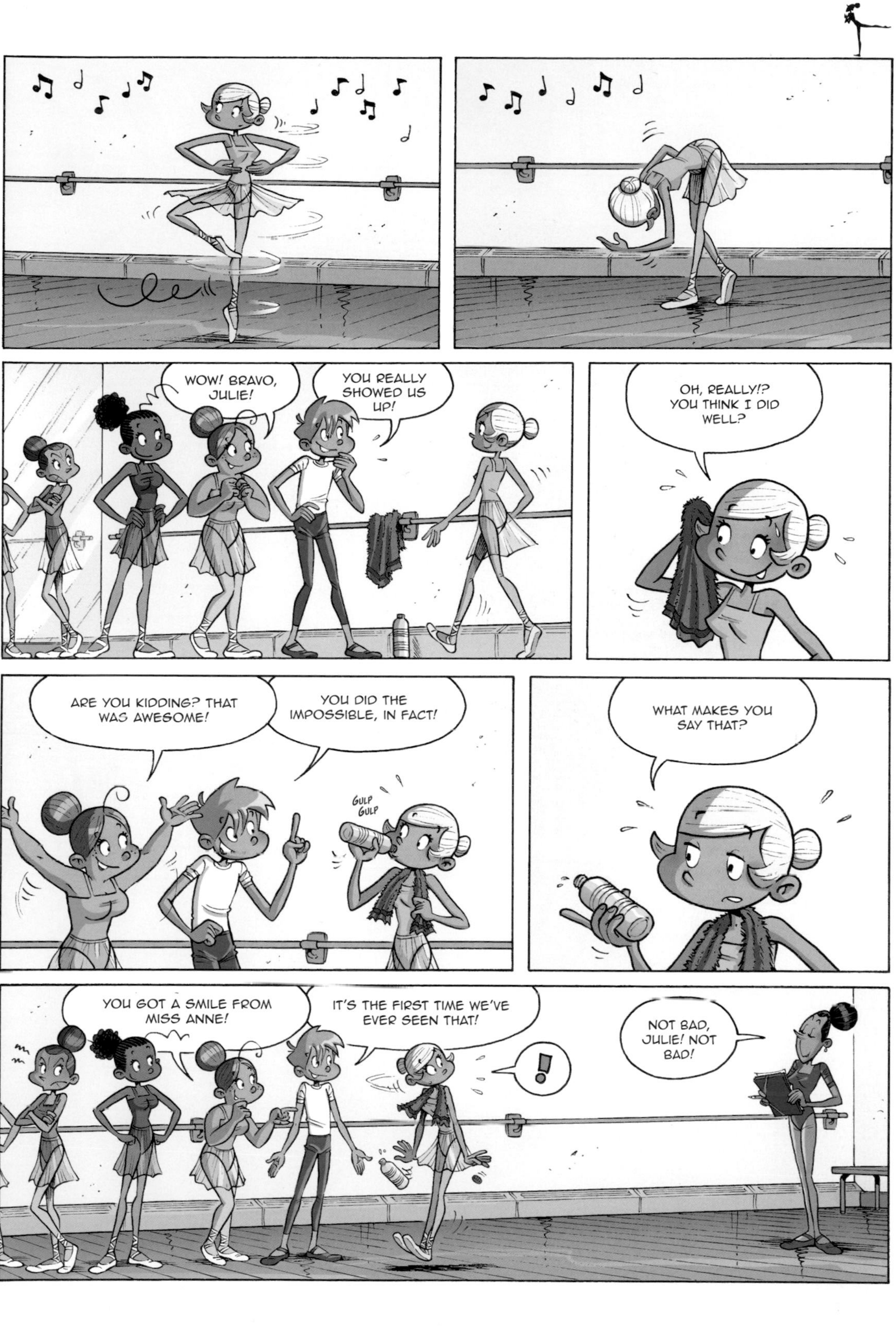
WOW! BRAVO, JULIE!
YOU REALLY SHOWED US UP!
OH, REALLY!? YOU THINK I DID WELL?
ARE YOU KIDDING? THAT WAS AWESOME!
YOU DID THE IMPOSSIBLE, IN FACT!
GULP GULP
WHAT MAKES YOU SAY THAT?
YOU GOT A SMILE FROM MISS ANNE!
IT'S THE FIRST TIME WE'VE EVER SEEN THAT!
!
NOT BAD, JULIE! NOT BAD!

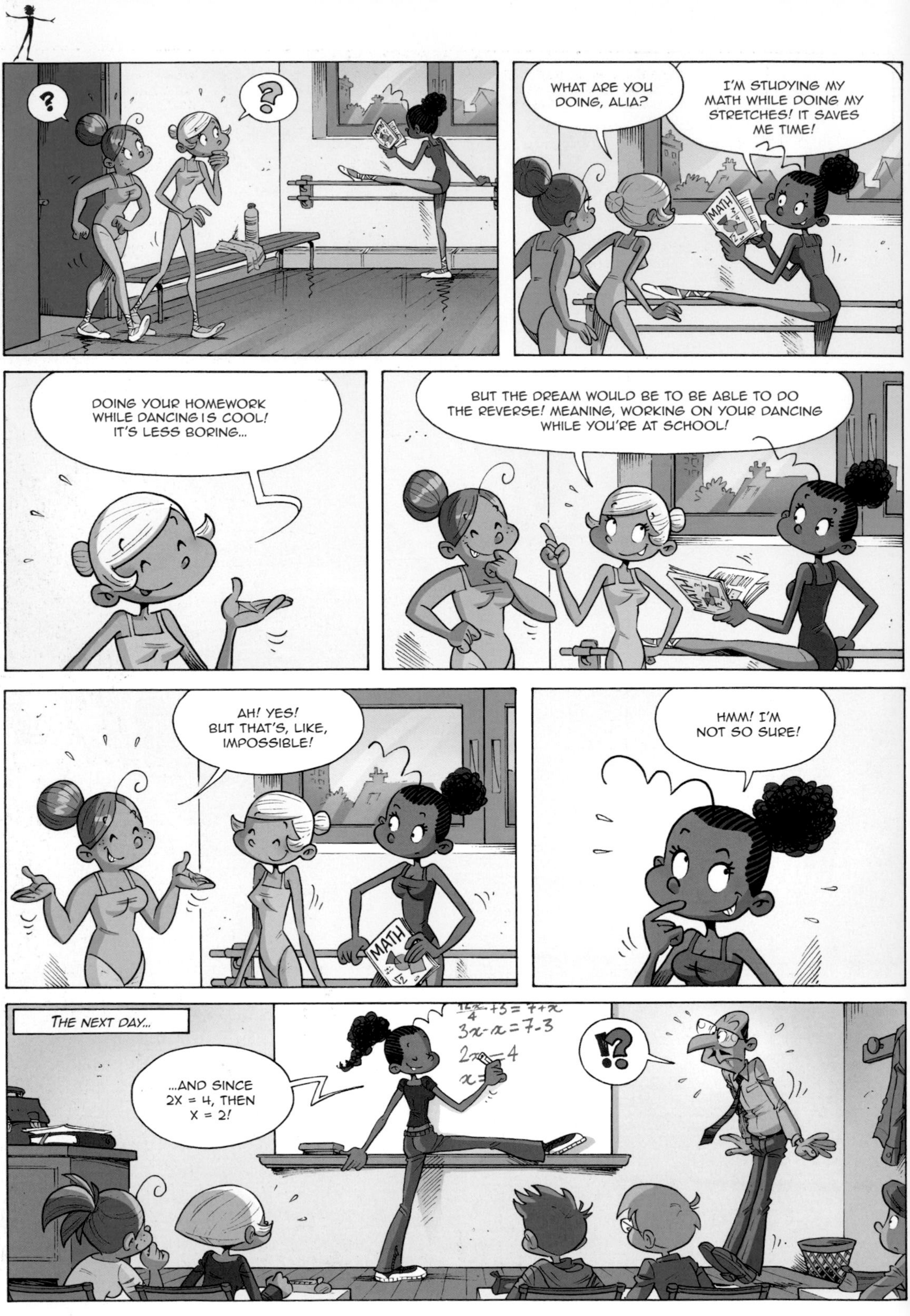

?
?
WHAT ARE YOU DOING, ALIA?
I'M STUDYING MY MATH WHILE DOING MY STRETCHES! IT SAVES ME TIME!
MATH
DOING YOUR HOMEWORK WHILE DANCING IS COOL! IT'S LESS BORING...
BUT THE DREAM WOULD BE TO BE ABLE TO DO THE REVERSE! MEANING, WORKING ON YOUR DANCING WHILE YOU'RE AT SCHOOL!
MATH
AH! YES! BUT THAT'S, LIKE, IMPOSSIBLE!
MATH
HMM! I'M NOT SO SURE!
THE NEXT DAY...
3x-x=7-3
...AND SINCE 2X = 4, THEN X = 2!
!?

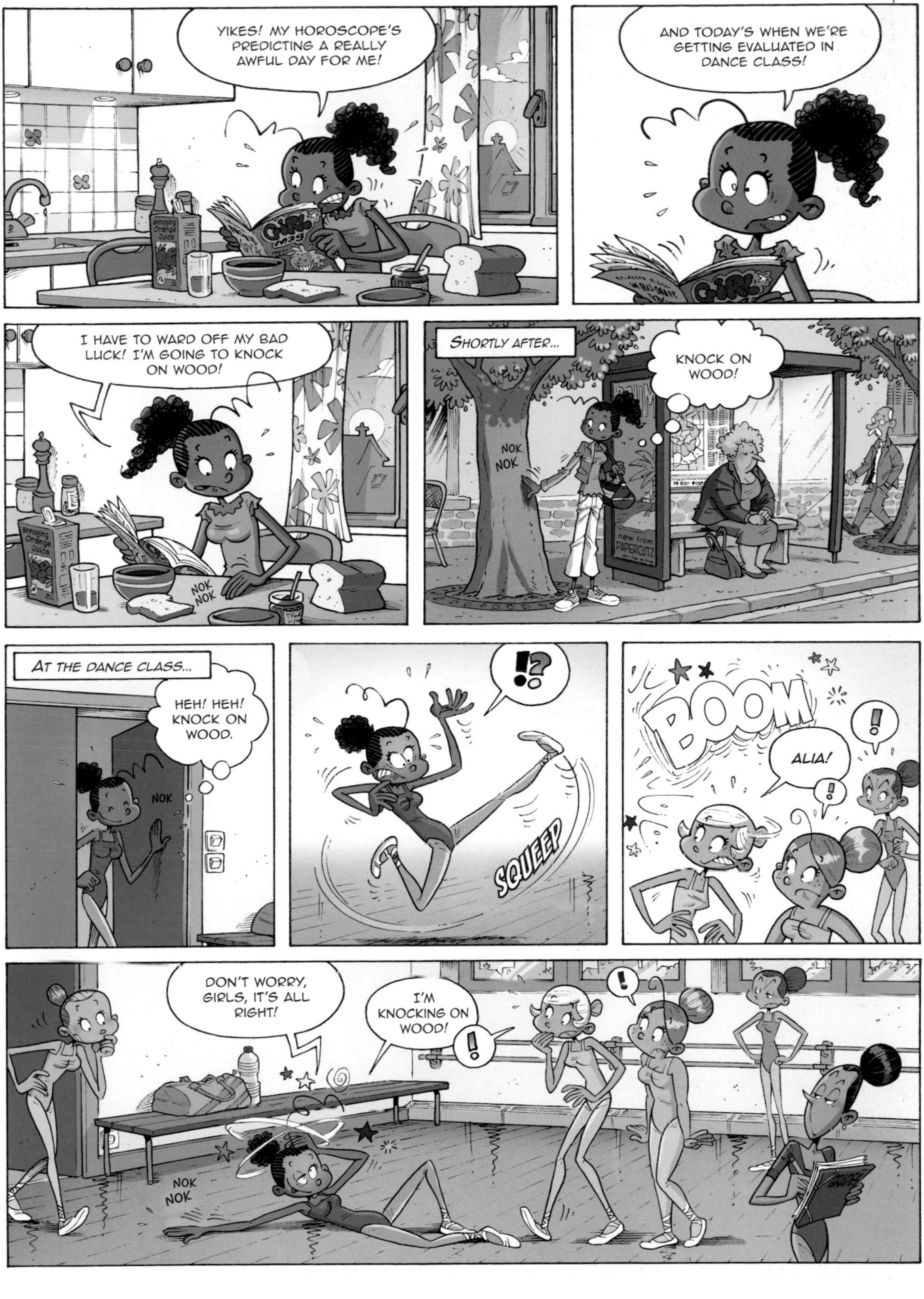
YIKES! MY HOROSCOPE'S PREDICTING A REALLY AWFUL DAY FOR ME!
AND TODAY'S WHEN WE'RE GETTING EVALUATED IN DANCE CLASS!
I HAVE TO WARD OFF MY BAD LUCK! I'M GOING TO KNOCK ON WOOD!
NOK NOK
SHORTLY AFTER...
KNOCK ON WOOD!
NOK NOK
new from PAPERCUTZ
AT THE DANCE CLASS...
HEH! HEH! KNOCK ON WOOD.
NOK
!?
SQUEEP
BOOM
ALIA!
!
!
DON'T WORRY, GIRLS, IT'S ALL RIGHT!
I'M KNOCKING ON WOOD!
!
!
NOK NOK

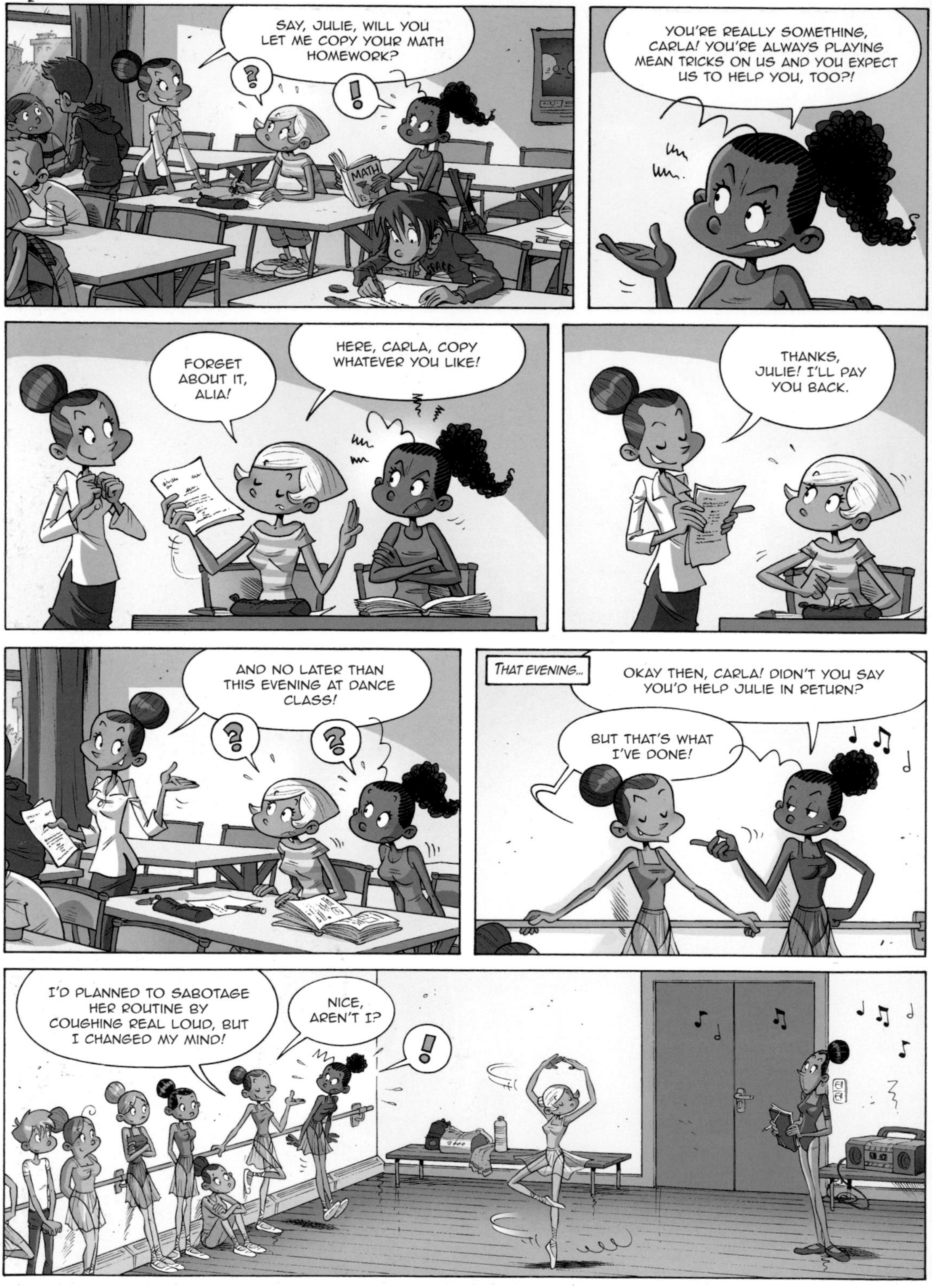
SAY, JULIE, WILL YOU LET ME COPY YOUR MATH HOMEWORK?
?
!
MATH
YOU'RE REALLY SOMETHING, CARLA! YOU'RE ALWAYS PLAYING MEAN TRICKS ON US AND YOU EXPECT US TO HELP YOU, TOO?!
FORGET ABOUT IT, ALIA!
HERE, CARLA, COPY WHATEVER YOU LIKE!
THANKS, JULIE! I'LL PAY YOU BACK.
AND NO LATER THAN THIS EVENING AT DANCE CLASS!
?
?
THAT EVENING...
OKAY THEN, CARLA! DIDN'T YOU SAY YOU'D HELP JULIE IN RETURN?
BUT THAT'S WHAT I'VE DONE!
I'D PLANNED TO SABOTAGE HER ROUTINE BY COUGHING REAL LOUD, BUT I CHANGED MY MIND!
NICE, AREN'T I?
!

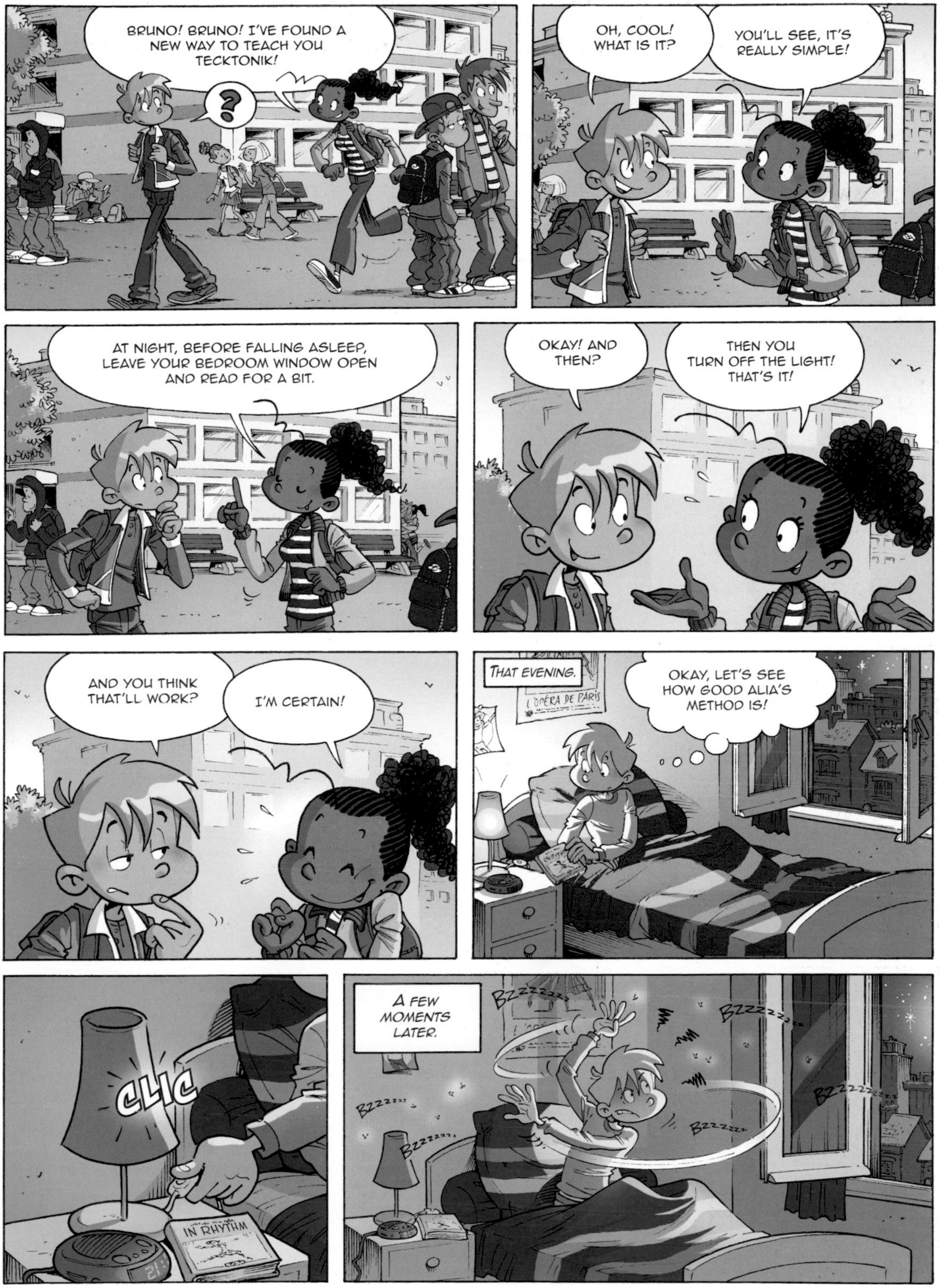
BRUNO! BRUNO! I'VE FOUND A NEW WAY TO TEACH YOU TECKTONIK!
?
OH, COOL! WHAT IS IT?
YOU'LL SEE, IT'S REALLY SIMPLE!
AT NIGHT, BEFORE FALLING ASLEEP, LEAVE YOUR BEDROOM WINDOW OPEN AND READ FOR A BIT.
OKAY! AND THEN?
THEN YOU TURN OFF THE LIGHT! THAT'S IT!
AND YOU THINK THAT'LL WORK?
I'M CERTAIN!
THAT EVENING.
L'OPÉRA DE PARIS
OKAY, LET'S SEE HOW GOOD ALIA'S METHOD IS!
CLIC
IN RHYTHM
A FEW MOMENTS LATER.
BZZZZZZZZ
BZZZZZZZZ
BZZZZZZ
BZZZZZZZ
BZZZZZZZ
BZZZZZZZZZ

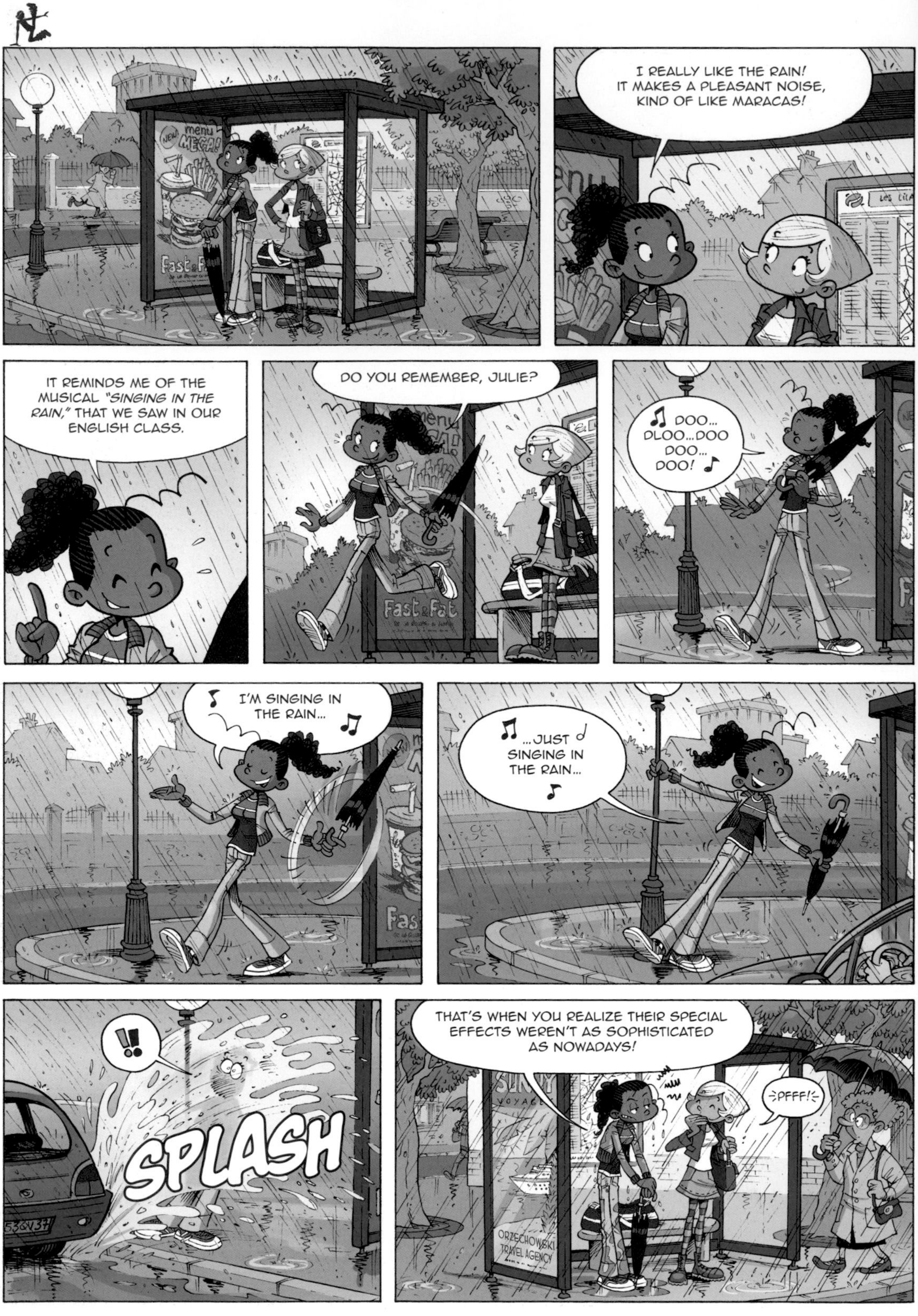
I REALLY LIKE THE RAIN! IT MAKES A PLEASANT NOISE, KIND OF LIKE MARACAS!
IT REMINDS ME OF THE MUSICAL "SINGING IN THE RAIN," THAT WE SAW IN OUR ENGLISH CLASS.
DO YOU REMEMBER, JULIE?
DOO... DLOO...DOO DOO... DOO!
I'M SINGING IN THE RAIN...
...JUST SINGING IN THE RAIN...
!!
SPLASH
THAT'S WHEN YOU REALIZE THEIR SPECIAL EFFECTS WEREN'T AS SOPHISTICATED AS NOWADAYS!
PFFF!
ORZECHOWSKI TRAVEL AGENCY

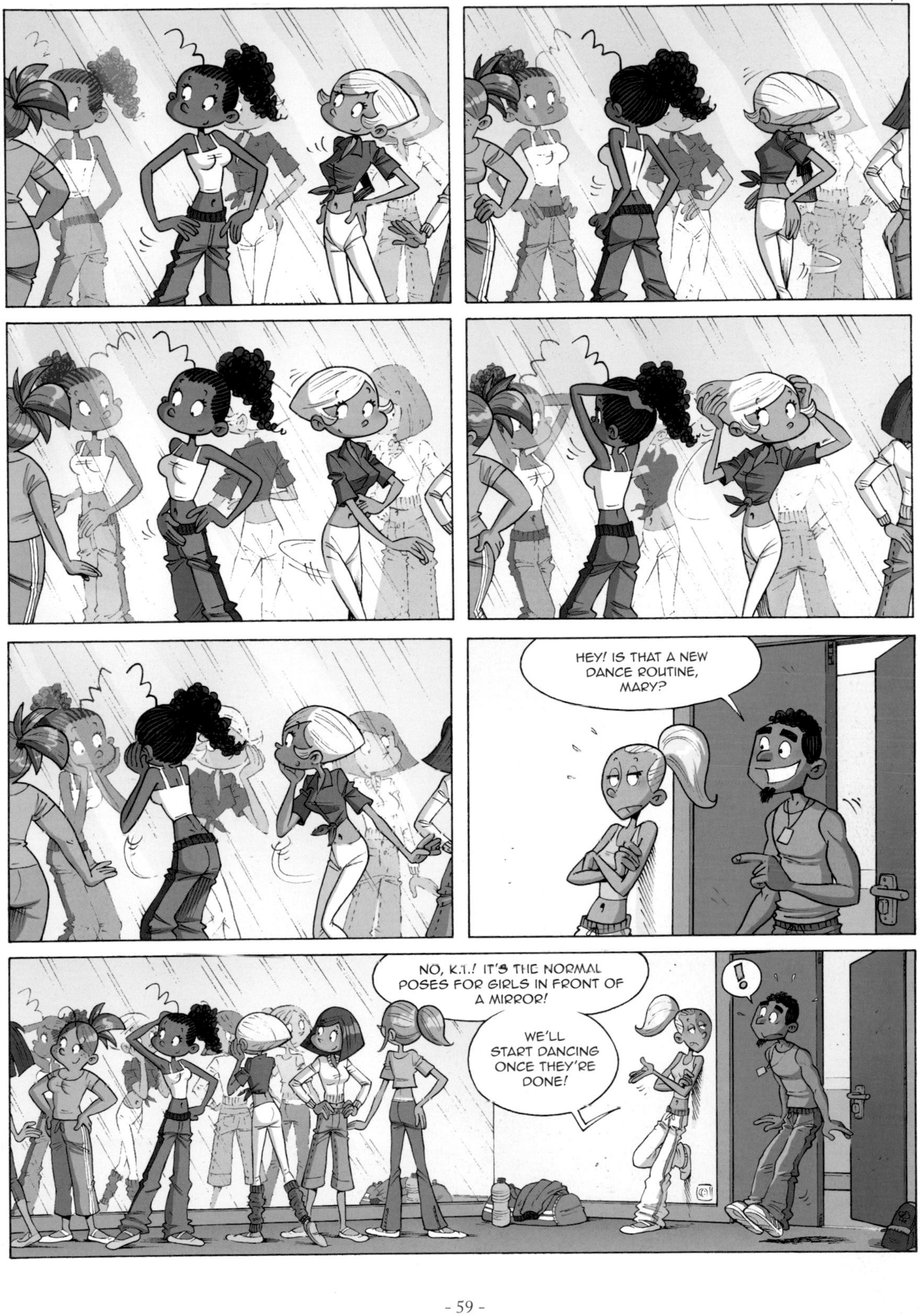
HEY! IS THAT A NEW DANCE ROUTINE, MARY?
NO, K.T.! IT'S THE NORMAL POSES FOR GIRLS IN FRONT OF A MIRROR!
WE'LL START DANCING ONCE THEY'RE DONE!
!

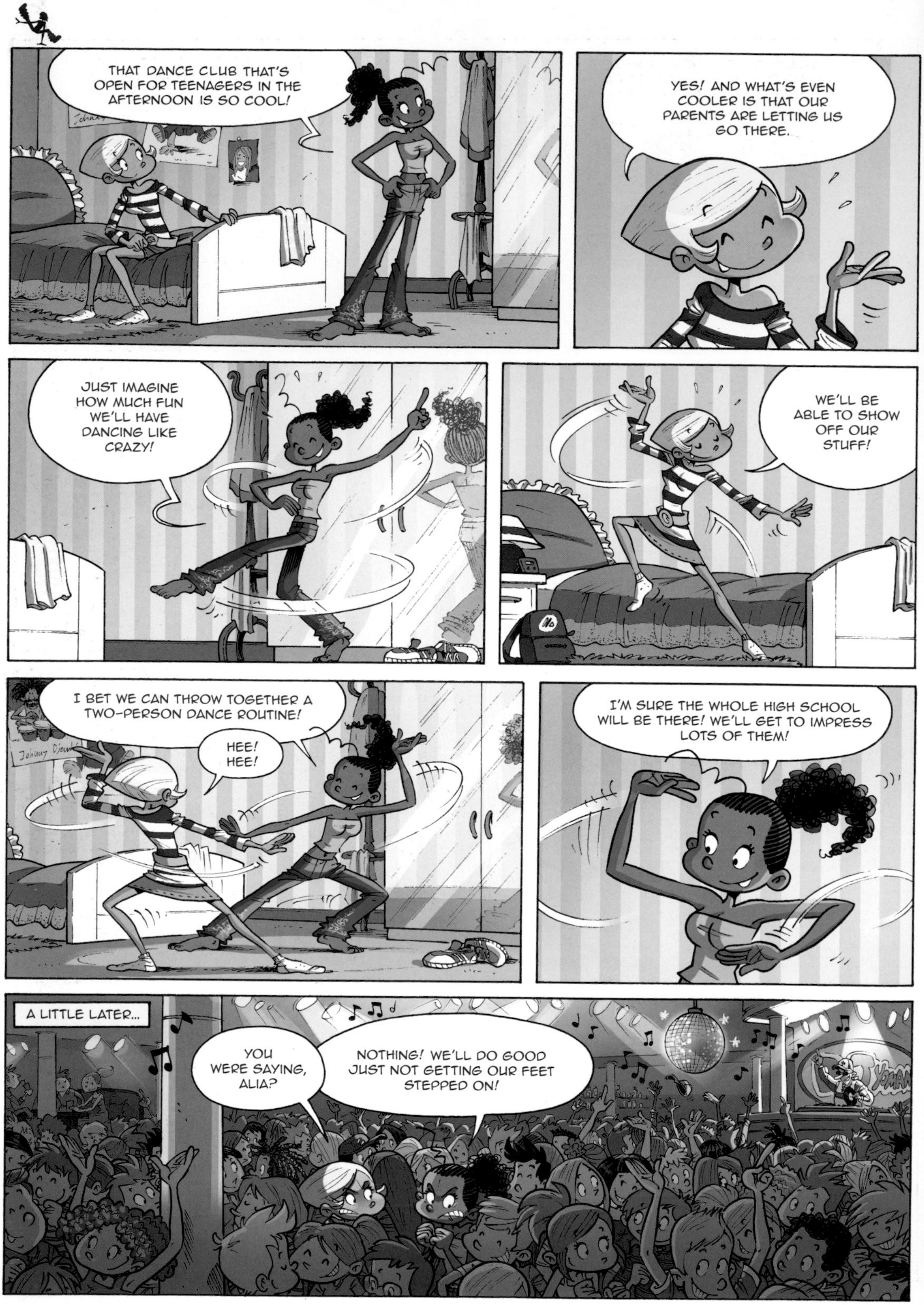

THAT DANCE CLUB THAT'S OPEN FOR TEENAGERS IN THE AFTERNOON IS SO COOL!
YES! AND WHAT'S EVEN COOLER IS THAT OUR PARENTS ARE LETTING US GO THERE.
JUST IMAGINE HOW MUCH FUN WE'LL HAVE DANCING LIKE CRAZY!
WE'LL BE ABLE TO SHOW OFF OUR STUFF!
I BET WE CAN THROW TOGETHER A TWO-PERSON DANCE ROUTINE!
HEE! HEE!
I'M SURE THE WHOLE HIGH SCHOOL WILL BE THERE! WE'LL GET TO IMPRESS LOTS OF THEM!
A LITTLE LATER...
YOU WERE SAYING, ALIA?
NOTHING! WE'LL DO GOOD JUST NOT GETTING OUR FEET STEPPED ON!

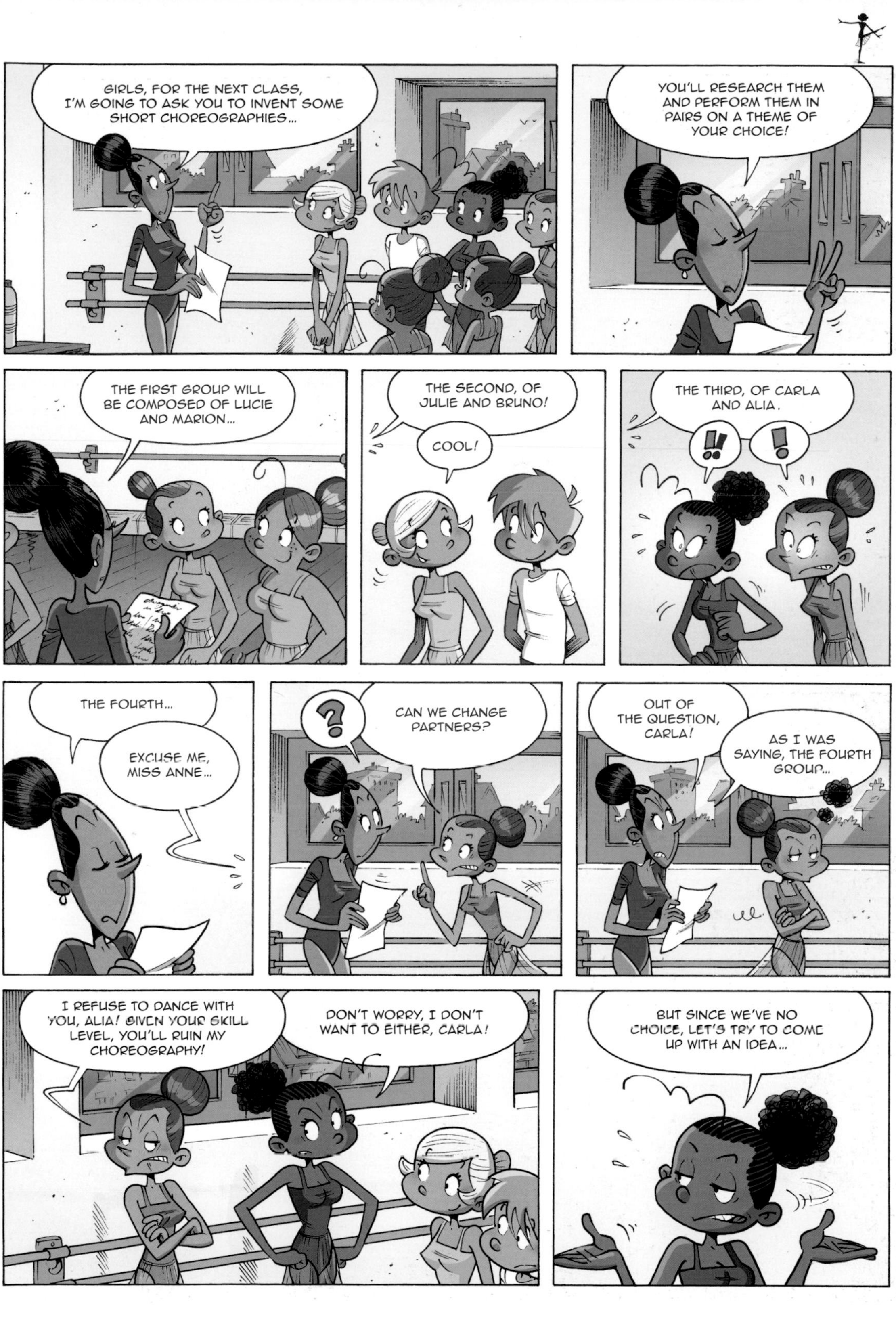
GIRLS, FOR THE NEXT CLASS, I'M GOING TO ASK YOU TO INVENT SOME SHORT CHOREOGRAPHIES...
YOU'LL RESEARCH THEM AND PERFORM THEM IN PAIRS ON A THEME OF YOUR CHOICE!
THE FIRST GROUP WILL BE COMPOSED OF LUCIE AND MARION...
THE SECOND, OF JULIE AND BRUNO!
COOL!
THE THIRD, OF CARLA AND ALIA.
!!
!
THE FOURTH...
EXCUSE ME, MISS ANNE...
?
CAN WE CHANGE PARTNERS?
OUT OF THE QUESTION, CARLA!
AS I WAS SAYING, THE FOURTH GROUP...
I REFUSE TO DANCE WITH YOU, ALIA! GIVEN YOUR SKILL LEVEL, YOU'LL RUIN MY CHOREOGRAPHY!
DON'T WORRY, I DON'T WANT TO EITHER, CARLA!
BUT SINCE WE'VE NO CHOICE, LET'S TRY TO COME UP WITH AN IDEA...

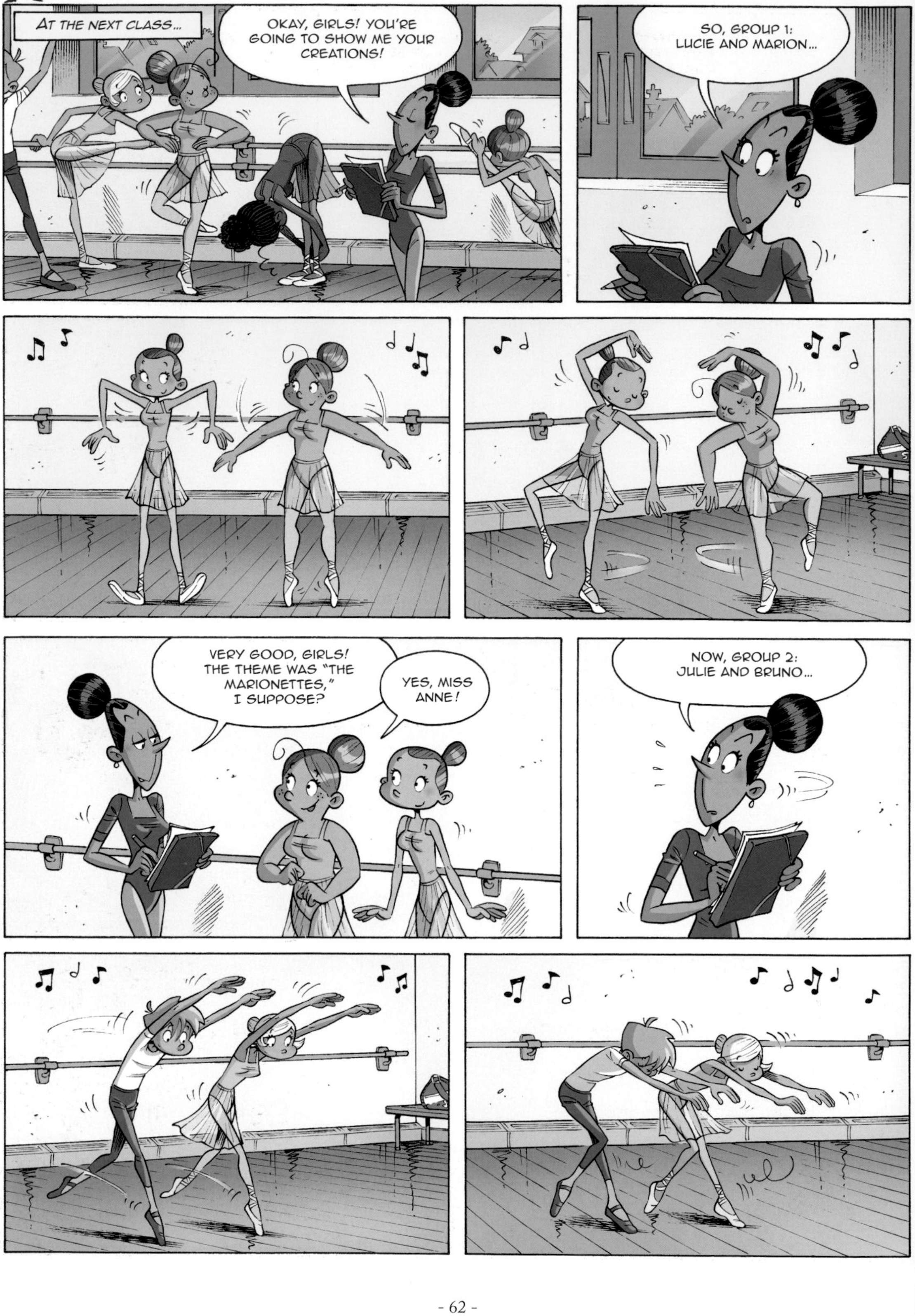

AT THE NEXT CLASS...
OKAY, GIRLS! YOU'RE GOING TO SHOW ME YOUR CREATIONS!
SO, GROUP 1: LUCIE AND MARION...
VERY GOOD, GIRLS! THE THEME WAS "THE MARIONETTES," I SUPPOSE?
YES, MISS ANNE!
NOW, GROUP 2: JULIE AND BRUNO...

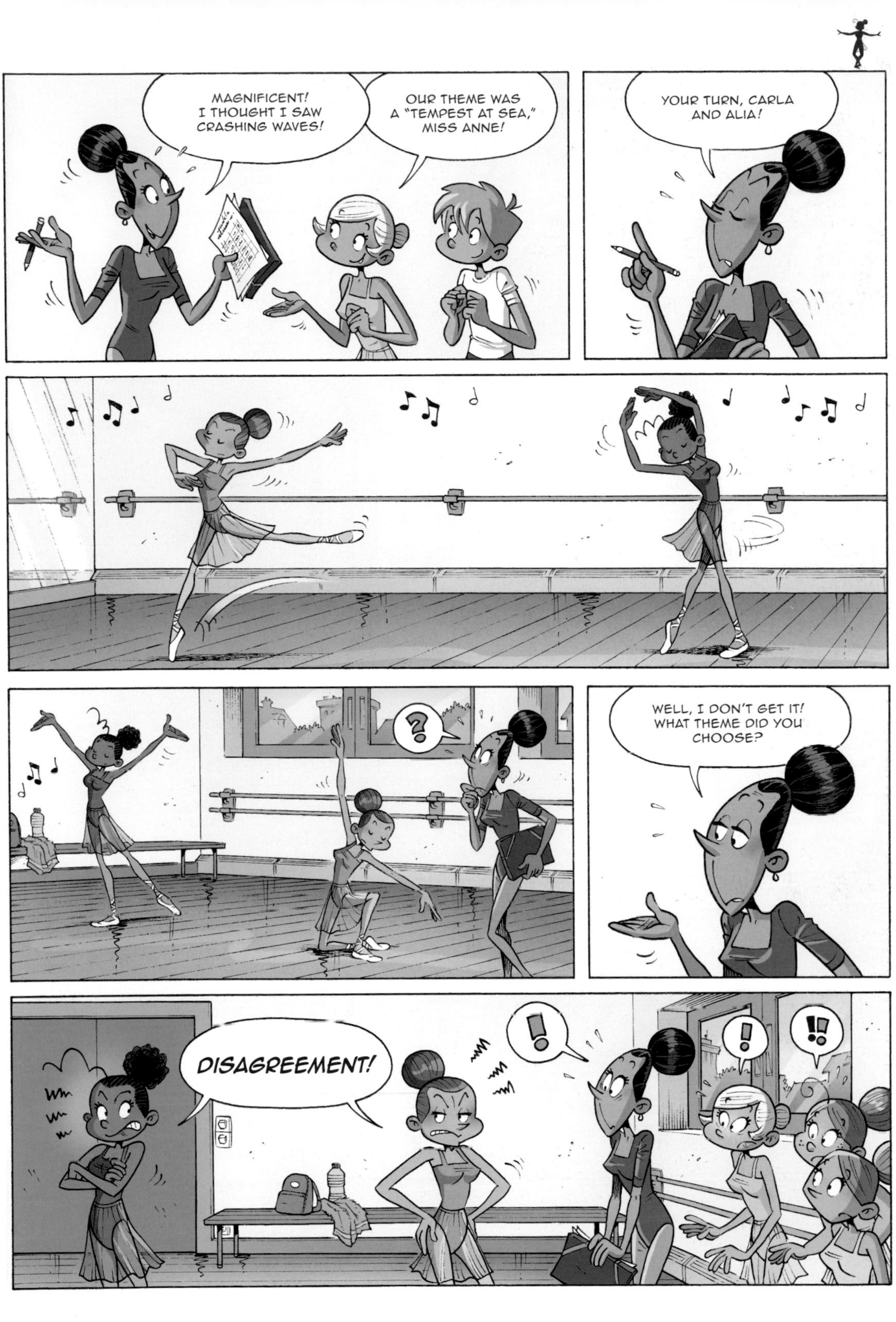
MAGNIFICENT! I THOUGHT I SAW CRASHING WAVES!
OUR THEME WAS A "TEMPEST AT SEA," MISS ANNE!
YOUR TURN, CARLA AND ALIA!
?
WELL, I DON'T GET IT! WHAT THEME DID YOU CHOOSE?
DISAGREEMENT!
!
!
!!

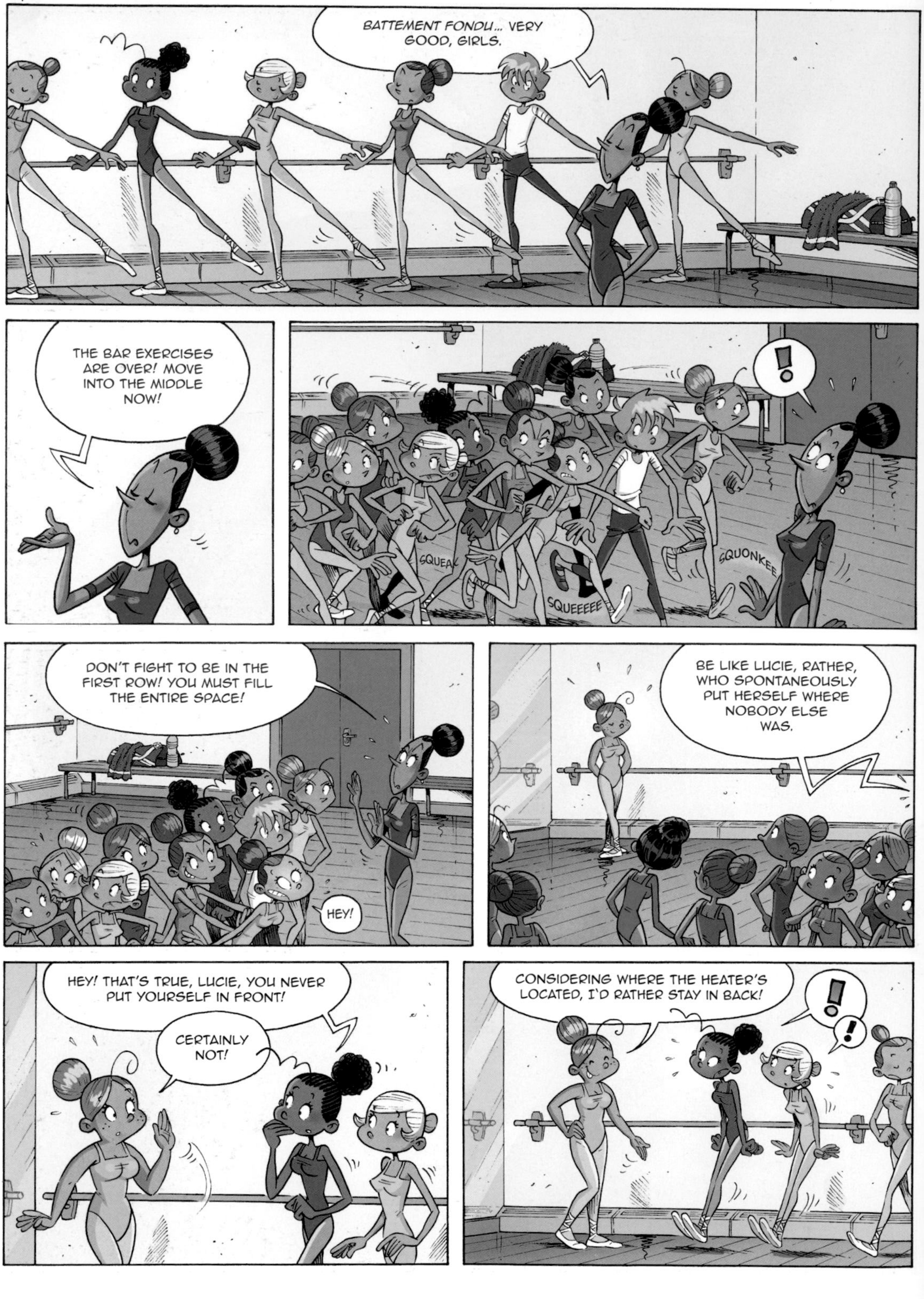

BATTEMENT FONDU... VERY GOOD, GIRLS.
THE BAR EXERCISES ARE OVER! MOVE INTO THE MIDDLE NOW!
!
SQUEAK
SQUEEEEEE
SQUONKEE
DON'T FIGHT TO BE IN THE FIRST ROW! YOU MUST FILL THE ENTIRE SPACE!
HEY!
BE LIKE LUCIE, RATHER, WHO SPONTANEOUSLY PUT HERSELF WHERE NOBODY ELSE WAS.
HEY! THAT'S TRUE, LUCIE, YOU NEVER PUT YOURSELF IN FRONT!
CERTAINLY NOT!
CONSIDERING WHERE THE HEATER'S LOCATED, I'D RATHER STAY IN BACK!
!
!

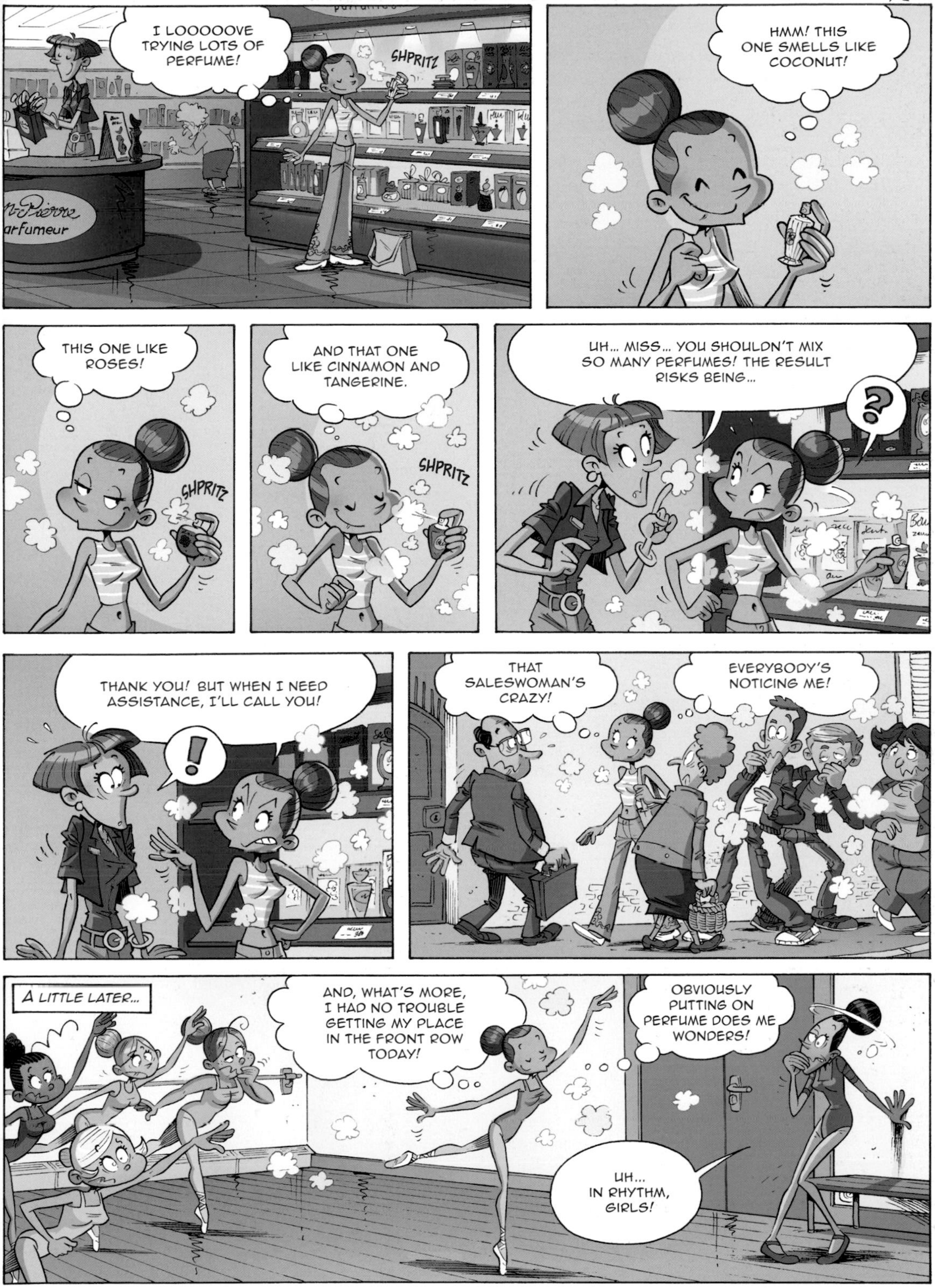
I LOOOOOVE TRYING LOTS OF PERFUME!
SHPRITZ
HMM! THIS ONE SMELLS LIKE COCONUT!
THIS ONE LIKE ROSES!
SHPRITZ
AND THAT ONE LIKE CINNAMON AND TANGERINE.
SHPRITZ
UH... MISS... YOU SHOULDN'T MIX SO MANY PERFUMES! THE RESULT RISKS BEING...
?
THANK YOU! BUT WHEN I NEED ASSISTANCE, I'LL CALL YOU!
!
THAT SALESWOMAN'S CRAZY!
EVERYBODY'S NOTICING ME!
A LITTLE LATER...
AND, WHAT'S MORE, I HAD NO TROUBLE GETTING MY PLACE IN THE FRONT ROW TODAY!
OBVIOUSLY PUTTING ON PERFUME DOES ME WONDERS!
UH... IN RHYTHM, GIRLS!

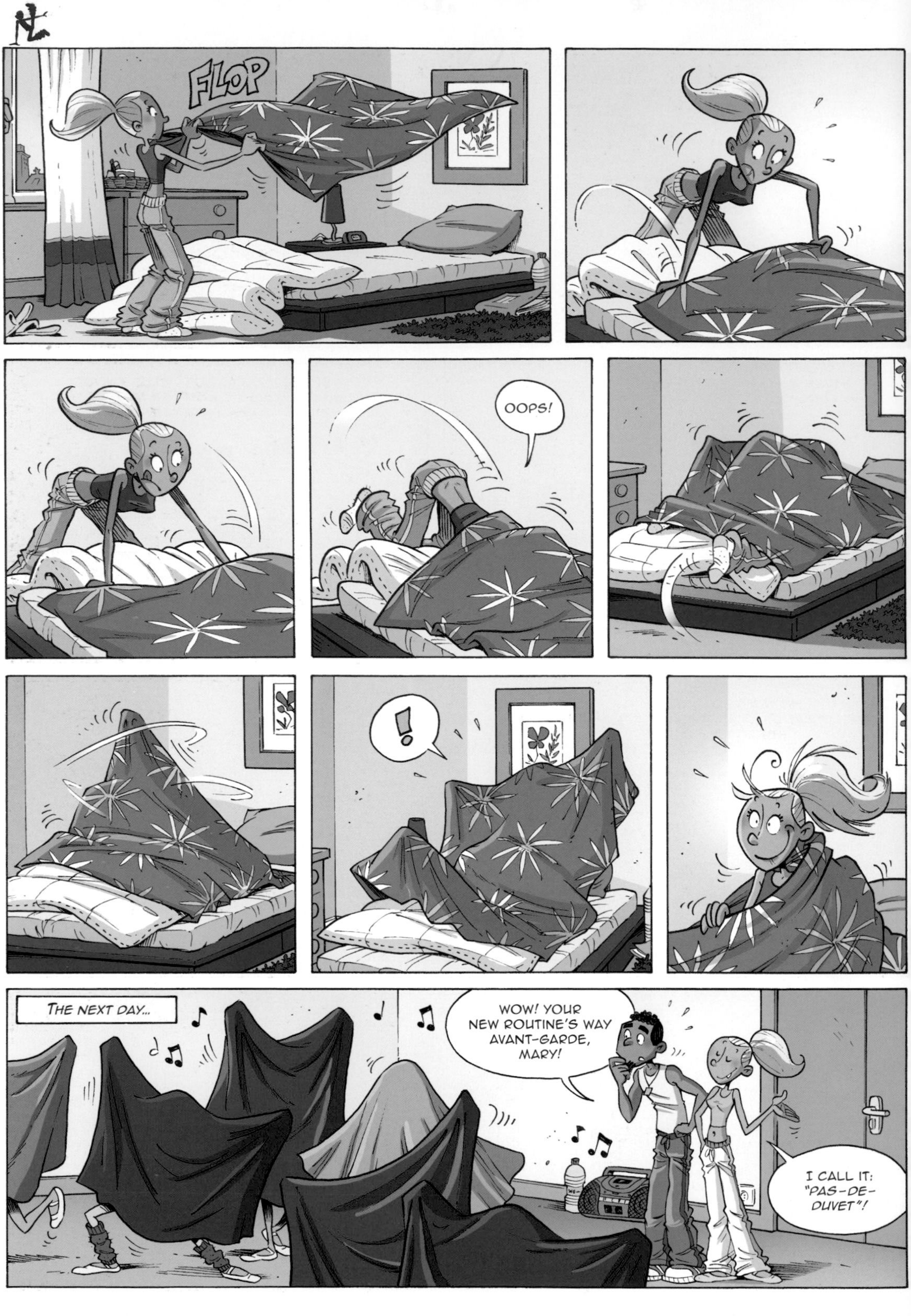
FLOP
OOPS!
!
THE NEXT DAY...
WOW! YOUR NEW ROUTINE'S WAY AVANT-GARDE, MARY!
I CALL IT: "PAS-DE-DUVET"!

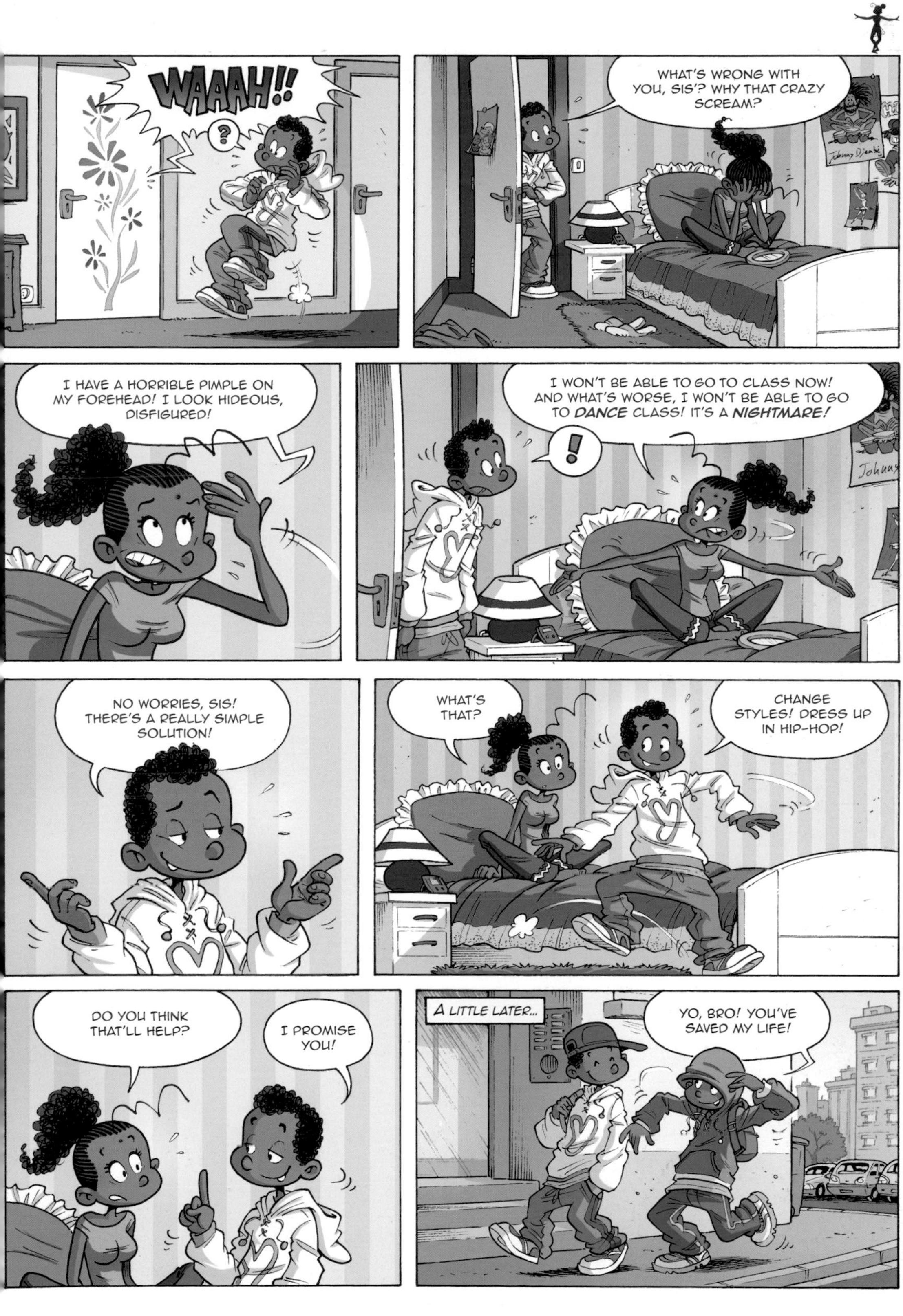
WAAAH!!
?
WHAT'S WRONG WITH YOU, SIS'? WHY THAT CRAZY SCREAM?
Johnny Djembé
I HAVE A HORRIBLE PIMPLE ON MY FOREHEAD! I LOOK HIDEOUS, DISFIGURED!
I WON'T BE ABLE TO GO TO CLASS NOW! AND WHAT'S WORSE, I WON'T BE ABLE TO GO TO DANCE CLASS! IT'S A NIGHTMARE!
!
NO WORRIES, SIS! THERE'S A REALLY SIMPLE SOLUTION!
WHAT'S THAT?
CHANGE STYLES! DRESS UP IN HIP-HOP!
DO YOU THINK THAT'LL HELP?
I PROMISE YOU!
A LITTLE LATER...
YO, BRO! YOU'VE SAVED MY LIFE!

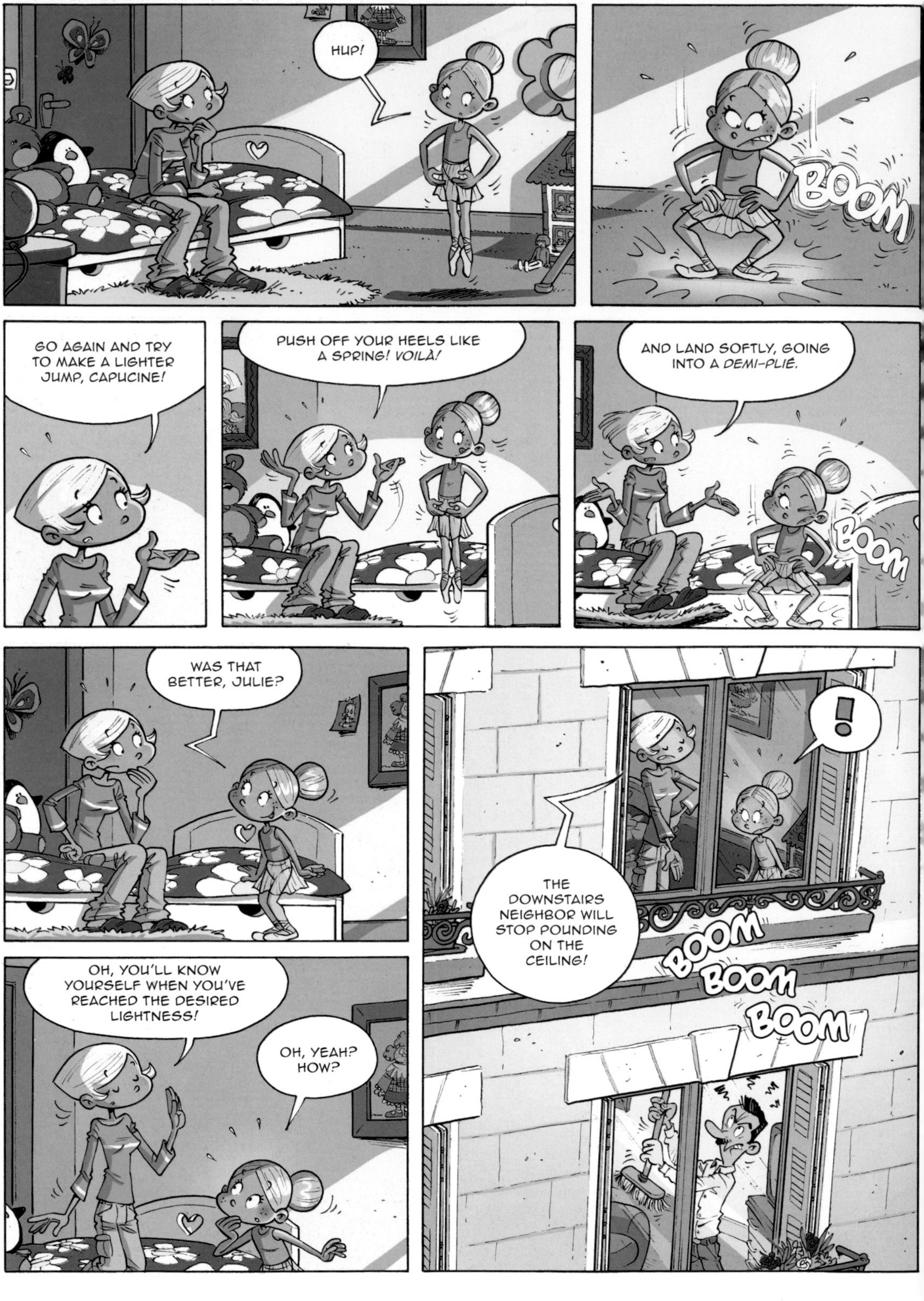
HUP!
BOOM
GO AGAIN AND TRY TO MAKE A LIGHTER JUMP, CAPUCINE!
PUSH OFF YOUR HEELS LIKE A SPRING! *VOILÀ!*
AND LAND SOFTLY, GOING INTO A *DEMI-PLIÉ*.
BOOM
WAS THAT BETTER, JULIE?
OH, YOU'LL KNOW YOURSELF WHEN YOU'VE REACHED THE DESIRED LIGHTNESS!
OH, YEAH? HOW?
!
THE DOWNSTAIRS NEIGHBOR WILL STOP POUNDING ON THE CEILING!
BOOM
BOOM
BOOM

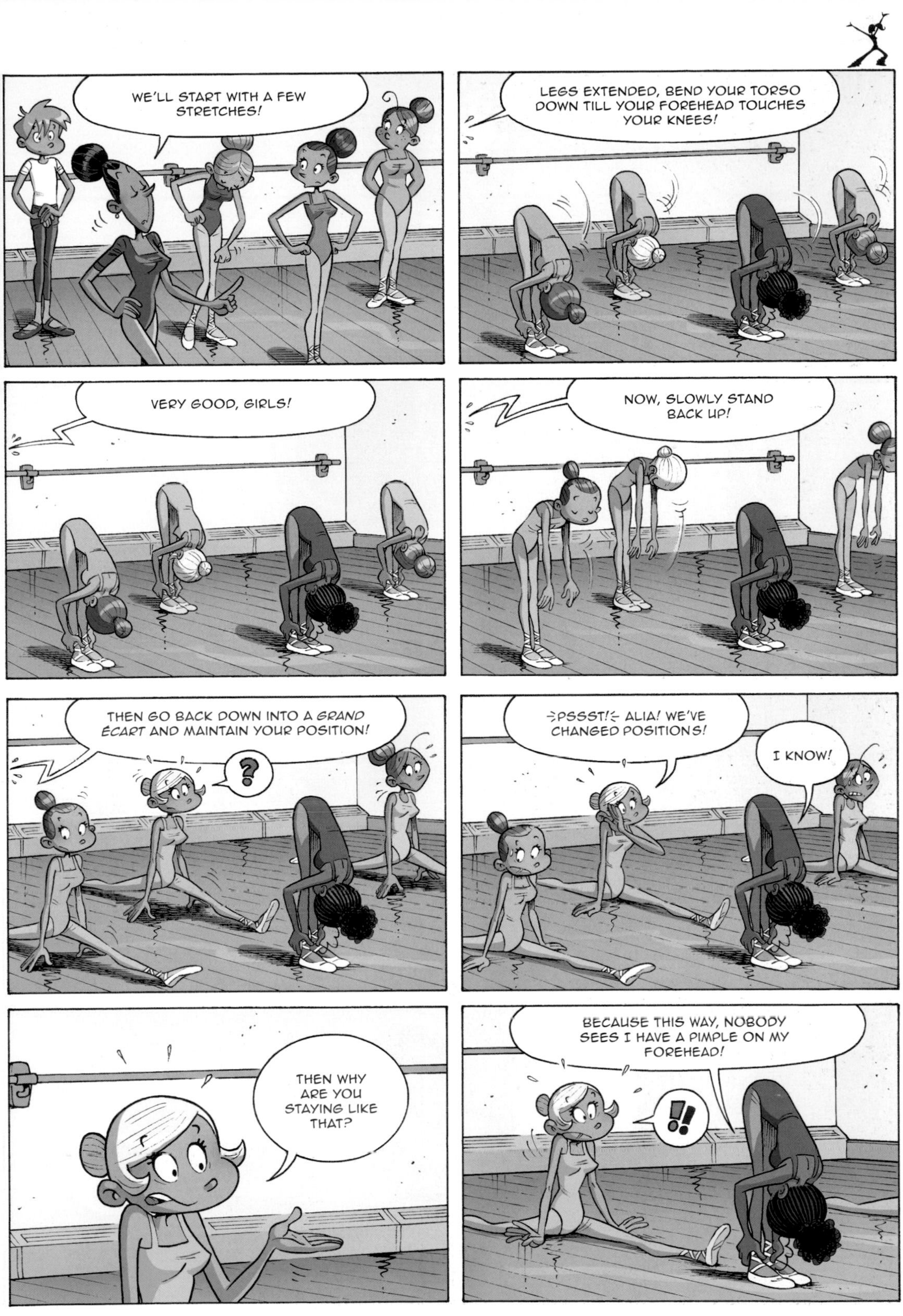

WE'LL START WITH A FEW STRETCHES!
LEGS EXTENDED, BEND YOUR TORSO DOWN TILL YOUR FOREHEAD TOUCHES YOUR KNEES!
VERY GOOD, GIRLS!
NOW, SLOWLY STAND BACK UP!
THEN GO BACK DOWN INTO A *GRAND ÉCART* AND MAINTAIN YOUR POSITION!
?
PSSST! ALIA! WE'VE CHANGED POSITIONS!
I KNOW!
THEN WHY ARE YOU STAYING LIKE THAT?
BECAUSE THIS WAY, NOBODY SEES I HAVE A PIMPLE ON MY FOREHEAD!
!!

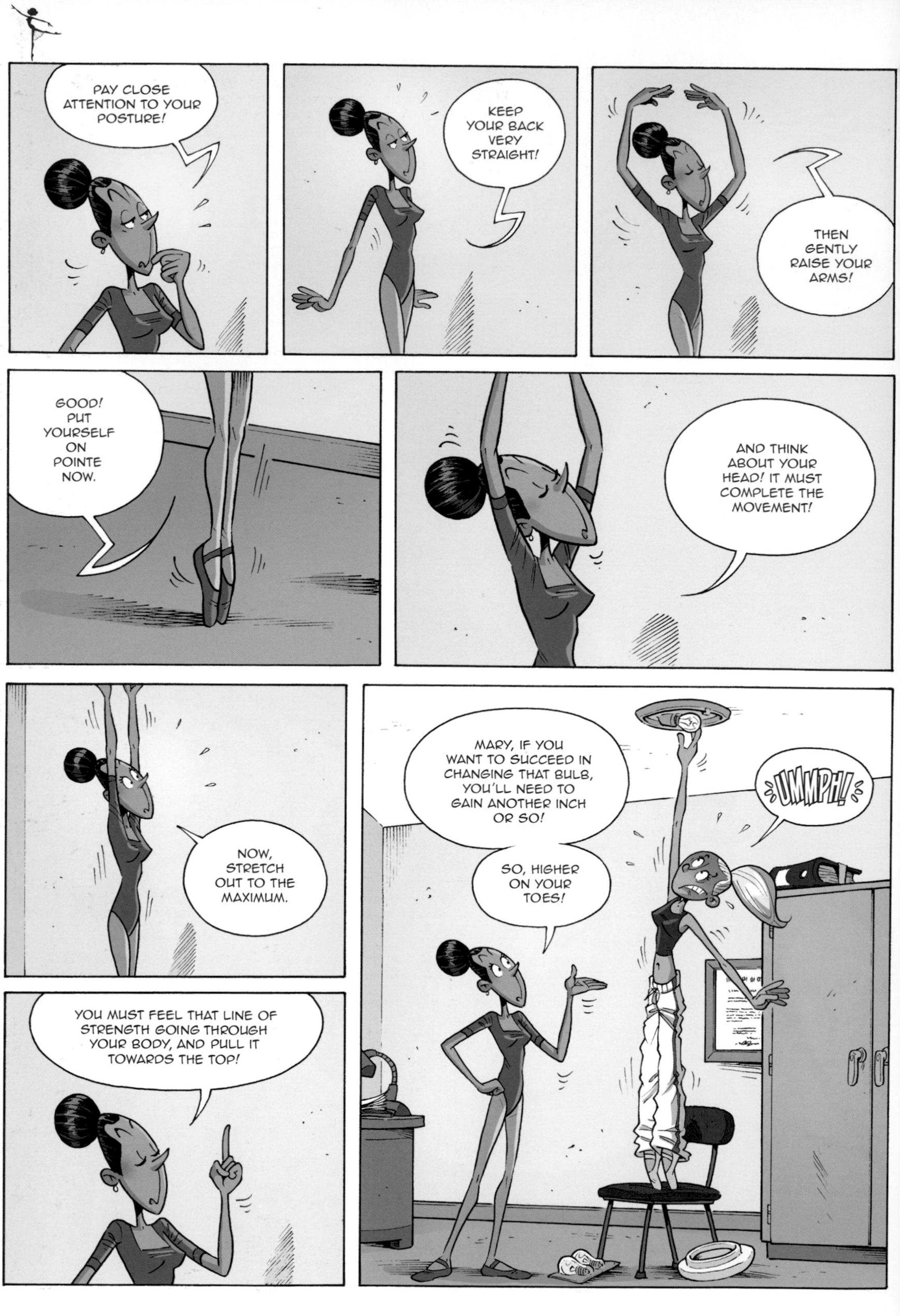
PAY CLOSE ATTENTION TO YOUR POSTURE!
KEEP YOUR BACK VERY STRAIGHT!
THEN GENTLY RAISE YOUR ARMS!
GOOD! PUT YOURSELF ON POINTE NOW.
AND THINK ABOUT YOUR HEAD! IT MUST COMPLETE THE MOVEMENT!
NOW, STRETCH OUT TO THE MAXIMUM.
YOU MUST FEEL THAT LINE OF STRENGTH GOING THROUGH YOUR BODY, AND PULL IT TOWARDS THE TOP!
MARY, IF YOU WANT TO SUCCEED IN CHANGING THAT BULB, YOU'LL NEED TO GAIN ANOTHER INCH OR SO!
SO, HIGHER ON YOUR TOES!
UMMPH!

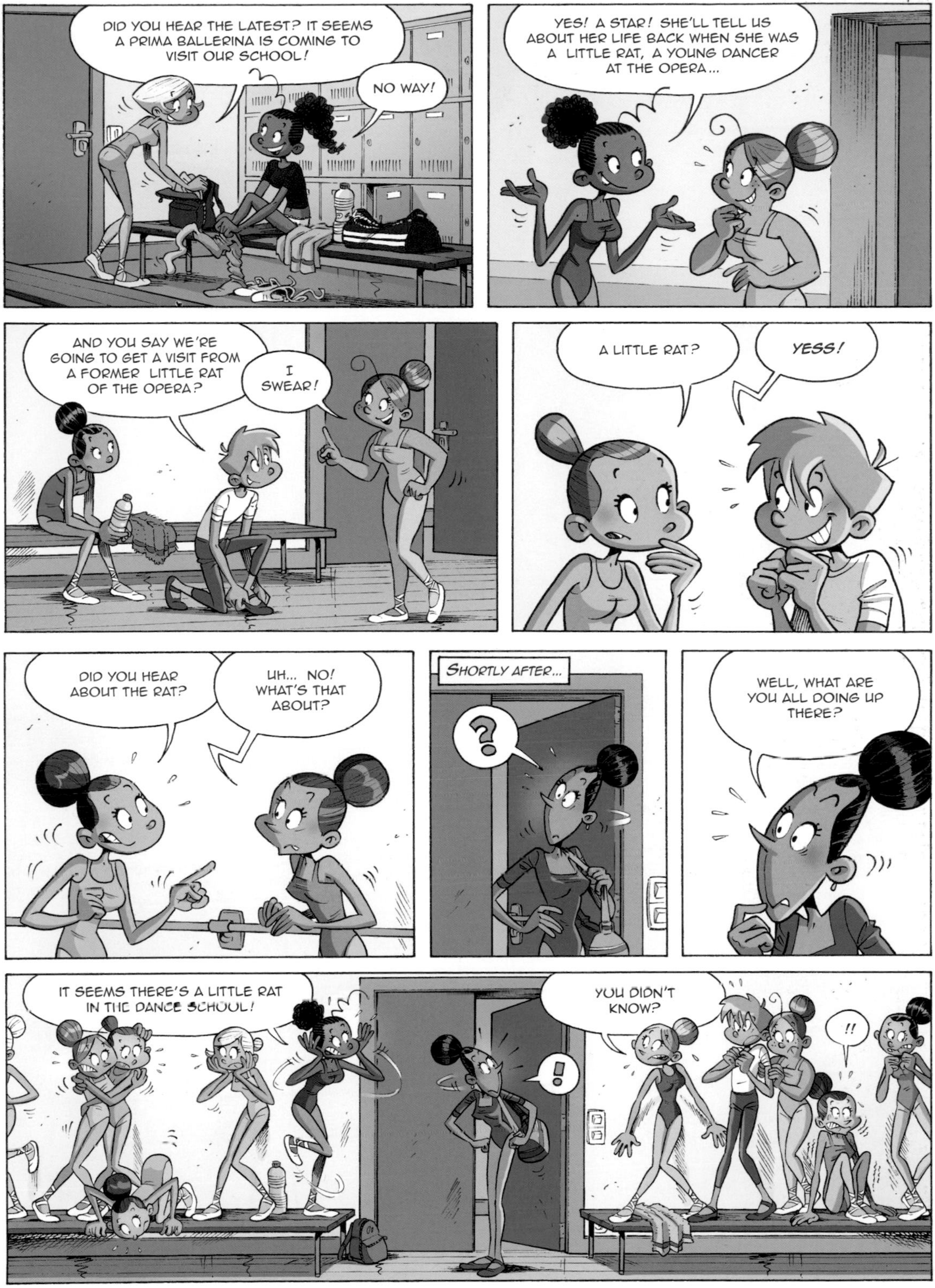
DID YOU HEAR THE LATEST? IT SEEMS A PRIMA BALLERINA IS COMING TO VISIT OUR SCHOOL!
NO WAY!
YES! A STAR! SHE'LL TELL US ABOUT HER LIFE BACK WHEN SHE WAS A LITTLE RAT, A YOUNG DANCER AT THE OPERA...
AND YOU SAY WE'RE GOING TO GET A VISIT FROM A FORMER LITTLE RAT OF THE OPERA?
I SWEAR!
A LITTLE RAT?
YESS!
DID YOU HEAR ABOUT THE RAT?
UH... NO! WHAT'S THAT ABOUT?
SHORTLY AFTER...
?
WELL, WHAT ARE YOU ALL DOING UP THERE?
IT SEEMS THERE'S A LITTLE RAT IN THE DANCE SCHOOL!
!
YOU DIDN'T KNOW?
!!

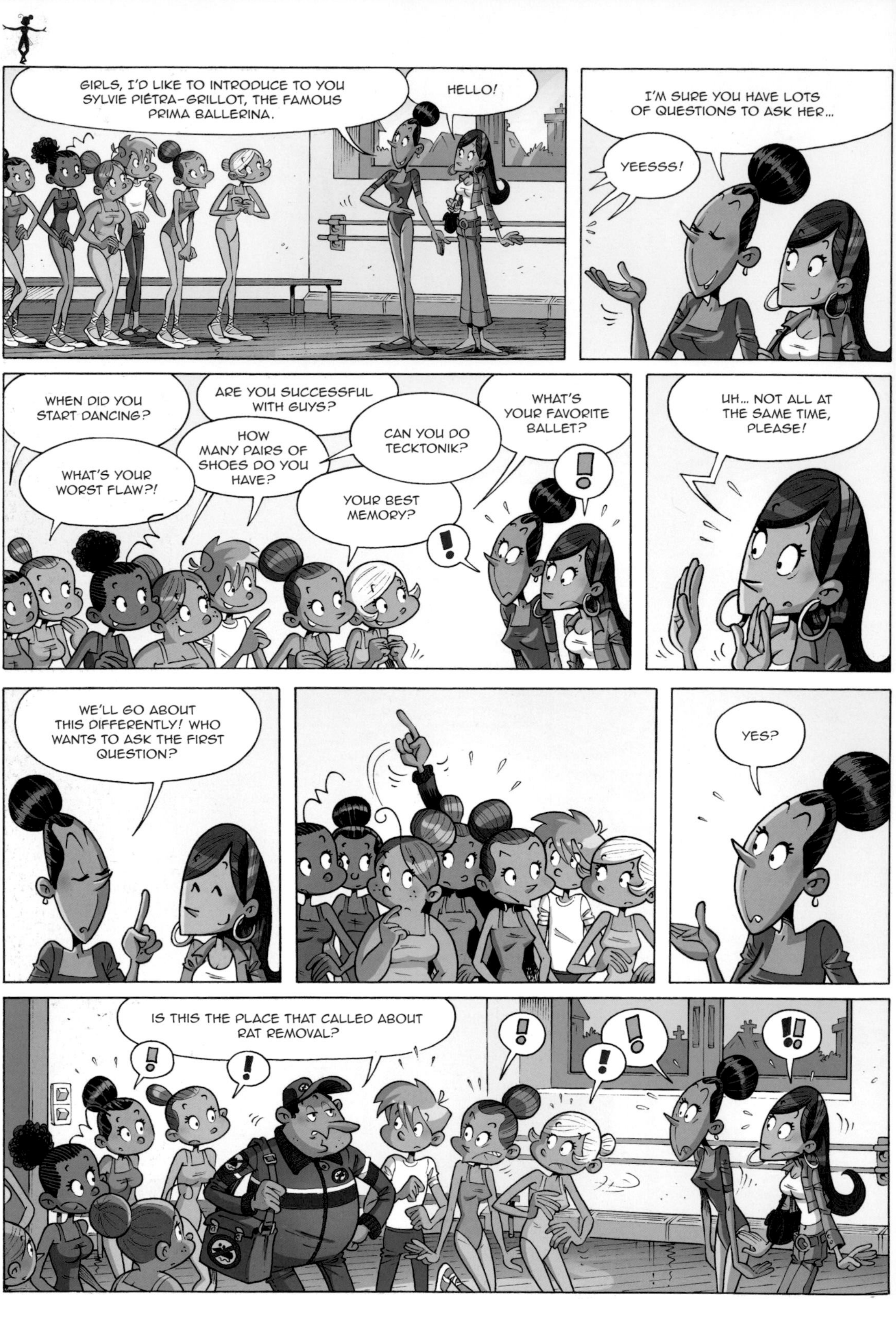
GIRLS, I'D LIKE TO INTRODUCE TO YOU SYLVIE PIÉTRA-GRILLOT, THE FAMOUS PRIMA BALLERINA.
HELLO!
I'M SURE YOU HAVE LOTS OF QUESTIONS TO ASK HER...
YEESSS!
WHEN DID YOU START DANCING?
ARE YOU SUCCESSFUL WITH GUYS?
WHAT'S YOUR FAVORITE BALLET?
HOW MANY PAIRS OF SHOES DO YOU HAVE?
CAN YOU DO TECKTONIK?
WHAT'S YOUR WORST FLAW?!
YOUR BEST MEMORY?
!
!
UH... NOT ALL AT THE SAME TIME, PLEASE!
WE'LL GO ABOUT THIS DIFFERENTLY! WHO WANTS TO ASK THE FIRST QUESTION?
YES?
IS THIS THE PLACE THAT CALLED ABOUT RAT REMOVAL?
!
!
!
!
!
!!

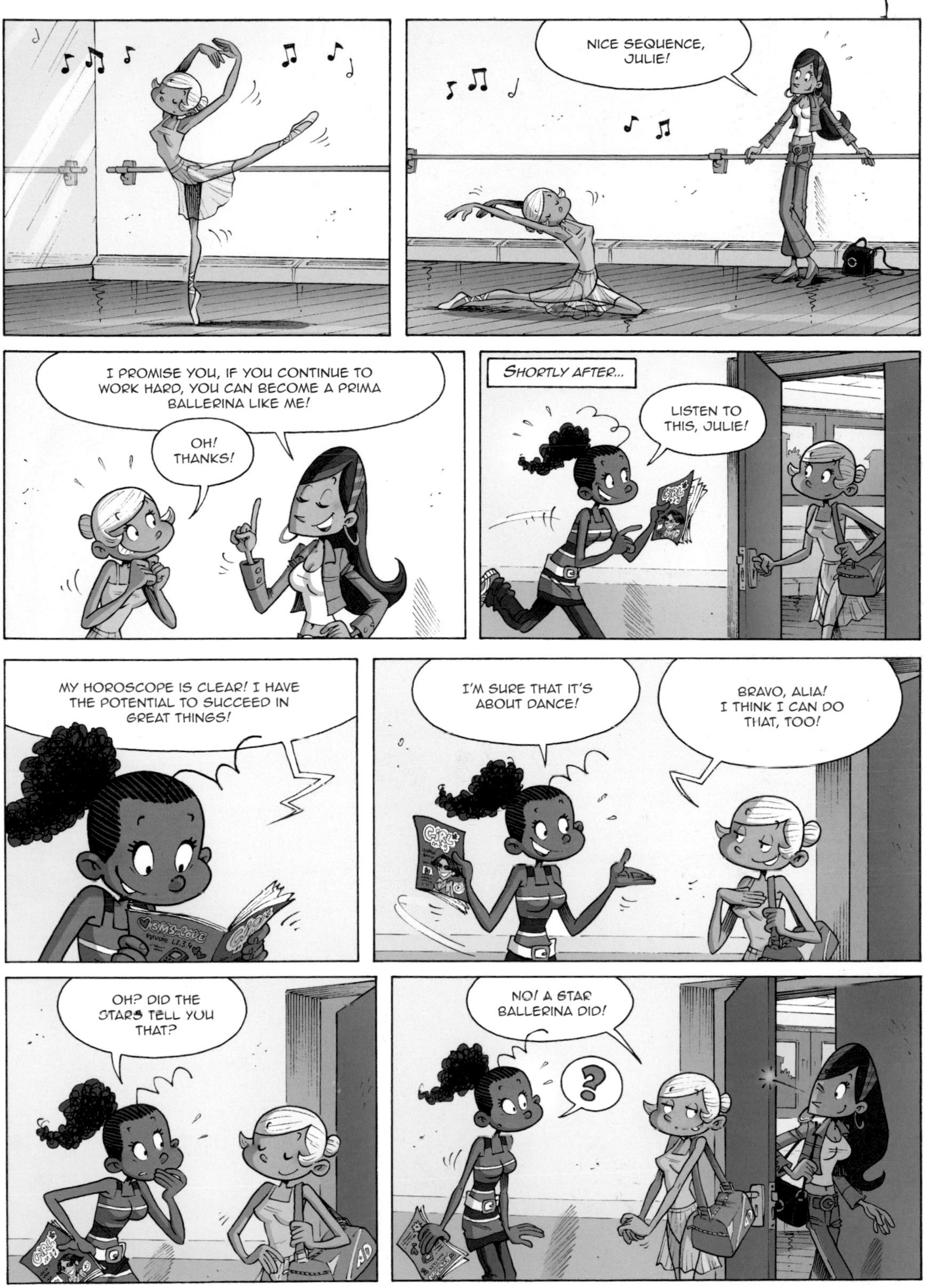
NICE SEQUENCE, JULIE!
I PROMISE YOU, IF YOU CONTINUE TO WORK HARD, YOU CAN BECOME A PRIMA BALLERINA LIKE ME!
OH! THANKS!
SHORTLY AFTER...
LISTEN TO THIS, JULIE!
MY HOROSCOPE IS CLEAR! I HAVE THE POTENTIAL TO SUCCEED IN GREAT THINGS!
I'M SURE THAT IT'S ABOUT DANCE!
BRAVO, ALIA! I THINK I CAN DO THAT, TOO!
OH? DID THE STARS TELL YOU THAT?
NO! A STAR BALLERINA DID!
?

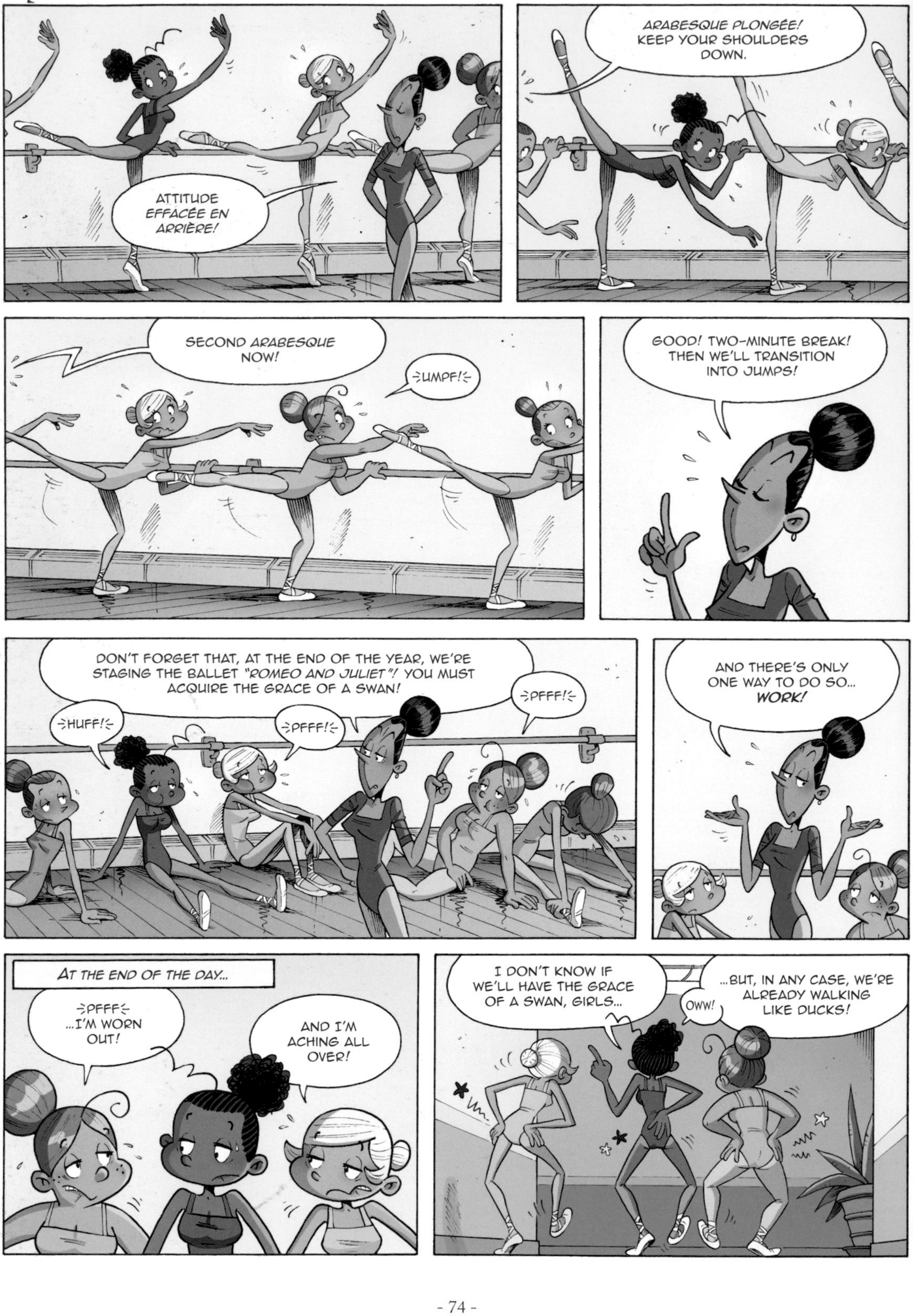
ATTITUDE EFFACÉE EN ARRIÈRE!
ARABESQUE PLONGÉE! KEEP YOUR SHOULDERS DOWN.
SECOND ARABESQUE NOW!
UMPF!
GOOD! TWO-MINUTE BREAK! THEN WE'LL TRANSITION INTO JUMPS!
DON'T FORGET THAT, AT THE END OF THE YEAR, WE'RE STAGING THE BALLET *"ROMEO AND JULIET"*! YOU MUST ACQUIRE THE GRACE OF A SWAN!
HUFF!
PFFF!
PFFF!
AND THERE'S ONLY ONE WAY TO DO SO... **WORK!**
AT THE END OF THE DAY...
PFFF ...I'M WORN OUT!
AND I'M ACHING ALL OVER!
I DON'T KNOW IF WE'LL HAVE THE GRACE OF A SWAN, GIRLS...
OWW!
...BUT, IN ANY CASE, WE'RE ALREADY WALKING LIKE DUCKS!

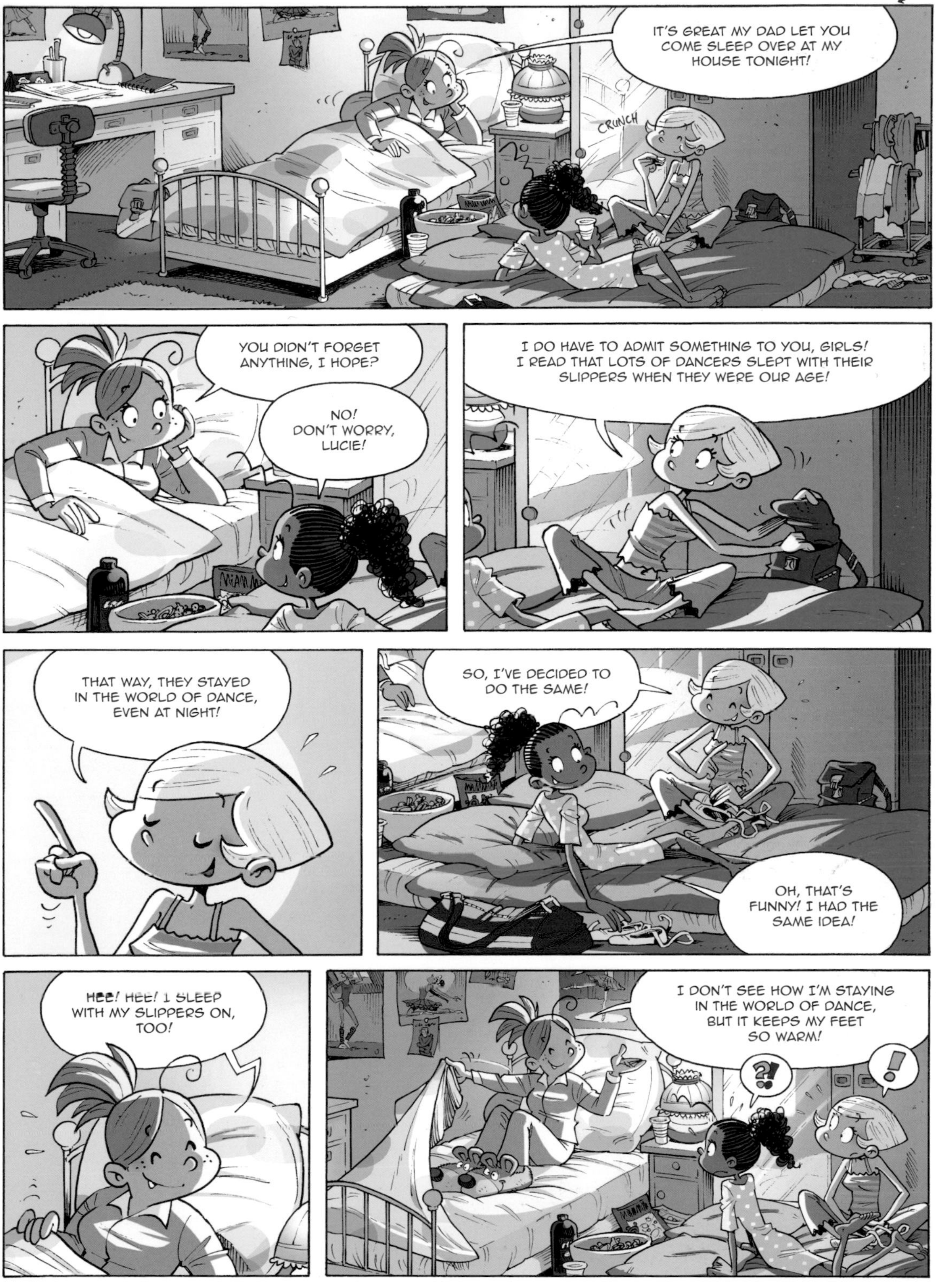
IT'S GREAT MY DAD LET YOU COME SLEEP OVER AT MY HOUSE TONIGHT!
CRUNCH
YOU DIDN'T FORGET ANYTHING, I HOPE?
NO! DON'T WORRY, LUCIE!
I DO HAVE TO ADMIT SOMETHING TO YOU, GIRLS! I READ THAT LOTS OF DANCERS SLEPT WITH THEIR SLIPPERS WHEN THEY WERE OUR AGE!
THAT WAY, THEY STAYED IN THE WORLD OF DANCE, EVEN AT NIGHT!
SO, I'VE DECIDED TO DO THE SAME!
OH, THAT'S FUNNY! I HAD THE SAME IDEA!
HEE! HEE! I SLEEP WITH MY SLIPPERS ON, TOO!
I DON'T SEE HOW I'M STAYING IN THE WORLD OF DANCE, BUT IT KEEPS MY FEET SO WARM!
?!
!

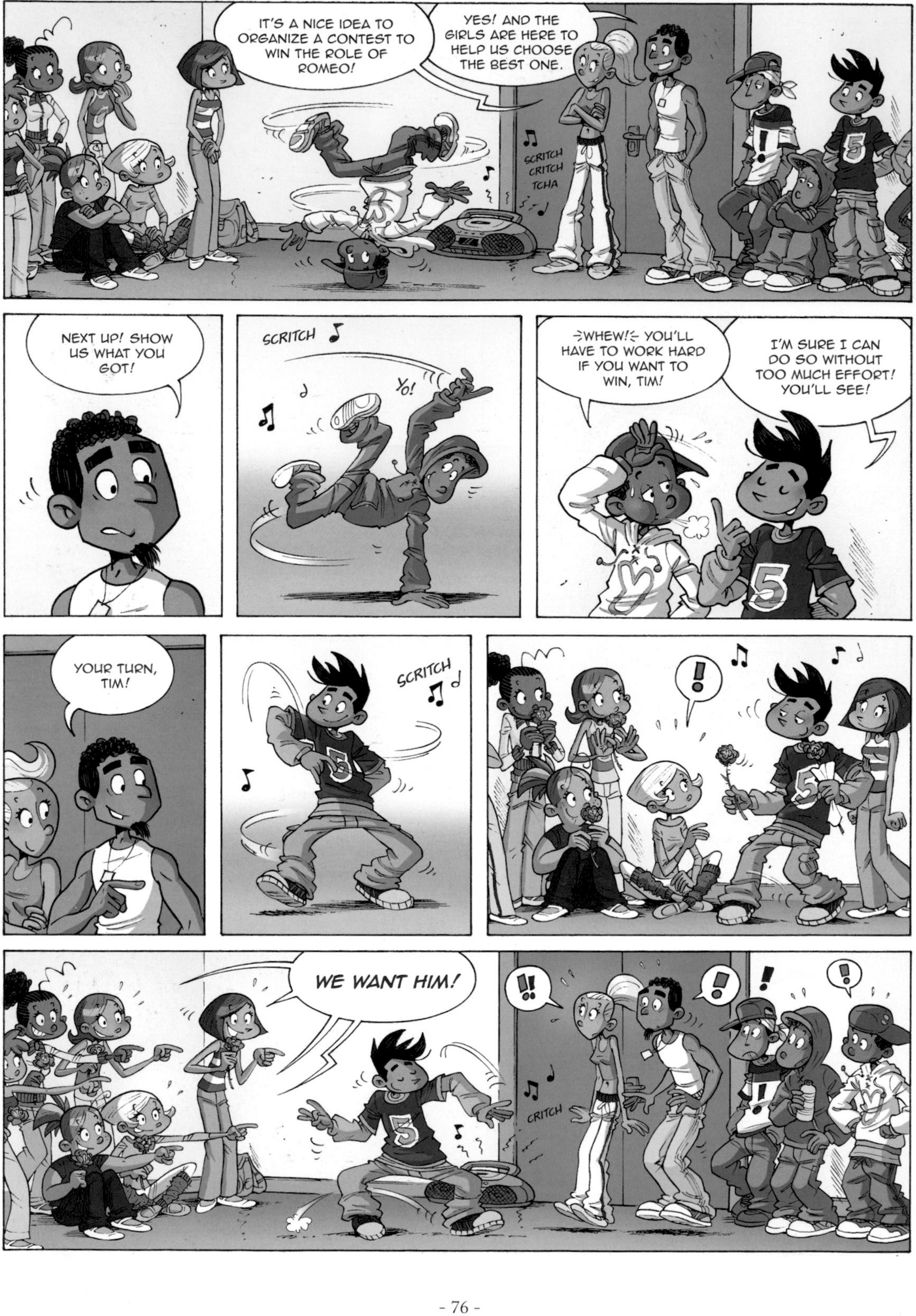
IT'S A NICE IDEA TO ORGANIZE A CONTEST TO WIN THE ROLE OF ROMEO!
YES! AND THE GIRLS ARE HERE TO HELP US CHOOSE THE BEST ONE.
SCRITCH CRITCH TCHA
NEXT UP! SHOW US WHAT YOU GOT!
SCRITCH
YO!
WHEW! YOU'LL HAVE TO WORK HARD IF YOU WANT TO WIN, TIM!
I'M SURE I CAN DO SO WITHOUT TOO MUCH EFFORT! YOU'LL SEE!
YOUR TURN, TIM!
SCRITCH
!
WE WANT HIM!
CRITCH
!!
!
!
!

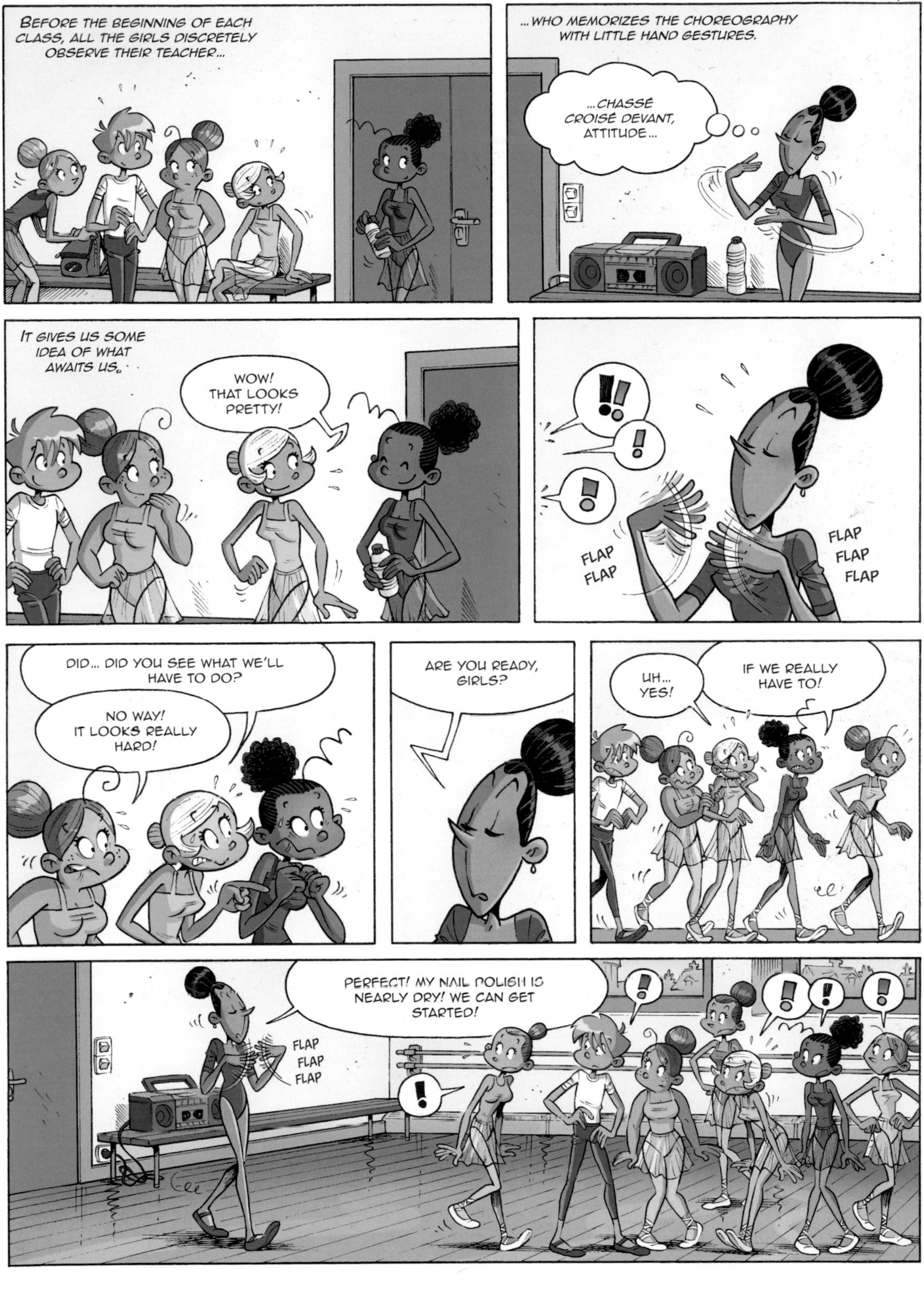
BEFORE THE BEGINNING OF EACH CLASS, ALL THE GIRLS DISCRETELY OBSERVE THEIR TEACHER...
...WHO MEMORIZES THE CHOREOGRAPHY WITH LITTLE HAND GESTURES.
...CHASSÉ CROISÉ DEVANT, ATTITUDE...
IT GIVES US SOME IDEA OF WHAT AWAITS US.
WOW! THAT LOOKS PRETTY!
!!
!
!
FLAP FLAP
FLAP FLAP FLAP
DID... DID YOU SEE WHAT WE'LL HAVE TO DO?
NO WAY! IT LOOKS REALLY HARD!
ARE YOU READY, GIRLS?
UH... YES!
IF WE REALLY HAVE TO!
PERFECT! MY NAIL POLISH IS NEARLY DRY! WE CAN GET STARTED!
FLAP FLAP FLAP
!
!
!
!
!
!

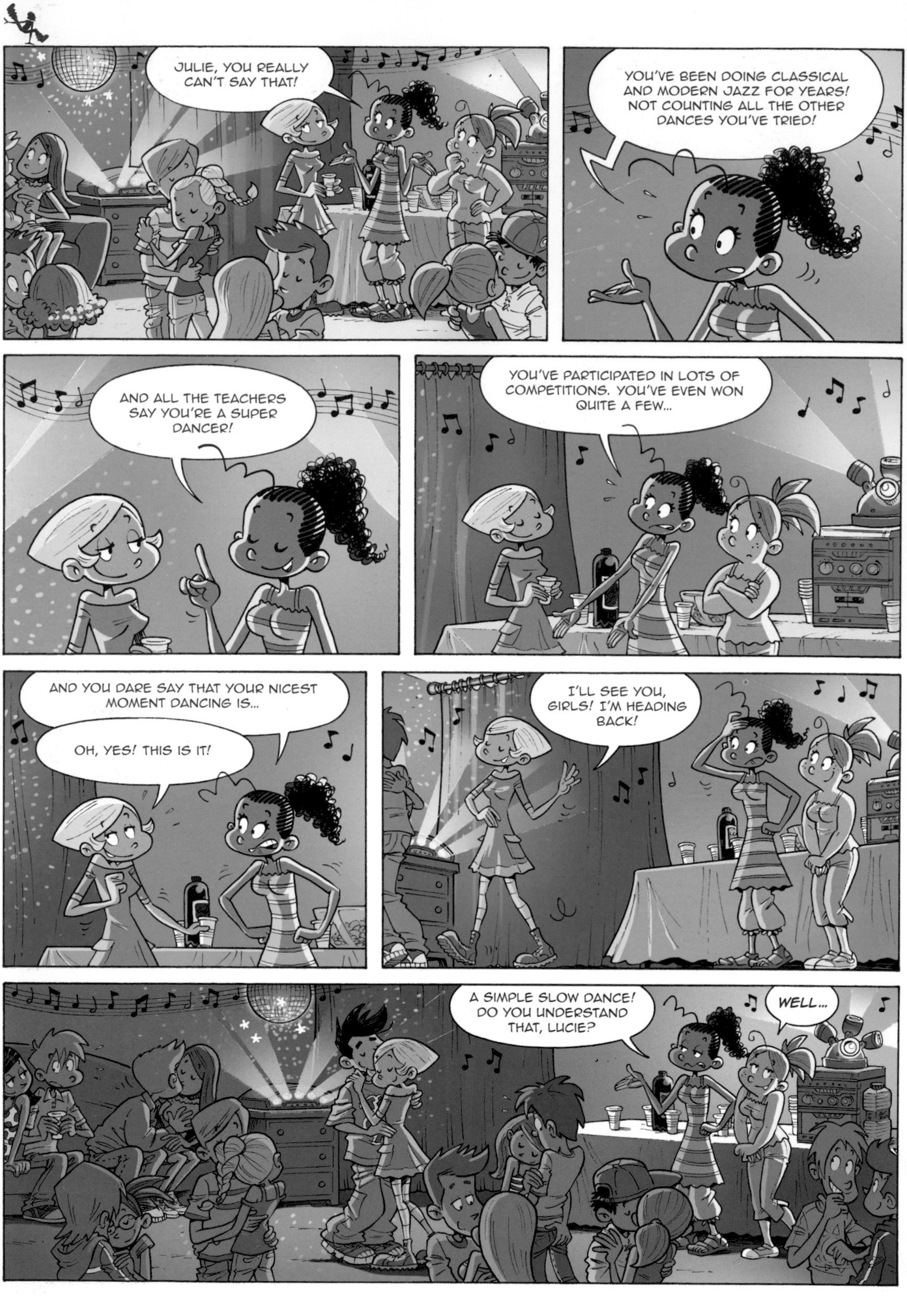
JULIE, YOU REALLY CAN'T SAY THAT!
YOU'VE BEEN DOING CLASSICAL AND MODERN JAZZ FOR YEARS! NOT COUNTING ALL THE OTHER DANCES YOU'VE TRIED!
AND ALL THE TEACHERS SAY YOU'RE A SUPER DANCER!
YOU'VE PARTICIPATED IN LOTS OF COMPETITIONS. YOU'VE EVEN WON QUITE A FEW...
AND YOU DARE SAY THAT YOUR NICEST MOMENT DANCING IS...
OH, YES! THIS IS IT!
I'LL SEE YOU, GIRLS! I'M HEADING BACK!
A SIMPLE SLOW DANCE! DO YOU UNDERSTAND THAT, LUCIE?
WELL...

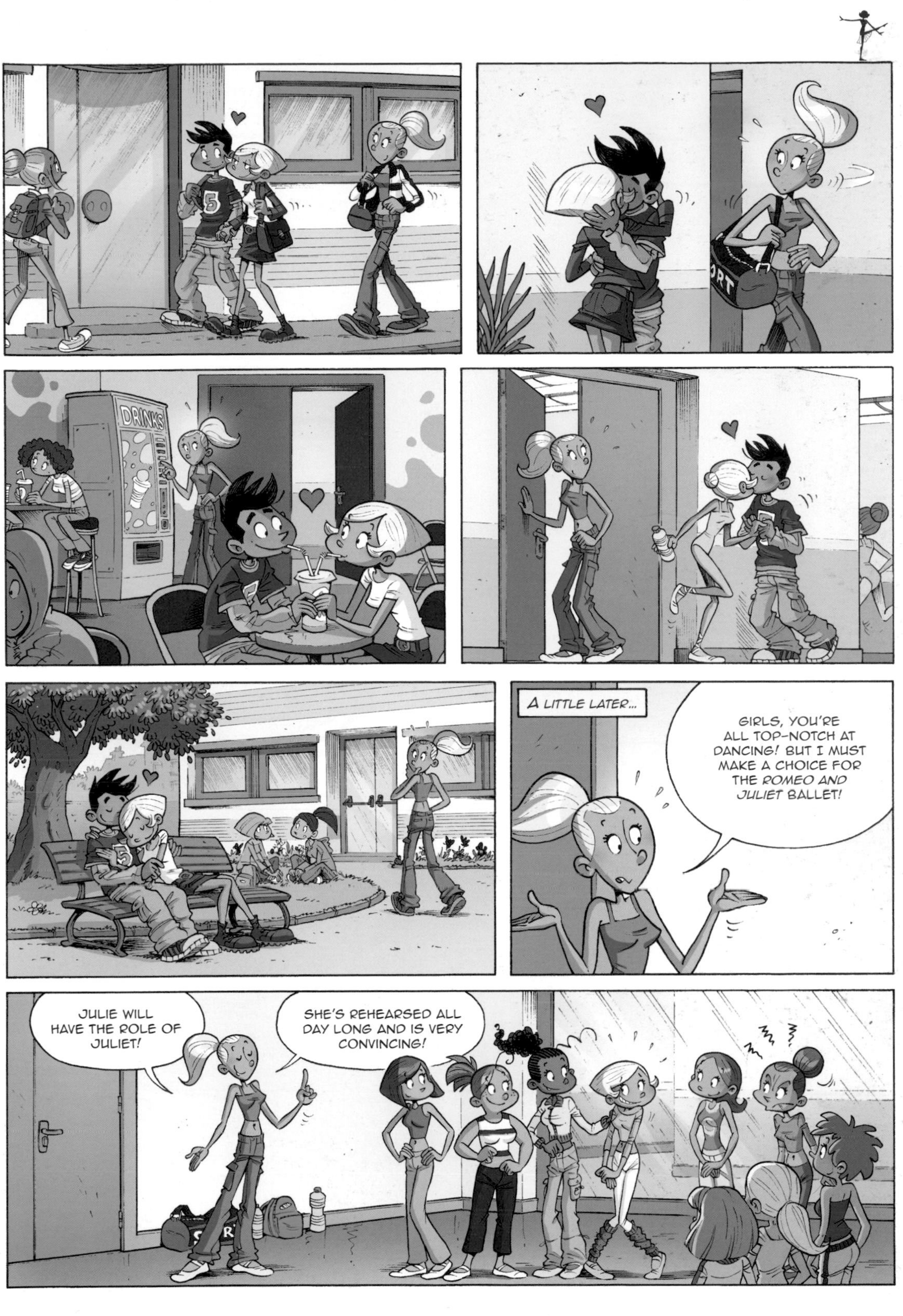
DRINKS
A LITTLE LATER...
GIRLS, YOU'RE ALL TOP-NOTCH AT DANCING! BUT I MUST MAKE A CHOICE FOR THE *ROMEO AND JULIET* BALLET!
JULIE WILL HAVE THE ROLE OF JULIET!
SHE'S REHEARSED ALL DAY LONG AND IS VERY CONVINCING!

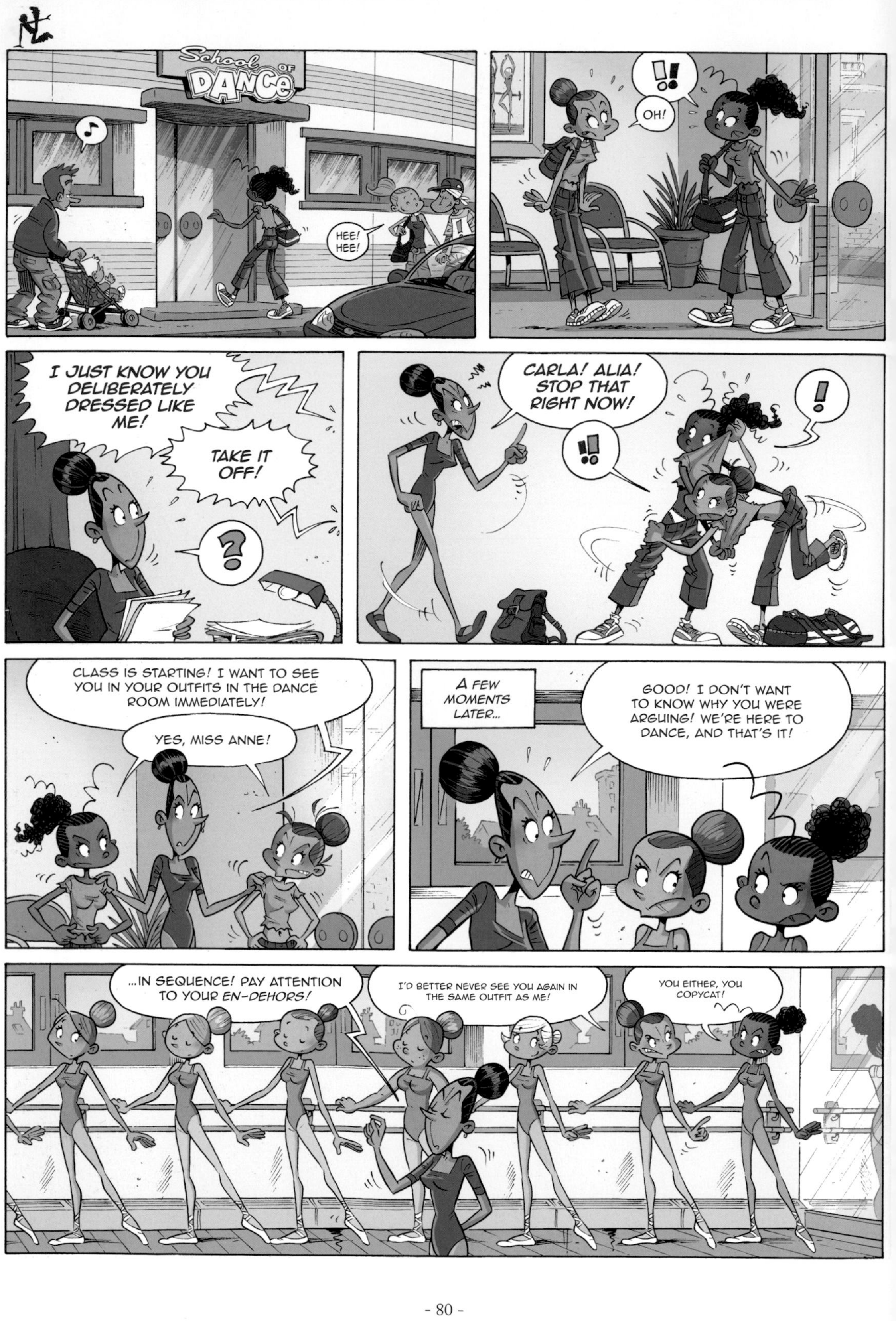

School of DANCE
HEE! HEE!
!!
OH!
I JUST KNOW YOU DELIBERATELY DRESSED LIKE ME!
TAKE IT OFF!
?
CARLA! ALIA! STOP THAT RIGHT NOW!
!!
!
CLASS IS STARTING! I WANT TO SEE YOU IN YOUR OUTFITS IN THE DANCE ROOM IMMEDIATELY!
YES, MISS ANNE!
A FEW MOMENTS LATER...
GOOD! I DON'T WANT TO KNOW WHY YOU WERE ARGUING! WE'RE HERE TO DANCE, AND THAT'S IT!
...IN SEQUENCE! PAY ATTENTION TO YOUR EN-DEHORS!
I'D BETTER NEVER SEE YOU AGAIN IN THE SAME OUTFIT AS ME!
YOU EITHER, YOU COPYCAT!

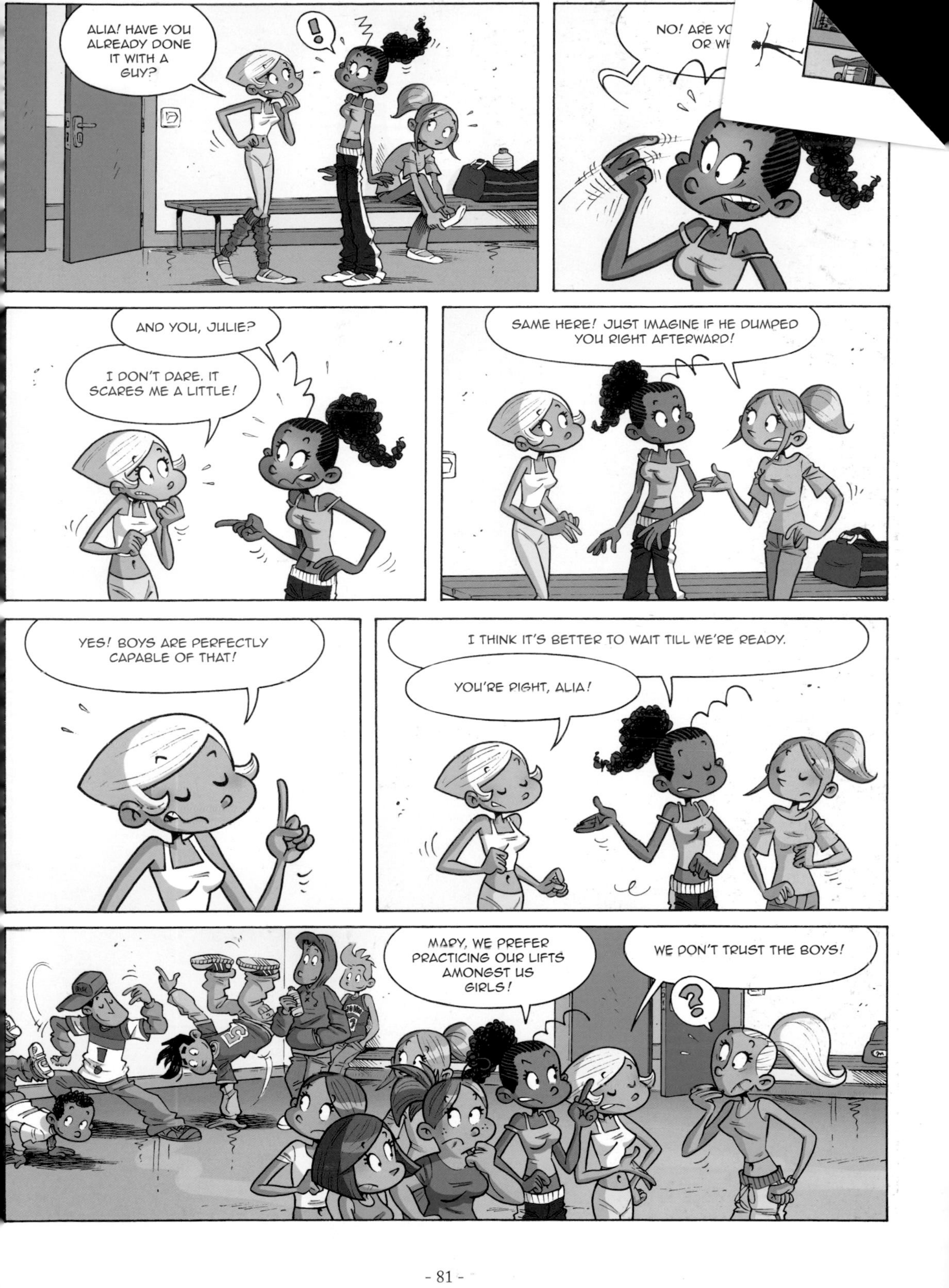
ALIA! HAVE YOU ALREADY DONE IT WITH A GUY?
!
NO! ARE YO
OR WH
AND YOU, JULIE?
I DON'T DARE. IT SCARES ME A LITTLE!
SAME HERE! JUST IMAGINE IF HE DUMPED YOU RIGHT AFTERWARD!
YES! BOYS ARE PERFECTLY CAPABLE OF THAT!
I THINK IT'S BETTER TO WAIT TILL WE'RE READY.
YOU'RE RIGHT, ALIA!
MARY, WE PREFER PRACTICING OUR LIFTS AMONGST US GIRLS!
WE DON'T TRUST THE BOYS!
?

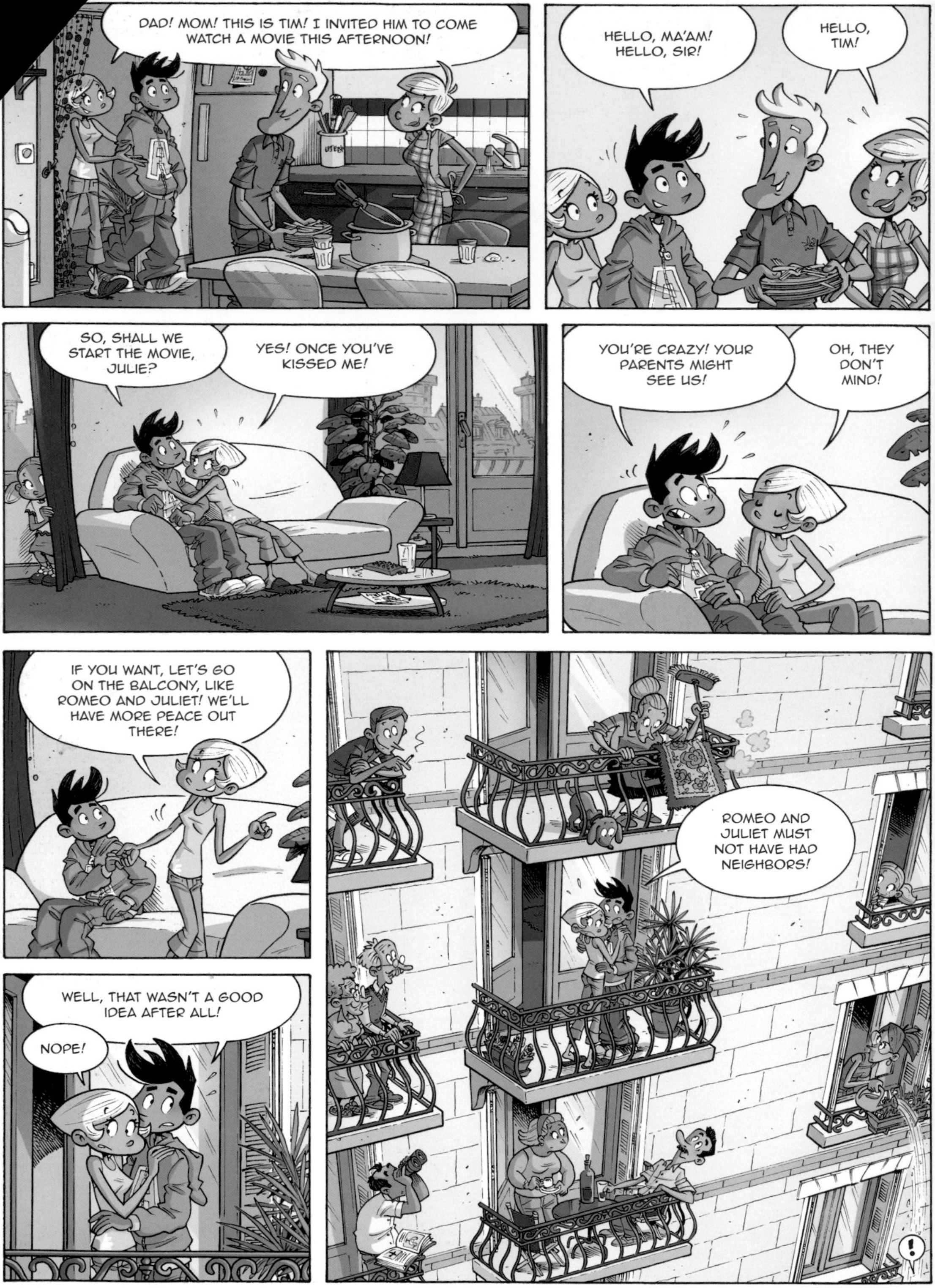
DAD! MOM! THIS IS TIM! I INVITED HIM TO COME WATCH A MOVIE THIS AFTERNOON!
HELLO, MA'AM! HELLO, SIR!
HELLO, TIM!
SO, SHALL WE START THE MOVIE, JULIE?
YES! ONCE YOU'VE KISSED ME!
YOU'RE CRAZY! YOUR PARENTS MIGHT SEE US!
OH, THEY DON'T MIND!
IF YOU WANT, LET'S GO ON THE BALCONY, LIKE ROMEO AND JULIET! WE'LL HAVE MORE PEACE OUT THERE!
WELL, THAT WASN'T A GOOD IDEA AFTER ALL!
NOPE!
ROMEO AND JULIET MUST NOT HAVE HAD NEIGHBORS!
!

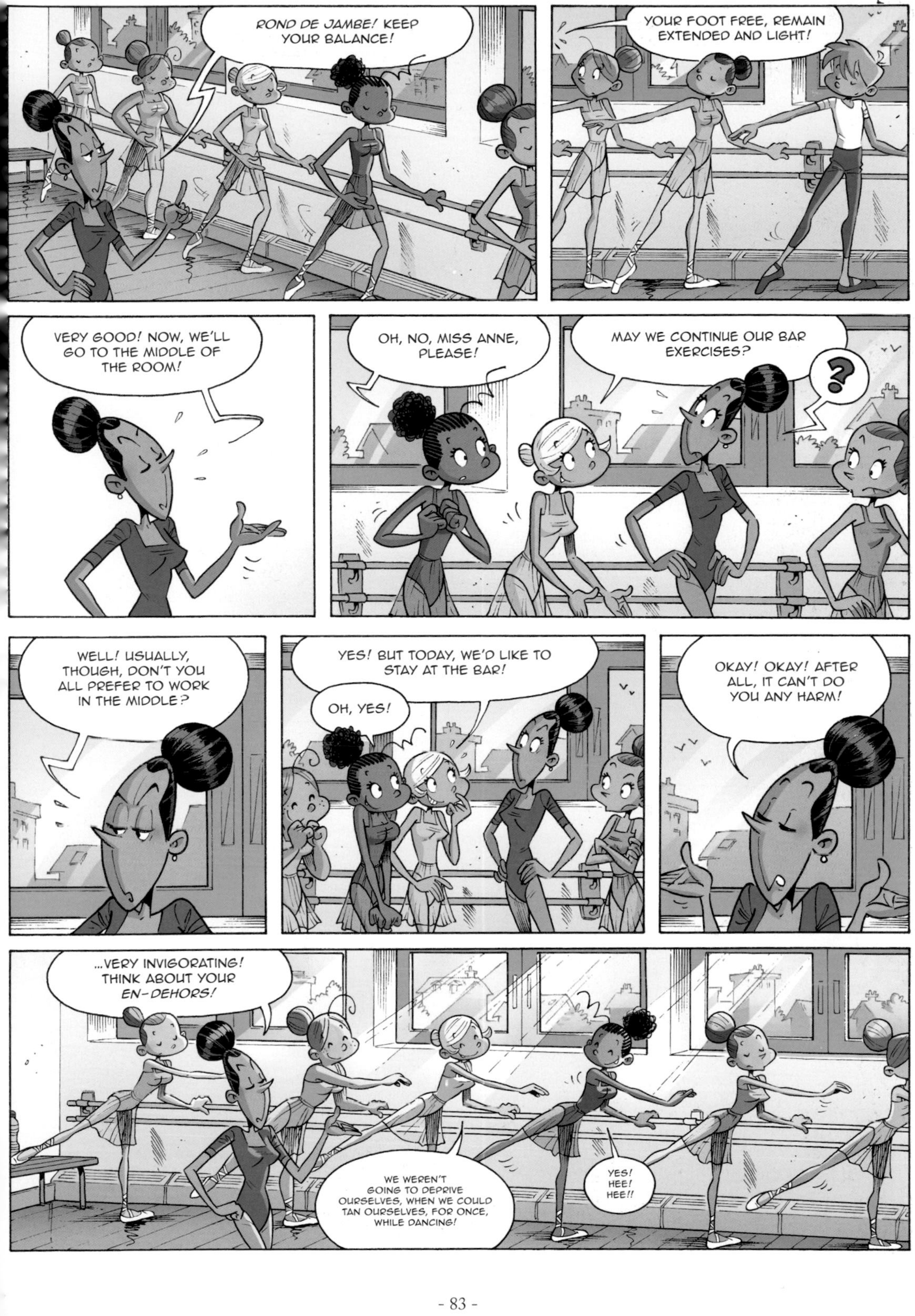

RONDE DE JAMBE! KEEP YOUR BALANCE!
YOUR FOOT FREE, REMAIN EXTENDED AND LIGHT!
VERY GOOD! NOW, WE'LL GO TO THE MIDDLE OF THE ROOM!
OH, NO, MISS ANNE, PLEASE!
MAY WE CONTINUE OUR BAR EXERCISES?
?
WELL! USUALLY, THOUGH, DON'T YOU ALL PREFER TO WORK IN THE MIDDLE?
YES! BUT TODAY, WE'D LIKE TO STAY AT THE BAR!
OH, YES!
OKAY! OKAY! AFTER ALL, IT CAN'T DO YOU ANY HARM!
...VERY INVIGORATING! THINK ABOUT YOUR *EN-DEHORS!*
WE WEREN'T GOING TO DEPRIVE OURSELVES, WHEN WE COULD TAN OURSELVES, FOR ONCE, WHILE DANCING!
YES! HEE! HEE!!

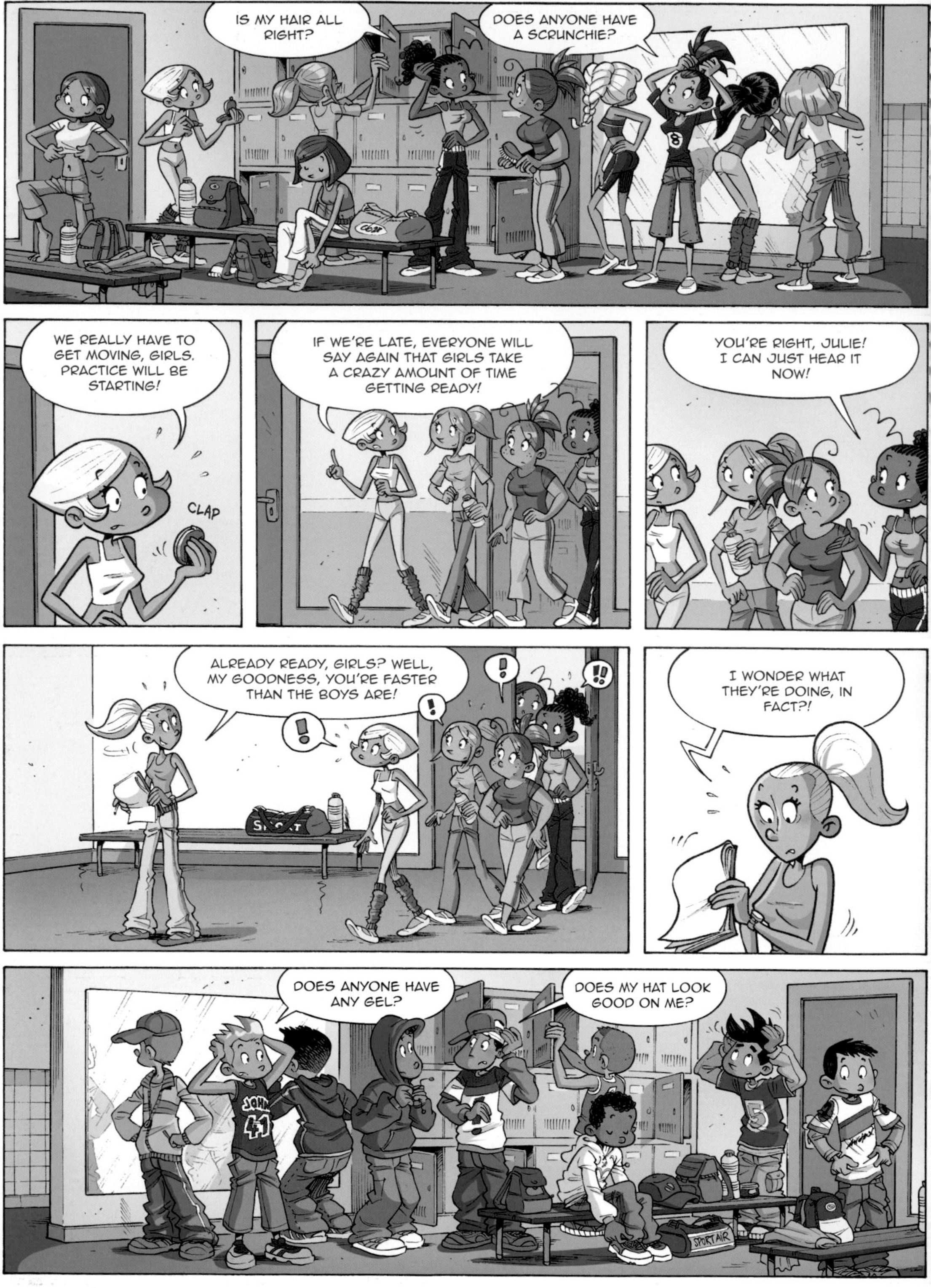
IS MY HAIR ALL RIGHT?
DOES ANYONE HAVE A SCRUNCHIE?
WE REALLY HAVE TO GET MOVING, GIRLS. PRACTICE WILL BE STARTING!
CLAP
IF WE'RE LATE, EVERYONE WILL SAY AGAIN THAT GIRLS TAKE A CRAZY AMOUNT OF TIME GETTING READY!
YOU'RE RIGHT, JULIE! I CAN JUST HEAR IT NOW!
ALREADY READY, GIRLS? WELL, MY GOODNESS, YOU'RE FASTER THAN THE BOYS ARE!
!
!
!
!!
I WONDER WHAT THEY'RE DOING, IN FACT?!
DOES ANYONE HAVE ANY GEL?
DOES MY HAT LOOK GOOD ON ME?

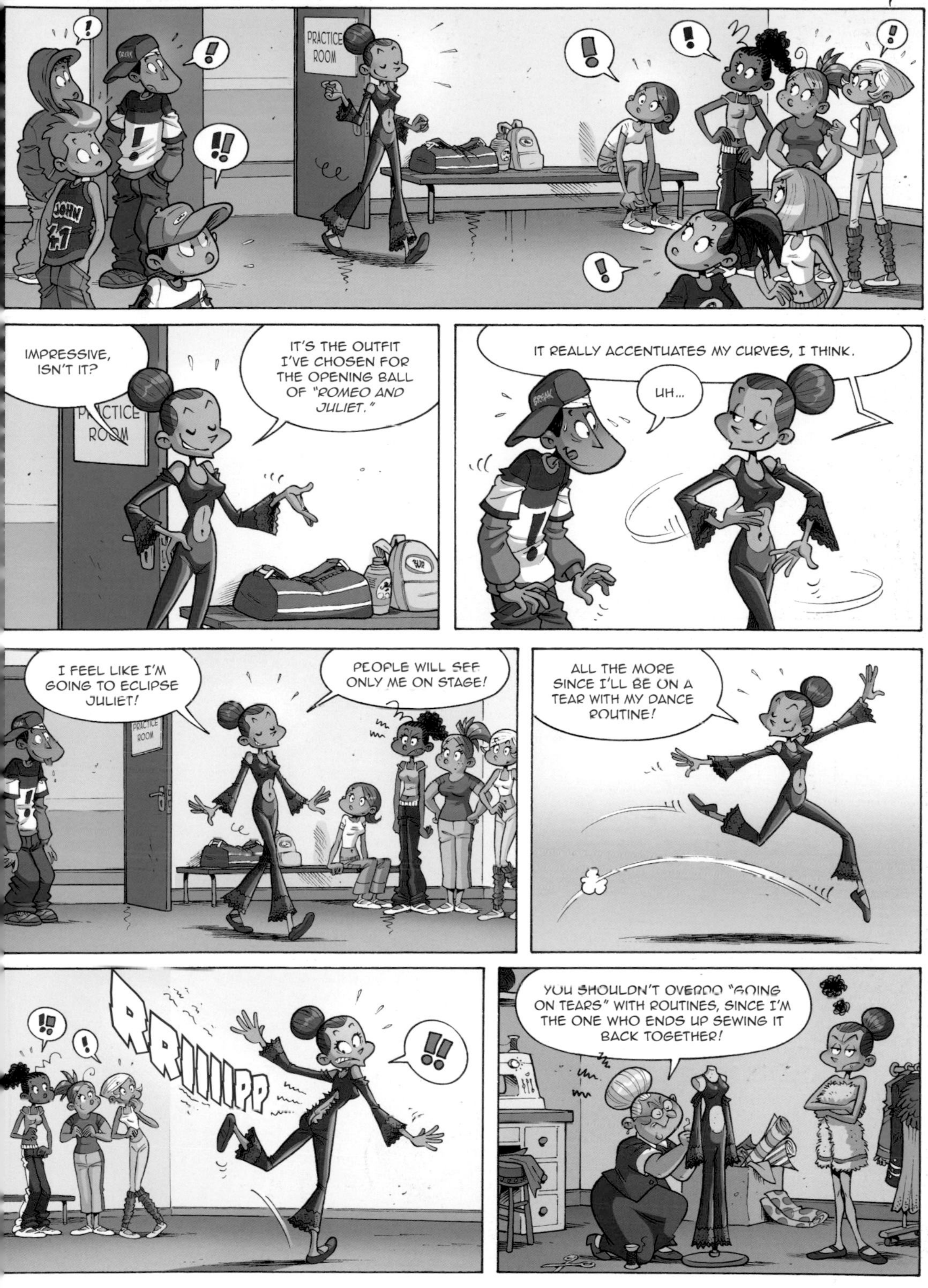

!
!
!!
PRACTICE ROOM
!
!
!
!
IMPRESSIVE, ISN'T IT?
IT'S THE OUTFIT I'VE CHOSEN FOR THE OPENING BALL OF "ROMEO AND JULIET."
IT REALLY ACCENTUATES MY CURVES, I THINK.
UH...
I FEEL LIKE I'M GOING TO ECLIPSE JULIET!
PEOPLE WILL SEE ONLY ME ON STAGE!
ALL THE MORE SINCE I'LL BE ON A TEAR WITH MY DANCE ROUTINE!
RRIIIIPP
!!
!
!!
YOU SHOULDN'T OVERDO "GOING ON TEARS" WITH ROUTINES, SINCE I'M THE ONE WHO ENDS UP SEWING IT BACK TOGETHER!

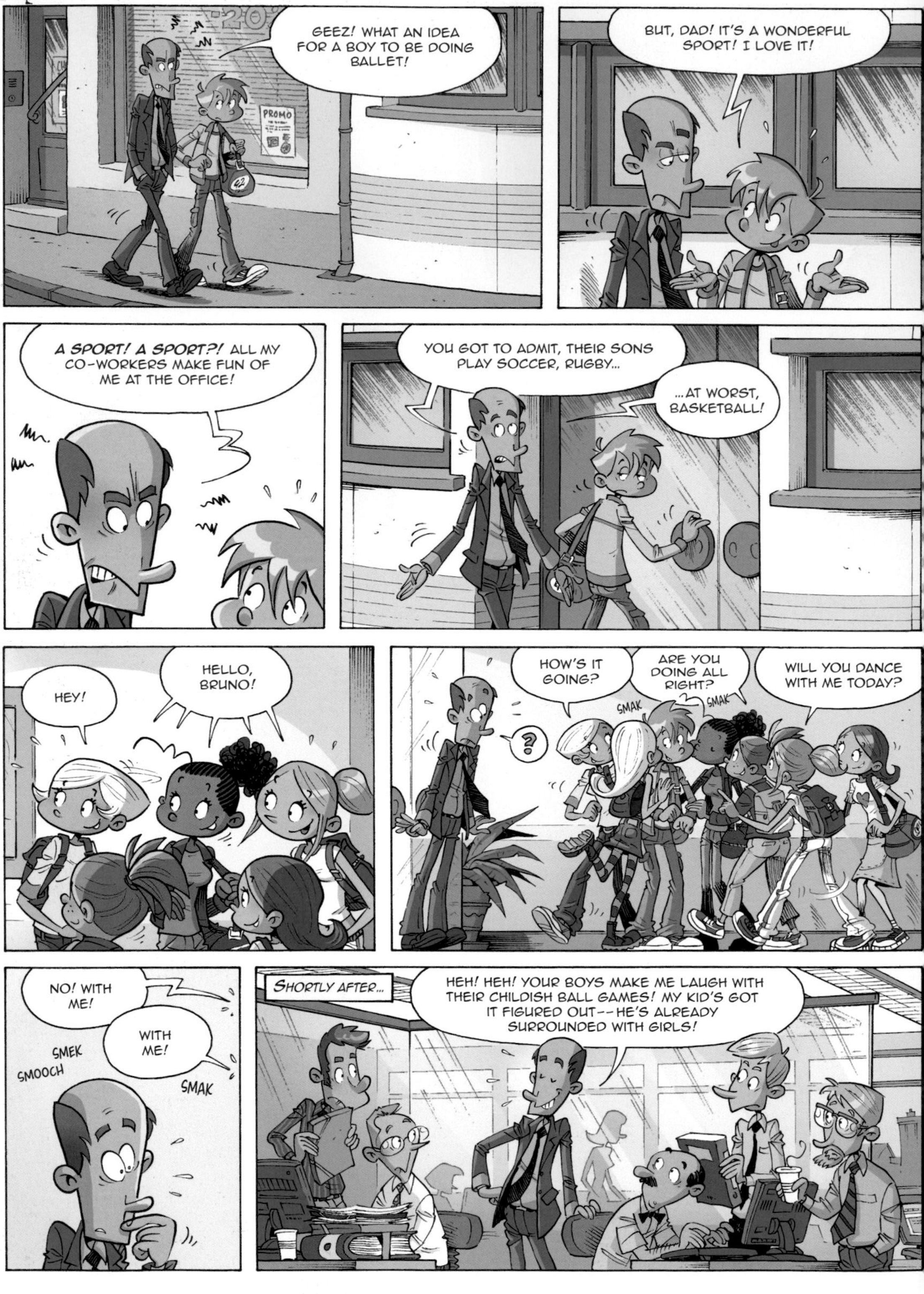
GEEZ! WHAT AN IDEA FOR A BOY TO BE DOING BALLET!
PROMO
BUT, DAD! IT'S A WONDERFUL SPORT! I LOVE IT!
A SPORT! A SPORT?! ALL MY CO-WORKERS MAKE FUN OF ME AT THE OFFICE!
YOU GOT TO ADMIT, THEIR SONS PLAY SOCCER, RUGBY...
...AT WORST, BASKETBALL!
HEY!
HELLO, BRUNO!
HOW'S IT GOING?
ARE YOU DOING ALL RIGHT?
SMAK
SMAK
WILL YOU DANCE WITH ME TODAY?
?
NO! WITH ME!
WITH ME!
SMEK
SMOOCH
SMAK
SHORTLY AFTER...
HEH! HEH! YOUR BOYS MAKE ME LAUGH WITH THEIR CHILDISH BALL GAMES! MY KID'S GOT IT FIGURED OUT--HE'S ALREADY SURROUNDED WITH GIRLS!

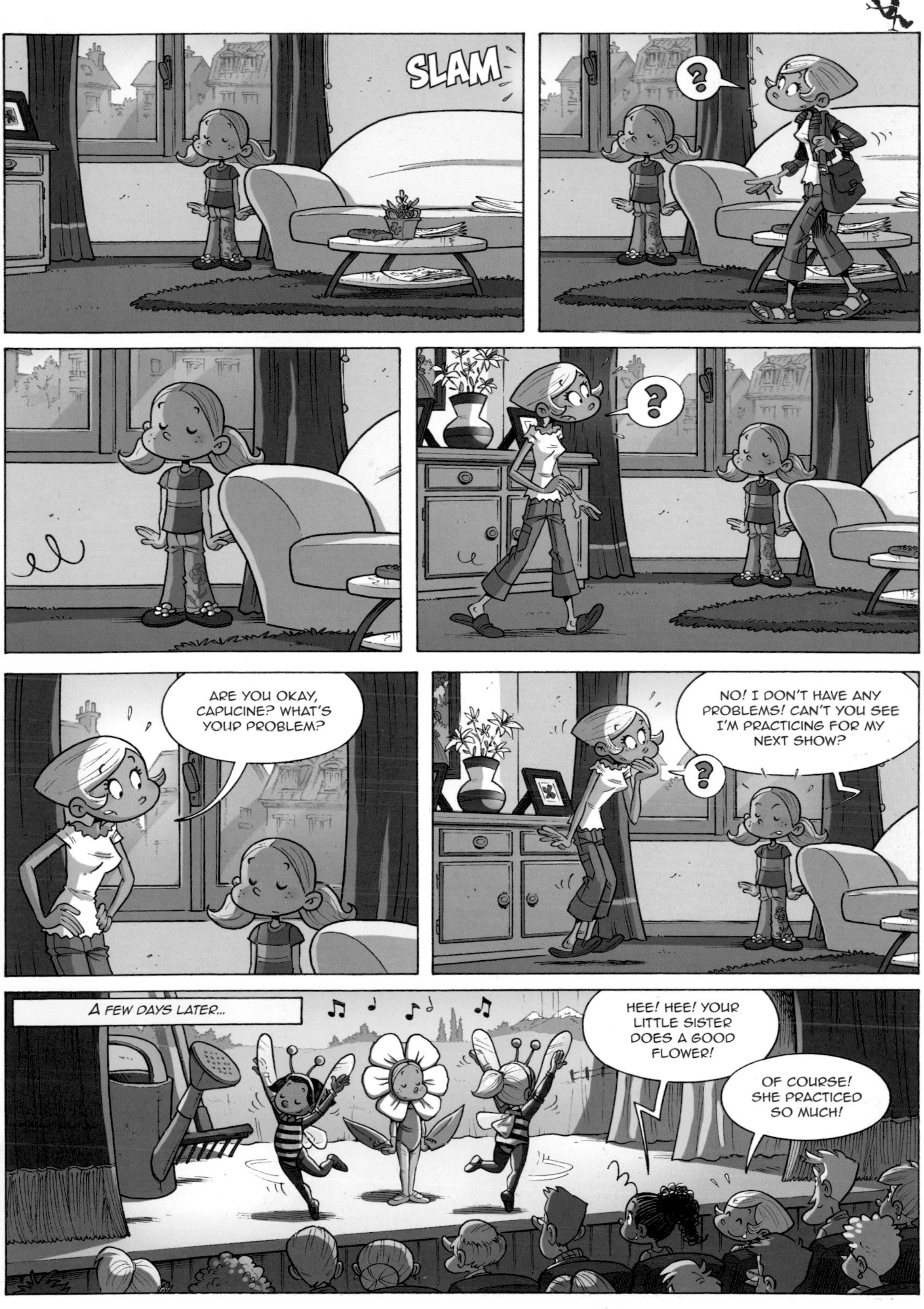
SLAM
?
?
ARE YOU OKAY, CAPUCINE? WHAT'S YOUR PROBLEM?
NO! I DON'T HAVE ANY PROBLEMS! CAN'T YOU SEE I'M PRACTICING FOR MY NEXT SHOW?
?
A FEW DAYS LATER...
HEE! HEE! YOUR LITTLE SISTER DOES A GOOD FLOWER!
OF COURSE! SHE PRACTICED SO MUCH!

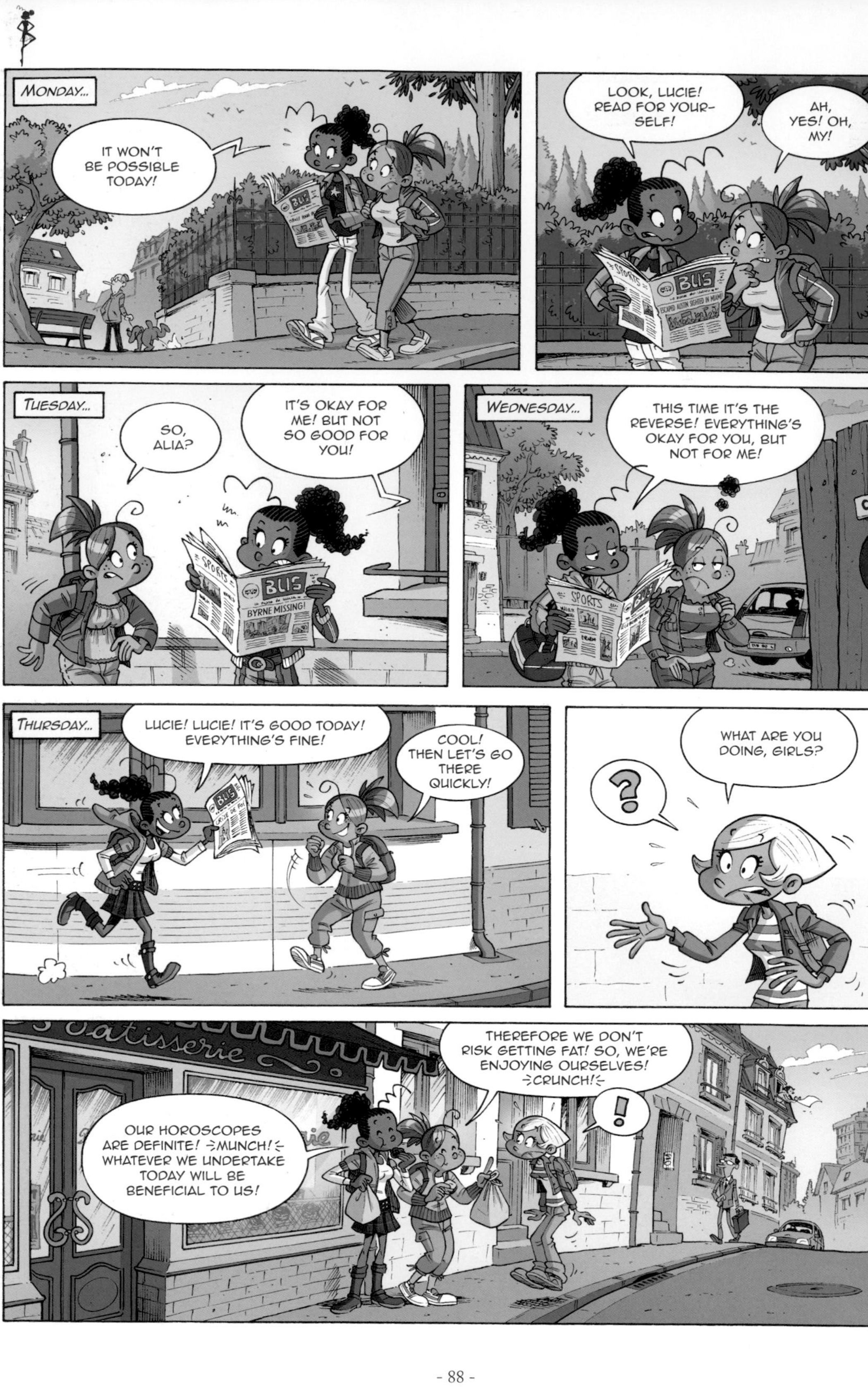
MONDAY...
IT WON'T BE POSSIBLE TODAY!
LOOK, LUCIE! READ FOR YOURSELF!
AH, YES! OH, MY!
BUS
ESCAPED AUSTIN SIGHTED IN MIAMI
TUESDAY...
SO, ALIA?
IT'S OKAY FOR ME! BUT NOT SO GOOD FOR YOU!
SPORTS
BUS
BYRNE MISSING!
WEDNESDAY...
THIS TIME IT'S THE REVERSE! EVERYTHING'S OKAY FOR YOU, BUT NOT FOR ME!
SPORTS
CHANT
THURSDAY...
LUCIE! LUCIE! IT'S GOOD TODAY! EVERYTHING'S FINE!
BUS
COOL! THEN LET'S GO THERE QUICKLY!
?
WHAT ARE YOU DOING, GIRLS?
Patisserie
OUR HOROSCOPES ARE DEFINITE! MUNCH! WHATEVER WE UNDERTAKE TODAY WILL BE BENEFICIAL TO US!
THEREFORE WE DON'T RISK GETTING FAT! SO, WE'RE ENJOYING OURSELVES! CRUNCH!
!

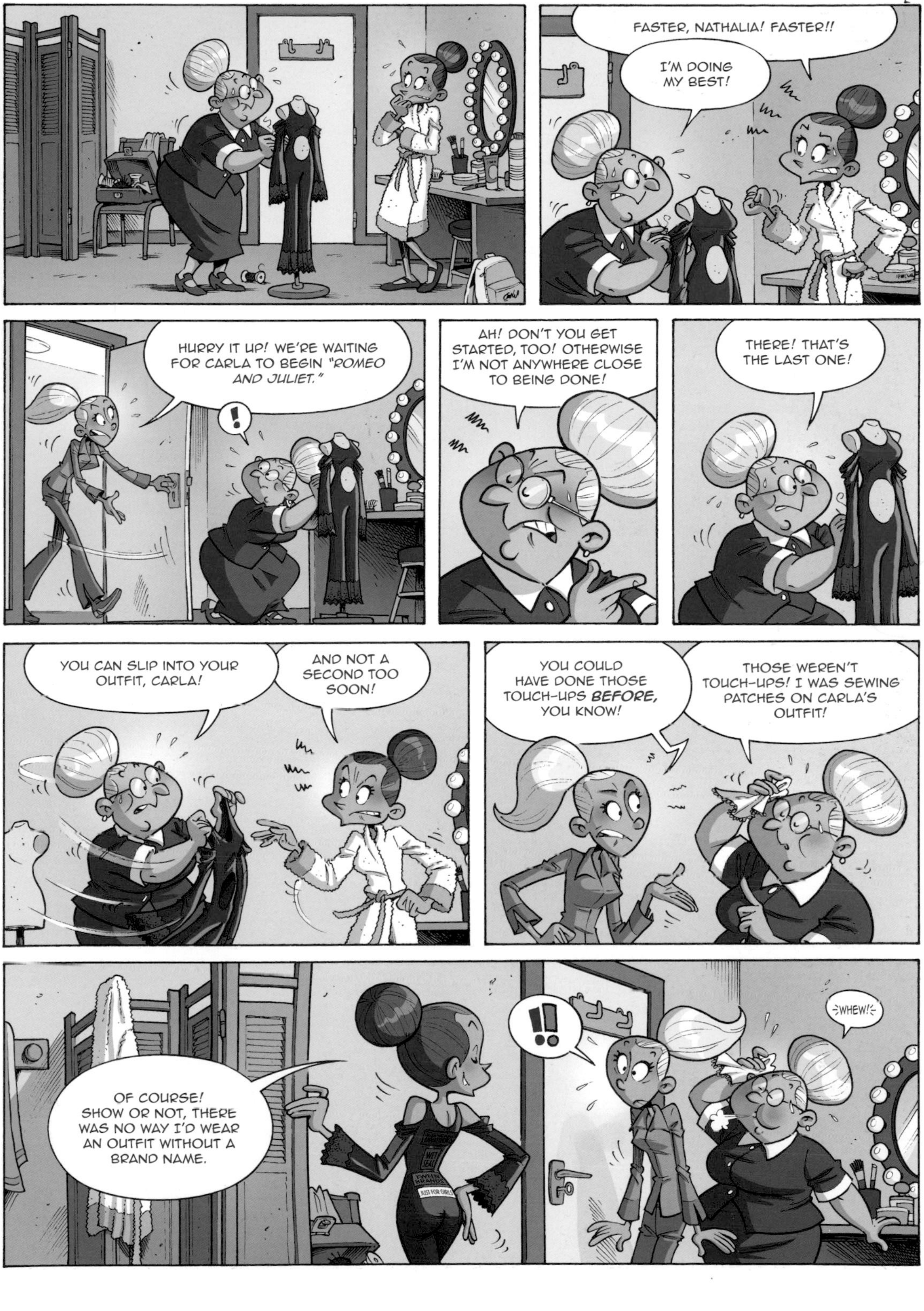

FASTER, NATHALIA! FASTER!!
I'M DOING MY BEST!
HURRY IT UP! WE'RE WAITING FOR CARLA TO BEGIN *"ROMEO AND JULIET."*
!
AH! DON'T YOU GET STARTED, TOO! OTHERWISE I'M NOT ANYWHERE CLOSE TO BEING DONE!
THERE! THAT'S THE LAST ONE!
YOU CAN SLIP INTO YOUR OUTFIT, CARLA!
AND NOT A SECOND TOO SOON!
YOU COULD HAVE DONE THOSE TOUCH-UPS **BEFORE,** YOU KNOW!
THOSE WEREN'T TOUCH-UPS! I WAS SEWING PATCHES ON CARLA'S OUTFIT!
OF COURSE! SHOW OR NOT, THERE WAS NO WAY I'D WEAR AN OUTFIT WITHOUT A BRAND NAME.
!!
WHEW!
JUST FOR GIRLS

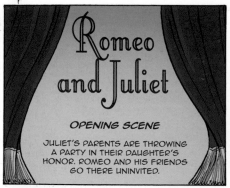

Romeo and Juliet

OPENING SCENE

JULIET'S PARENTS ARE THROWING A PARTY IN THEIR DAUGHTER'S HONOR. ROMEO AND HIS FRIENDS GO THERE UNINVITED.

AAAH! I LOVE THE MOMENT WHEN ROMEO CATCHES JULIET'S GAZE!

THE MUSIC STOPS... AND IT'S LOVE AT FIRST SIGHT!

SCRITCH

CRITCH

HEY! K.T., ARE YOU THE ONE WHO ADDED HIP-HOP "SCRATCHING" TO THIS SCENE?

UH... NO! IT WAS SUPPOSED TO BE QUIET!

SCRITCH

CRITCH

I REALLY DON'T UNDERSTAND WHERE THOSE NOISES ARE COMING FROM.

SCRITCH

?

?

MMM! THESE CELERY STICKS ARE EXCELLENT!

SCRITCH

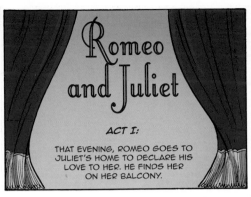

Romeo and Juliet

ACT I:

THAT EVENING, ROMEO GOES TO JULIET'S HOME TO DECLARE HIS LOVE TO HER. HE FINDS HER ON HER BALCONY.

BACKSTAGE...

TIM! JULIE! THERE'S BEEN A SLIGHT, LAST-MINUTE CHANGE!

TIM, YOU MUST ENTER ON THIS SIDE! AND YOU, JULIE, MUST GO THROUGH THERE!

ARE YOU SURE, CARLA? I THOUGHT IT WAS THE OPPOSITE!

IT'S BEEN CHANGED, I TELL YOU! HURRY, YOU'RE GOING TO BE LATE!

EH! HEH! I GOT THEM GOOD! THAT'LL TEACH JULIE TO ALWAYS ROB ME OF THE MAIN ROLE!

RUB RUB

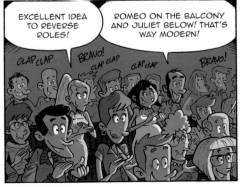

EXCELLENT IDEA TO REVERSE ROLES!

ROMEO ON THE BALCONY AND JULIET BELOW! THAT'S WAY MODERN!

CLAP CLAP BRAVO! CLAP CLAP CLAP CLAP BRAVO!

WAS THAT YOUR IDEA, CARLA? BRAVO! IT'S A HUGE SUCCESS!

YOU'D MAKE A GREAT STAGE DIRECTOR!

CLAP CLAP CLAP CLAP CLAP CLAP

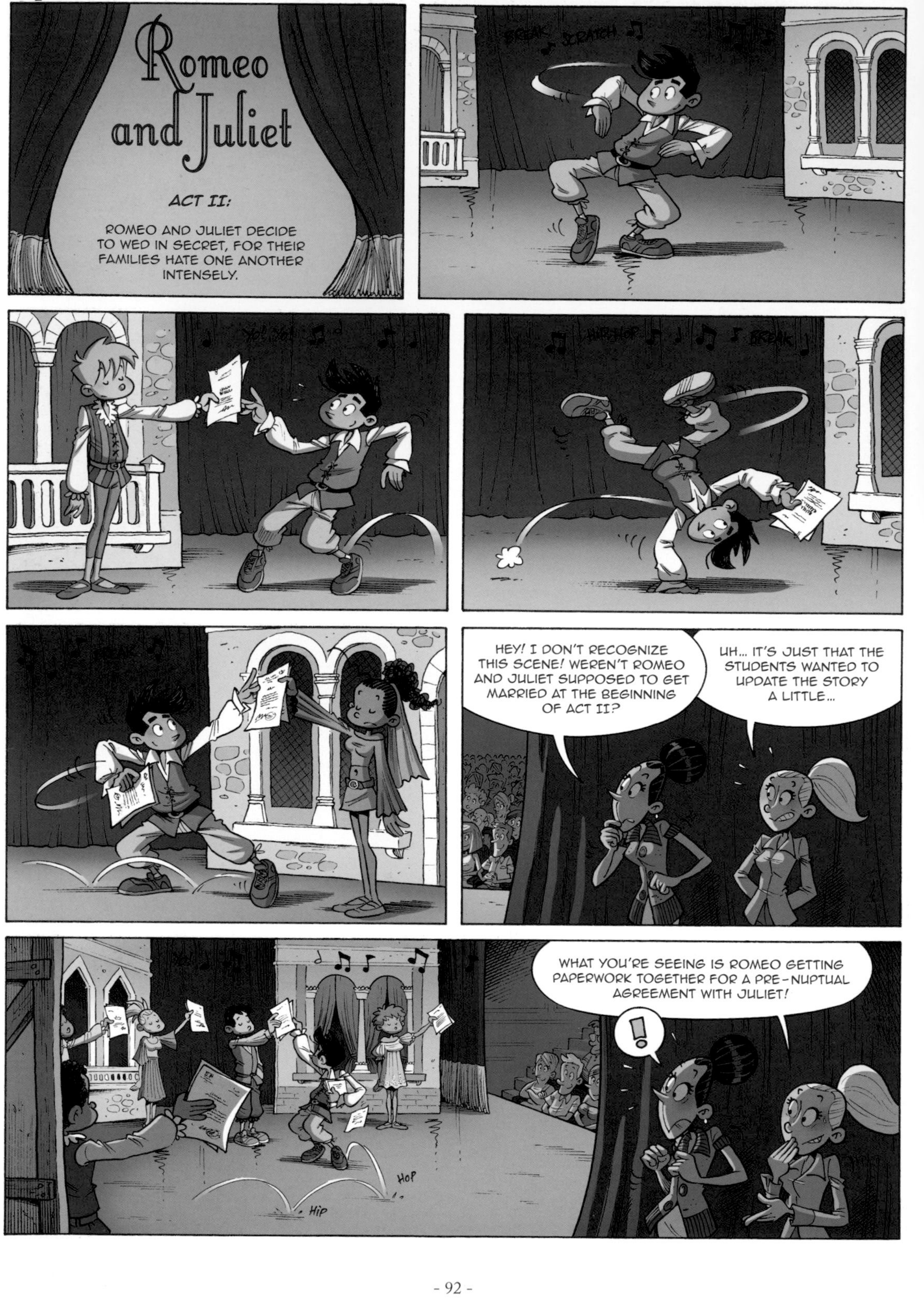
Romeo and Juliet
ACT II:
ROMEO AND JULIET DECIDE TO WED IN SECRET, FOR THEIR FAMILIES HATE ONE ANOTHER INTENSELY.
BREAK SCRATCH
YO! YO!
HIP-HOP
BREAK
HEY! I DON'T RECOGNIZE THIS SCENE! WEREN'T ROMEO AND JULIET SUPPOSED TO GET MARRIED AT THE BEGINNING OF ACT II?
UH... IT'S JUST THAT THE STUDENTS WANTED TO UPDATE THE STORY A LITTLE...
WHAT YOU'RE SEEING IS ROMEO GETTING PAPERWORK TOGETHER FOR A PRE-NUPTUAL AGREEMENT WITH JULIET!
!
HOP
HIP

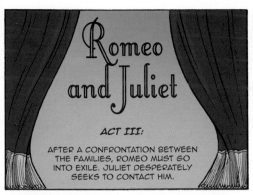

Romeo and Juliet

ACT III:

AFTER A CONFRONTATION BETWEEN THE FAMILIES, ROMEO MUST GO INTO EXILE. JULIET DESPERATELY SEEKS TO CONTACT HIM.

HEY! JULIET'S GOT A FUNNY WAY OF TRYING TO SEND A MESSAGE TO ROMEO!

WHY, YES! IT'S STILL THE MODERN VERSION!

SHE'S TRYING TO CALL HIM ON HER CELL PHONE, BUT SHE HAS NO RECEPTION!

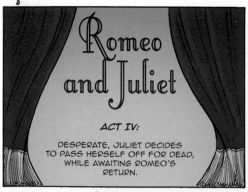

Romeo and Juliet

ACT IV:

DESPERATE, JULIET DECIDES TO PASS HERSELF OFF FOR DEAD, WHILE AWAITING ROMEO'S RETURN.

IF I UNDERSTAND CORRECTLY, JULIET'S TRYING ONE LAST TIME TO REACH ROMEO TO EXPLAIN HER PLAN TO HIM!

THAT'S EXACTLY RIGHT, ANNE!

TADA *TADA*

AH! THAT'S WHY SHE DOESN'T REACH ROMEO! SHE HAS THE WRONG NUMBER!

UH... NO!

THAT RING WASN'T PLANNED! IT'S SOMEONE WHO MUST HAVE FORGOTTEN TO TURN OFF HIS PHONE!

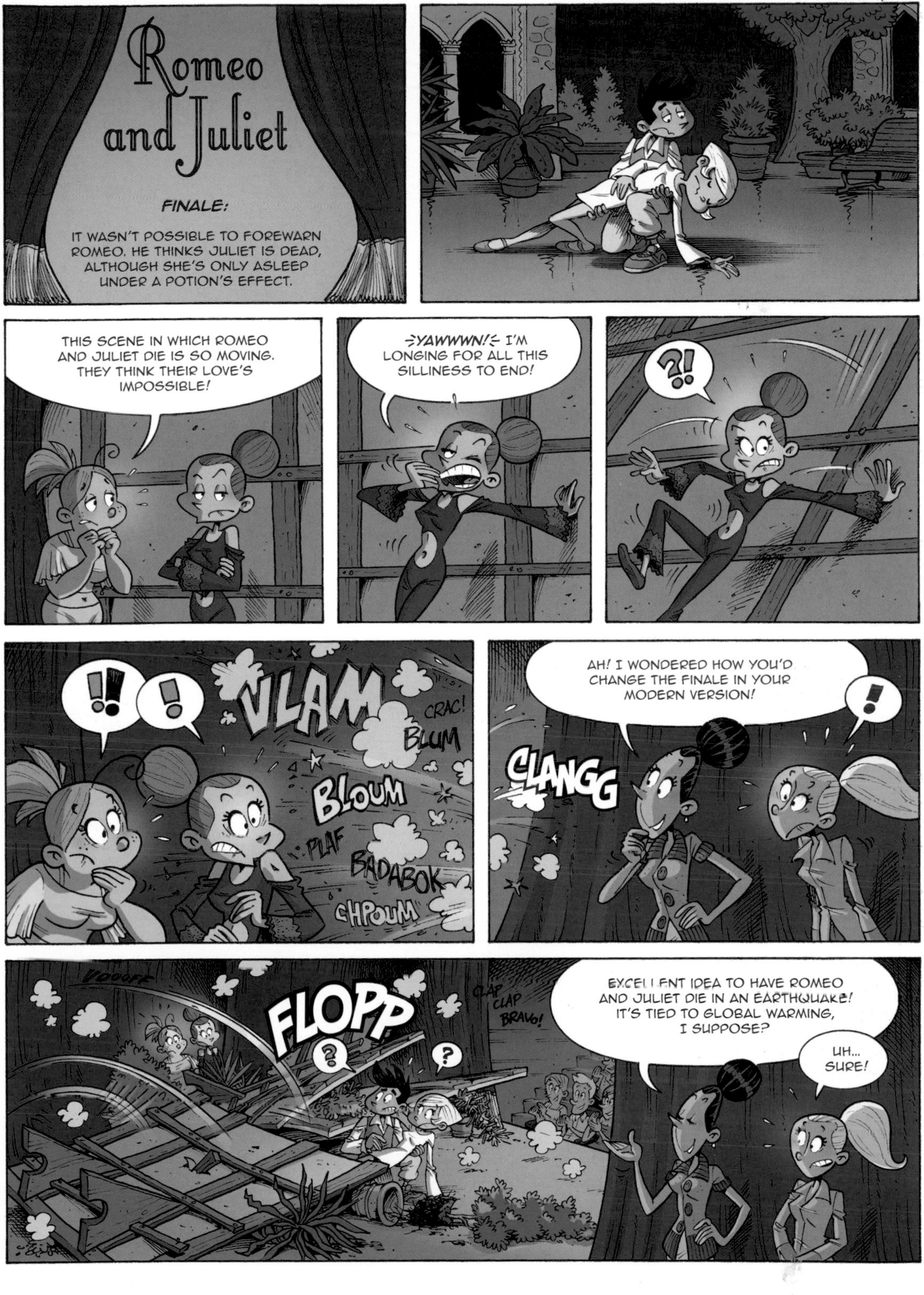
Romeo and Juliet
FINALE:
IT WASN'T POSSIBLE TO FOREWARN ROMEO. HE THINKS JULIET IS DEAD, ALTHOUGH SHE'S ONLY ASLEEP UNDER A POTION'S EFFECT.
THIS SCENE IN WHICH ROMEO AND JULIET DIE IS SO MOVING. THEY THINK THEIR LOVE'S IMPOSSIBLE!
YAWWWN! I'M LONGING FOR ALL THIS SILLINESS TO END!
?!
!!
!
VLAM
CRAC!
BLUM
BLOUM
PLAF
BADABOK
CHPOUM
CLANGG
AH! I WONDERED HOW YOU'D CHANGE THE FINALE IN YOUR MODERN VERSION!
!
VOOOFF
FLOPP
CLAP CLAP
BRAVO!
?
?
EXCELLENT IDEA TO HAVE ROMEO AND JULIET DIE IN AN EARTHQUAKE! IT'S TIED TO GLOBAL WARMING, I SUPPOSE?
UH... SURE!

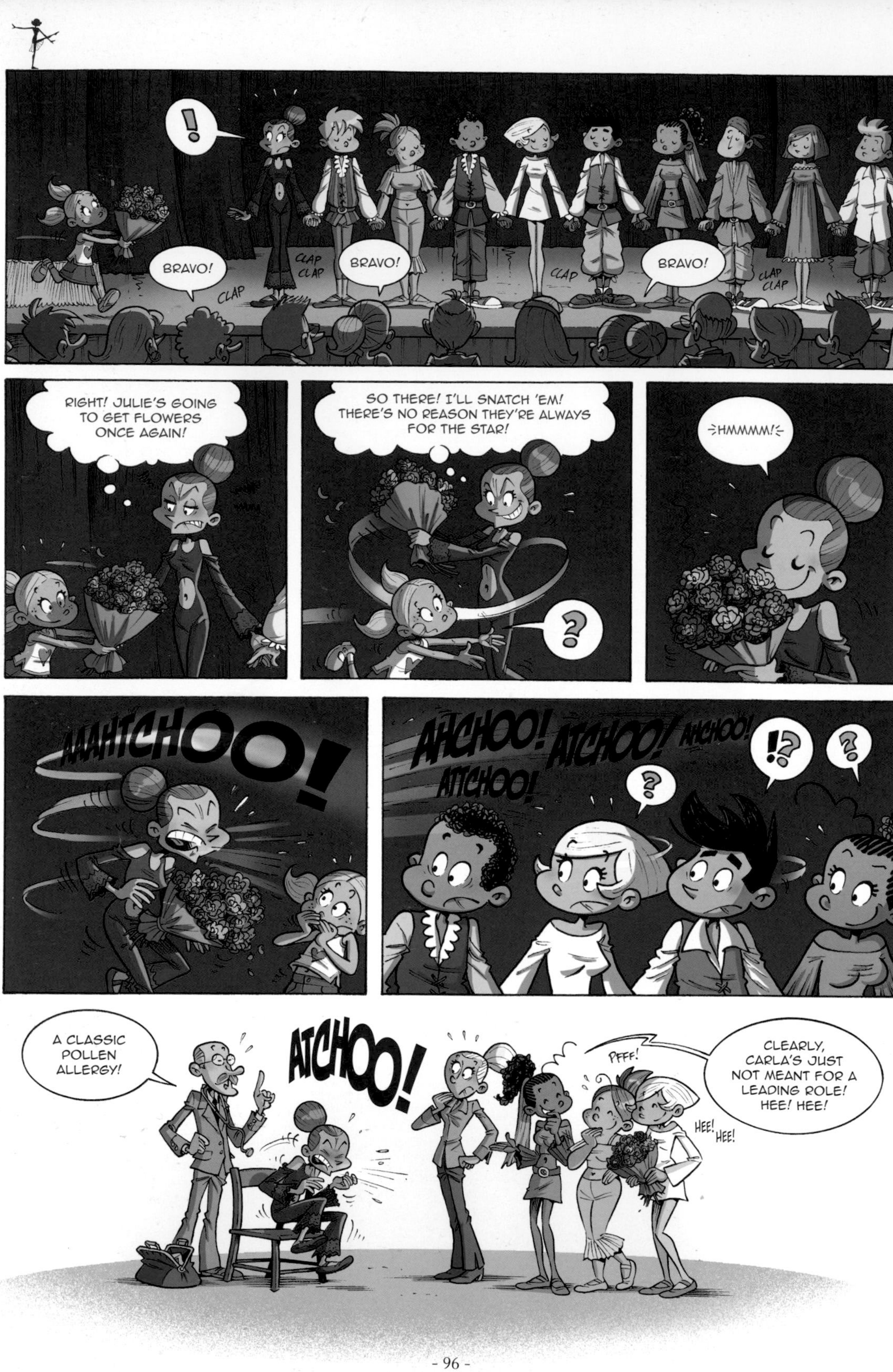
!
BRAVO!
CLAP
CLAP CLAP
BRAVO!
CLAP
BRAVO!
CLAP CLAP
RIGHT! JULIE'S GOING TO GET FLOWERS ONCE AGAIN!
SO THERE! I'LL SNATCH 'EM! THERE'S NO REASON THEY'RE ALWAYS FOR THE STAR!
?
HMMMM!
AAAHTCHOO!
AHCHOO! ATCHOO! AHCHOO!
ATCHOO!
?
!?
?
A CLASSIC POLLEN ALLERGY!
ATCHOO!
PFFF!
CLEARLY, CARLA'S JUST NOT MEANT FOR A LEADING ROLE! HEE! HEE!
HEE! HEE!

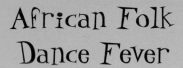

African Folk Dance Fever

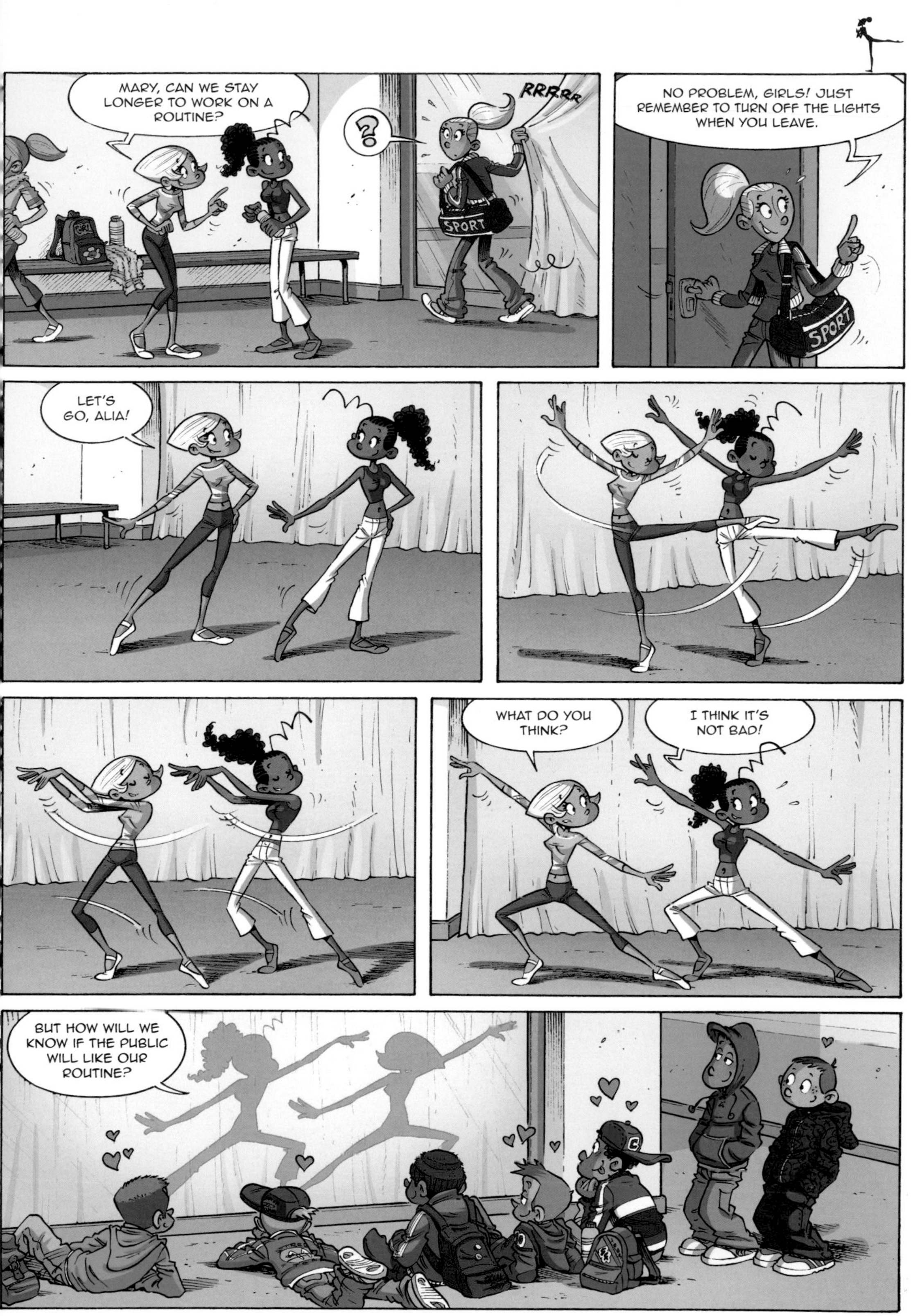
MARY, CAN WE STAY LONGER TO WORK ON A ROUTINE?
?
RRRRRR
NO PROBLEM, GIRLS! JUST REMEMBER TO TURN OFF THE LIGHTS WHEN YOU LEAVE.
SPORT
LET'S GO, ALIA!
WHAT DO YOU THINK?
I THINK IT'S NOT BAD!
BUT HOW WILL WE KNOW IF THE PUBLIC WILL LIKE OUR ROUTINE?

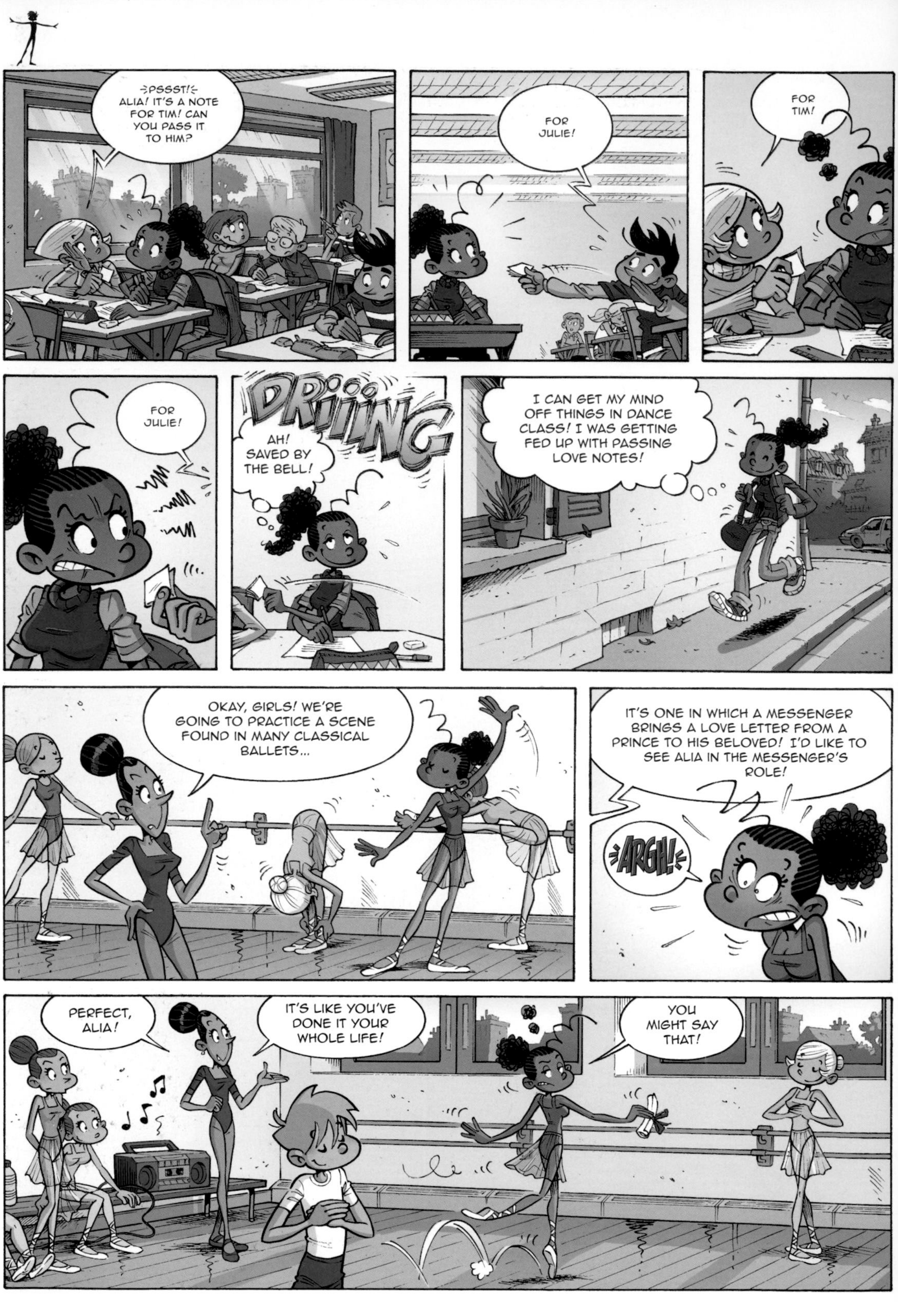

PSSST! ALIA! IT'S A NOTE FOR TIM! CAN YOU PASS IT TO HIM?
FOR JULIE!
FOR TIM!
FOR JULIE!
DRiiiiNG
AH! SAVED BY THE BELL!
I CAN GET MY MIND OFF THINGS IN DANCE CLASS! I WAS GETTING FED UP WITH PASSING LOVE NOTES!
OKAY, GIRLS! WE'RE GOING TO PRACTICE A SCENE FOUND IN MANY CLASSICAL BALLETS...
IT'S ONE IN WHICH A MESSENGER BRINGS A LOVE LETTER FROM A PRINCE TO HIS BELOVED! I'D LIKE TO SEE ALIA IN THE MESSENGER'S ROLE!
ARGH!
PERFECT, ALIA!
IT'S LIKE YOU'VE DONE IT YOUR WHOLE LIFE!
YOU MIGHT SAY THAT!

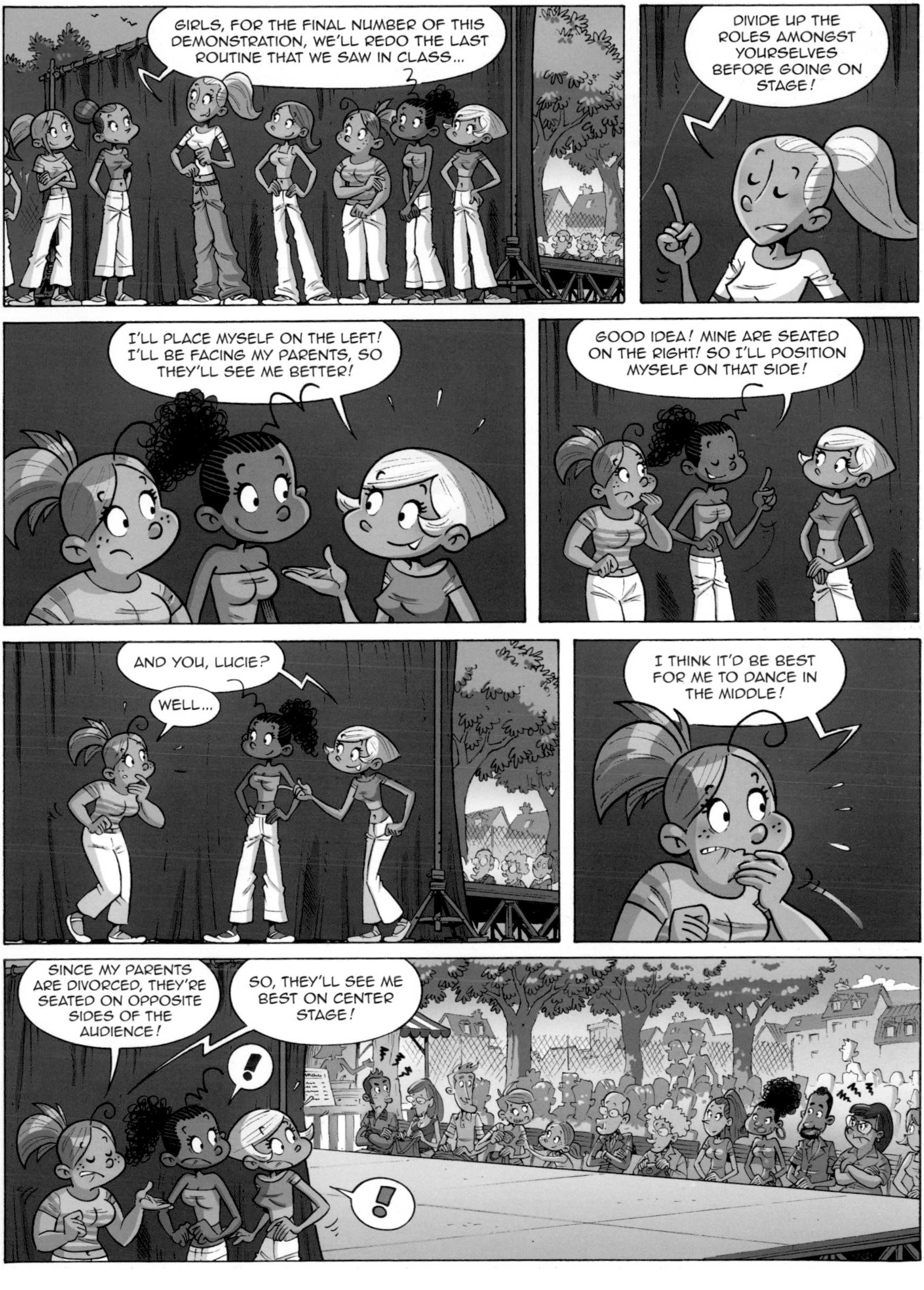

GIRLS, FOR THE FINAL NUMBER OF THIS DEMONSTRATION, WE'LL REDO THE LAST ROUTINE THAT WE SAW IN CLASS...
DIVIDE UP THE ROLES AMONGST YOURSELVES BEFORE GOING ON STAGE!
I'LL PLACE MYSELF ON THE LEFT! I'LL BE FACING MY PARENTS, SO THEY'LL SEE ME BETTER!
GOOD IDEA! MINE ARE SEATED ON THE RIGHT! SO I'LL POSITION MYSELF ON THAT SIDE!
AND YOU, LUCIE?
WELL...
I THINK IT'D BE BEST FOR ME TO DANCE IN THE MIDDLE!
SINCE MY PARENTS ARE DIVORCED, THEY'RE SEATED ON OPPOSITE SIDES OF THE AUDIENCE!
SO, THEY'LL SEE ME BEST ON CENTER STAGE!
!
!

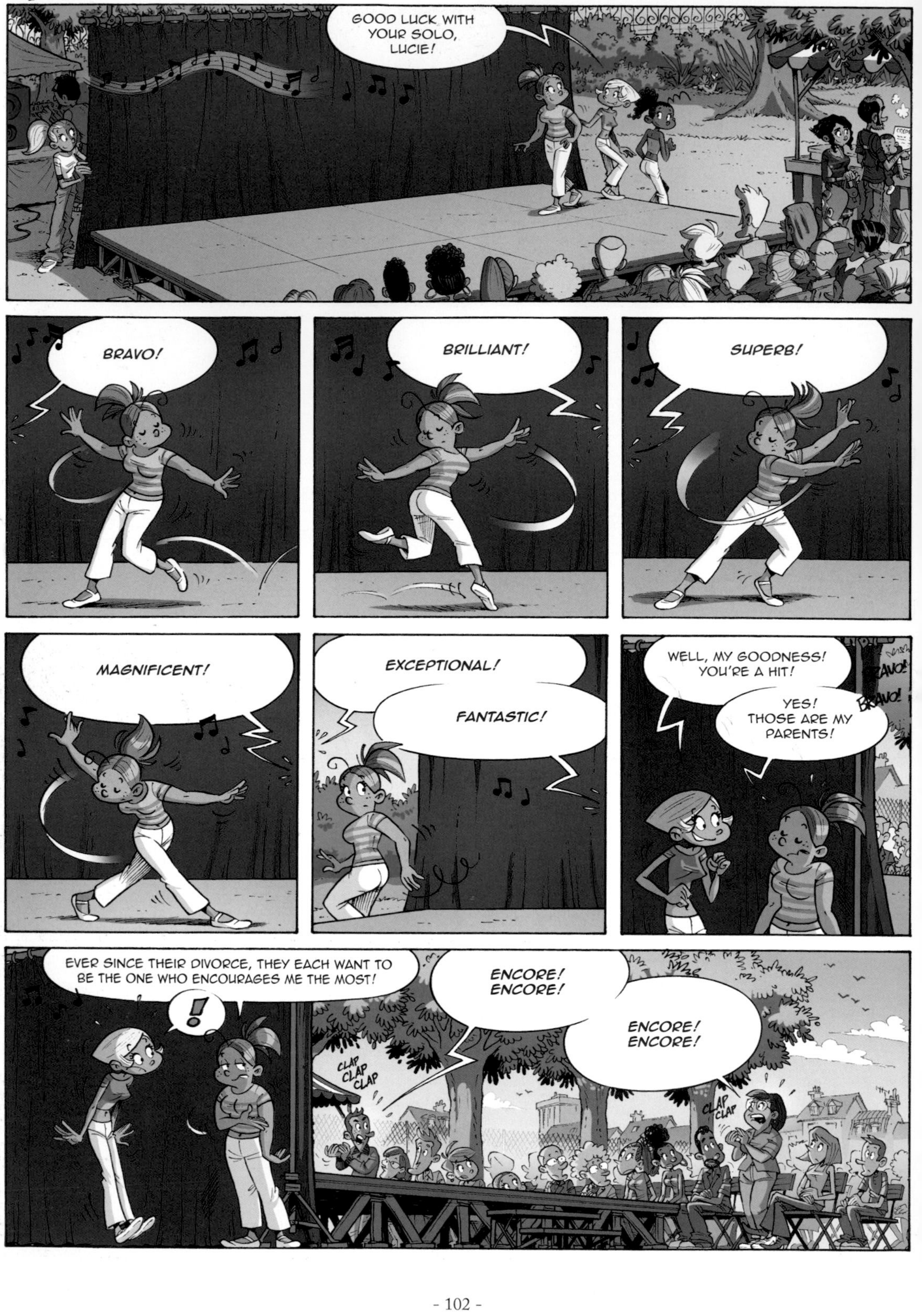
GOOD LUCK WITH YOUR SOLO, LUCIE!
BRAVO!
BRILLIANT!
SUPERB!
MAGNIFICENT!
EXCEPTIONAL!
FANTASTIC!
WELL, MY GOODNESS! YOU'RE A HIT!
YES! THOSE ARE MY PARENTS!
BRAVO!
EVER SINCE THEIR DIVORCE, THEY EACH WANT TO BE THE ONE WHO ENCOURAGES ME THE MOST!
!
ENCORE! ENCORE!
ENCORE! ENCORE!
CLAP CLAP CLAP
CLAP CLAP

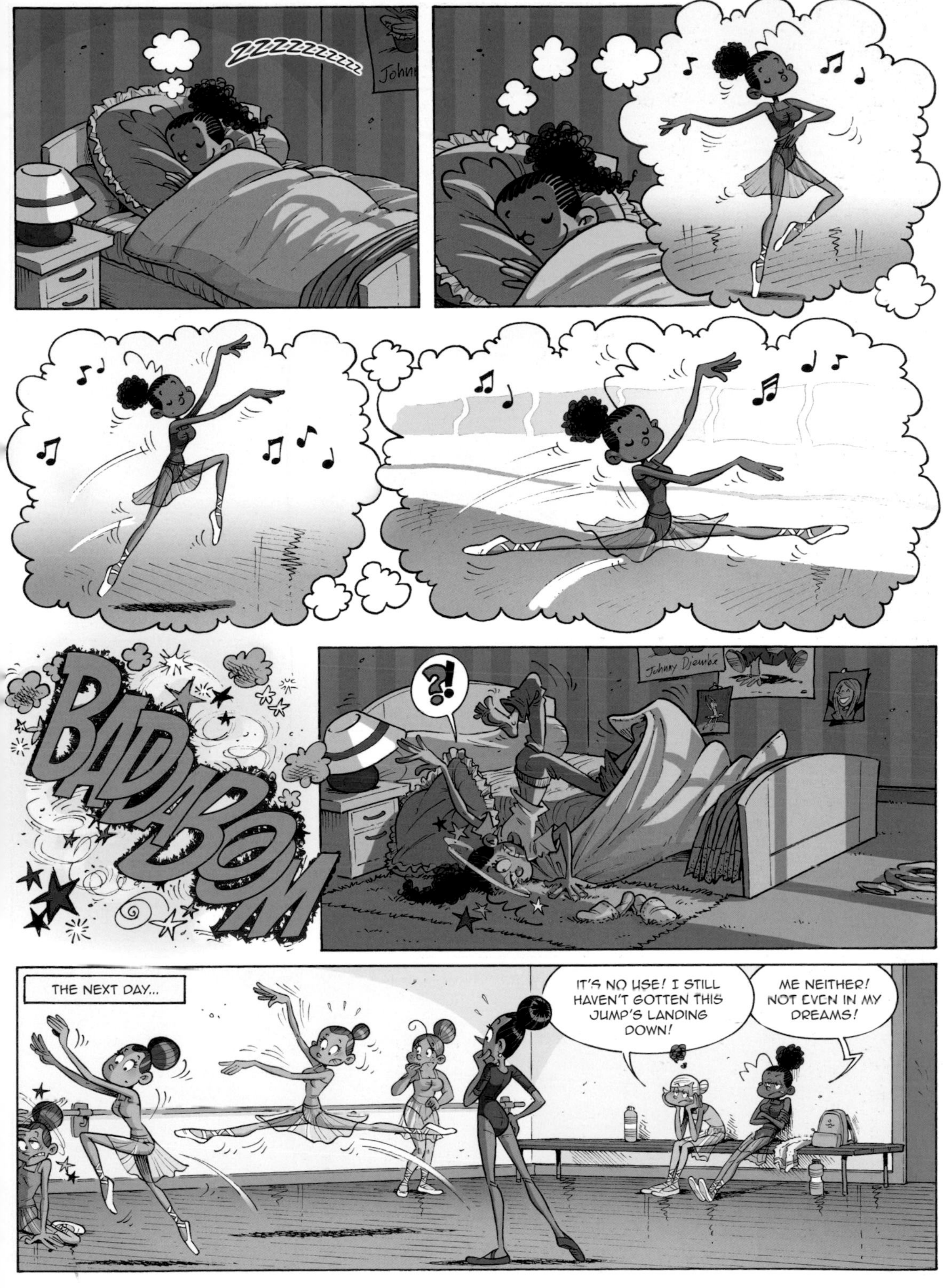
ZZZZZZZZZZZ
Johnny Djembé
BADABOOM
?!
THE NEXT DAY...
IT'S NO USE! I STILL HAVEN'T GOTTEN THIS JUMP'S LANDING DOWN!
ME NEITHER! NOT EVEN IN MY DREAMS!

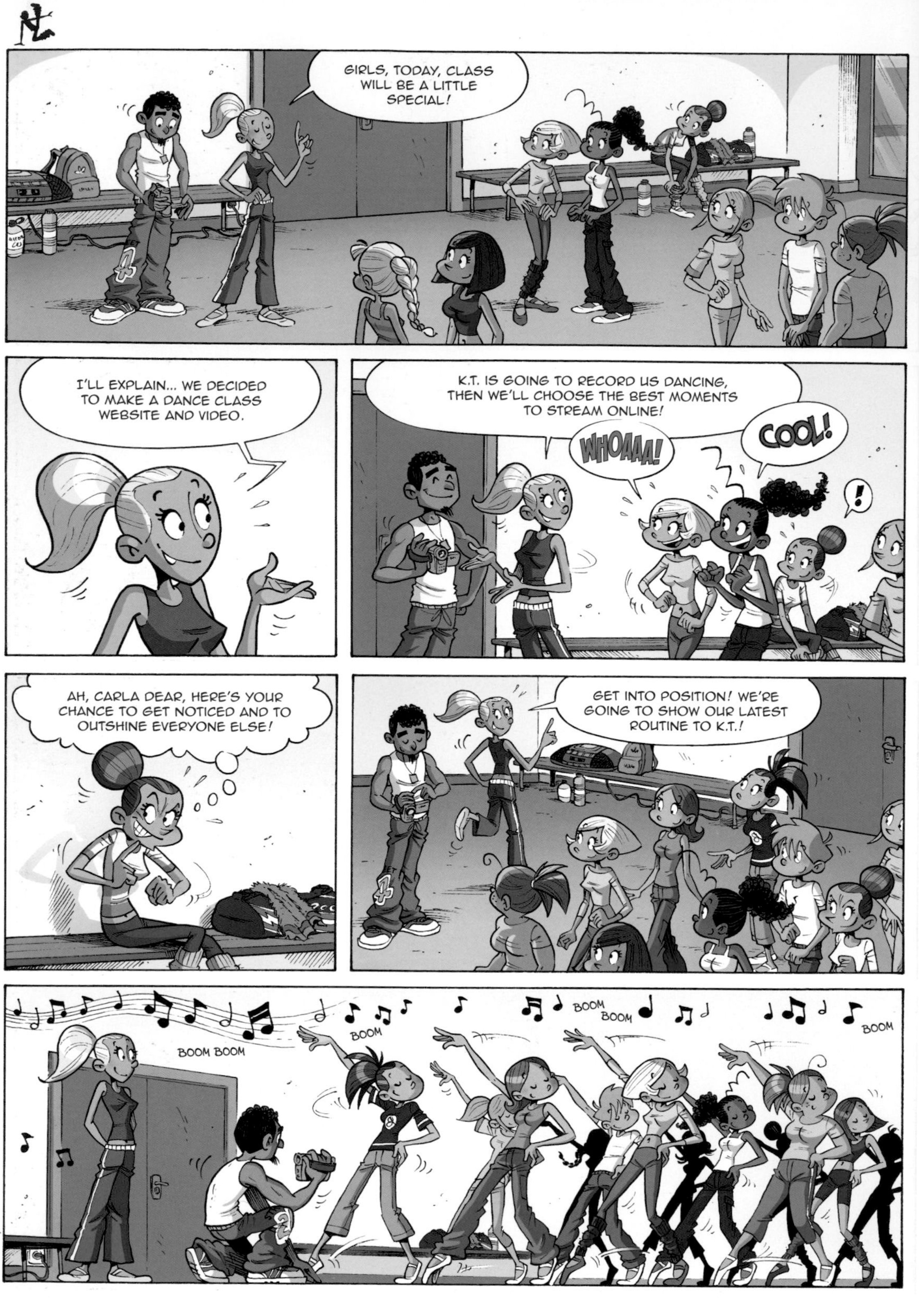
GIRLS, TODAY, CLASS WILL BE A LITTLE SPECIAL!
I'LL EXPLAIN... WE DECIDED TO MAKE A DANCE CLASS WEBSITE AND VIDEO.
K.T. IS GOING TO RECORD US DANCING, THEN WE'LL CHOOSE THE BEST MOMENTS TO STREAM ONLINE!
WHOAAA!
COOL!
!
AH, CARLA DEAR, HERE'S YOUR CHANCE TO GET NOTICED AND TO OUTSHINE EVERYONE ELSE!
GET INTO POSITION! WE'RE GOING TO SHOW OUR LATEST ROUTINE TO K.T.!
BOOM BOOM
BOOM
BOOM BOOM
BOOM

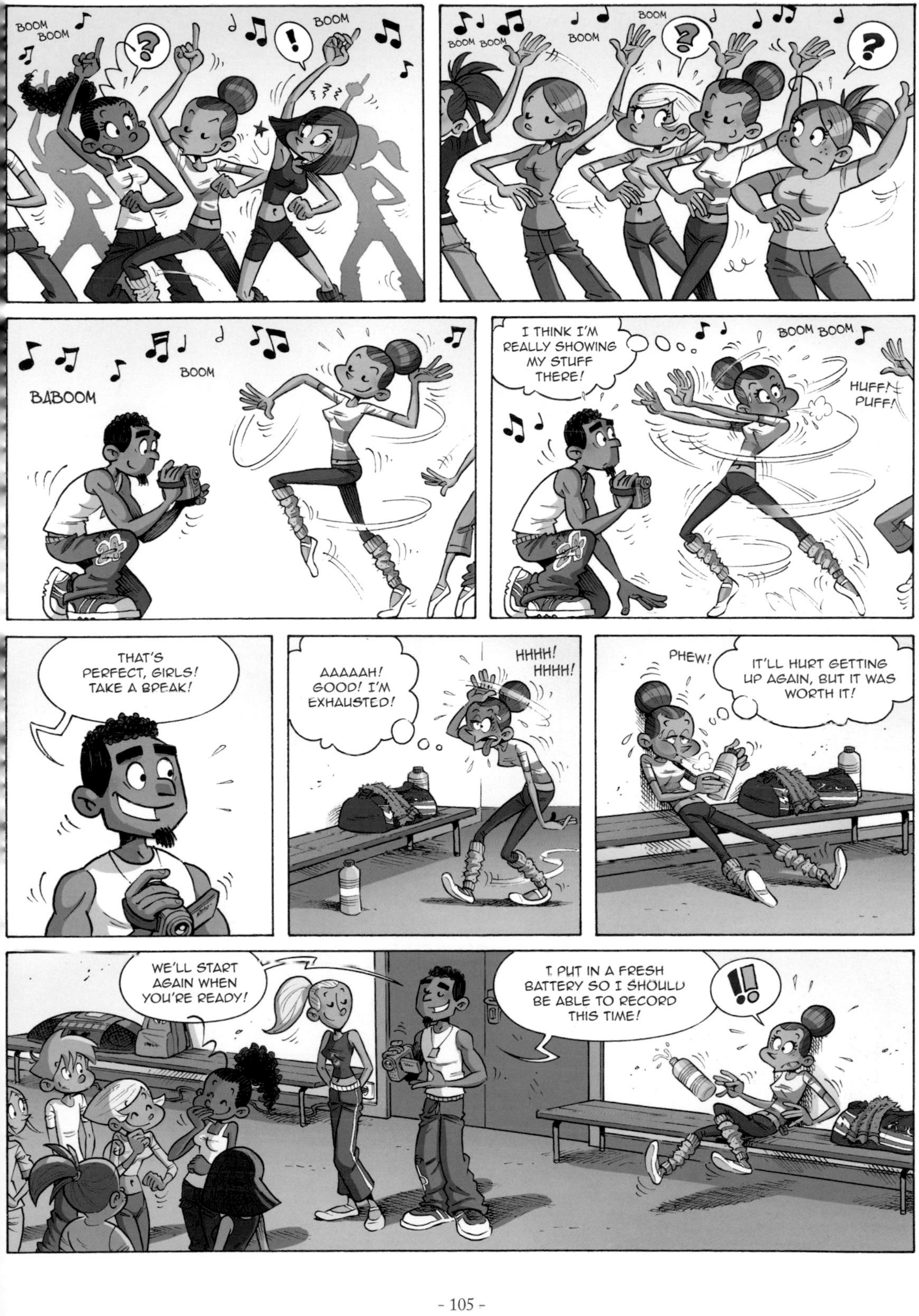
BOOM
BOOM
BOOM
BOOM BOOM
BOOM
BOOM
BABOOM
BOOM
I THINK I'M REALLY SHOWING MY STUFF THERE!
BOOM BOOM
HUFF! PUFF!
THAT'S PERFECT, GIRLS! TAKE A BREAK!
AAAAAH! GOOD! I'M EXHAUSTED!
HHHH! HHHH!
PHEW!
IT'LL HURT GETTING UP AGAIN, BUT IT WAS WORTH IT!
WE'LL START AGAIN WHEN YOU'RE READY!
I PUT IN A FRESH BATTERY SO I SHOULD BE ABLE TO RECORD THIS TIME!

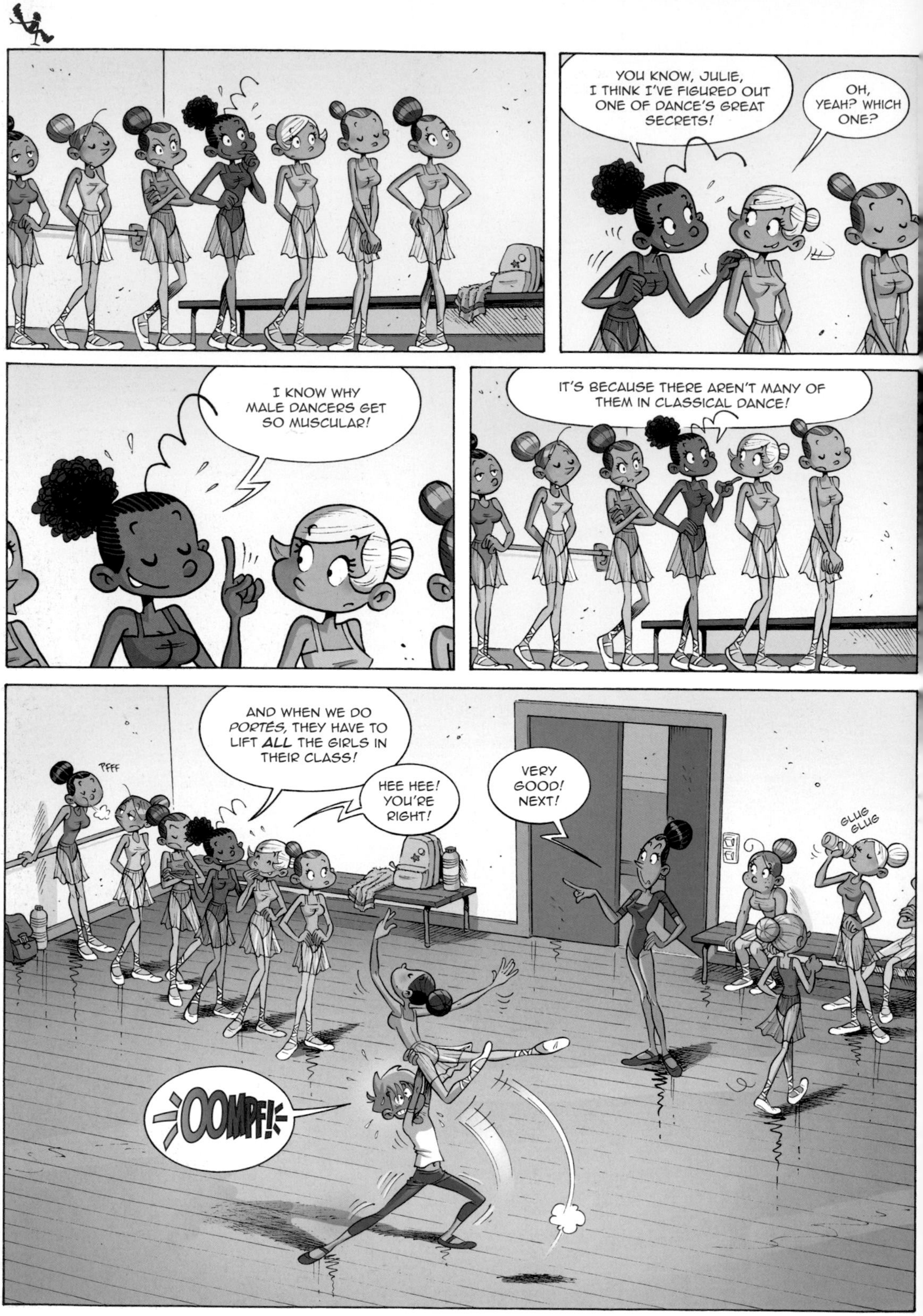
YOU KNOW, JULIE, I THINK I'VE FIGURED OUT ONE OF DANCE'S GREAT SECRETS!
OH, YEAH? WHICH ONE?
I KNOW WHY MALE DANCERS GET SO MUSCULAR!
IT'S BECAUSE THERE AREN'T MANY OF THEM IN CLASSICAL DANCE!
PFFF
AND WHEN WE DO *PORTÉS,* THEY HAVE TO LIFT **ALL** THE GIRLS IN THEIR CLASS!
HEE HEE! YOU'RE RIGHT!
VERY GOOD! NEXT!
GLUG GLUG
OOMPF!

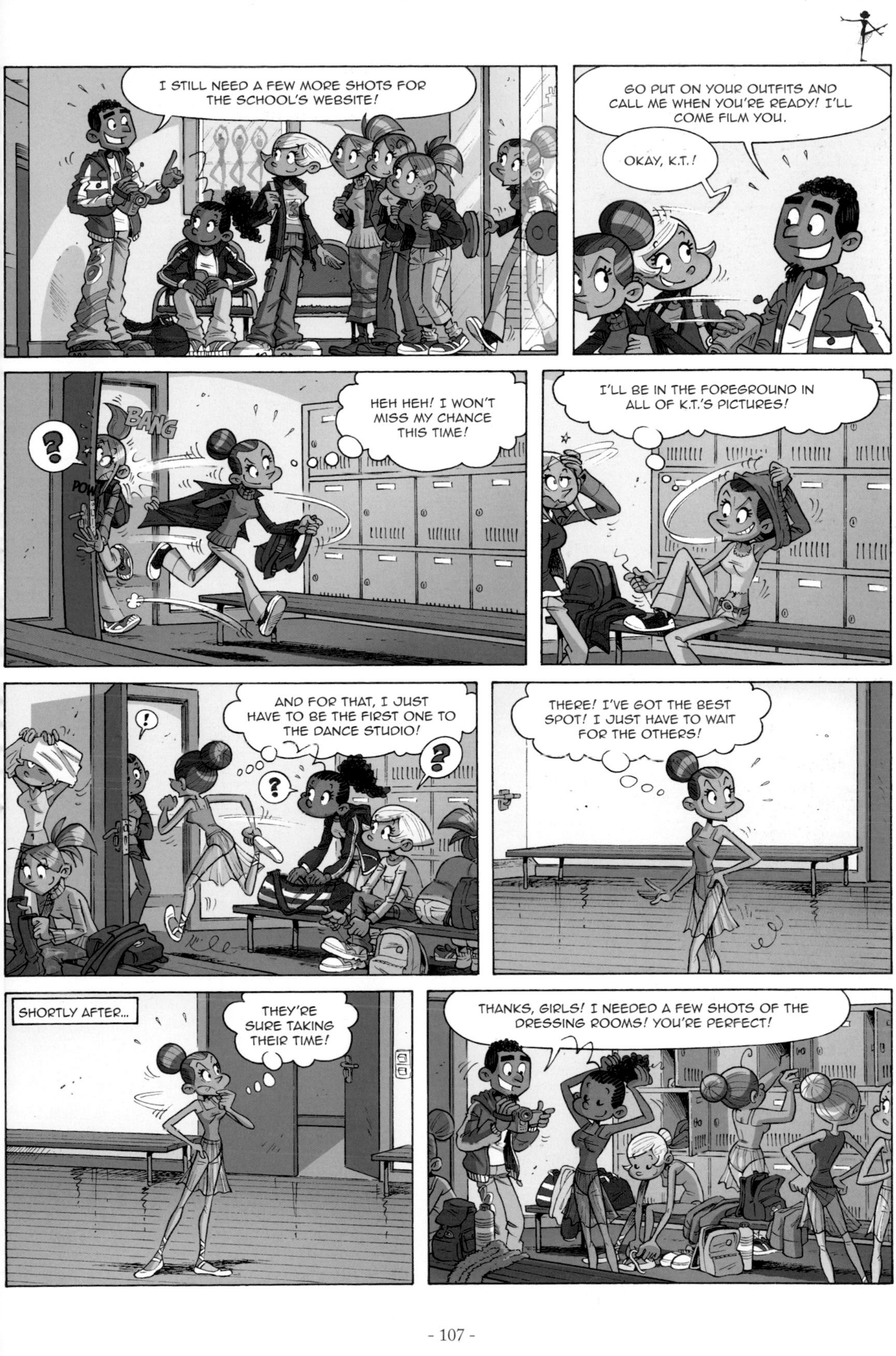
I STILL NEED A FEW MORE SHOTS FOR THE SCHOOL'S WEBSITE!
GO PUT ON YOUR OUTFITS AND CALL ME WHEN YOU'RE READY! I'LL COME FILM YOU.
OKAY, K.T.!
BANG
POW
?
HEH HEH! I WON'T MISS MY CHANCE THIS TIME!
I'LL BE IN THE FOREGROUND IN ALL OF K.T.'S PICTURES!
!
AND FOR THAT, I JUST HAVE TO BE THE FIRST ONE TO THE DANCE STUDIO!
?
?
THERE! I'VE GOT THE BEST SPOT! I JUST HAVE TO WAIT FOR THE OTHERS!
SHORTLY AFTER...
THEY'RE SURE TAKING THEIR TIME!
THANKS, GIRLS! I NEEDED A FEW SHOTS OF THE DRESSING ROOMS! YOU'RE PERFECT!

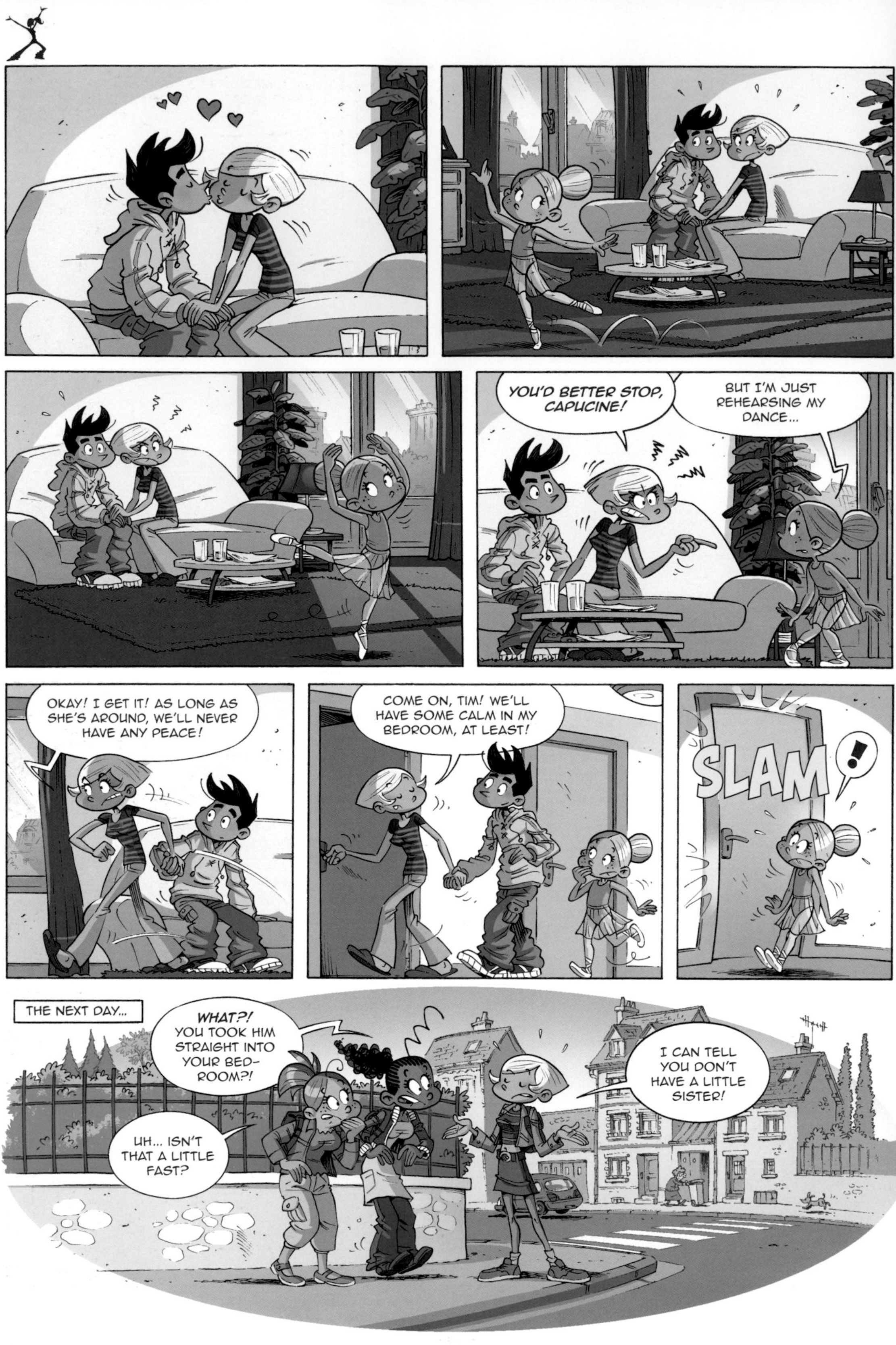
YOU'D BETTER STOP, CAPUCINE!
BUT I'M JUST REHEARSING MY DANCE...
OKAY! I GET IT! AS LONG AS SHE'S AROUND, WE'LL NEVER HAVE ANY PEACE!
COME ON, TIM! WE'LL HAVE SOME CALM IN MY BEDROOM, AT LEAST!
SLAM
!
THE NEXT DAY...
WHAT?! YOU TOOK HIM STRAIGHT INTO YOUR BED-ROOM?!
UH... ISN'T THAT A LITTLE FAST?
I CAN TELL YOU DON'T HAVE A LITTLE SISTER!

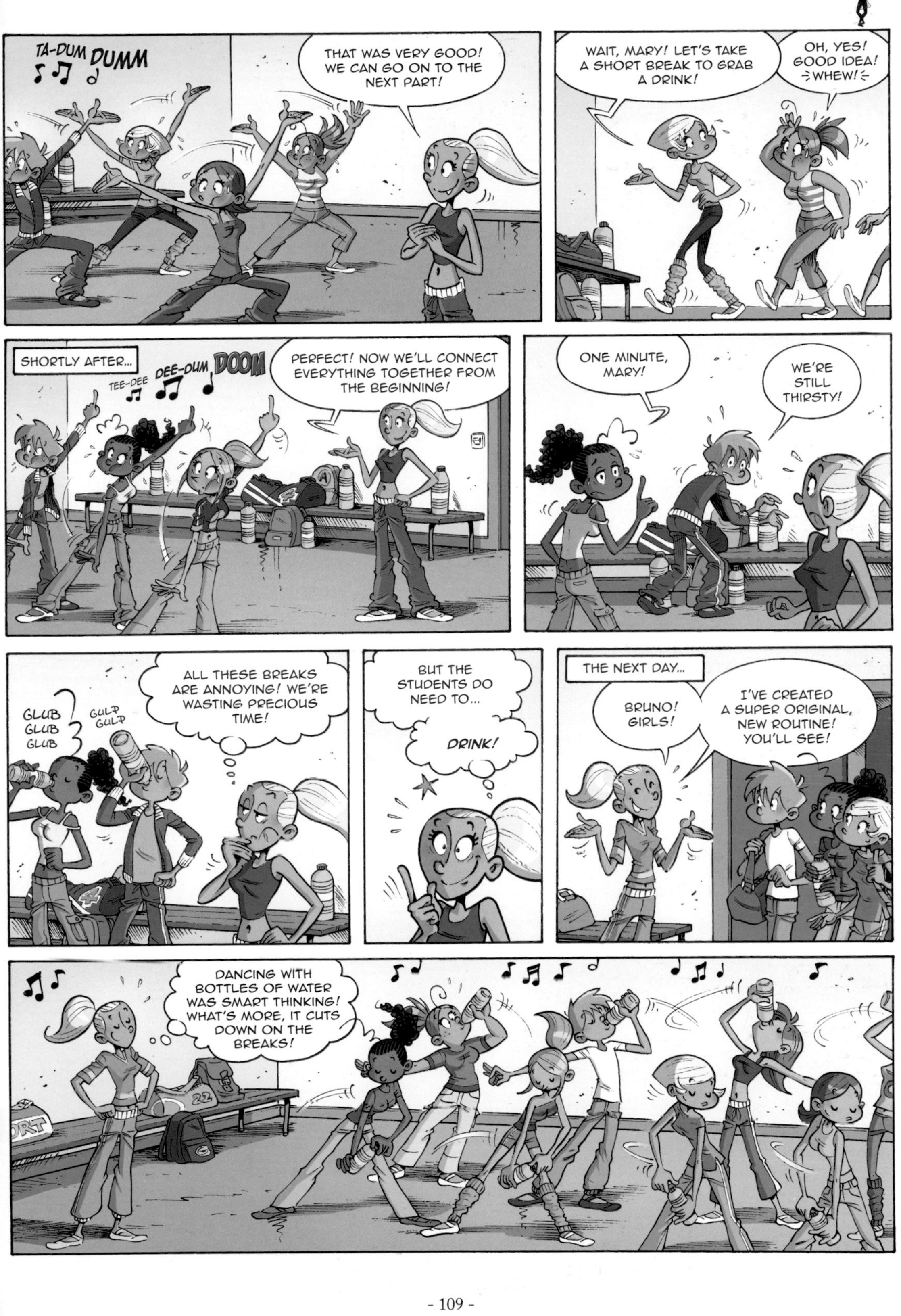
TA-DUM DUMM
THAT WAS VERY GOOD! WE CAN GO ON TO THE NEXT PART!
WAIT, MARY! LET'S TAKE A SHORT BREAK TO GRAB A DRINK!
OH, YES! GOOD IDEA! WHEW!
SHORTLY AFTER...
TEE-DEE DEE-DUM DOOM
PERFECT! NOW WE'LL CONNECT EVERYTHING TOGETHER FROM THE BEGINNING!
ONE MINUTE, MARY!
WE'RE STILL THIRSTY!
GLUB GLUB GLUB
GULP GULP
ALL THESE BREAKS ARE ANNOYING! WE'RE WASTING PRECIOUS TIME!
BUT THE STUDENTS DO NEED TO...
DRINK!
THE NEXT DAY...
BRUNO! GIRLS!
I'VE CREATED A SUPER ORIGINAL, NEW ROUTINE! YOU'LL SEE!
DANCING WITH BOTTLES OF WATER WAS SMART THINKING! WHAT'S MORE, IT CUTS DOWN ON THE BREAKS!

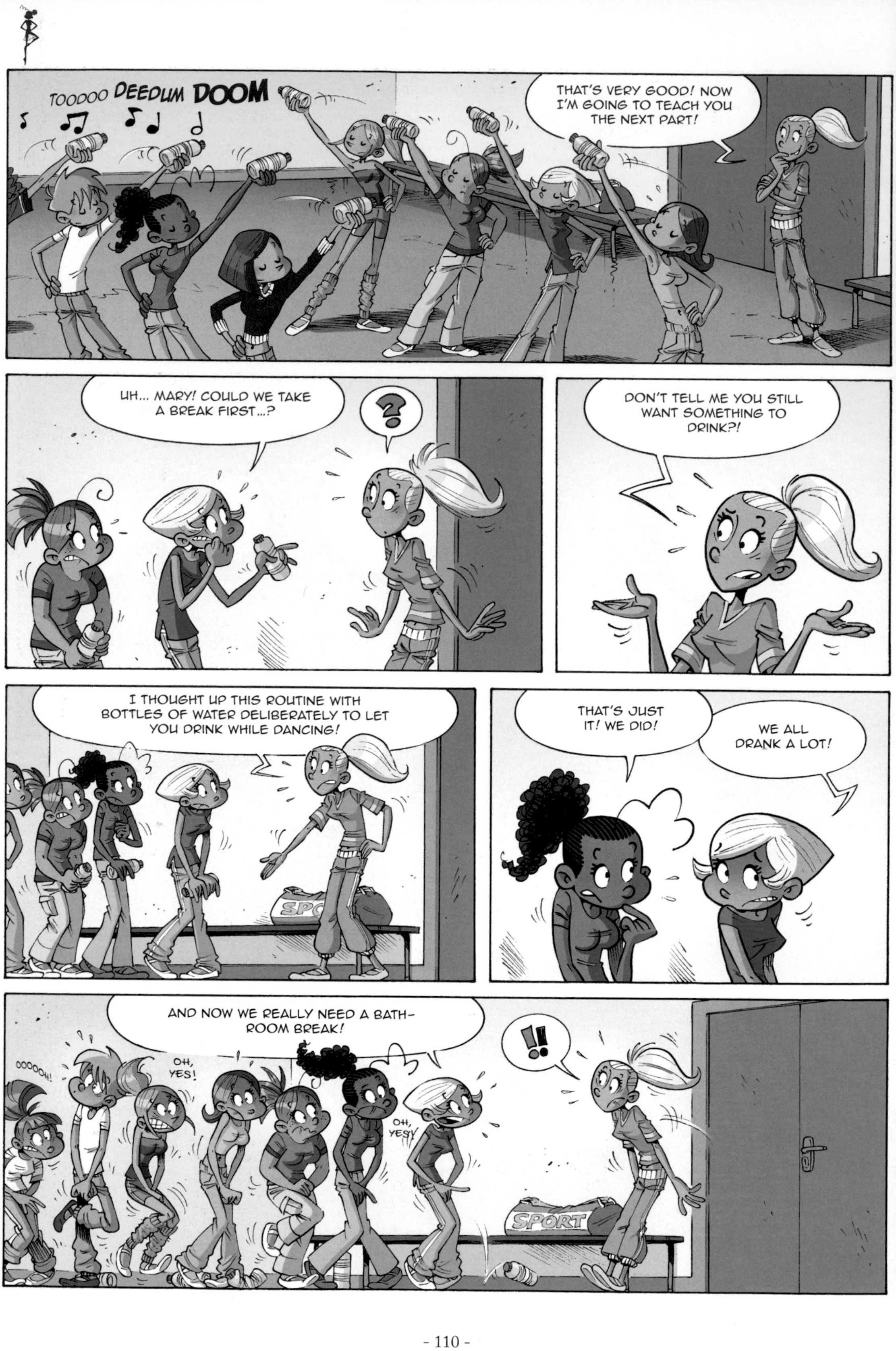
TOODOO DEEDUM DOOM
THAT'S VERY GOOD! NOW I'M GOING TO TEACH YOU THE NEXT PART!
UH... MARY! COULD WE TAKE A BREAK FIRST...?
?
DON'T TELL ME YOU STILL WANT SOMETHING TO DRINK?!
I THOUGHT UP THIS ROUTINE WITH BOTTLES OF WATER DELIBERATELY TO LET YOU DRINK WHILE DANCING!
SPORT
THAT'S JUST IT! WE DID!
WE ALL DRANK A LOT!
AND NOW WE REALLY NEED A BATH-ROOM BREAK!
OOOOOH!
OH, YES!
OH, YES!
!!
SPORT

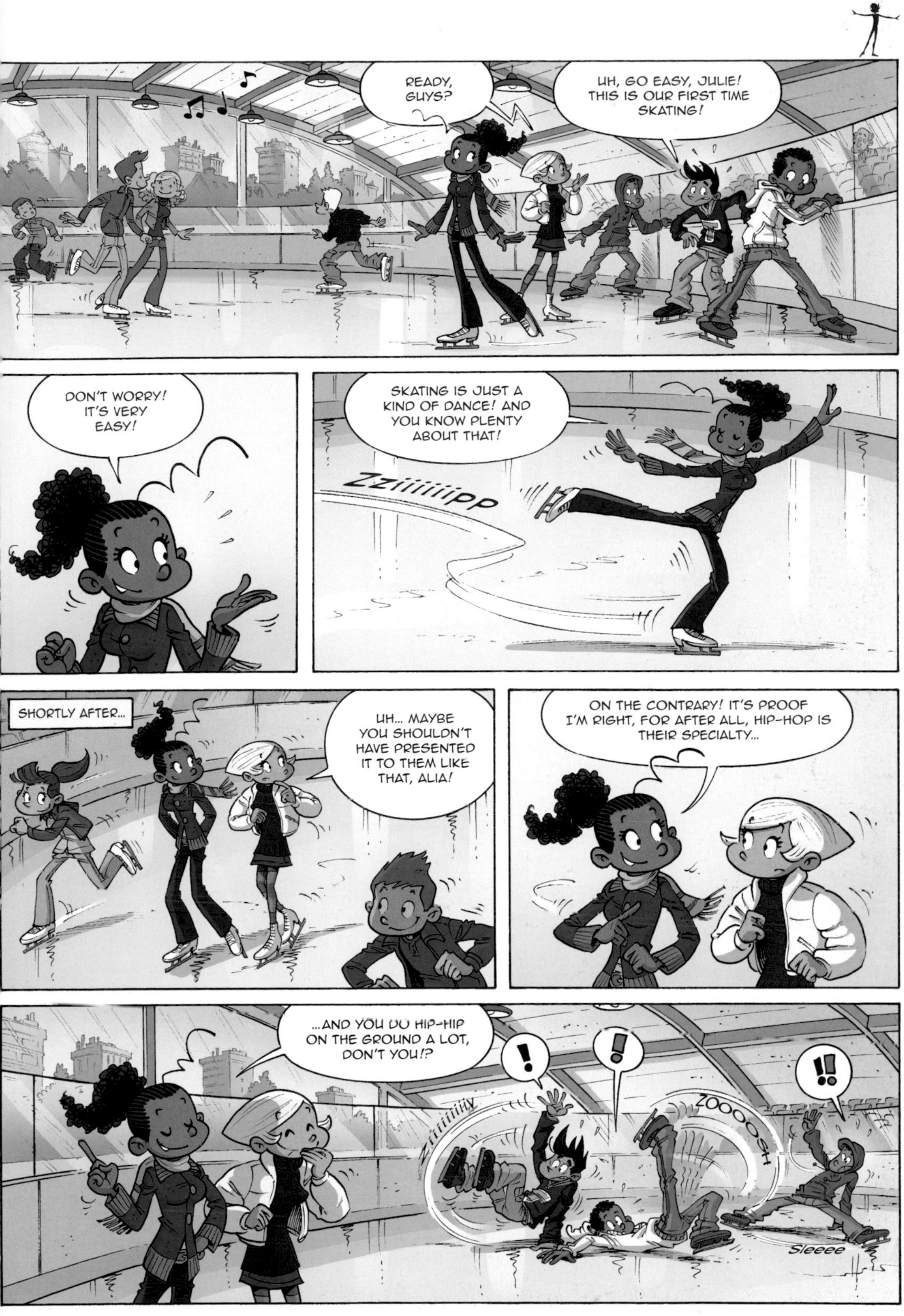
READY, GUYS?
UH, GO EASY, JULIE! THIS IS OUR FIRST TIME SKATING!
DON'T WORRY! IT'S VERY EASY!
SKATING IS JUST A KIND OF DANCE! AND YOU KNOW PLENTY ABOUT THAT!
Zziiiiiipp
SHORTLY AFTER...
UH... MAYBE YOU SHOULDN'T HAVE PRESENTED IT TO THEM LIKE THAT, ALIA!
ON THE CONTRARY! IT'S PROOF I'M RIGHT, FOR AFTER ALL, HIP-HOP IS THEIR SPECIALTY...
...AND YOU DO HIP-HIP ON THE GROUND A LOT, DON'T YOU!?
!
!
!!
ZOOOOSH
Sleeee

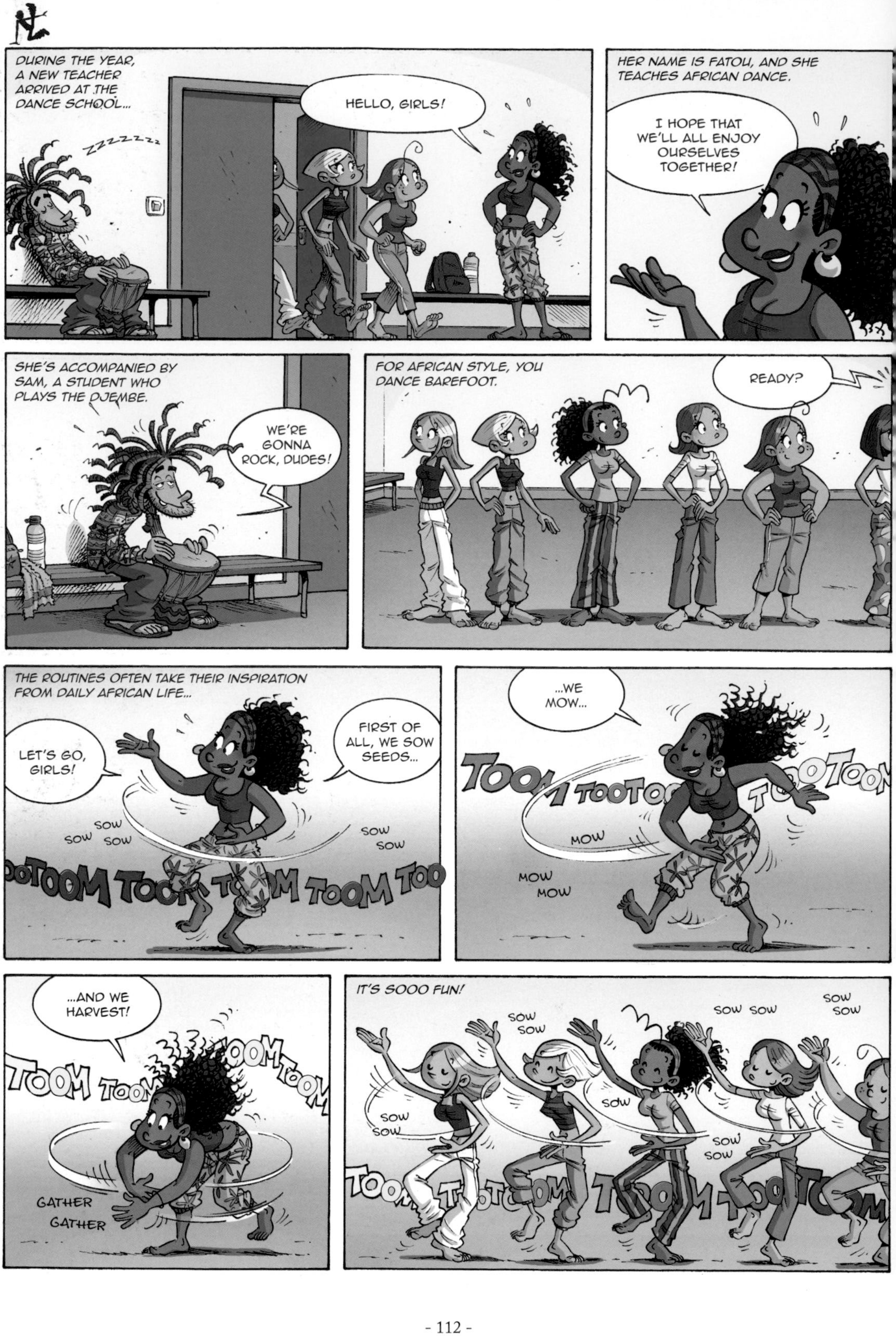
DURING THE YEAR, A NEW TEACHER ARRIVED AT THE DANCE SCHOOL...
ZZZZZZZ
HELLO, GIRLS!
HER NAME IS FATOU, AND SHE TEACHES AFRICAN DANCE.
I HOPE THAT WE'LL ALL ENJOY OURSELVES TOGETHER!
SHE'S ACCOMPANIED BY SAM, A STUDENT WHO PLAYS THE DJEMBE.
WE'RE GONNA ROCK, DUDES!
FOR AFRICAN STYLE, YOU DANCE BAREFOOT.
READY?
THE ROUTINES OFTEN TAKE THEIR INSPIRATION FROM DAILY AFRICAN LIFE...
LET'S GO, GIRLS!
FIRST OF ALL, WE SOW SEEDS...
SOW SOW SOW
SOW SOW
TOOTOOM TOOM TOOM TOOM TOO
...WE MOW...
TOOM TOOTOO TOOTOOM
MOW
MOW MOW
...AND WE HARVEST!
TOOM TOOM TOOMTOOM
GATHER GATHER
IT'S SOOO FUN!
SOW SOW
SOW SOW
SOW SOW
SOW
SOW SOW
SOW SOW
TOOM TOOTOOM TOOM TOOTOOM

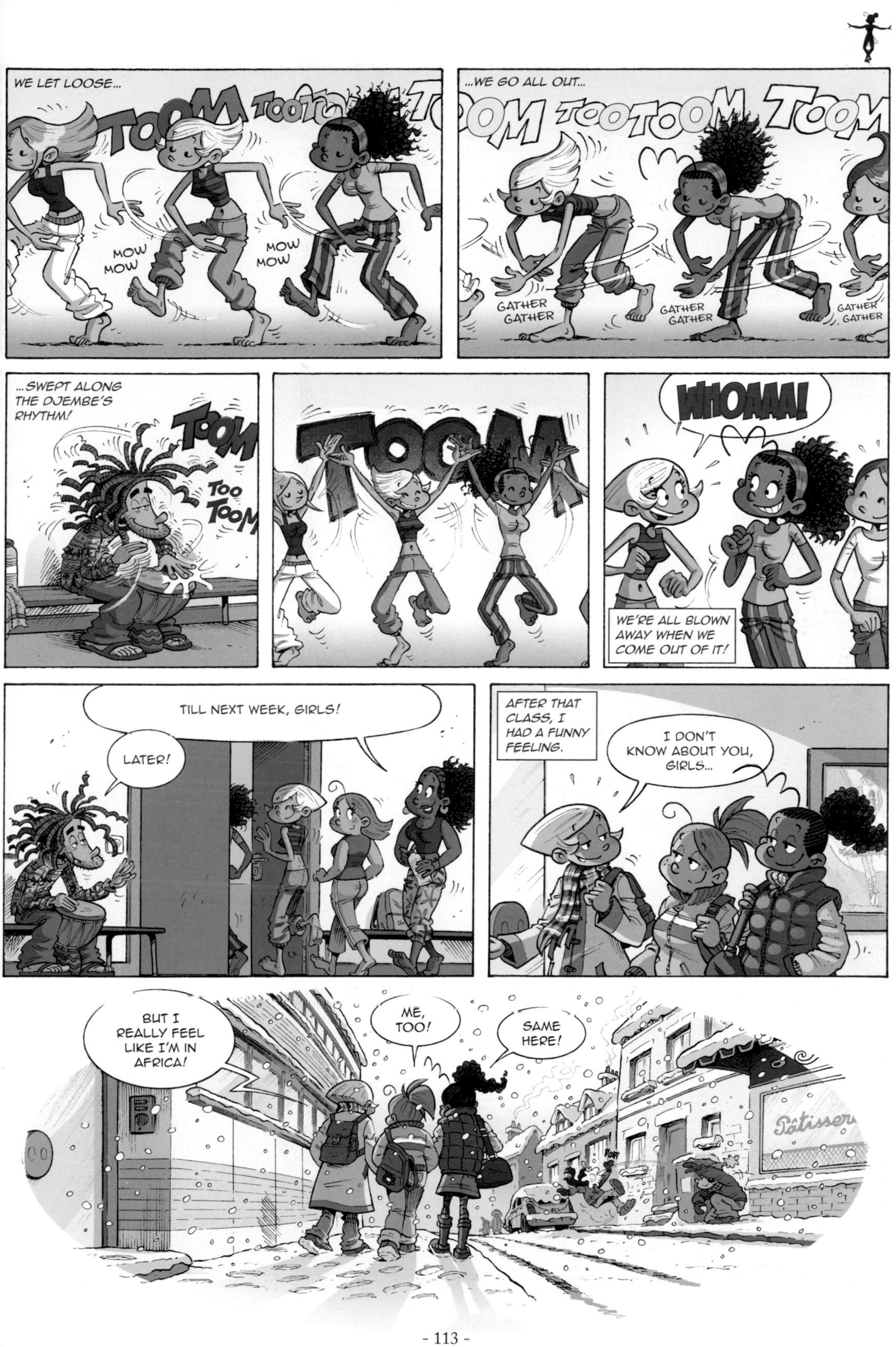
WE LET LOOSE...
TOOM TOOTOOM TOOM
MOW MOW
MOW MOW
...WE GO ALL OUT...
TOOM TOOTOOM TOOM
GATHER GATHER
GATHER GATHER
GATHER GATHER
...SWEPT ALONG THE DJEMBE'S RHYTHM!
TOOM
TOO TOOM
TOOM
WHOAAA!
WE'RE ALL BLOWN AWAY WHEN WE COME OUT OF IT!
TILL NEXT WEEK, GIRLS!
LATER!
AFTER THAT CLASS, I HAD A FUNNY FEELING.
I DON'T KNOW ABOUT YOU, GIRLS...
BUT I REALLY FEEL LIKE I'M IN AFRICA!
ME, TOO!
SAME HERE!

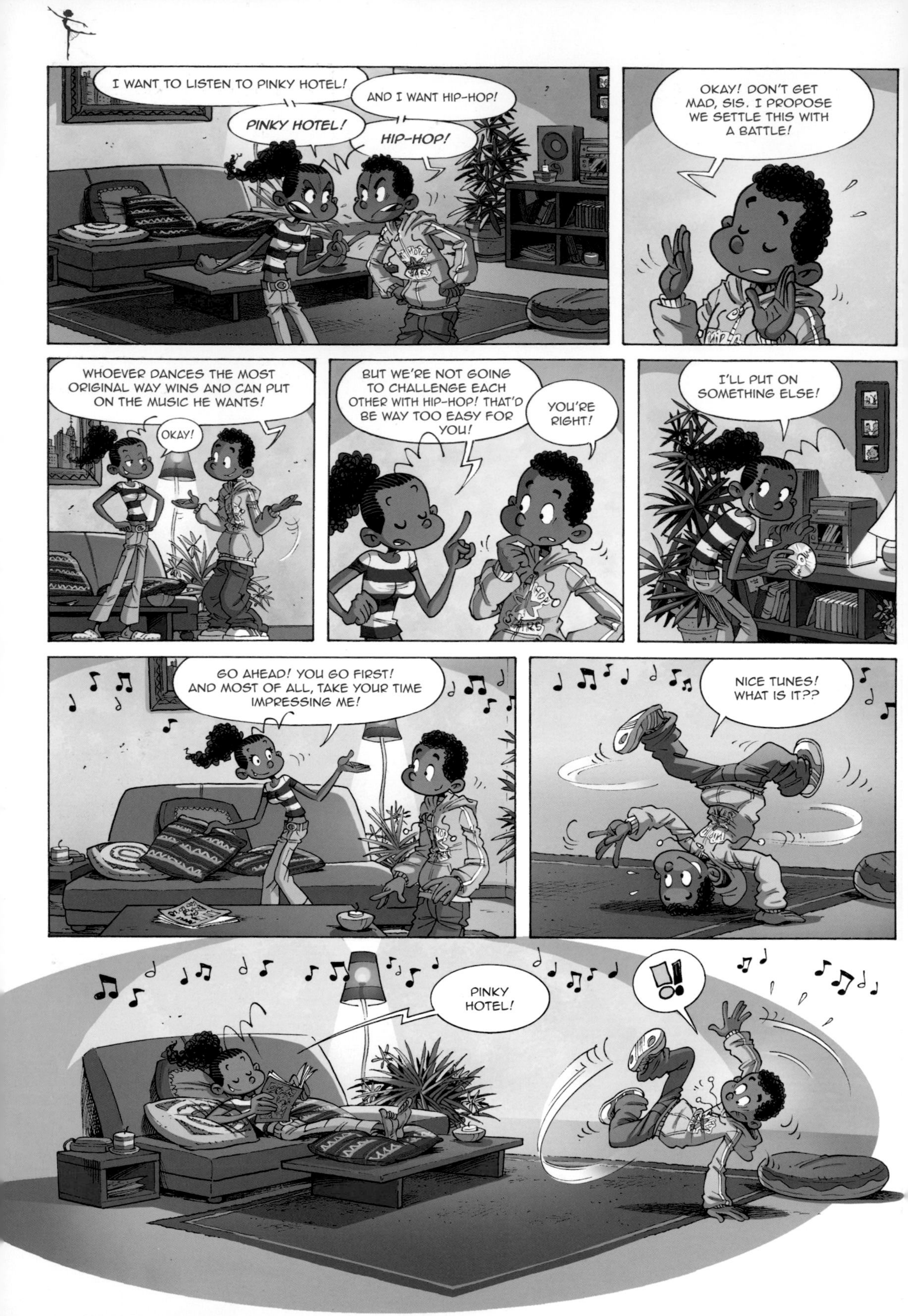
I WANT TO LISTEN TO PINKY HOTEL!
AND I WANT HIP-HOP!
PINKY HOTEL!
HIP-HOP!
OKAY! DON'T GET MAD, SIS. I PROPOSE WE SETTLE THIS WITH A BATTLE!
WHOEVER DANCES THE MOST ORIGINAL WAY WINS AND CAN PUT ON THE MUSIC HE WANTS!
OKAY!
BUT WE'RE NOT GOING TO CHALLENGE EACH OTHER WITH HIP-HOP! THAT'D BE WAY TOO EASY FOR YOU!
YOU'RE RIGHT!
I'LL PUT ON SOMETHING ELSE!
GO AHEAD! YOU GO FIRST! AND MOST OF ALL, TAKE YOUR TIME IMPRESSING ME!
NICE TUNES! WHAT IS IT??
PINKY HOTEL!
!

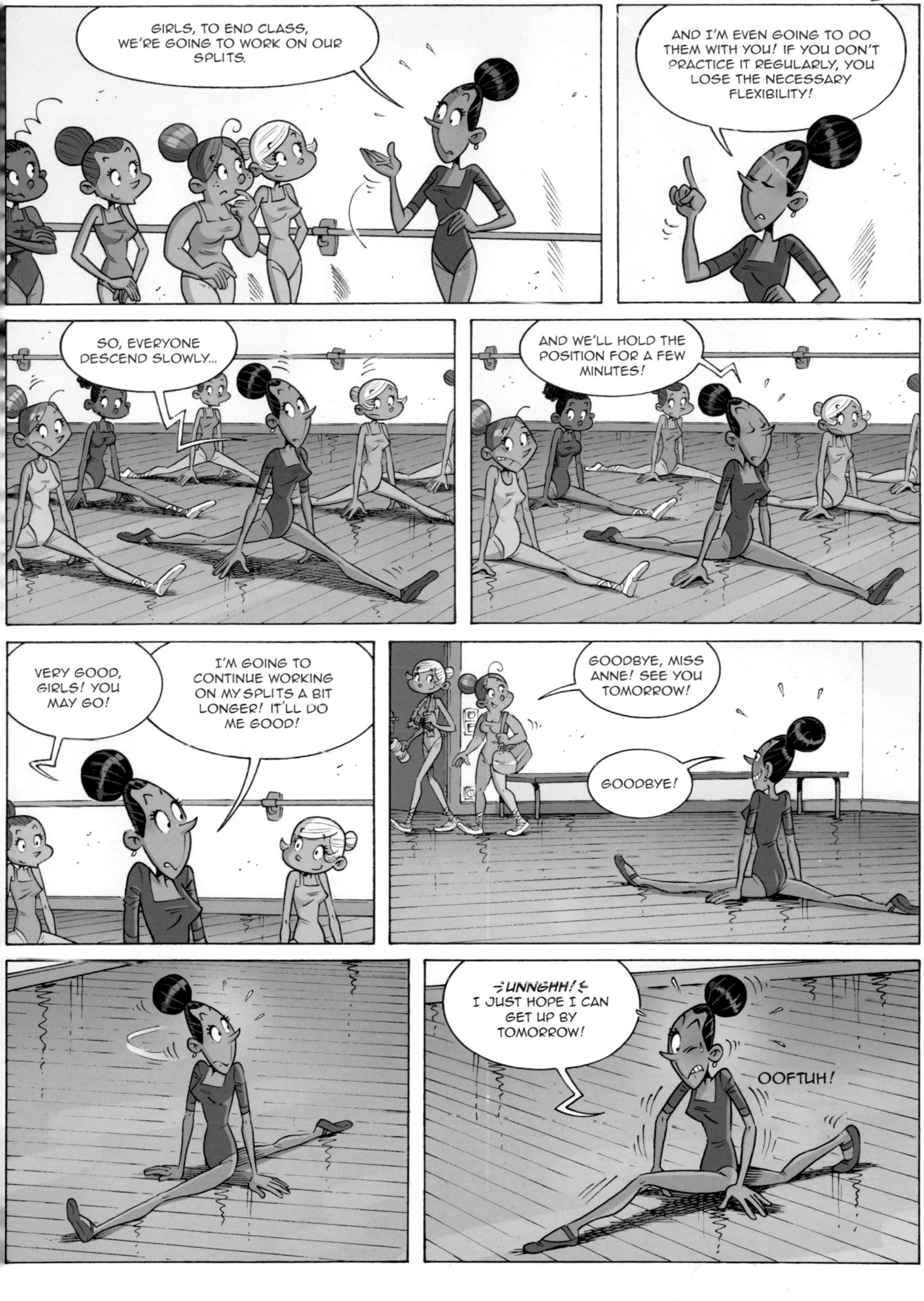
GIRLS, TO END CLASS, WE'RE GOING TO WORK ON OUR SPLITS.
AND I'M EVEN GOING TO DO THEM WITH YOU! IF YOU DON'T PRACTICE IT REGULARLY, YOU LOSE THE NECESSARY FLEXIBILITY!
SO, EVERYONE DESCEND SLOWLY...
AND WE'LL HOLD THE POSITION FOR A FEW MINUTES!
VERY GOOD, GIRLS! YOU MAY GO!
I'M GOING TO CONTINUE WORKING ON MY SPLITS A BIT LONGER! IT'LL DO ME GOOD!
GOODBYE, MISS ANNE! SEE YOU TOMORROW!
GOODBYE!
UNNGHH! I JUST HOPE I CAN GET UP BY TOMORROW!
OOFTUH!

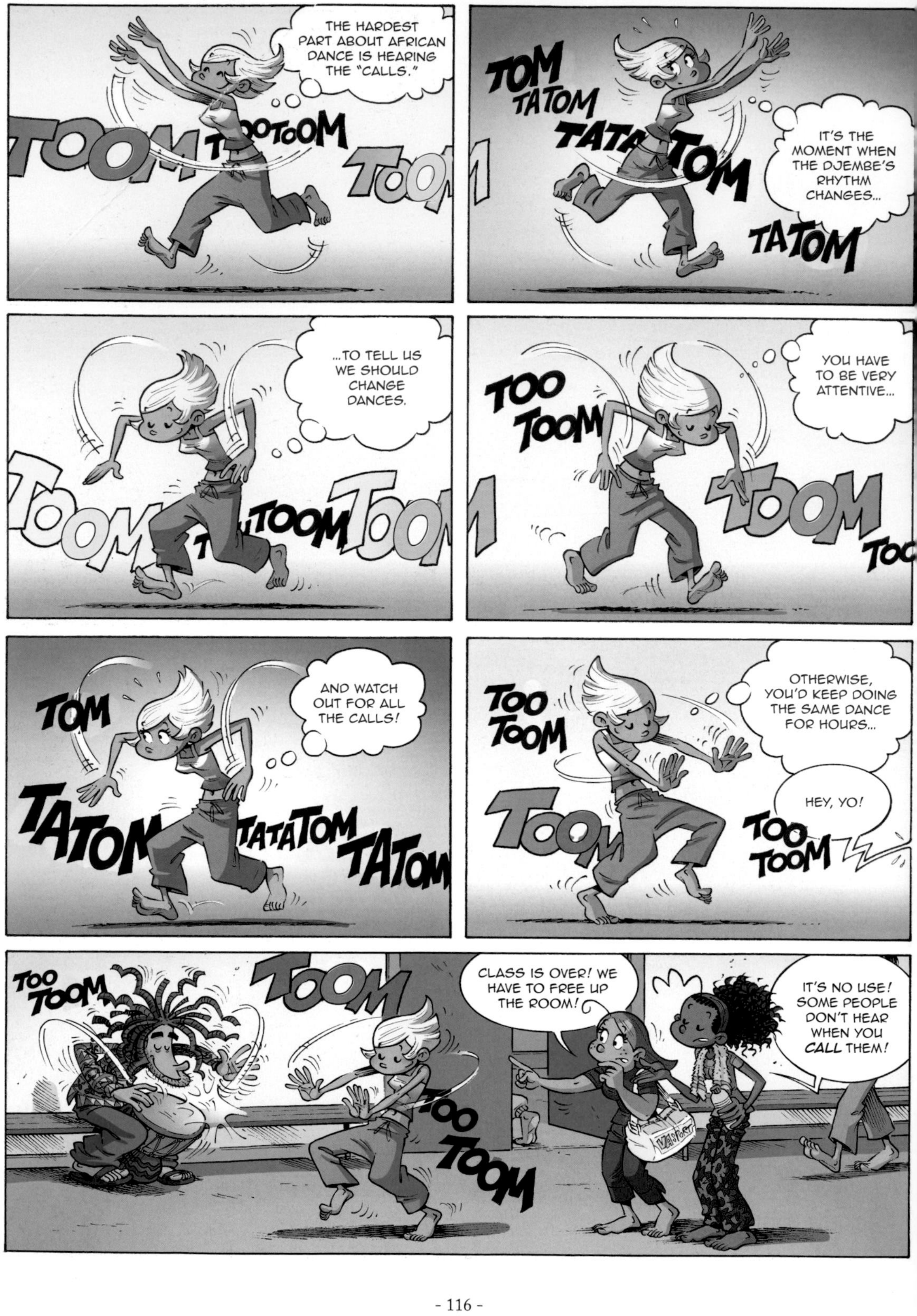
THE HARDEST PART ABOUT AFRICAN DANCE IS HEARING THE "CALLS."
TOOM TOOTOOM TOOM
TOM TATOM TATATOM TATOM
IT'S THE MOMENT WHEN THE DJEMBE'S RHYTHM CHANGES...
...TO TELL US WE SHOULD CHANGE DANCES.
TOOM TOOM TOOM
TOO TOOM
YOU HAVE TO BE VERY ATTENTIVE...
TOOM
TOM
AND WATCH OUT FOR ALL THE CALLS!
TATOM TATATOM TATOM
TOO TOOM
OTHERWISE, YOU'D KEEP DOING THE SAME DANCE FOR HOURS...
TOOM
HEY, YO!
TOO TOOM
TOO TOOM
TOOM
TOO TOOM
CLASS IS OVER! WE HAVE TO FREE UP THE ROOM!
IT'S NO USE! SOME PEOPLE DON'T HEAR WHEN YOU *CALL* THEM!

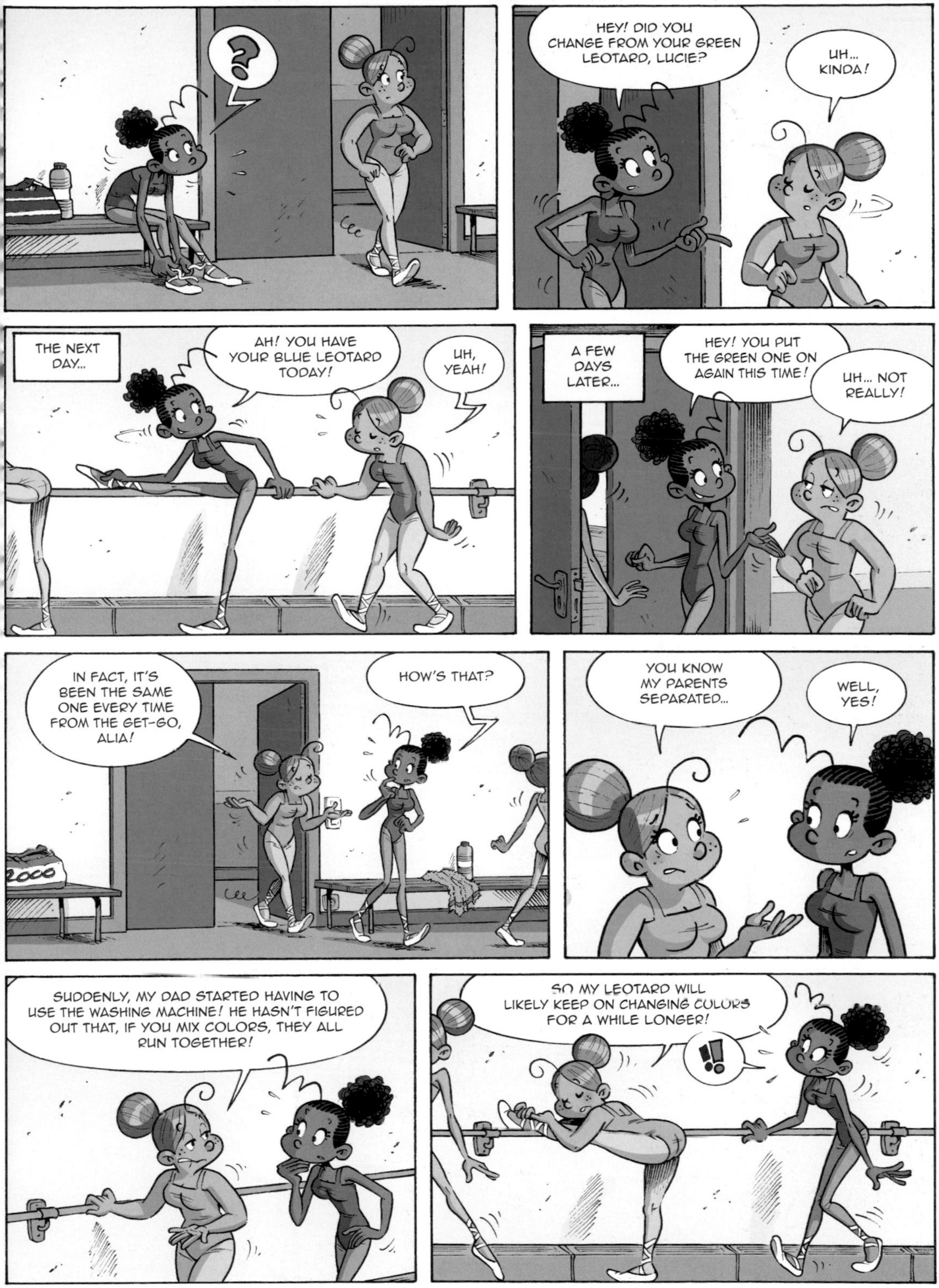
?
HEY! DID YOU CHANGE FROM YOUR GREEN LEOTARD, LUCIE?
UH... KINDA!
THE NEXT DAY...
AH! YOU HAVE YOUR BLUE LEOTARD TODAY!
UH, YEAH!
A FEW DAYS LATER...
HEY! YOU PUT THE GREEN ONE ON AGAIN THIS TIME!
UH... NOT REALLY!
IN FACT, IT'S BEEN THE SAME ONE EVERY TIME FROM THE GET-GO, ALIA!
HOW'S THAT?
YOU KNOW MY PARENTS SEPARATED...
WELL, YES!
SUDDENLY, MY DAD STARTED HAVING TO USE THE WASHING MACHINE! HE HASN'T FIGURED OUT THAT, IF YOU MIX COLORS, THEY ALL RUN TOGETHER!
SO MY LEOTARD WILL LIKELY KEEP ON CHANGING COLORS FOR A WHILE LONGER!
!!

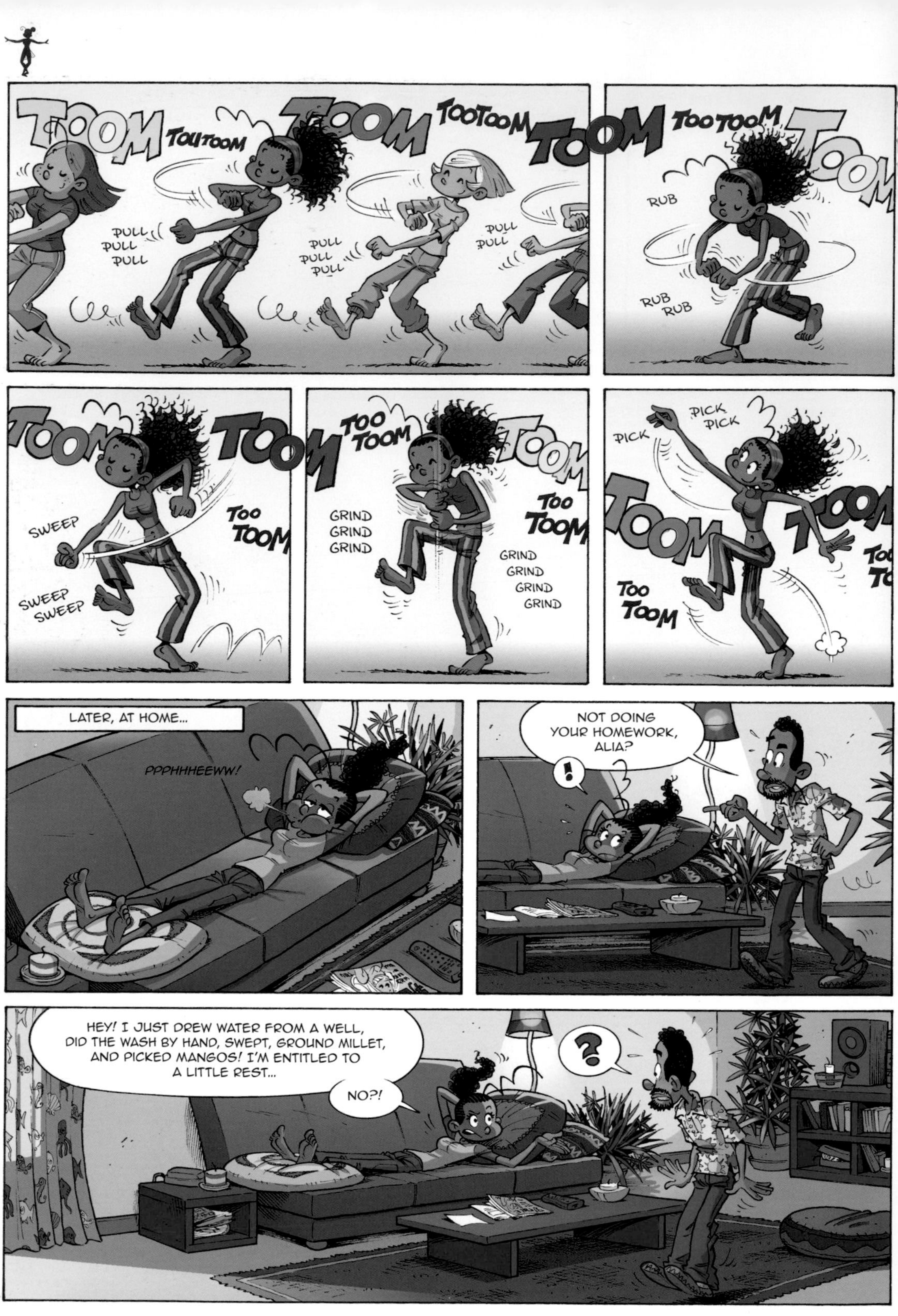
TOOM
TOUTOOM
TOOM
PULL PULL PULL
PULL PULL PULL
TOOTOOM
PULL PULL
TOOM
TOO TOOM
TOOM
RUB
RUB RUB
TOOM
SWEEP
SWEEP SWEEP
TOOM
TOO TOOM
TOO TOOM
GRIND GRIND GRIND
TOOM
TOO TOOM
GRIND GRIND GRIND GRIND
PICK
PICK PICK
TOOM
TOOM
TOO TOOM
LATER, AT HOME...
PPPHHHEEWW!
NOT DOING YOUR HOMEWORK, ALIA?
!
HEY! I JUST DREW WATER FROM A WELL, DID THE WASH BY HAND, SWEPT, GROUND MILLET, AND PICKED MANGOS! I'M ENTITLED TO A LITTLE REST...
NO?!
?

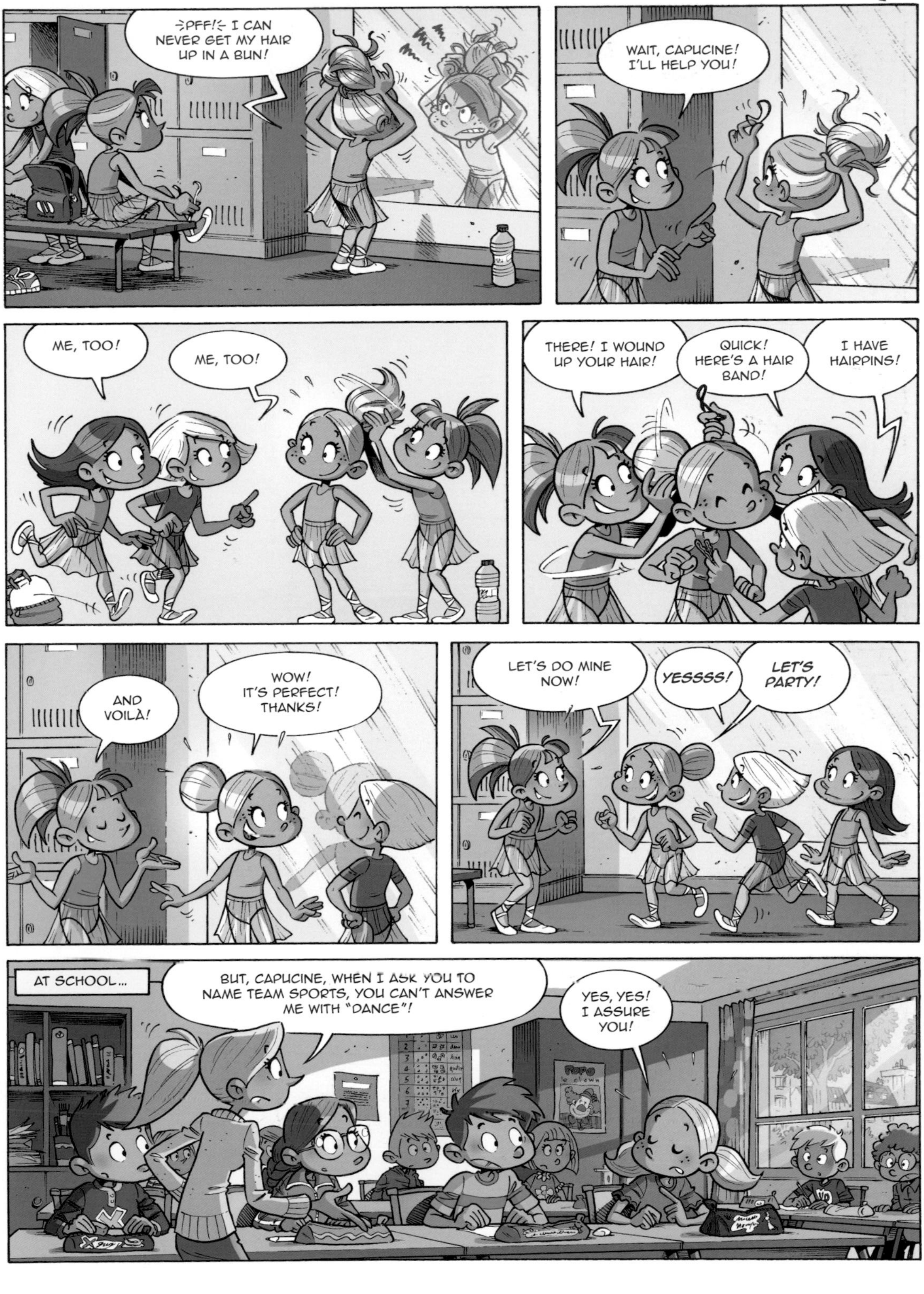

PFF! I CAN NEVER GET MY HAIR UP IN A BUN!
WAIT, CAPUCINE! I'LL HELP YOU!
ME, TOO!
ME, TOO!
THERE! I WOUND UP YOUR HAIR!
QUICK! HERE'S A HAIR BAND!
I HAVE HAIRPINS!
AND VOILÀ!
WOW! IT'S PERFECT! THANKS!
LET'S DO MINE NOW!
YESSSS!
LET'S PARTY!
AT SCHOOL...
BUT, CAPUCINE, WHEN I ASK YOU TO NAME TEAM SPORTS, YOU CAN'T ANSWER ME WITH "DANCE"!
YES, YES! I ASSURE YOU!

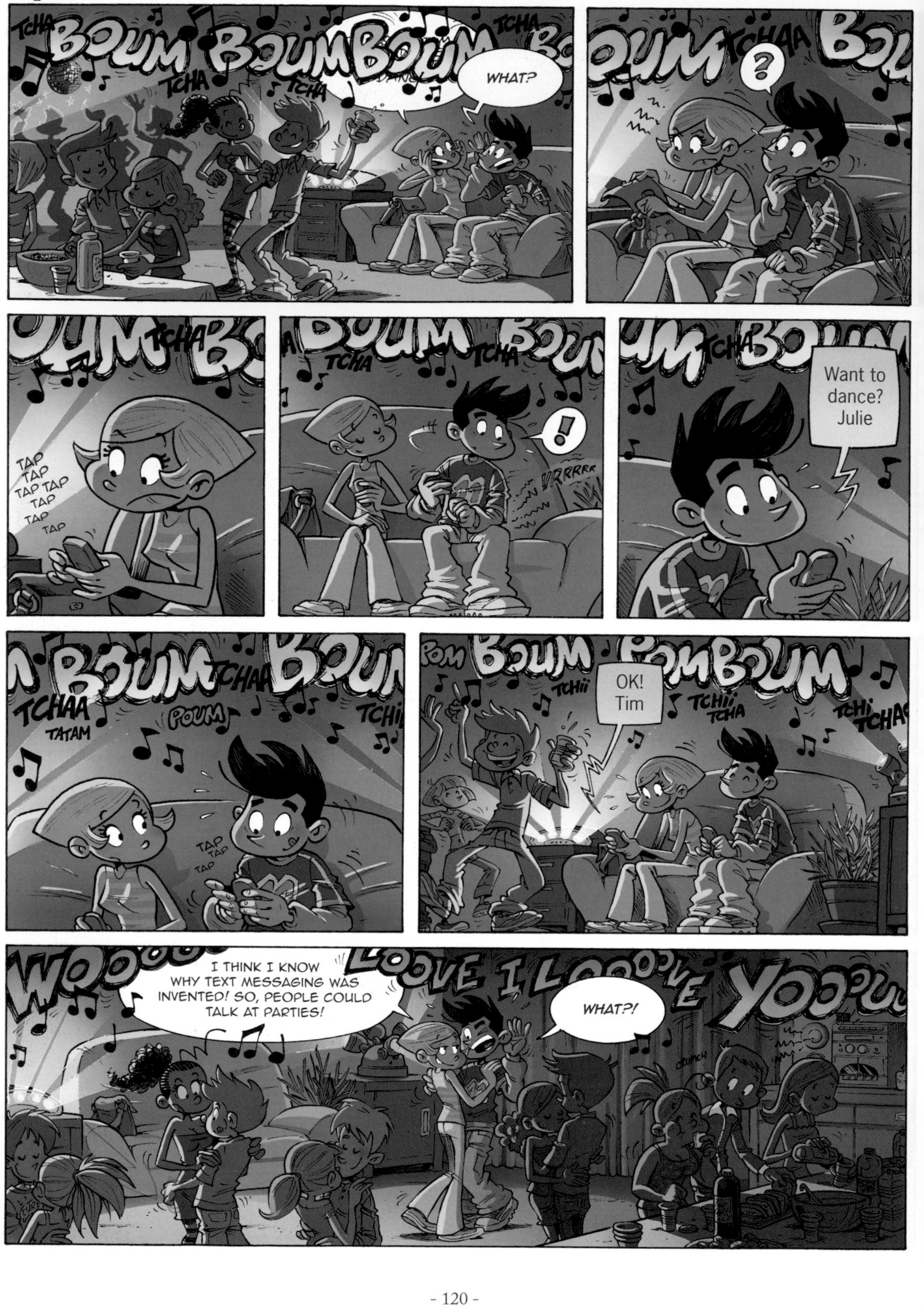
TCHA
BOUM BOUMBOUM
TCHA
TCHA
TCHA
WHAT?
TCHA
OUM
TCHAA
BOU
?
OUM
TCHA
B
TAP
TAP
TAP TAP
TAP
TAP
TAP
BOUM
TCHA
TCHA
BOU
!
VRRRRR
UM
TCHA
BOU
Want to dance? Julie
BOUM
TCHAA
BOUM
TCHAA
TATAM
POUM
TCHI
TAP
TAP
TAP
POM BOUM
POMBOUM
TCHII
TCHII
TCHA
TCHI
TCHA
OK! Tim
WOOO
LOOOVE I LOOOOVE
YOOOU
I THINK I KNOW WHY TEXT MESSAGING WAS INVENTED! SO, PEOPLE COULD TALK AT PARTIES!
WHAT?!
CRUNCH

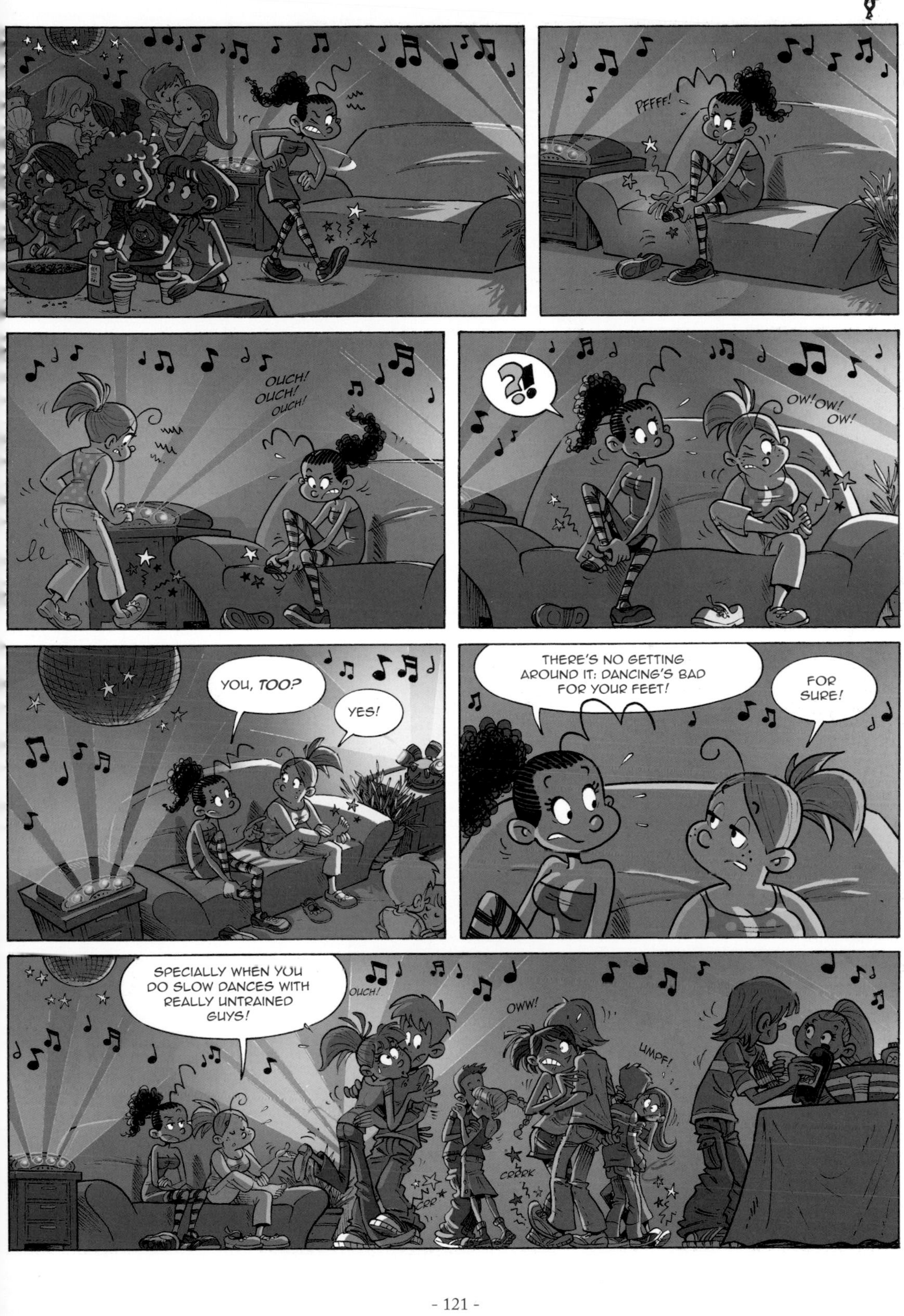
PFFFF!
OUCH! OUCH! OUCH!
OW! OW! OW!
?!
YOU, TOO?
YES!
THERE'S NO GETTING AROUND IT: DANCING'S BAD FOR YOUR FEET!
FOR SURE!
SPECIALLY WHEN YOU DO SLOW DANCES WITH REALLY UNTRAINED GUYS!
OUCH!
OWW!
UMPF!
CRRRK

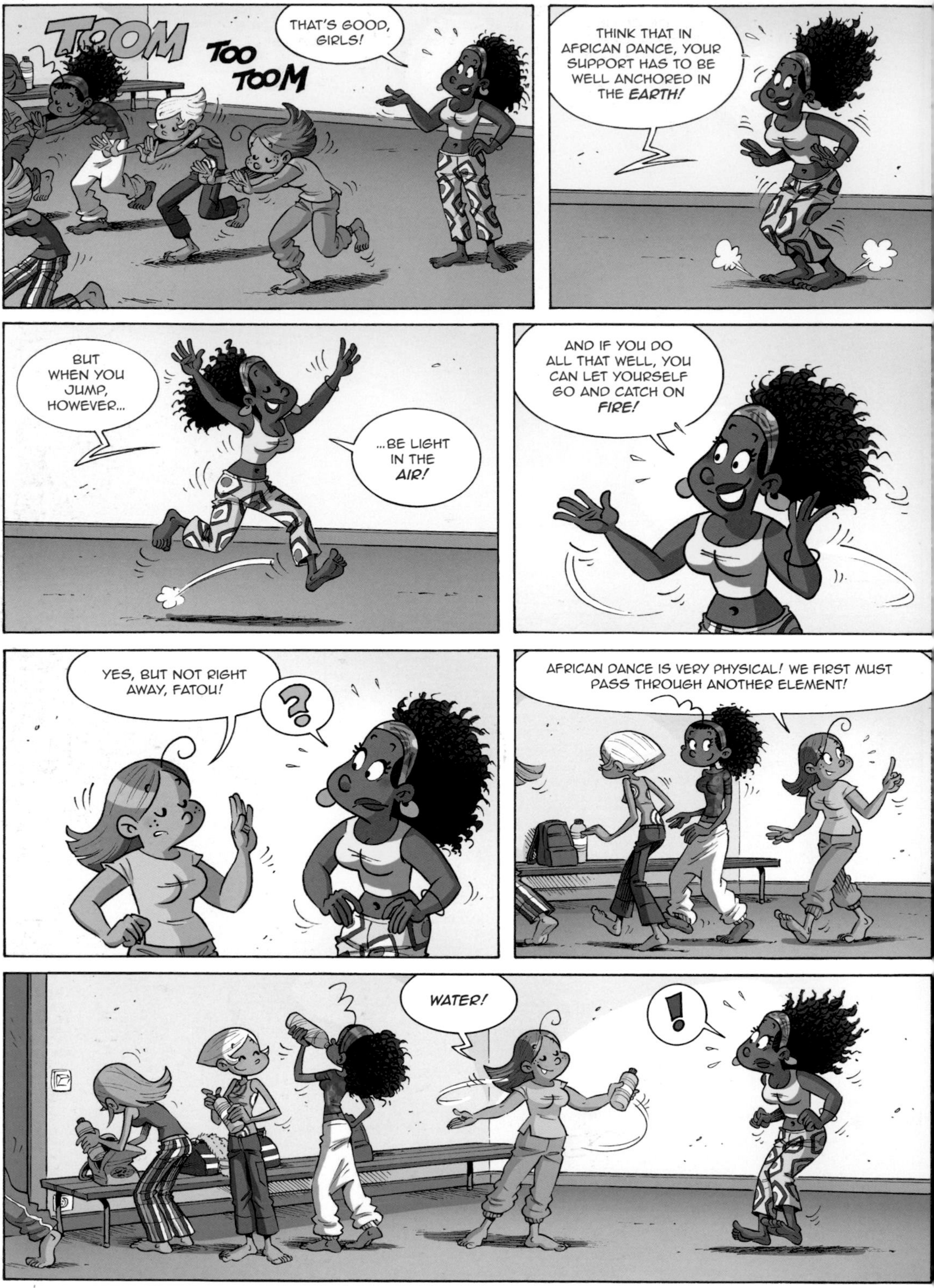
TOOM TOO TOOM
THAT'S GOOD, GIRLS!
THINK THAT IN AFRICAN DANCE, YOUR SUPPORT HAS TO BE WELL ANCHORED IN THE EARTH!
BUT WHEN YOU JUMP, HOWEVER...
...BE LIGHT IN THE AIR!
AND IF YOU DO ALL THAT WELL, YOU CAN LET YOURSELF GO AND CATCH ON FIRE!
YES, BUT NOT RIGHT AWAY, FATOU!
?
AFRICAN DANCE IS VERY PHYSICAL! WE FIRST MUST PASS THROUGH ANOTHER ELEMENT!
WATER!
!

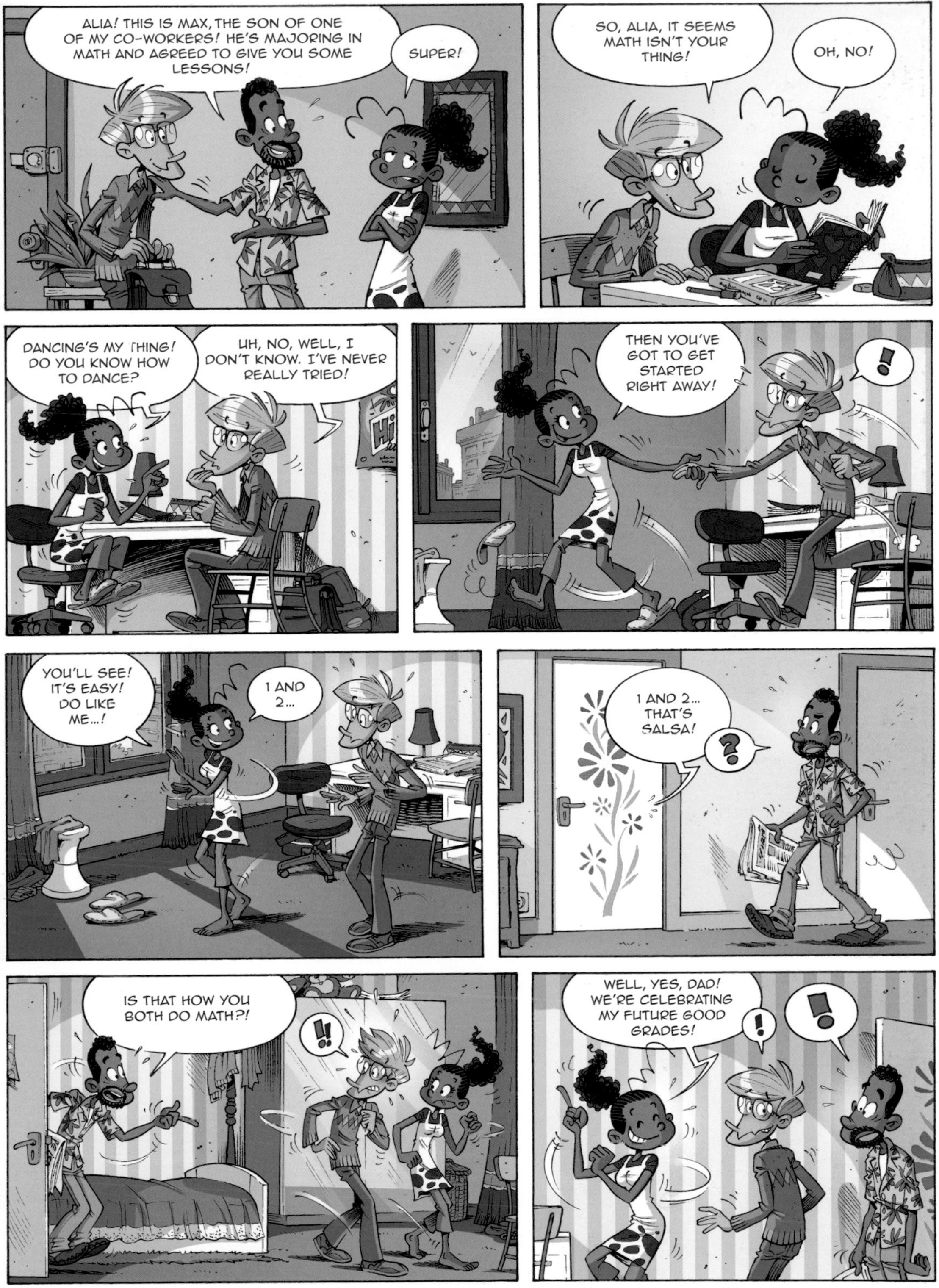
ALIA! THIS IS MAX, THE SON OF ONE OF MY CO-WORKERS! HE'S MAJORING IN MATH AND AGREED TO GIVE YOU SOME LESSONS!
SUPER!
SO, ALIA, IT SEEMS MATH ISN'T YOUR THING!
OH, NO!
DANCING'S MY THING! DO YOU KNOW HOW TO DANCE?
UH, NO, WELL, I DON'T KNOW. I'VE NEVER REALLY TRIED!
THEN YOU'VE GOT TO GET STARTED RIGHT AWAY!
!
YOU'LL SEE! IT'S EASY! DO LIKE ME...!
1 AND 2...
1 AND 2... THAT'S SALSA!
?
IS THAT HOW YOU BOTH DO MATH?!
!!
WELL, YES, DAD! WE'RE CELEBRATING MY FUTURE GOOD GRADES!
!
!

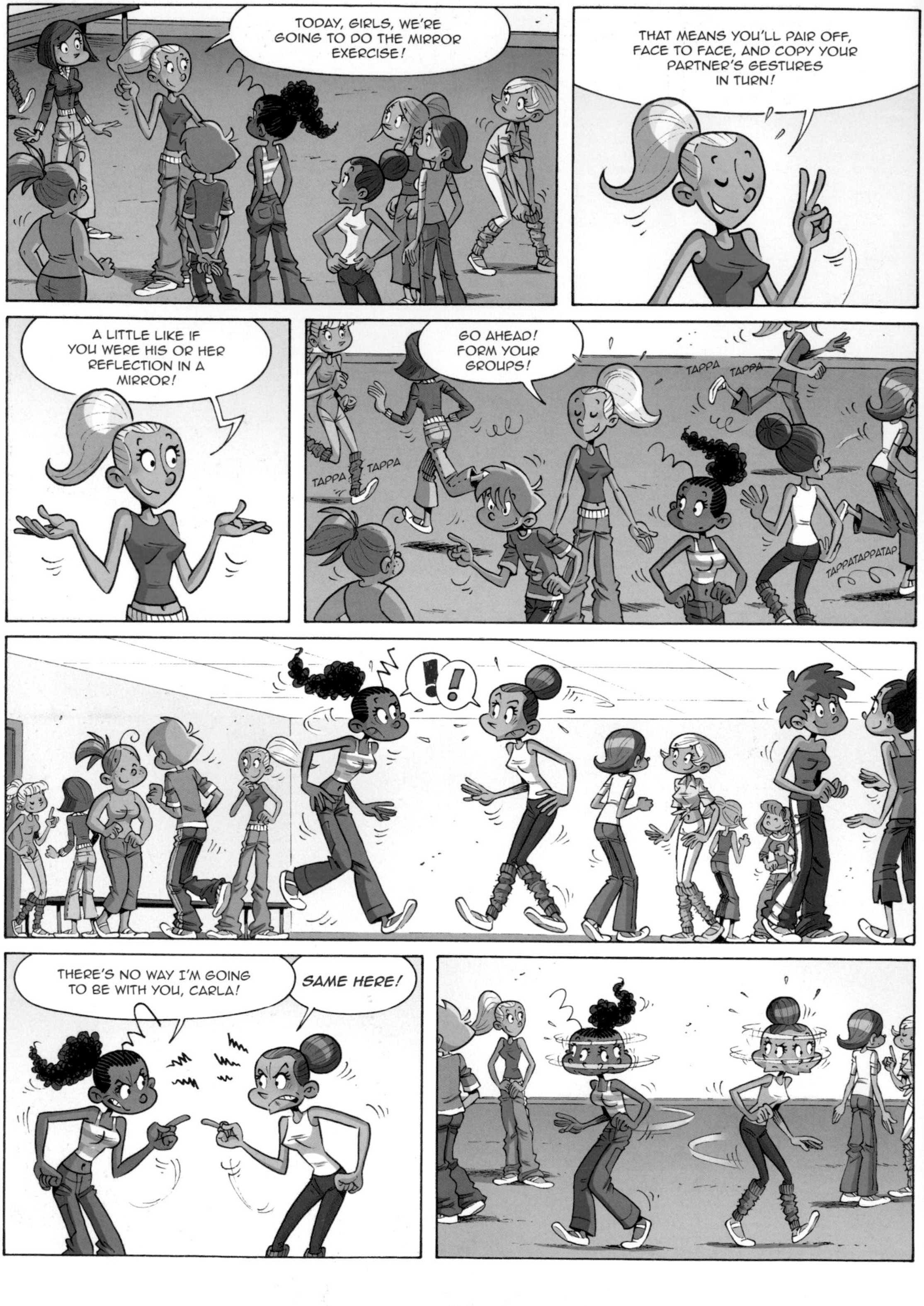
TODAY, GIRLS, WE'RE GOING TO DO THE MIRROR EXERCISE!
THAT MEANS YOU'LL PAIR OFF, FACE TO FACE, AND COPY YOUR PARTNER'S GESTURES IN TURN!
A LITTLE LIKE IF YOU WERE HIS OR HER REFLECTION IN A MIRROR!
GO AHEAD! FORM YOUR GROUPS!
TAPPA TAPPA
TAPPA TAPPA
TAPPATAPPATAP
!
!
THERE'S NO WAY I'M GOING TO BE WITH YOU, CARLA!
SAME HERE!

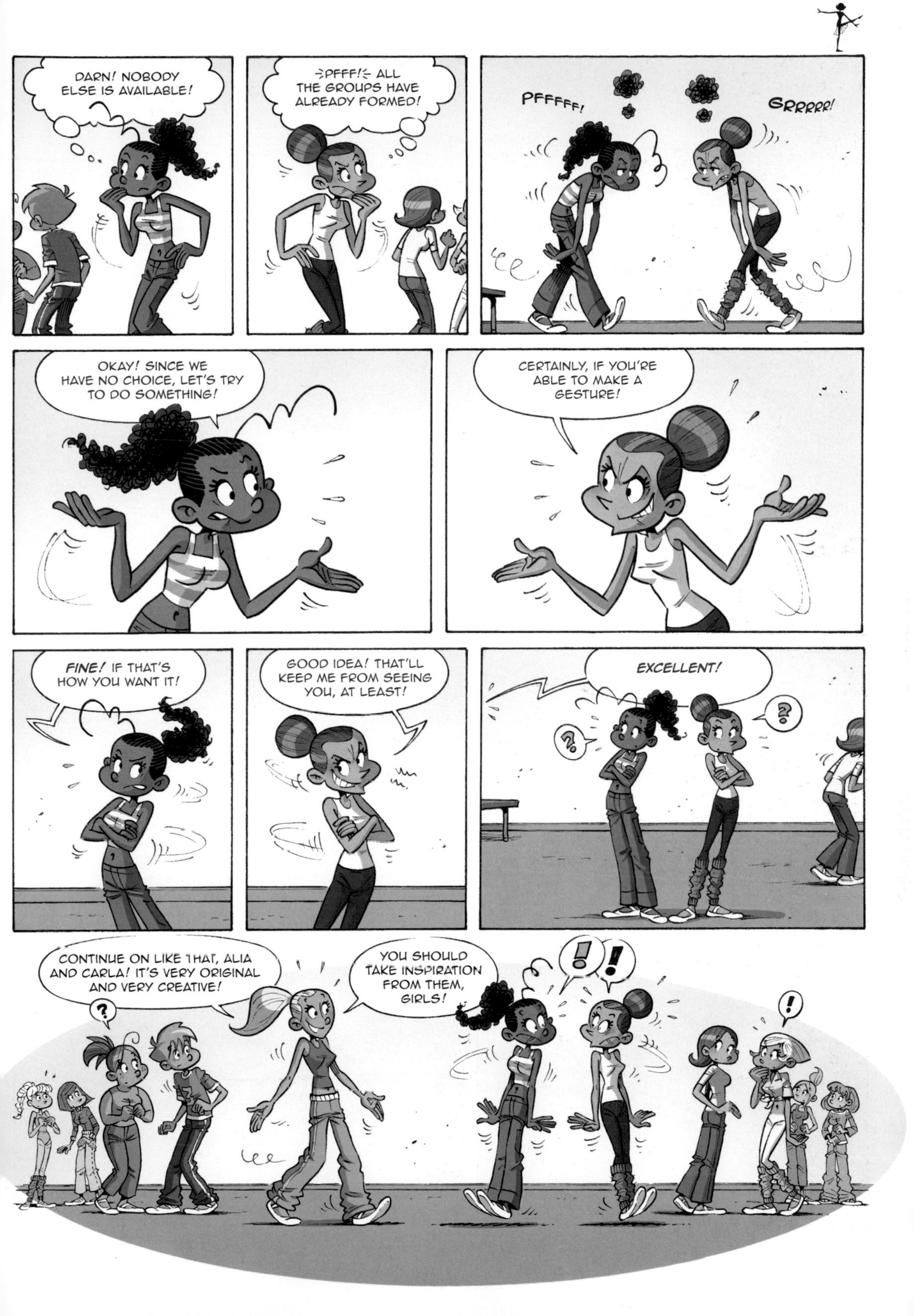
DARN! NOBODY ELSE IS AVAILABLE!
PFFF! ALL THE GROUPS HAVE ALREADY FORMED!
PFFFFF!
GRRRRR!
OKAY! SINCE WE HAVE NO CHOICE, LET'S TRY TO DO SOMETHING!
CERTAINLY, IF YOU'RE ABLE TO MAKE A GESTURE!
FINE! IF THAT'S HOW YOU WANT IT!
GOOD IDEA! THAT'LL KEEP ME FROM SEEING YOU, AT LEAST!
EXCELLENT!
?
?
CONTINUE ON LIKE THAT, ALIA AND CARLA! IT'S VERY ORIGINAL AND VERY CREATIVE!
?
YOU SHOULD TAKE INSPIRATION FROM THEM, GIRLS!
!
!
!

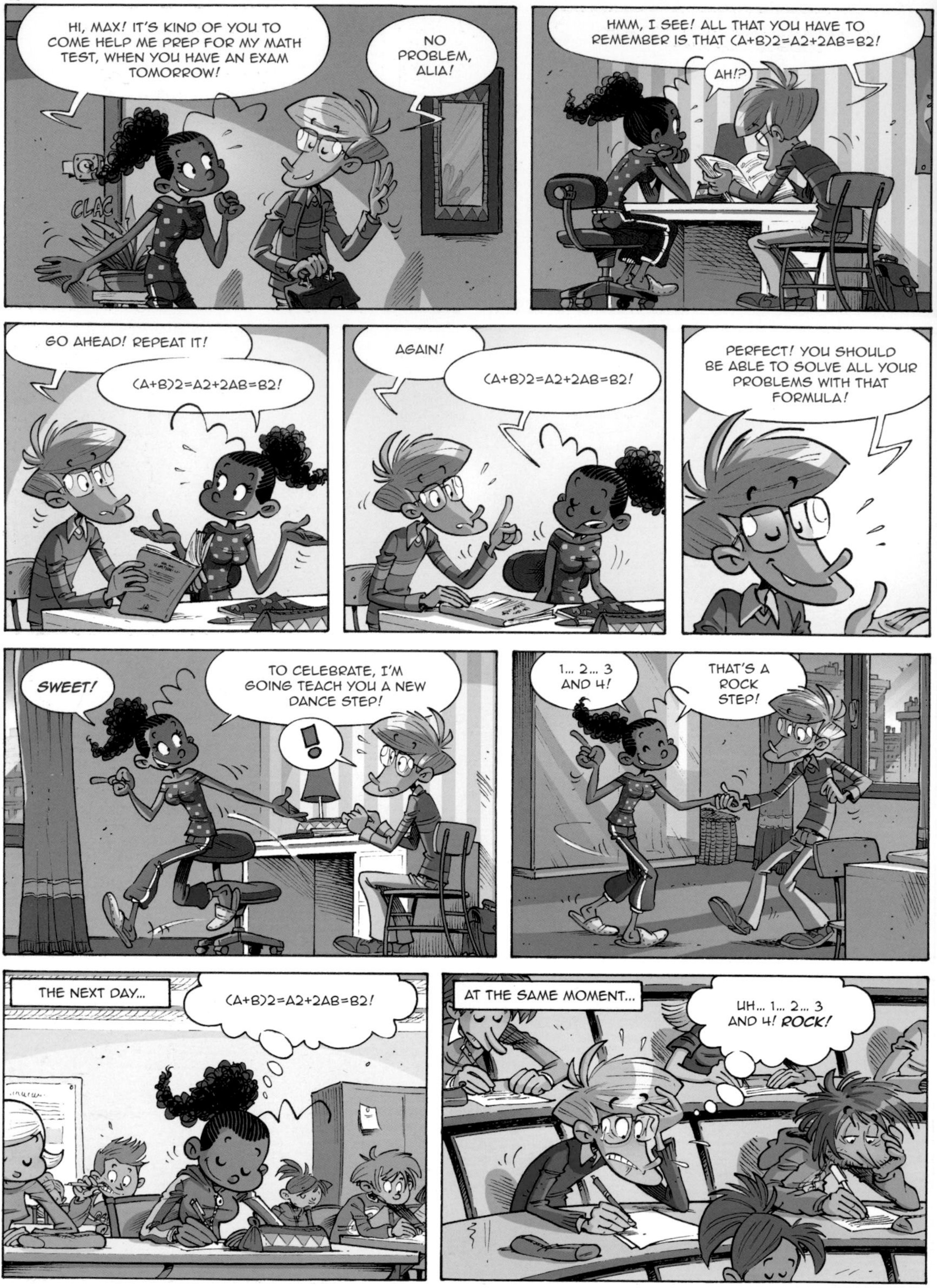
HI, MAX! IT'S KIND OF YOU TO COME HELP ME PREP FOR MY MATH TEST, WHEN YOU HAVE AN EXAM TOMORROW!
NO PROBLEM, ALIA!
CLAC
HMM, I SEE! ALL THAT YOU HAVE TO REMEMBER IS THAT (A+B)2=A2+2AB=B2!
AH!?
GO AHEAD! REPEAT IT!
(A+B)2=A2+2AB=B2!
AGAIN!
(A+B)2=A2+2AB=B2!
PERFECT! YOU SHOULD BE ABLE TO SOLVE ALL YOUR PROBLEMS WITH THAT FORMULA!
SWEET!
TO CELEBRATE, I'M GOING TEACH YOU A NEW DANCE STEP!
!
1... 2... 3 AND 4!
THAT'S A ROCK STEP!
THE NEXT DAY...
(A+B)2=A2+2AB=B2!
AT THE SAME MOMENT...
UH... 1... 2... 3 AND 4! ROCK!

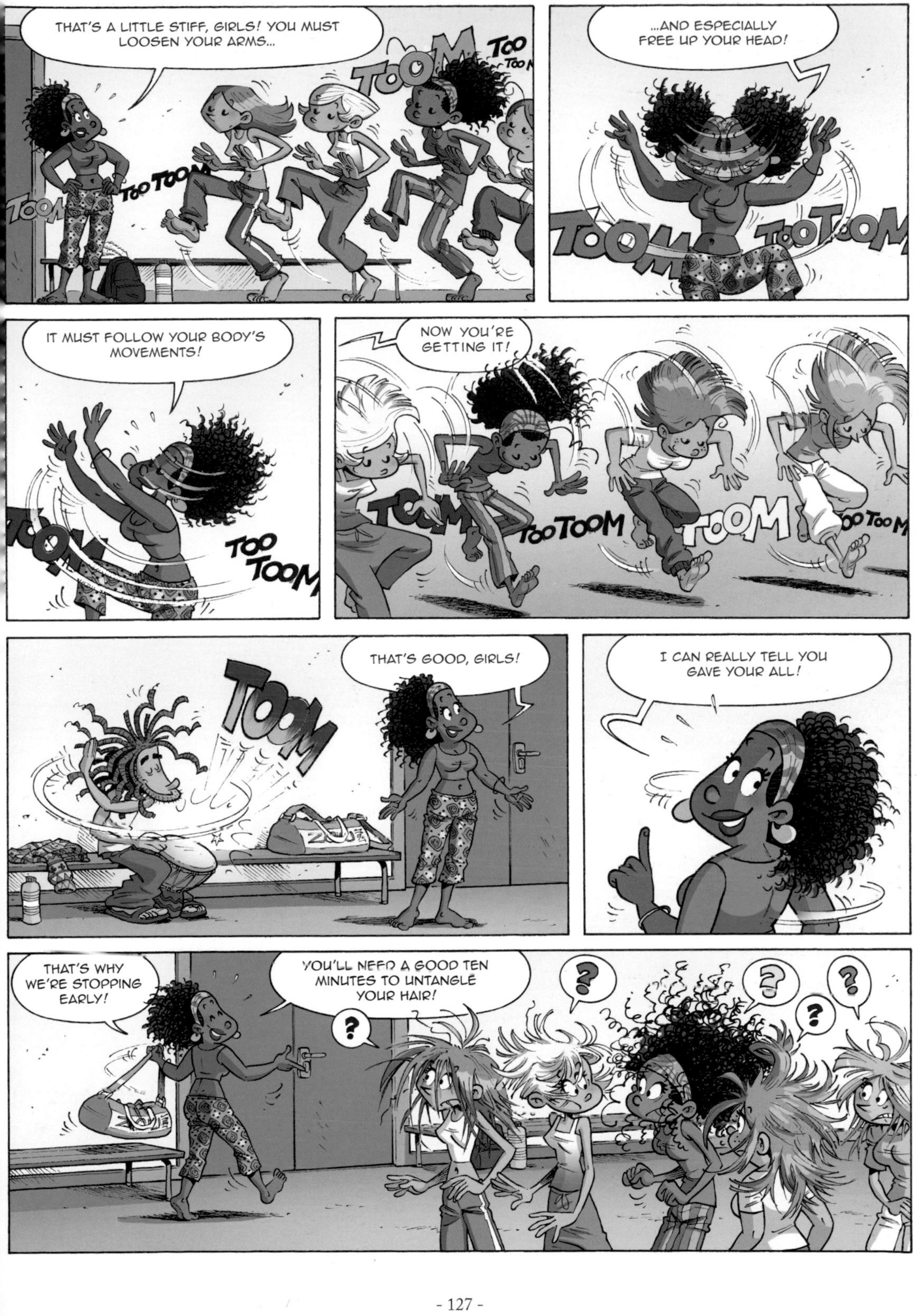
THAT'S A LITTLE STIFF, GIRLS! YOU MUST LOOSEN YOUR ARMS...
TOOM
TOO TOOM
TOOM
TOO TOOM
...AND ESPECIALLY FREE UP YOUR HEAD!
TOOM
TOO TOOM
IT MUST FOLLOW YOUR BODY'S MOVEMENTS!
TOOM
TOO TOOM
NOW YOU'RE GETTING IT!
TOOM
TOO TOOM
TOOM
TOO TOOM
TOOM
THAT'S GOOD, GIRLS!
I CAN REALLY TELL YOU GAVE YOUR ALL!
THAT'S WHY WE'RE STOPPING EARLY!
YOU'LL NEED A GOOD TEN MINUTES TO UNTANGLE YOUR HAIR!
?
?
?
?
?

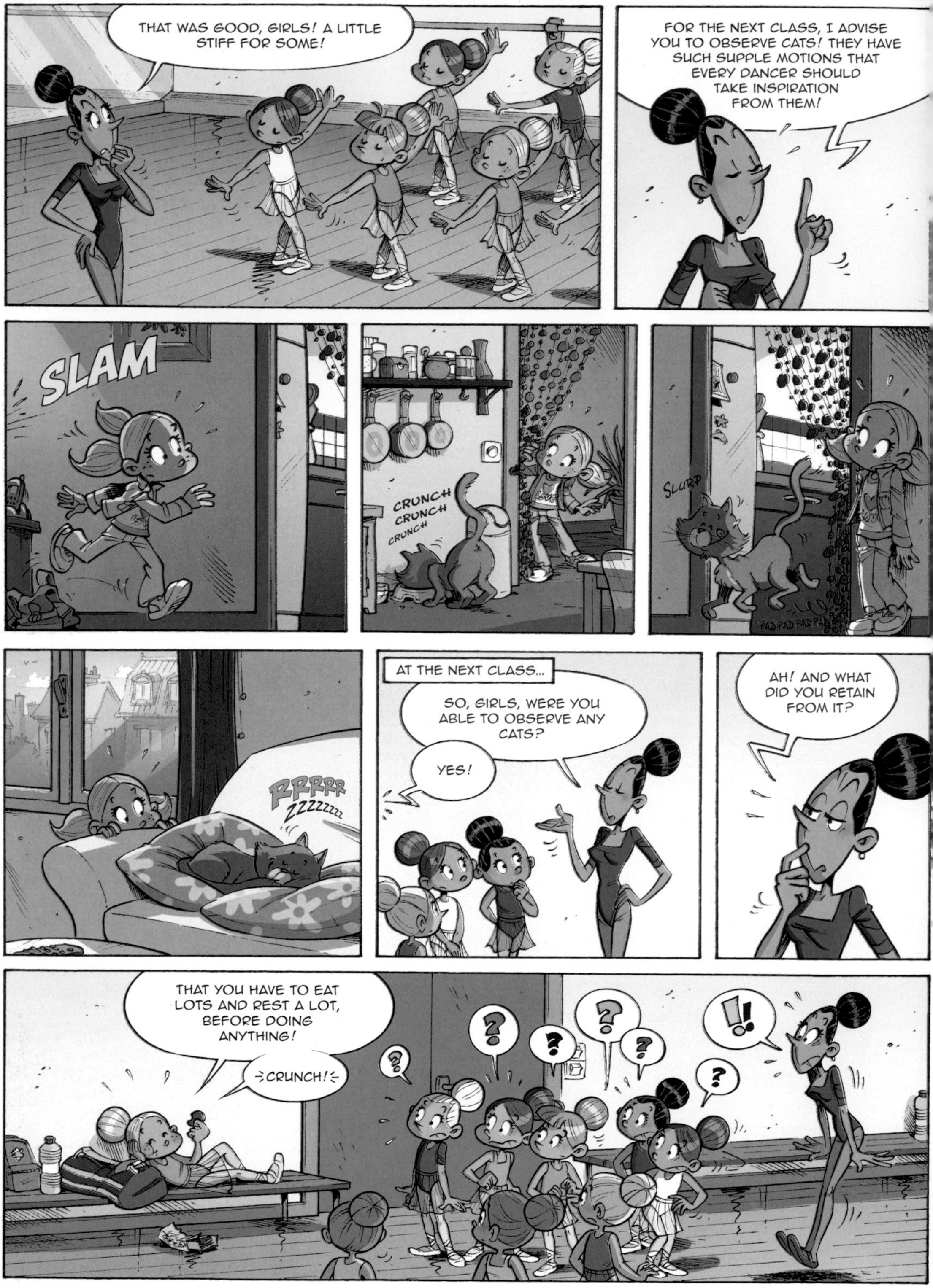

THAT WAS GOOD, GIRLS! A LITTLE STIFF FOR SOME!
FOR THE NEXT CLASS, I ADVISE YOU TO OBSERVE CATS! THEY HAVE SUCH SUPPLE MOTIONS THAT EVERY DANCER SHOULD TAKE INSPIRATION FROM THEM!
SLAM
CRUNCH
CRUNCH
CRUNCH
SLURP
PAD PAD PAD PAD
RRRRR
ZZZZZZZZ
AT THE NEXT CLASS...
SO, GIRLS, WERE YOU ABLE TO OBSERVE ANY CATS?
YES!
AH! AND WHAT DID YOU RETAIN FROM IT?
THAT YOU HAVE TO EAT LOTS AND REST A LOT, BEFORE DOING ANYTHING!
CRUNCH!
?
?
?
?
?
?
!!

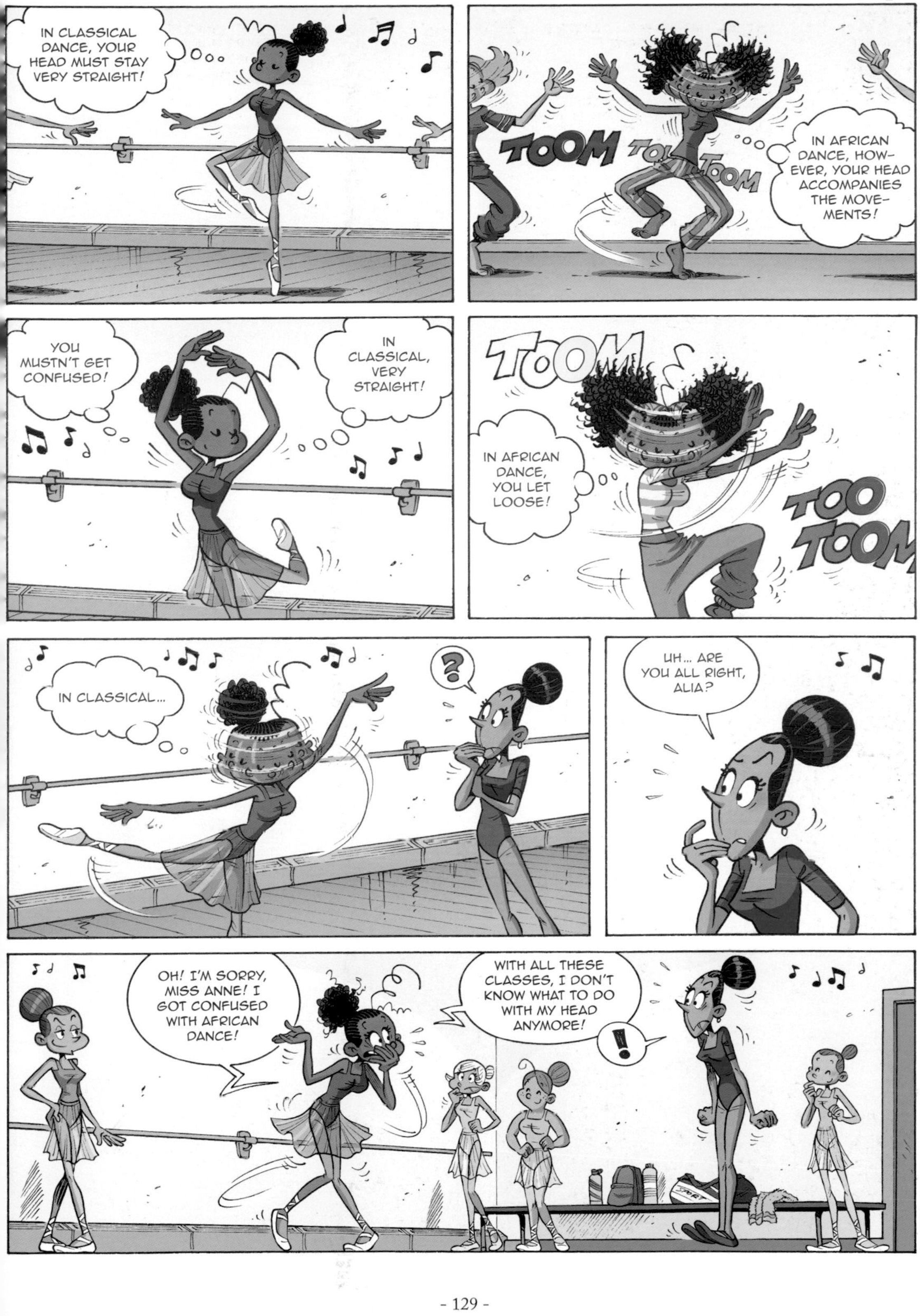
IN CLASSICAL DANCE, YOUR HEAD MUST STAY VERY STRAIGHT!
TOOM TO! TOOM
IN AFRICAN DANCE, HOW-EVER, YOUR HEAD ACCOMPANIES THE MOVE-MENTS!
YOU MUSTN'T GET CONFUSED!
IN CLASSICAL, VERY STRAIGHT!
TOOM
IN AFRICAN DANCE, YOU LET LOOSE!
TOO TOOM
IN CLASSICAL...
?
UH... ARE YOU ALL RIGHT, ALIA?
OH! I'M SORRY, MISS ANNE! I GOT CONFUSED WITH AFRICAN DANCE!
WITH ALL THESE CLASSES, I DON'T KNOW WHAT TO DO WITH MY HEAD ANYMORE!
!

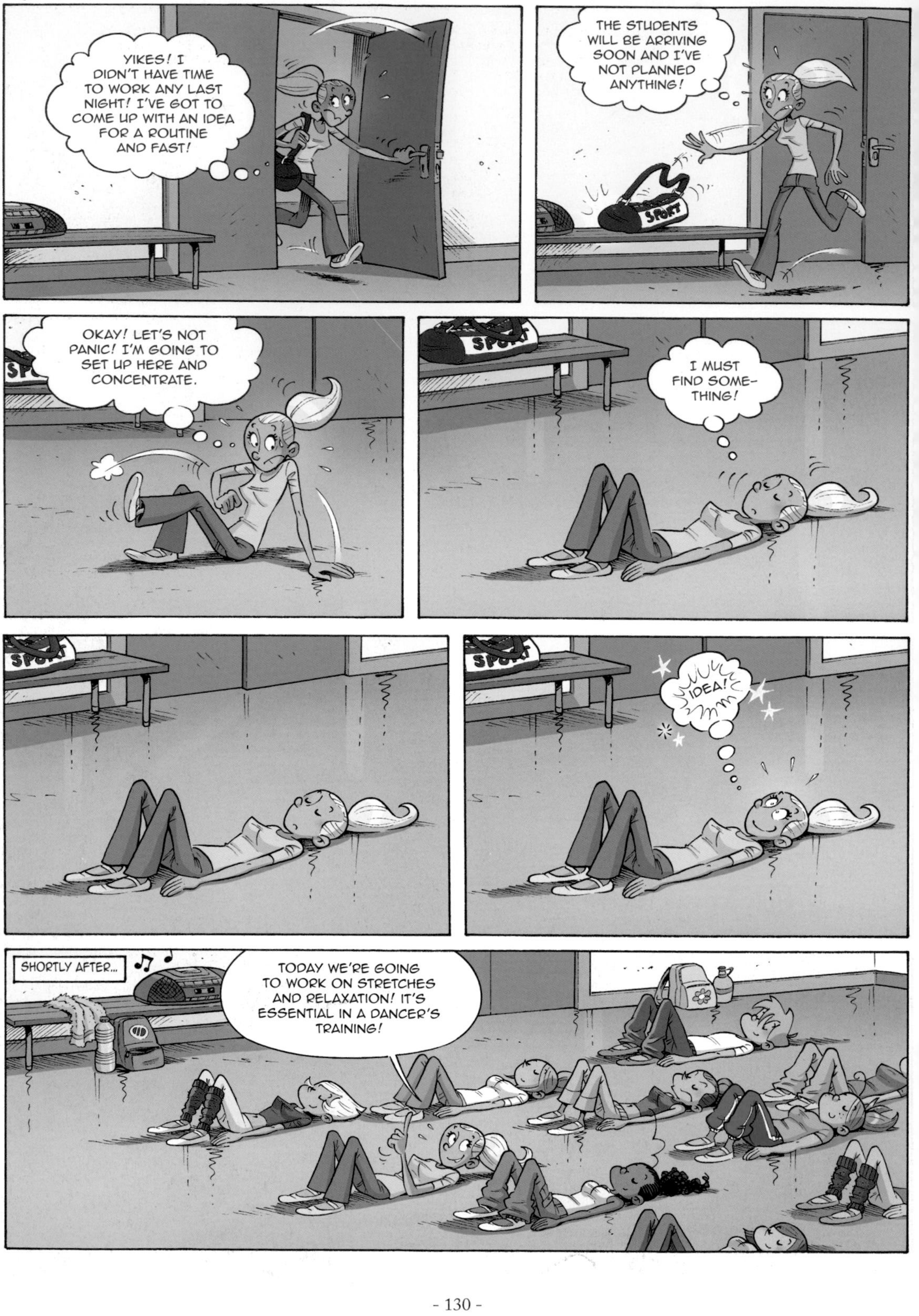
YIKES! I DIDN'T HAVE TIME TO WORK ANY LAST NIGHT! I'VE GOT TO COME UP WITH AN IDEA FOR A ROUTINE AND FAST!
THE STUDENTS WILL BE ARRIVING SOON AND I'VE NOT PLANNED ANYTHING!
SPORT
OKAY! LET'S NOT PANIC! I'M GOING TO SET UP HERE AND CONCENTRATE.
I MUST FIND SOME-THING!
IDEA!
SHORTLY AFTER...
TODAY WE'RE GOING TO WORK ON STRETCHES AND RELAXATION! IT'S ESSENTIAL IN A DANCER'S TRAINING!

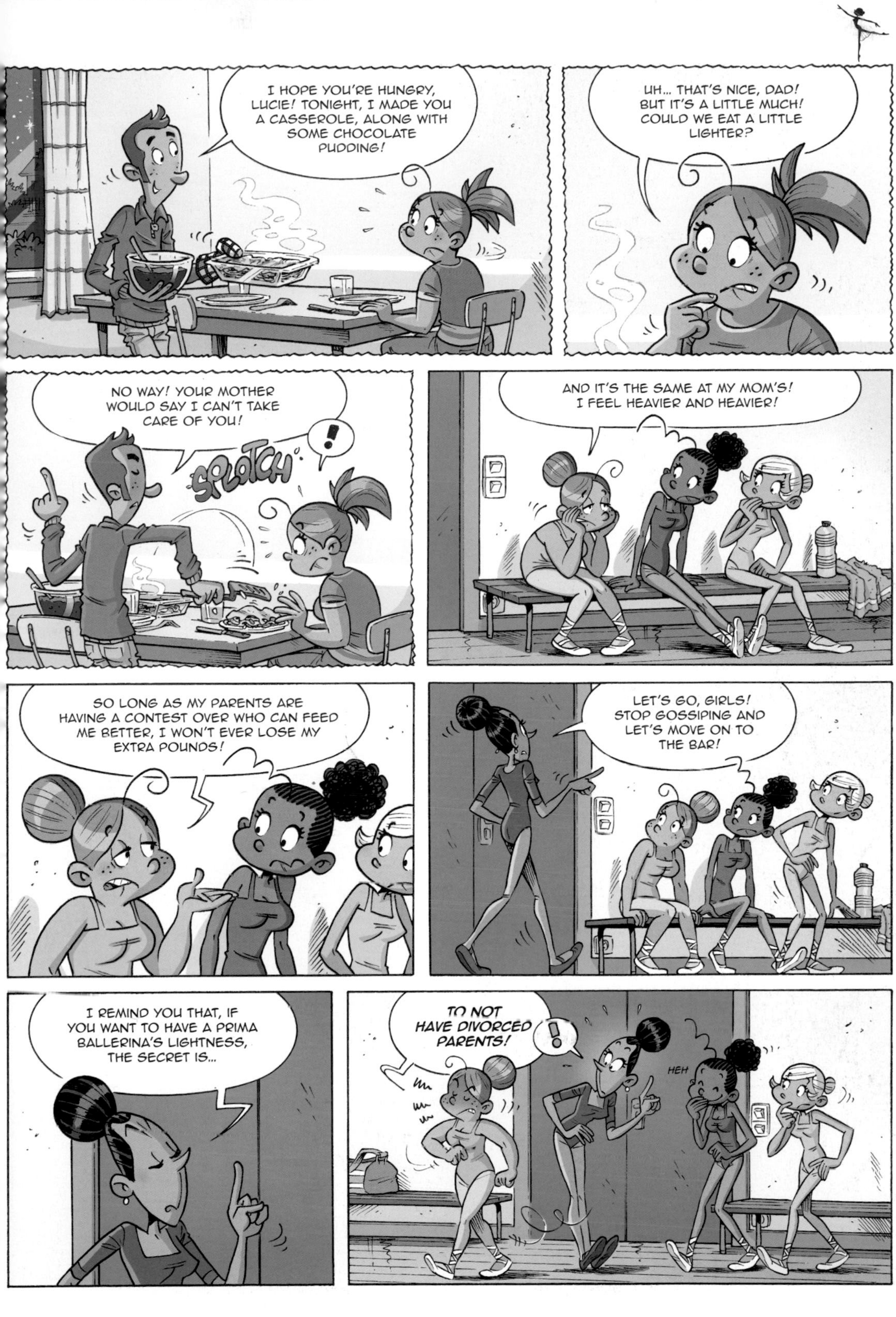

I HOPE YOU'RE HUNGRY, LUCIE! TONIGHT, I MADE YOU A CASSEROLE, ALONG WITH SOME CHOCOLATE PUDDING!
UH... THAT'S NICE, DAD! BUT IT'S A LITTLE MUCH! COULD WE EAT A LITTLE LIGHTER?
NO WAY! YOUR MOTHER WOULD SAY I CAN'T TAKE CARE OF YOU!
SPLOTCH
!
AND IT'S THE SAME AT MY MOM'S! I FEEL HEAVIER AND HEAVIER!
SO LONG AS MY PARENTS ARE HAVING A CONTEST OVER WHO CAN FEED ME BETTER, I WON'T EVER LOSE MY EXTRA POUNDS!
LET'S GO, GIRLS! STOP GOSSIPING AND LET'S MOVE ON TO THE BAR!
I REMIND YOU THAT, IF YOU WANT TO HAVE A PRIMA BALLERINA'S LIGHTNESS, THE SECRET IS...
TO NOT HAVE DIVORCED PARENTS!
!
HEH

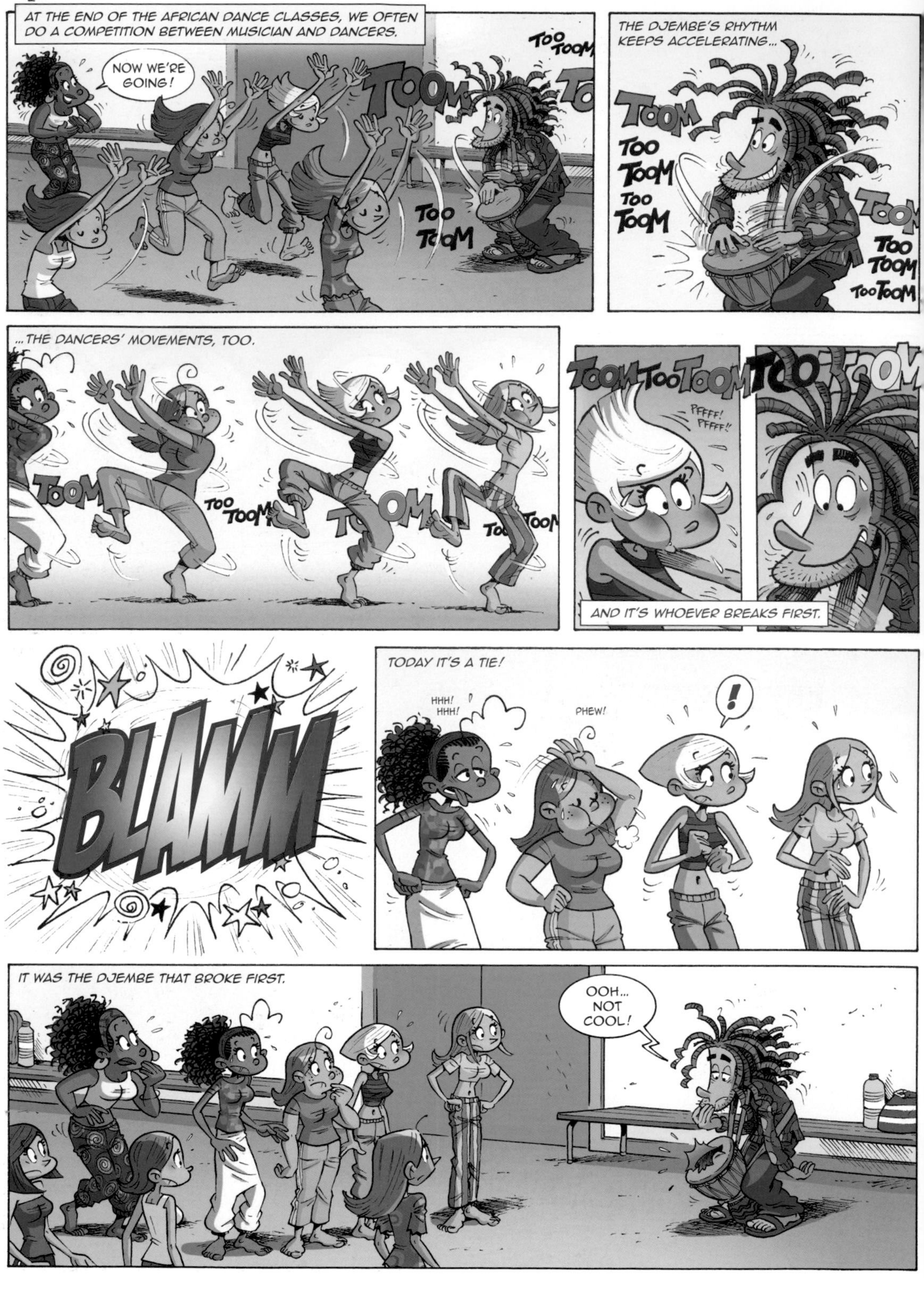
AT THE END OF THE AFRICAN DANCE CLASSES, WE OFTEN DO A COMPETITION BETWEEN MUSICIAN AND DANCERS.
NOW WE'RE GOING!
TOO TOOM
TOOM
TOO TOOM
THE DJEMBE'S RHYTHM KEEPS ACCELERATING...
TOOM
TOO TOOM
TOO TOOM
TOO TOOM TOO TOOM
...THE DANCERS' MOVEMENTS, TOO.
TOOM
TOO TOOM
PFFFF! PFFFF!
AND IT'S WHOEVER BREAKS FIRST.
BLAMM
TODAY IT'S A TIE!
HHH! HHH!
PHEW!
!
IT WAS THE DJEMBE THAT BROKE FIRST.
OOH... NOT COOL!

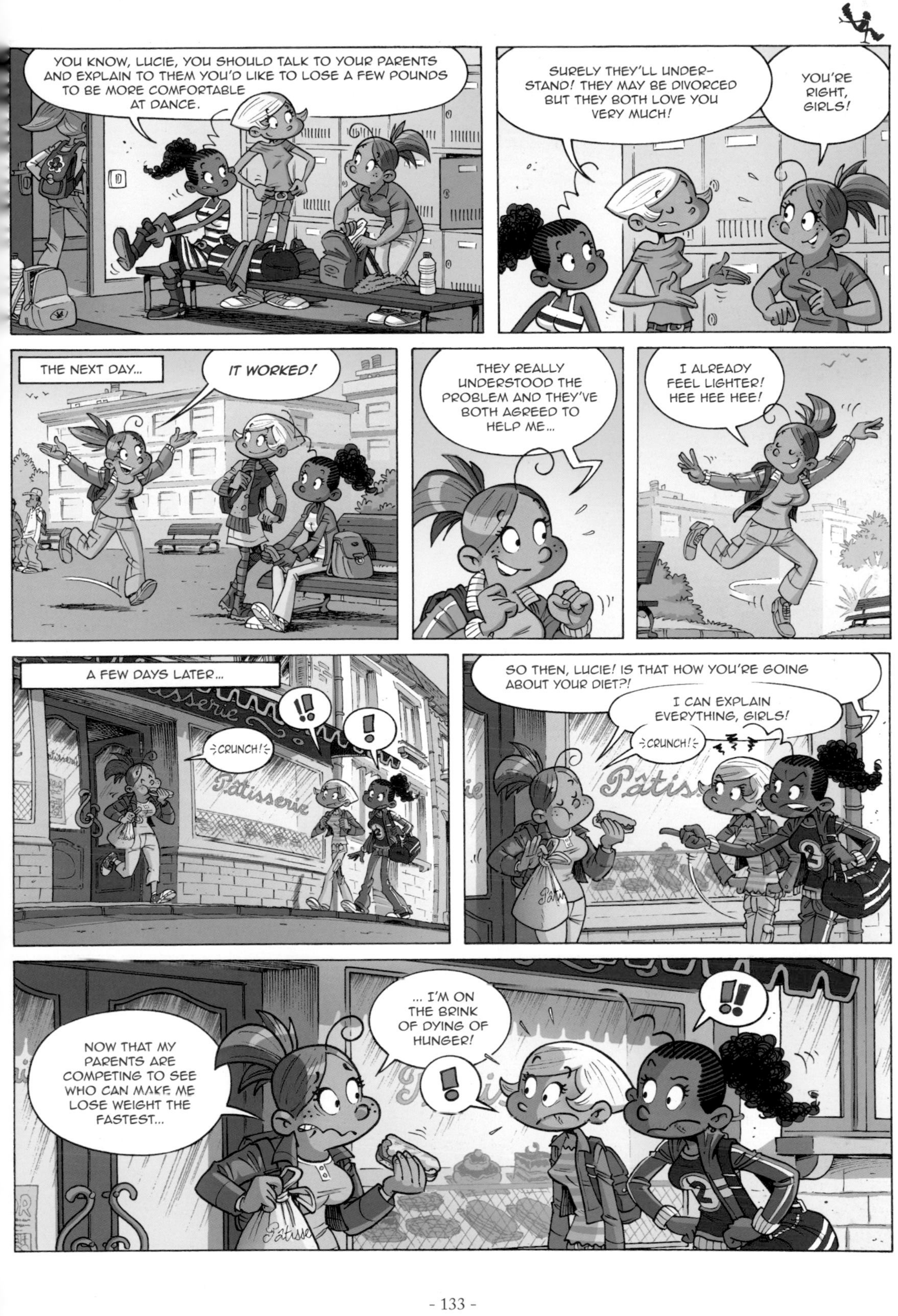
YOU KNOW, LUCIE, YOU SHOULD TALK TO YOUR PARENTS AND EXPLAIN TO THEM YOU'D LIKE TO LOSE A FEW POUNDS TO BE MORE COMFORTABLE AT DANCE.
SURELY THEY'LL UNDER-STAND! THEY MAY BE DIVORCED BUT THEY BOTH LOVE YOU VERY MUCH!
YOU'RE RIGHT, GIRLS!
THE NEXT DAY...
IT WORKED!
THEY REALLY UNDERSTOOD THE PROBLEM AND THEY'VE BOTH AGREED TO HELP ME...
I ALREADY FEEL LIGHTER! HEE HEE HEE!
A FEW DAYS LATER...
CRUNCH!
!!
!
Pâtisserie
SO THEN, LUCIE! IS THAT HOW YOU'RE GOING ABOUT YOUR DIET?!
I CAN EXPLAIN EVERYTHING, GIRLS!
CRUNCH!
NOW THAT MY PARENTS ARE COMPETING TO SEE WHO CAN MAKE ME LOSE WEIGHT THE FASTEST...
... I'M ON THE BRINK OF DYING OF HUNGER!
!
!!

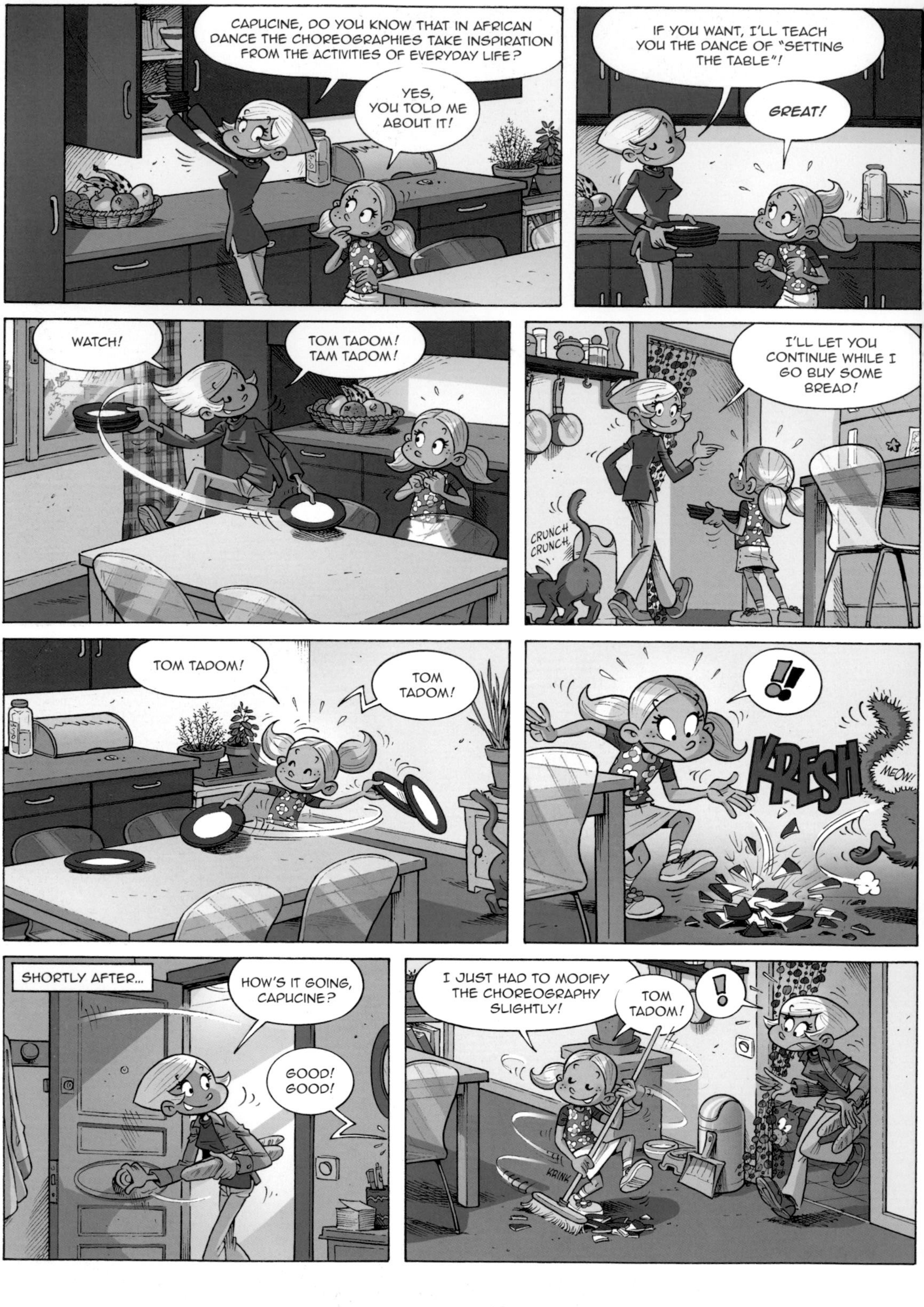
CAPUCINE, DO YOU KNOW THAT IN AFRICAN DANCE THE CHOREOGRAPHIES TAKE INSPIRATION FROM THE ACTIVITIES OF EVERYDAY LIFE?
YES, YOU TOLD ME ABOUT IT!
IF YOU WANT, I'LL TEACH YOU THE DANCE OF "SETTING THE TABLE"!
GREAT!
WATCH!
TOM TADOM! TAM TADOM!
I'LL LET YOU CONTINUE WHILE I GO BUY SOME BREAD!
CRUNCH CRUNCH
TOM TADOM!
TOM TADOM!
!!
KRESH
MEOW!
SHORTLY AFTER...
HOW'S IT GOING, CAPUCINE?
GOOD! GOOD!
I JUST HAD TO MODIFY THE CHOREOGRAPHY SLIGHTLY!
TOM TADOM!
!
KRINK

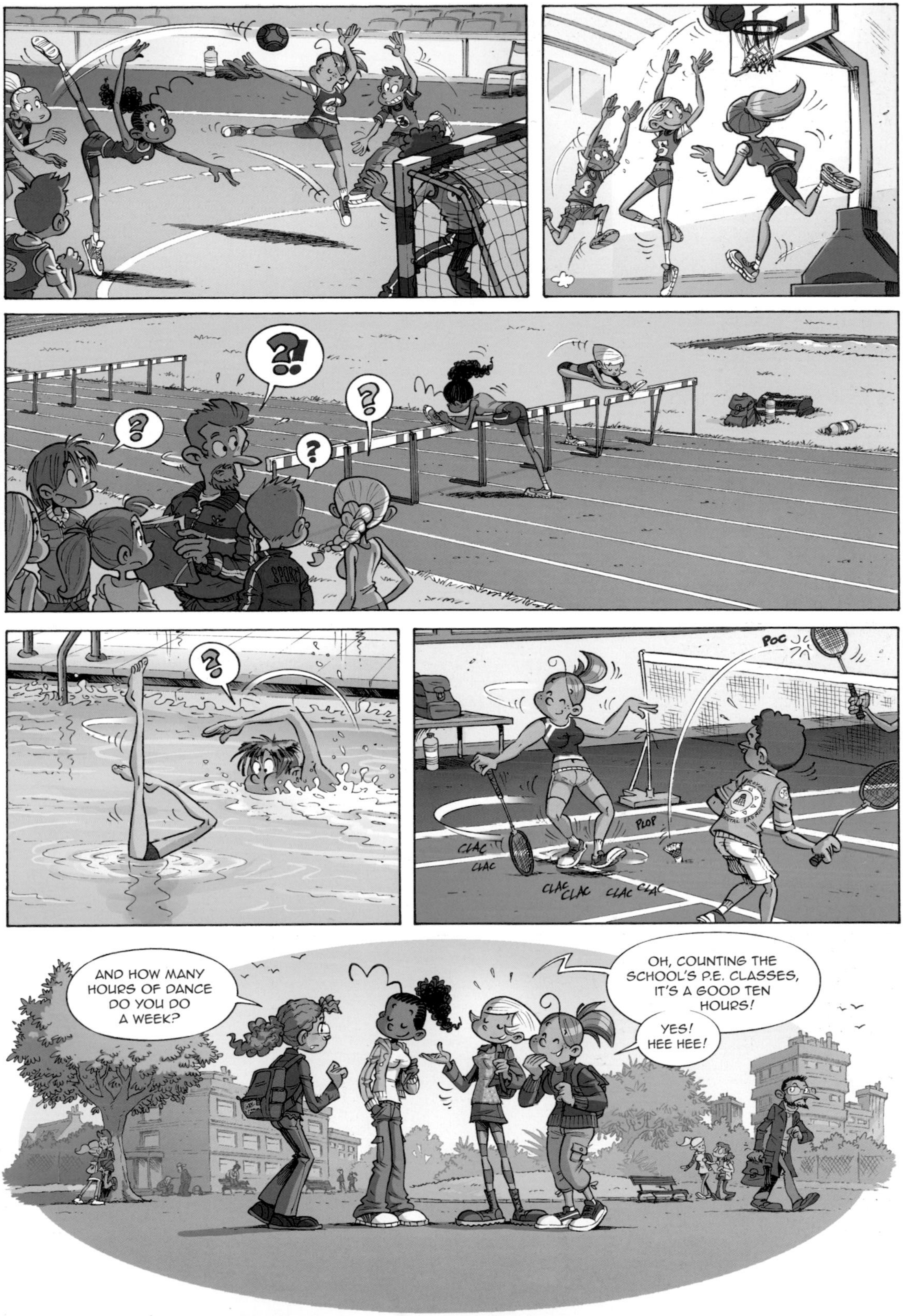
?!
?
?
?
?
POC
PLOP
CLAC
CLAC
CLAC CLAC CLAC CLAC
AND HOW MANY HOURS OF DANCE DO YOU DO A WEEK?
OH, COUNTING THE SCHOOL'S P.E. CLASSES, IT'S A GOOD TEN HOURS!
YES! HEE HEE!

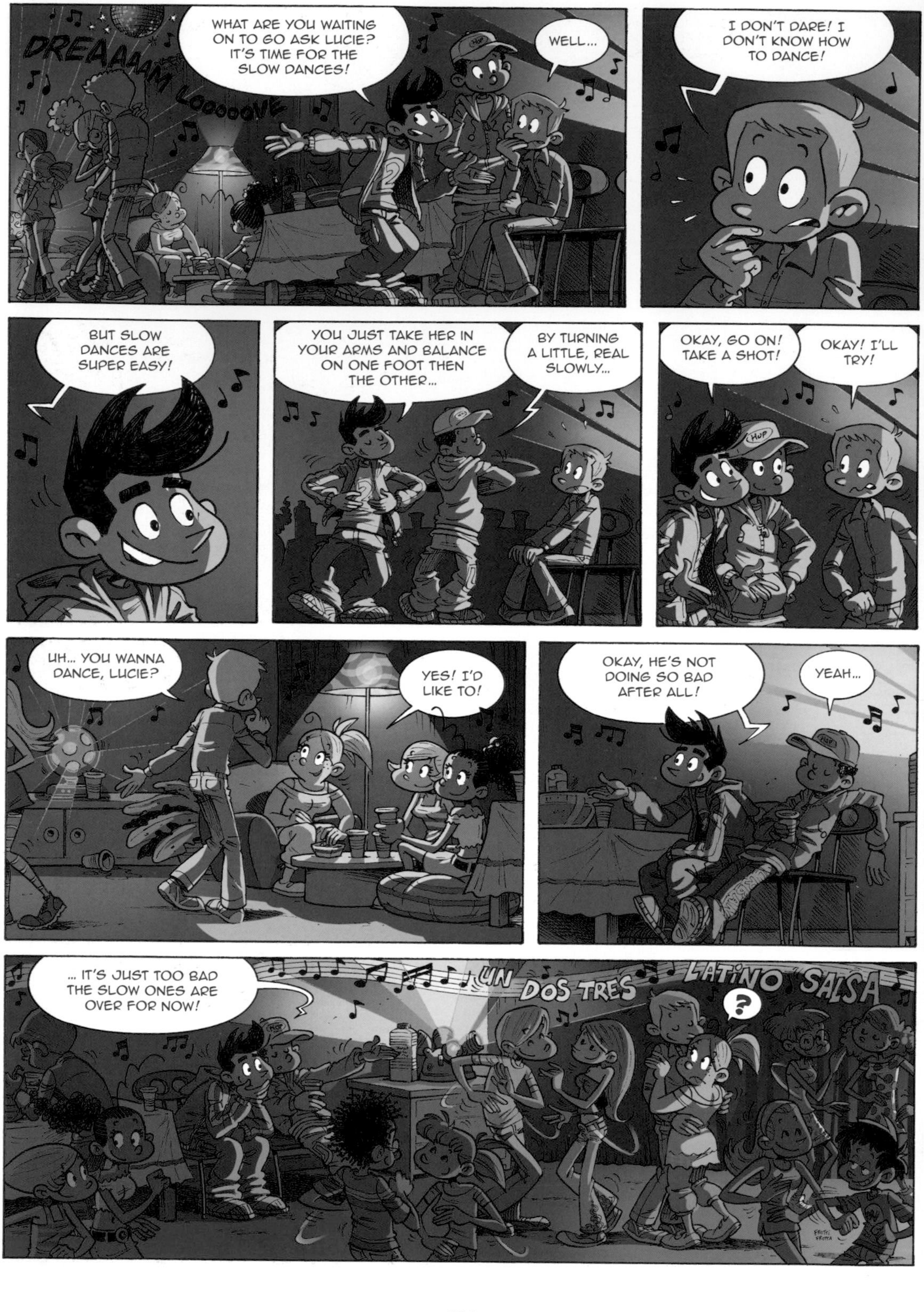
DREAAAAAM LOOOOOOVE
WHAT ARE YOU WAITING ON TO GO ASK LUCIE? IT'S TIME FOR THE SLOW DANCES!
WELL...
I DON'T DARE! I DON'T KNOW HOW TO DANCE!
BUT SLOW DANCES ARE SUPER EASY!
YOU JUST TAKE HER IN YOUR ARMS AND BALANCE ON ONE FOOT THEN THE OTHER...
BY TURNING A LITTLE, REAL SLOWLY...
OKAY, GO ON! TAKE A SHOT!
OKAY! I'LL TRY!
UH... YOU WANNA DANCE, LUCIE?
YES! I'D LIKE TO!
OKAY, HE'S NOT DOING SO BAD AFTER ALL!
YEAH...
... IT'S JUST TOO BAD THE SLOW ONES ARE OVER FOR NOW!
UN DOS TRES LATINO SALSA
?

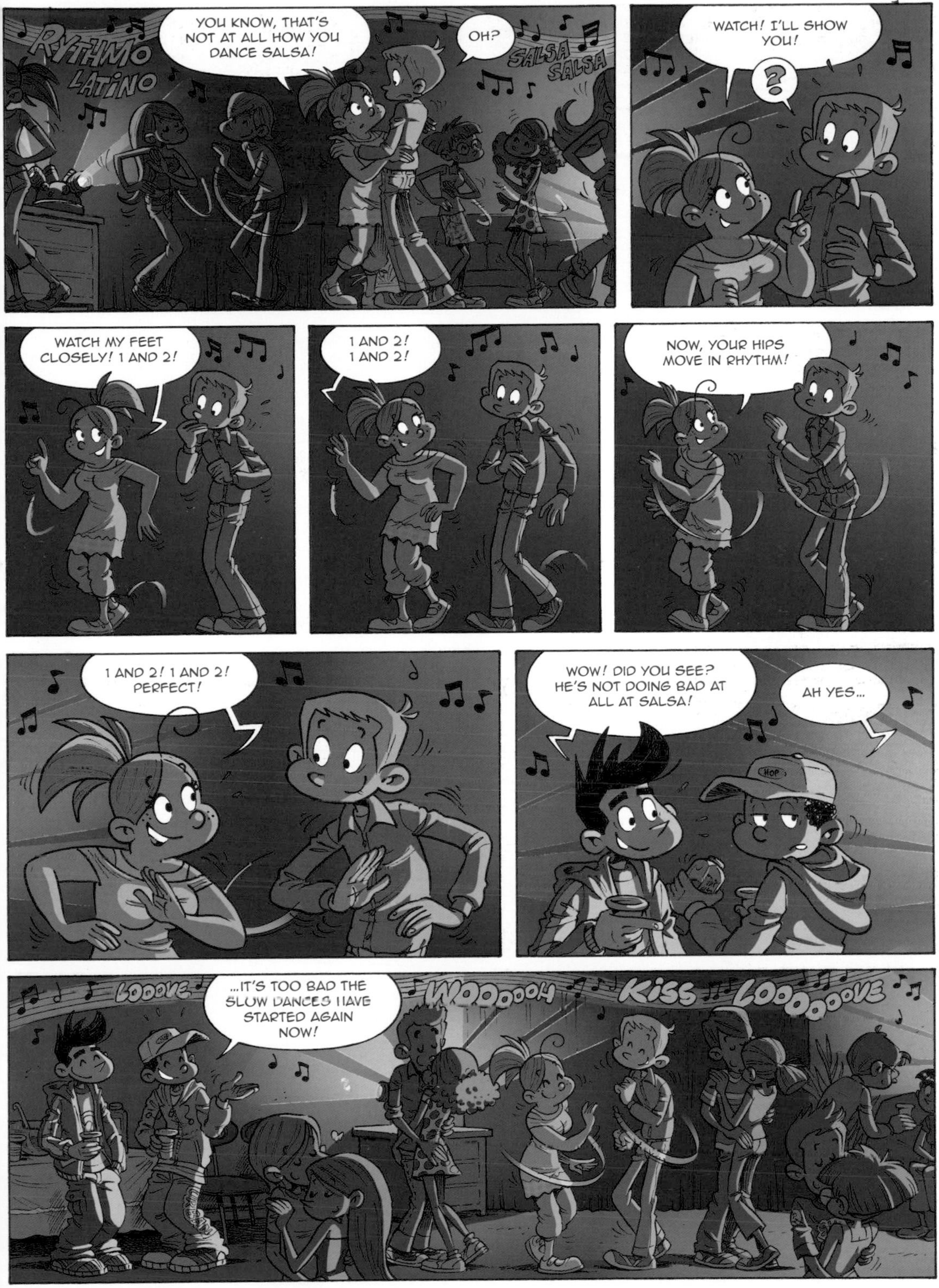
RYTHMO LATINO
YOU KNOW, THAT'S NOT AT ALL HOW YOU DANCE SALSA!
OH?
SALSA SALSA
WATCH! I'LL SHOW YOU!
?
WATCH MY FEET CLOSELY! 1 AND 2!
1 AND 2! 1 AND 2!
NOW, YOUR HIPS MOVE IN RHYTHM!
1 AND 2! 1 AND 2! PERFECT!
WOW! DID YOU SEE? HE'S NOT DOING BAD AT ALL AT SALSA!
AH YES...
HOP
LOOOVE
...IT'S TOO BAD THE SLOW DANCES HAVE STARTED AGAIN NOW!
WOOOOOOH
KISS
LOOOOOOVE

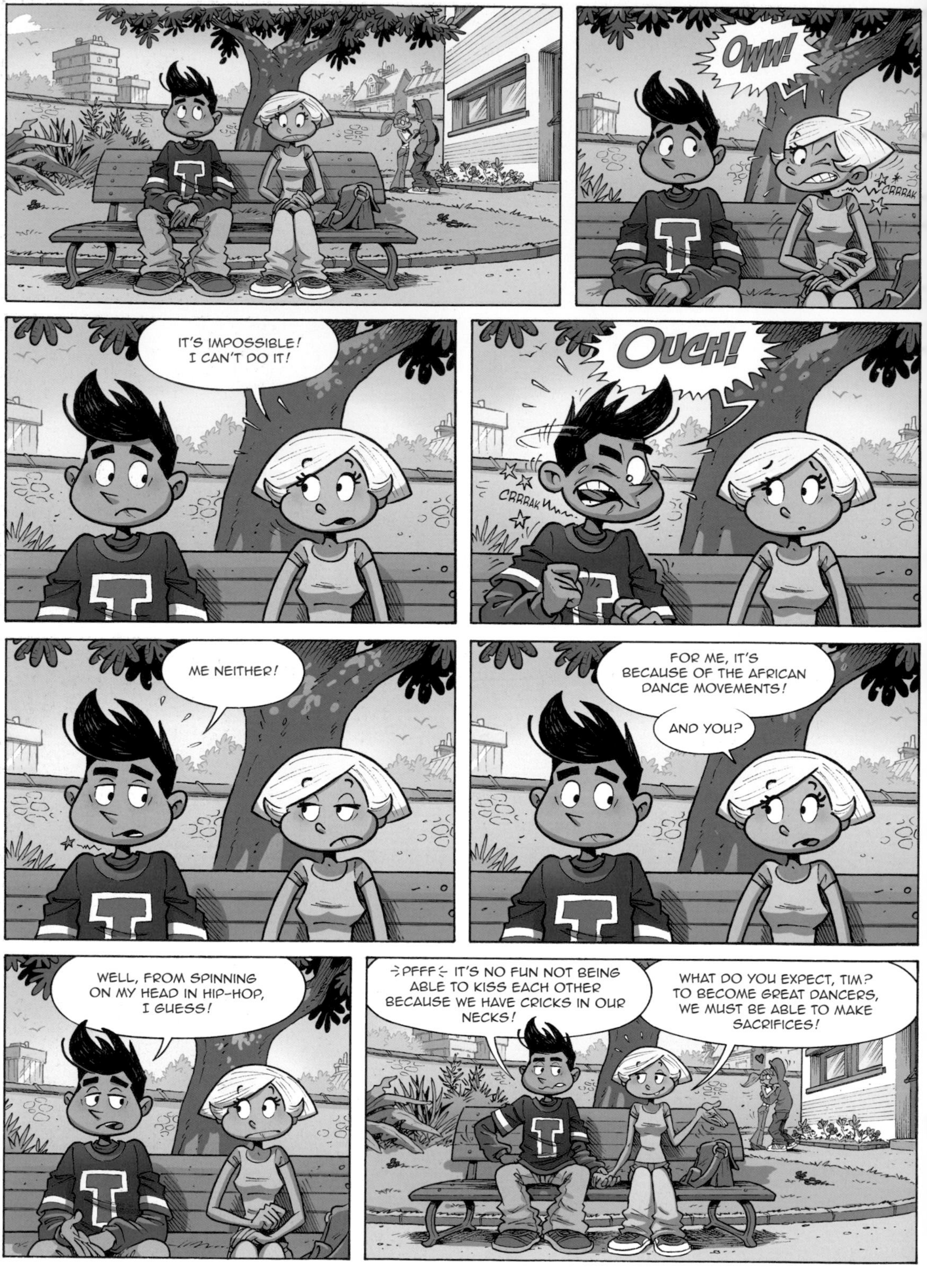
OWW!
CRRRAK
IT'S IMPOSSIBLE! I CAN'T DO IT!
OUCH!
CRRRAK
ME NEITHER!
FOR ME, IT'S BECAUSE OF THE AFRICAN DANCE MOVEMENTS!
AND YOU?
WELL, FROM SPINNING ON MY HEAD IN HIP-HOP, I GUESS!
⇒PFFF⇐ IT'S NO FUN NOT BEING ABLE TO KISS EACH OTHER BECAUSE WE HAVE CRICKS IN OUR NECKS!
WHAT DO YOU EXPECT, TIM? TO BECOME GREAT DANCERS, WE MUST BE ABLE TO MAKE SACRIFICES!

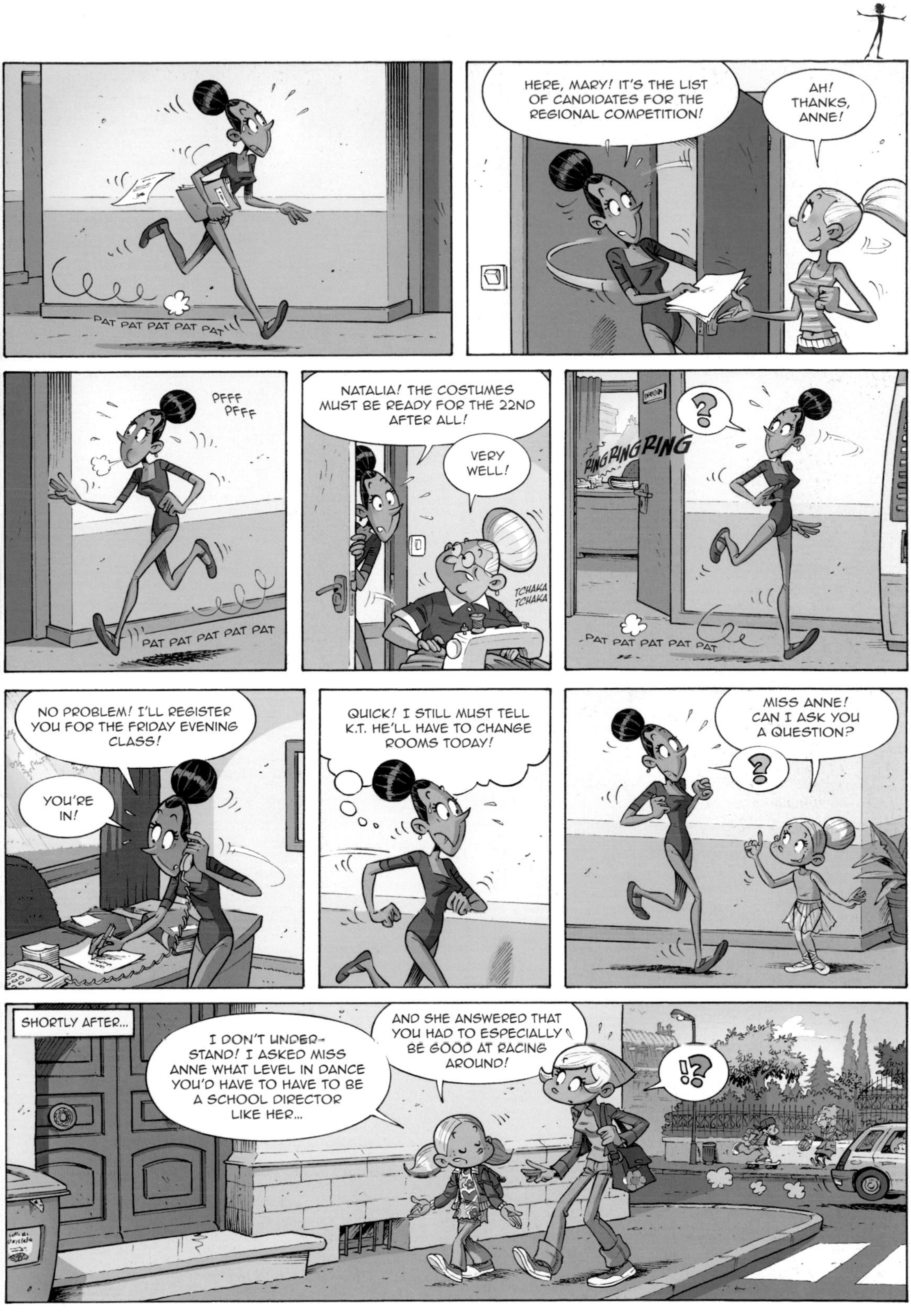
PAT PAT PAT PAT PAT
HERE, MARY! IT'S THE LIST OF CANDIDATES FOR THE REGIONAL COMPETITION!
AH! THANKS, ANNE!
PFFF PFFF
PAT PAT PAT PAT PAT
NATALIA! THE COSTUMES MUST BE READY FOR THE 22ND AFTER ALL!
VERY WELL!
TCHAKA TCHAKA
RING RING RING
?
PAT PAT PAT PAT PAT
NO PROBLEM! I'LL REGISTER YOU FOR THE FRIDAY EVENING CLASS!
YOU'RE IN!
QUICK! I STILL MUST TELL K.T. HE'LL HAVE TO CHANGE ROOMS TODAY!
MISS ANNE! CAN I ASK YOU A QUESTION?
?
SHORTLY AFTER...
I DON'T UNDER-STAND! I ASKED MISS ANNE WHAT LEVEL IN DANCE YOU'D HAVE TO HAVE TO BE A SCHOOL DIRECTOR LIKE HER...
AND SHE ANSWERED THAT YOU HAD TO ESPECIALLY BE GOOD AT RACING AROUND!
!?

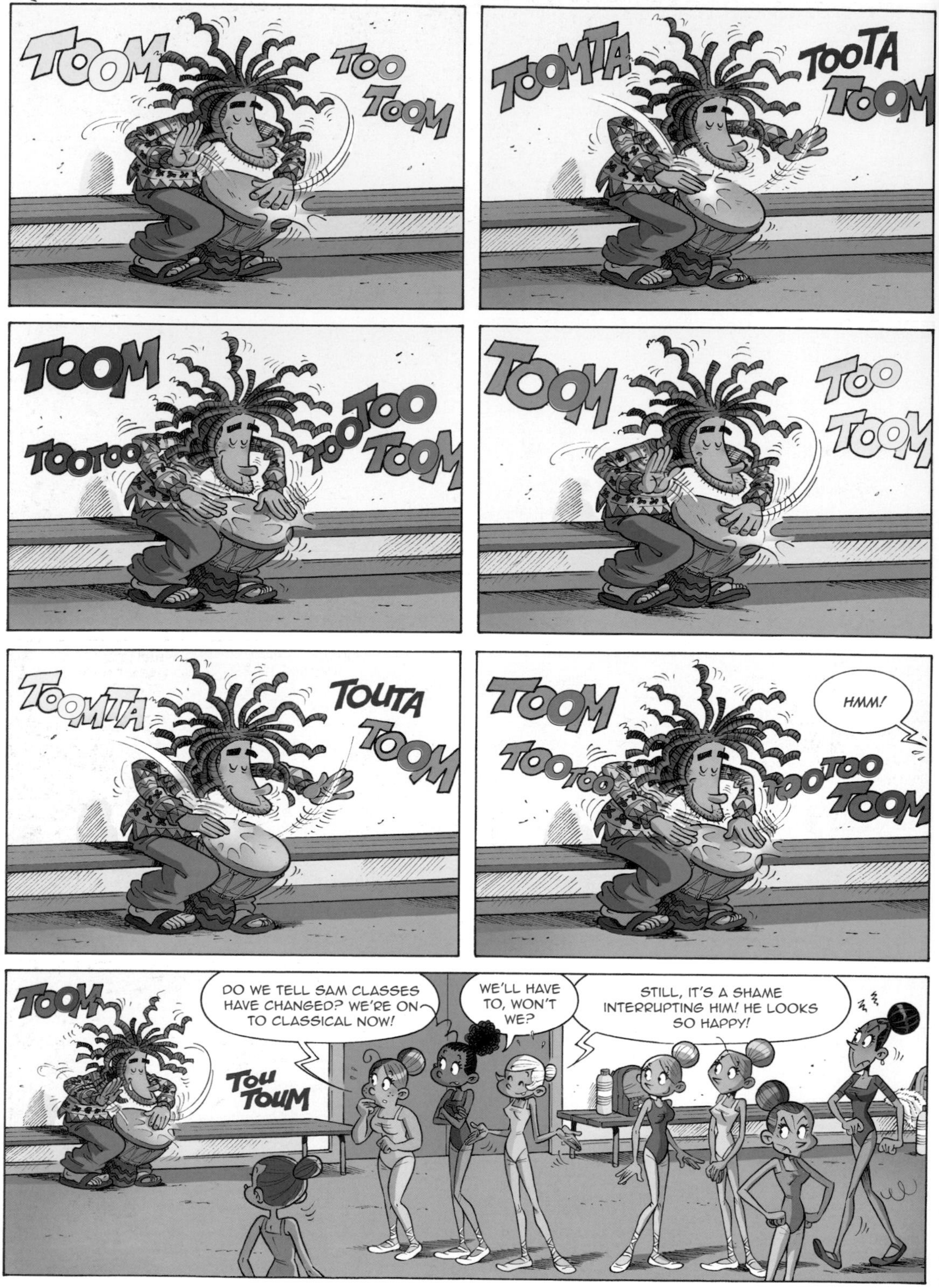
TOOM
TOO
TOOM
TOOMTA
TOOTA
TOOM
TOOM
TOOTOO
TOOTOO
TOOM
TOOM
TOO
TOOM
TOOMTA
TOUTA
TOOM
TOOM
HMM!
TOOTOO
TOOTOO
TOOM
TOOM
TOU
TOUM
DO WE TELL SAM CLASSES HAVE CHANGED? WE'RE ON TO CLASSICAL NOW!
WE'LL HAVE TO, WON'T WE?
STILL, IT'S A SHAME INTERRUPTING HIM! HE LOOKS SO HAPPY!

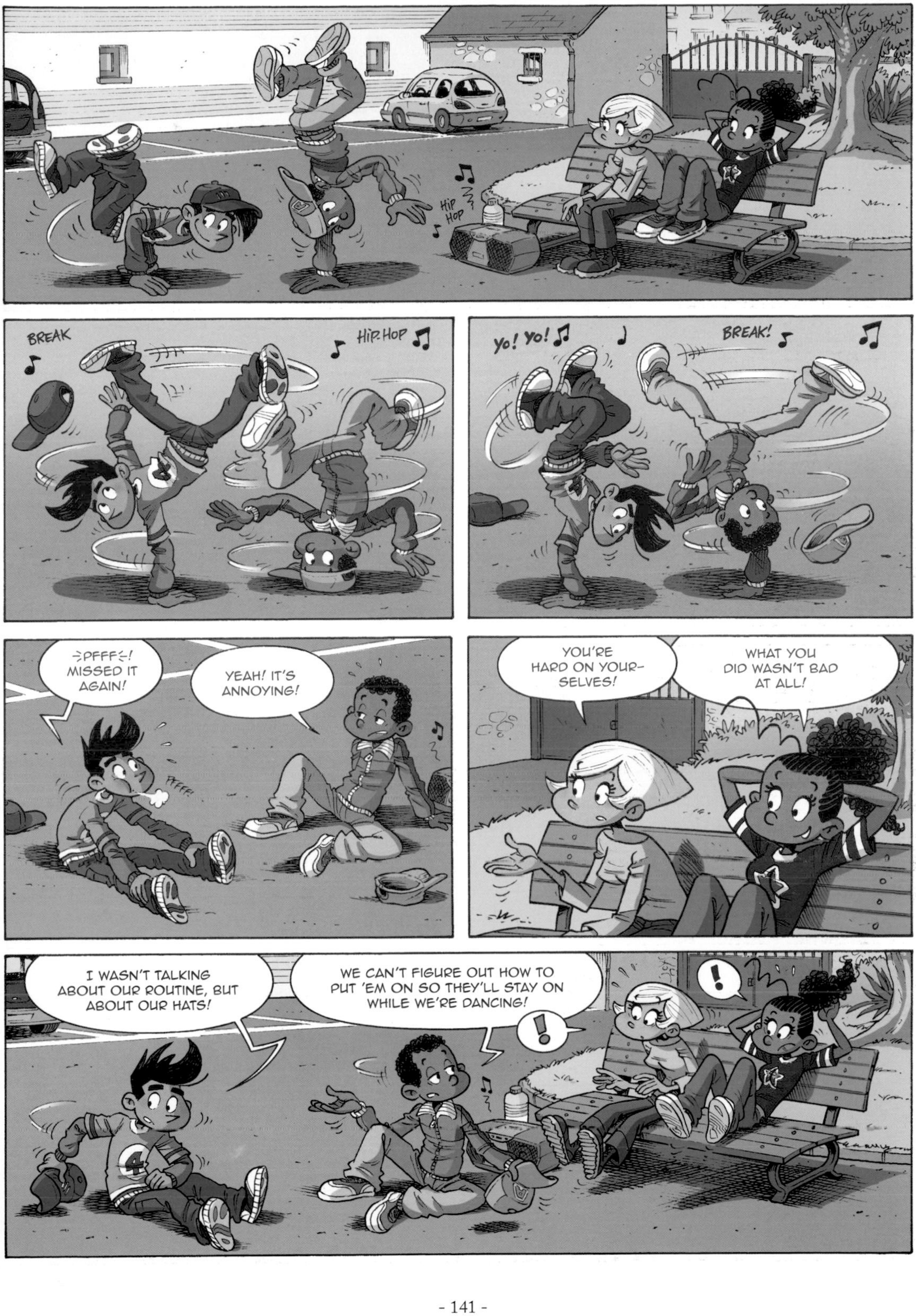

HIP HOP
BREAK
HIP-HOP
YO! YO!
BREAK!
PFFF! MISSED IT AGAIN!
PFFF!
YEAH! IT'S ANNOYING!
YOU'RE HARD ON YOURSELVES!
WHAT YOU DID WASN'T BAD AT ALL!
I WASN'T TALKING ABOUT OUR ROUTINE, BUT ABOUT OUR HATS!
WE CAN'T FIGURE OUT HOW TO PUT 'EM ON SO THEY'LL STAY ON WHILE WE'RE DANCING!
!
!

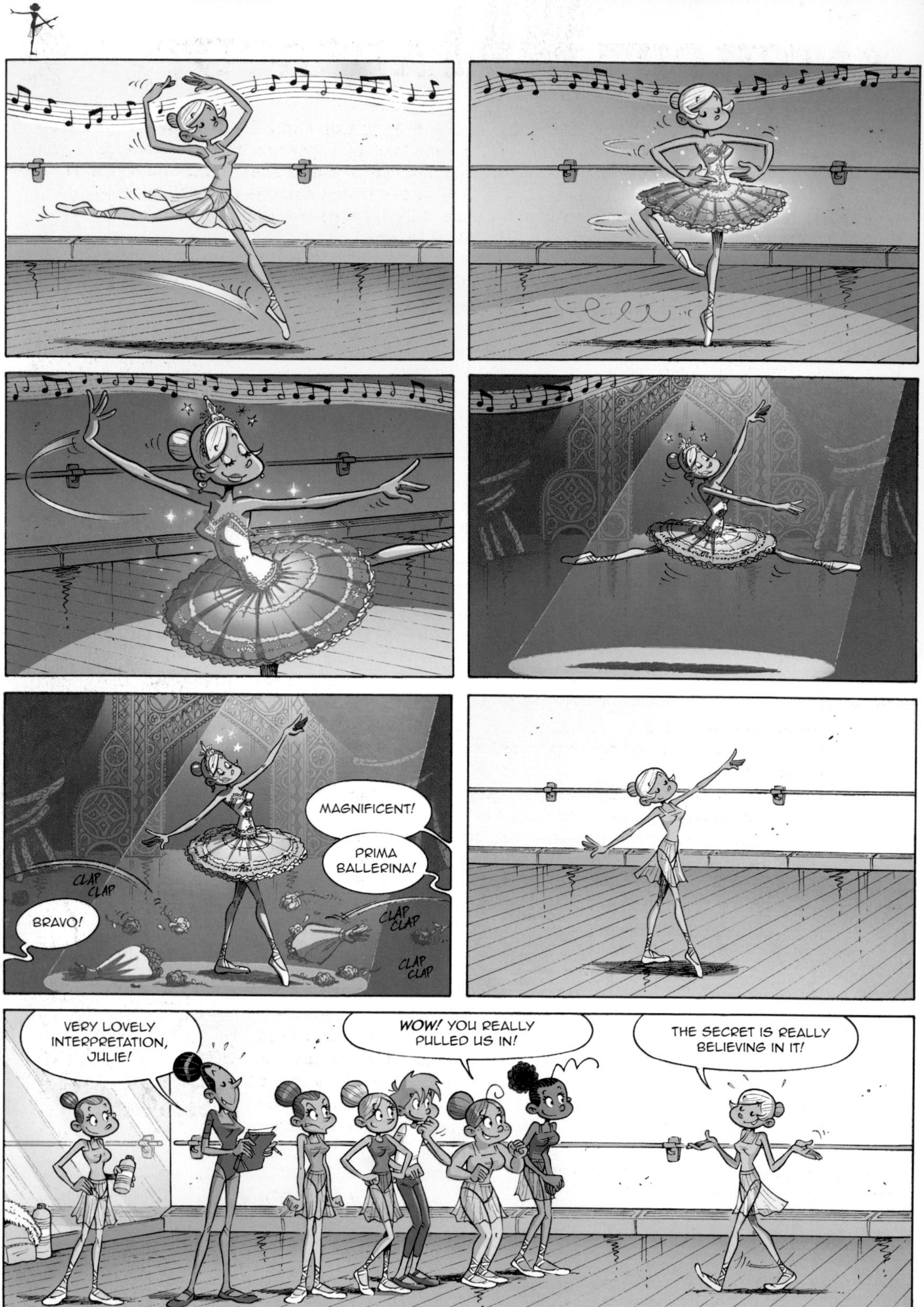
MAGNIFICENT!
PRIMA BALLERINA!
CLAP CLAP
BRAVO!
CLAP CLAP
CLAP CLAP
VERY LOVELY INTERPRETATION, JULIE!
WOW! YOU REALLY PULLED US IN!
THE SECRET IS REALLY BELIEVING IN IT!

WATCH OUT FOR PAPERCUTZ

Welcome to the premiere edition of DANCE CLASS 3 IN 1, by Crip and Béka. I'm Jim "Twinkle-toes" Salicrup, lapsed Ballroom Dance student and Editor-in-Chief of Papercutz, the non-dancing troupe dedicated to publishing great graphic novels for all ages. I'm here to offer a look behind-the-scenes, at the writers and artist who create DANCE CLASS. Since there are two writers and one artist, I'll be bringing you 3 short creator bios in 1 Watch Out for Papercutz page. 3 IN 1, get it? (Sometimes I feel like Luan Loud, Lincoln Loud's standup comedian sister from THE LOUD HOUSE.)

But wait, what this about there being "two" writers on DANCE CLASS? Doesn't it say "Béka – Writer" on page 4 of this graphic novel? Yes, it does, and that's because "Béka" is the name of the writing team of Bertrand Escaich and Caroline Roque. Just like it takes two to Tango, it takes two very talented writers to created DANCE CLASS stories…

Bertrand was born in 1973 in Ariège, France. Because he could only find his favorite *Tintin* and *Asterix* comics in small local bookstores, he was soon compelled to begin writing and drawing his own. Not knowing any artists, he later took his chances on sending a few stories to publishers that he drew himself. Luckily, he was accepted by the publisher *Vents d'Ouest* as an artist. There, he made the acquaintance of Bloz, the future artist of *Fonctionnaires*, and of Poupard, the future artist of *Rugbymen*. In 2002, thanks to Bamboo Editions, he could finally devote himself to his true passion: writing humorous stories. In collaboration with Caroline, he co-writes the gag series *Fourmidables*, *Footmaniacs*, and *Fonctionnaires*. They went on to create the *Rugbymen* and DANCE CLASS series.

Caroline Roque, the other half of the writing team known as Béka, was born in 1975 in Perpignan, France. She soon had her nose buried in books, first to color them, then to read them. Having studied chemistry to reassure her mom that she would find a good job one day, she decided instead to abandon her thesis and devote herself to writing comicbook scripts and novels. One of her stories received the prize for art house cinema in Toulouse, which encouraged her to continue in that direction. Around the time she abandoned her thesis, she met Bertrand and co-created the *Rugbymen* and DANCE CLASS graphic novel series with him.

Crip was born in Saumur, France in 1971. He grew up in Touraine where he spent his youth drawing. He has created illustrations for many publications, as well as posters and cards for various festivals. He has a parallel career as a comicbook artist under several pseudonyms, including Jésus, Prosper Hithonic, and Scriff Potiron. He has published work in anthologies, a small solo volume, and with the publishers La Sirène and Soleil for various volumes of the series *Tout sur*. He also hosts a studio at the Courteline cultural center to teach interested teenage fans how to make comics.

Papercutz has proudly published nine DANCE CLASS graphic novels, and we're now happy to be collecting them all in three volumes of DANCE CLASS 3 IN 1, of which this is the first, with two more to come. Béka and Crip have not only created a wonderful graphic novel series, but such delightful characters that we just can't get enough of them. If you love Julie, Alia, Lucie, and the rest of the wonderful DANCE CLASS cast of characters as much as we do, then we have truly wonderful news: Coming soon is the all-new tenth DANCE CLASS graphic novel "Letting It Go"! Look for it wherever books and/or e-books are sold, and, of course, at your local public library.

Now, I'm going to find a Dance Class where I can sign up for lessons…

Jim

STAY IN TOUCH!

EMAIL:	salicrup@papercutz.com
WEB:	papercutz.com
TWITTER:	@papercutzgn
INSTAGRAM:	@papercutzgn
FACEBOOK:	PAPERCUTZGRAPHICNOVELS
FAN MAIL:	Papercutz, 160 Broadway, Suite 700, East Wing, New York, NY 10038

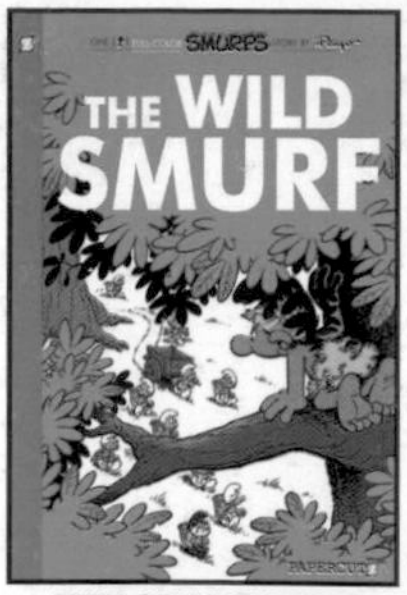
THE WILD SMURF
THE SMURFS #21

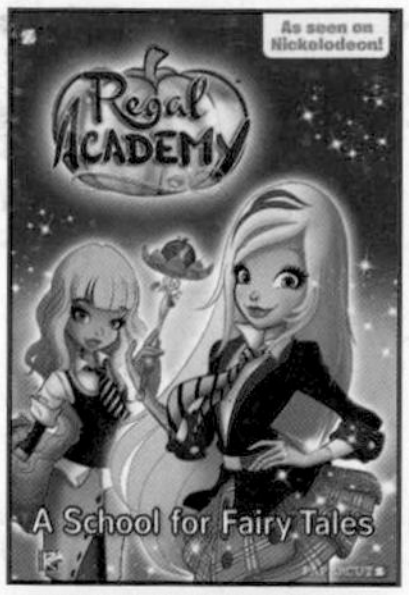
As seen on Nickelodeon!
Regal Academy
A School for Fairy Tales
REGAL ACADEMY #1

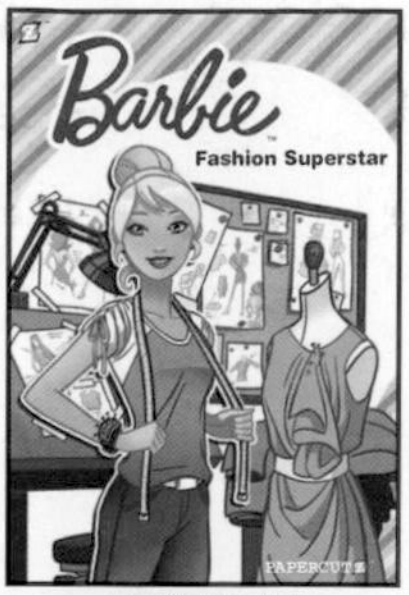
Barbie
Fashion Superstar
PAPERCUTZ
BARBIE #1

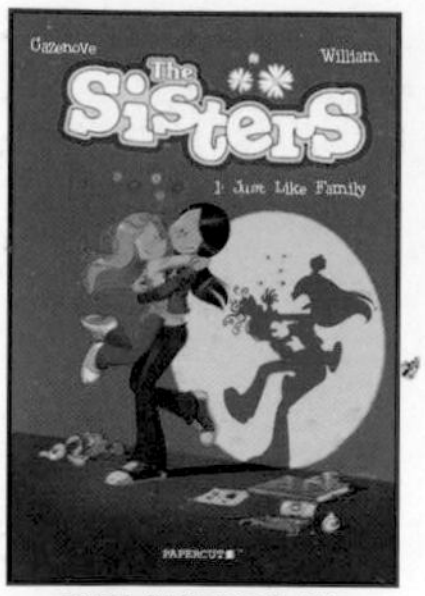
Cazenove
William
The Sisters
1 Just Like Family
PAPERCUTZ
THE SISTERS #1

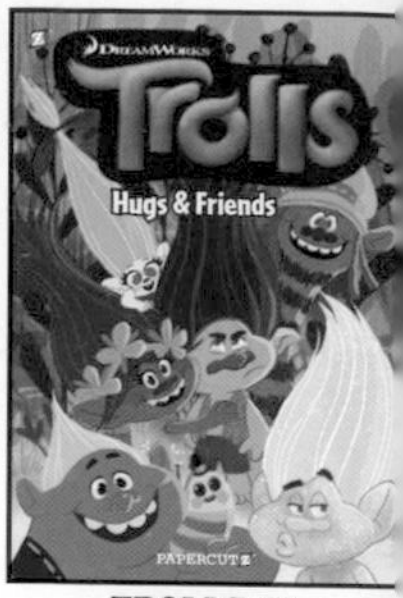
DREAMWORKS
Trolls
Hugs & Friends
PAPERCUTZ
TROLLS #1

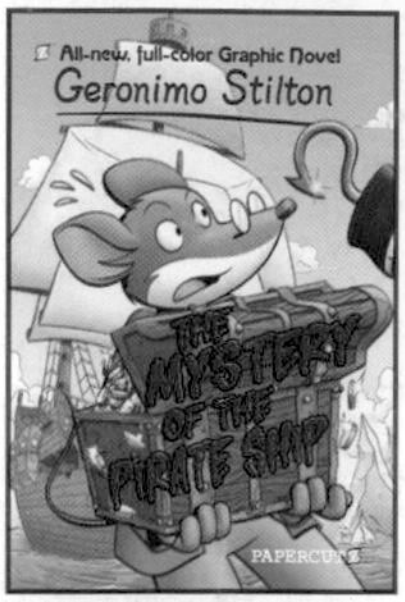
All-new, full-color Graphic Novel
Geronimo Stilton
The Mystery of the Pirate Ship
PAPERCUTZ
GERONIMO STILTON #17

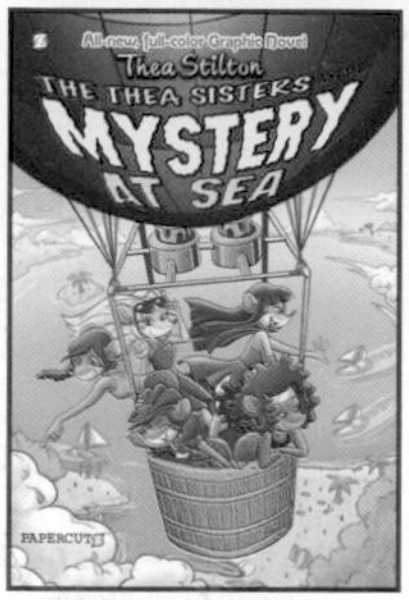
All-new, full-color Graphic Novel
Thea Stilton
The Thea Sisters
Mystery at Sea
PAPERCUTZ
THEA STILTON #6

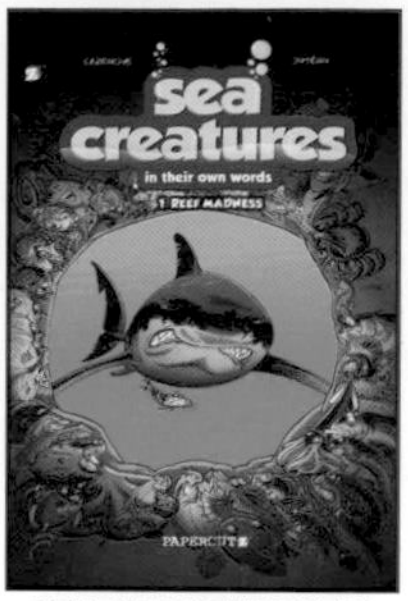
sea creatures
in their own words
PAPERCUTZ
SEA CREATURES #1

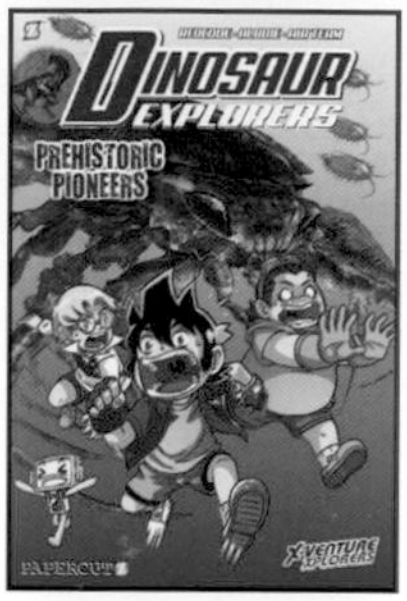
Dinosaur Explorers
Prehistoric Pioneers
PAPERCUTZ
DINOSAUR EXPLORERS #1

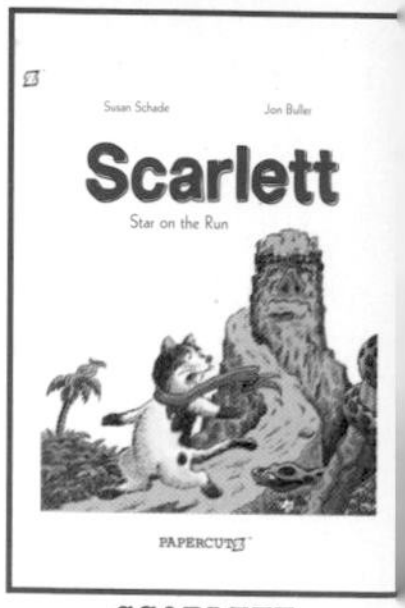
Susan Schade
Jon Buller
Scarlett
Star on the Run
PAPERCUTZ
SCARLETT

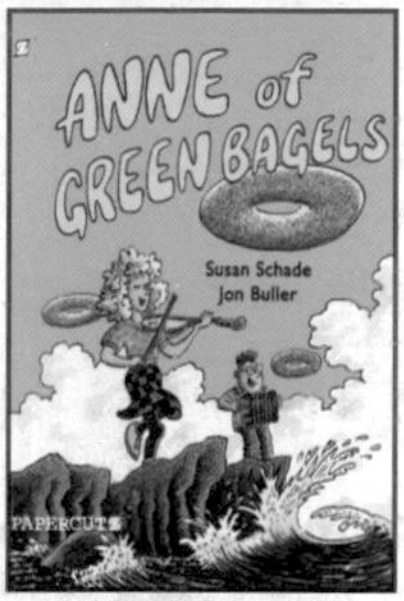
Anne of Green Bagels
Susan Schade
Jon Buller
PAPERCUTZ
ANNE OF GREEN BAGELS #1

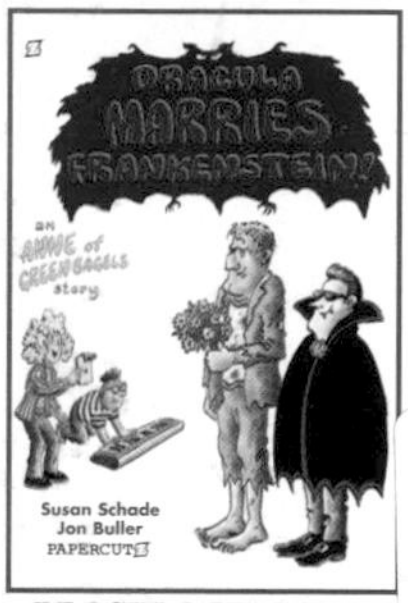
Dracula Marries Frankenstein!
an Anne of Green Bagels story
Susan Schade
Jon Buller
PAPERCUTZ
DRACULA MARRIES FRANKENSTEIN!

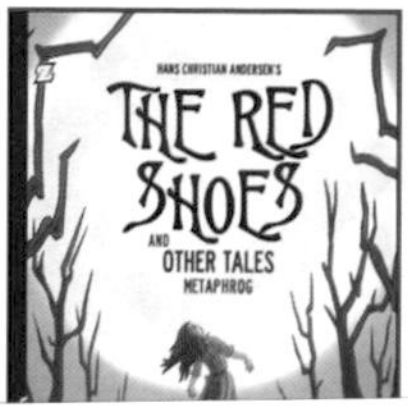
HANS CHRISTIAN ANDERSEN'S
The Red Shoes
and Other Tales
METAPHROG

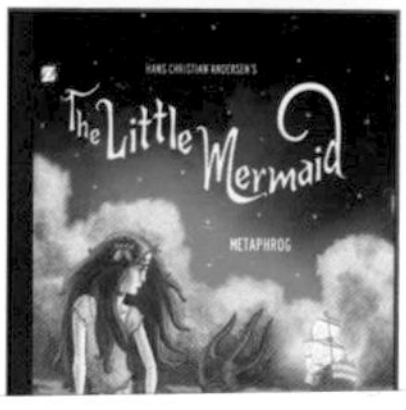
HANS CHRISTIAN ANDERSEN'S
The Little Mermaid
METAPHROG

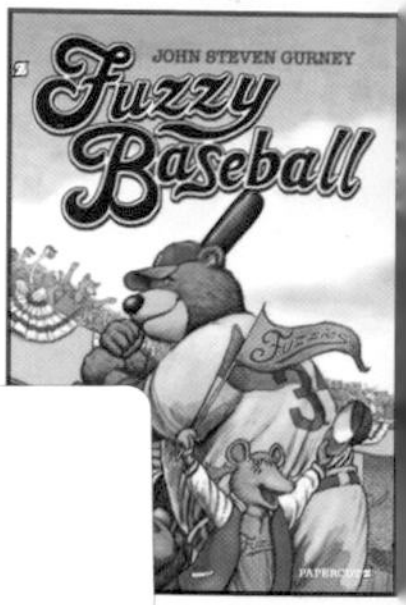
JOHN STEVEN GURNEY
Fuzzy Baseball
PAPERCUTZ
BASEBALL

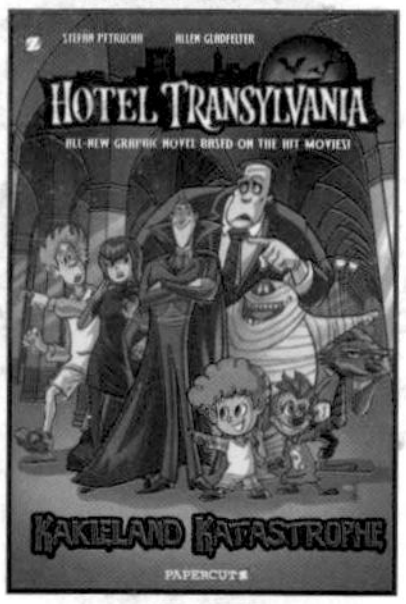
Hotel Transylvania
Kakieland Katastrophe
PAPERCUTZ
HOTEL TRANSYLVANIA #1

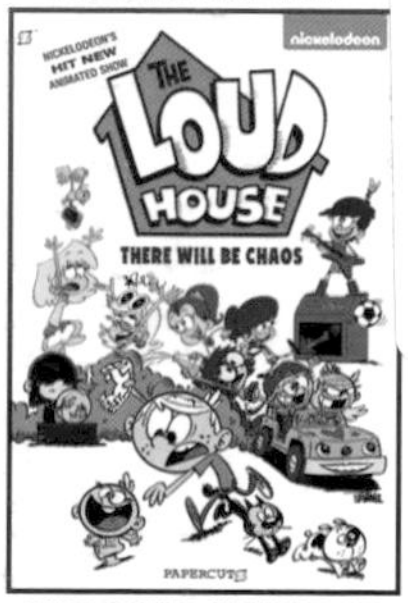
nickelodeon
The Loud House
There Will Be Chaos
PAPERCUTZ
THE LOUD HOUSE #1

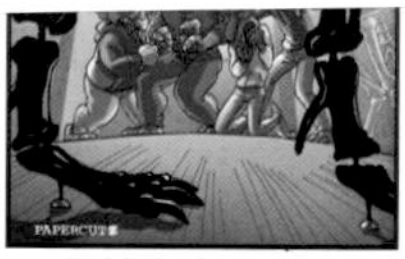
PAPERCUTZ
MANOSAURS #1

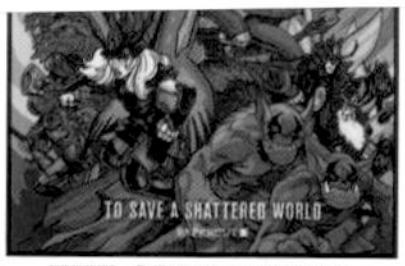
To Save a Shattered World
THE ONLY LIVING BOY #5

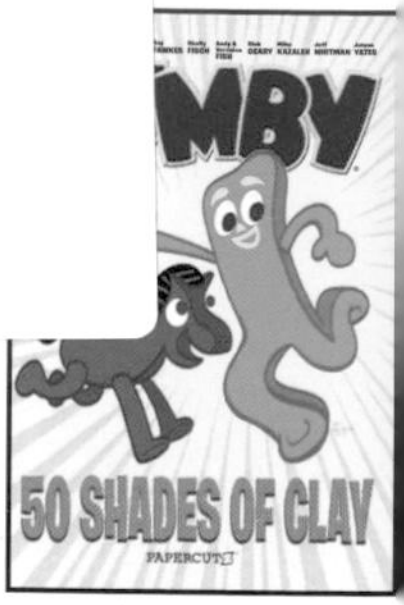
50 SHADES OF CLAY
PAPERCUTZ
GUMBY #1

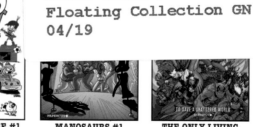